PALMETTO DREAMS

A SECOND CHANCE FOR LASTING LOVE

TERRY FOWLER

BARBOUR
PUBLISHING

Published by Barbour Publishing, Inc., P.O. Box 719, Uhrichsville, Ohio 44683, www.barbourbooks.com

Our mission is to publish and distribute inspirational products offering exceptional value and biblical encouragement to the masses.

ecpa Member of the
Evangelical Christian
Publishers Association

Printed in the United States of America.

Dear Reader,

Thank you for choosing *Palmetto Dreams*. This collection takes place in Myrtle Beach, South Carolina. I have many fond memories of the time I've spent along the Grand Strand. Though I live in neighboring North Carolina, I've had the pleasure of visiting the South Carolina sites you'll read about in these stories and highly recommend each of them.

I hope you'll also enjoy reading the stories of how each of my Cornerstone women find love. To me, their friendships are reminiscent of the bonds I've formed over the years with my own best friends. I feel blessed to have them in my life and definitely treasure them.

The theme of the stories is a simple one—that of God's love and forgiveness for each of us. Just as these characters forgave and loved each other, our heavenly Father wants to share His love with us. My prayer is that each of you know the gift of His love for you.

I love hearing from my readers. You can contact me through Barbour Publishing or visit my Web site at terryfowler.net.

Yours in Christ,
Terry Fowler

CHRISTMAS MOMMY

Dedication

To my family. Writing this story reminded me of the good things that come of being part of a large family.

Special thanks to Tammy and Mary for your help.

Chapter 1

I t's not that hard."

Julie Dennis almost laughed as she admonished her brother, the pastor. "Shame on you, Joey. You know it's wrong to fib."

"I'm not. It isn't," he insisted.

She leaned back in her chair to search the files on the cabinet behind her, never pausing in her work. "Maybe not for you and Mari. You're old hands at this kid stuff. I don't have your experience."

"Please, Julie. This trip is a lifelong dream of ours. Something we could never afford."

His statement caused Julie pain. She hated it when Joey dropped bombshells like this. How many times had she told them that if they needed or wanted anything they only had to ask? "Why didn't you say so?" she demanded. "I would have paid for it."

"And we'd have the same dilemma," he reminded.

"I don't mind staying with the kids. That's not the problem."

"I know. The timing could be better."

Julie agreed wholeheartedly. "No joke." She tapped the keyboard and the screen saver clicked off. After finding the information in the folder, she keyed the data and smiled when the programming problem solved itself. "Who goes off and leaves their kids at Christmastime? That's the most unbelievable thing I've ever heard."

"It's not really Christmas," Joey said. "And the kids won't even miss us. Having you around, spoiling them outrageously, will be tons more fun than having us here."

Her brother's attempt to sweet-talk her fell short. "Yeah, right. Laying it on with a trowel is not working here."

"Mari promises to write long, copious lists. You'll be able to handle this blindfolded with one hand tied behind your back."

"You think I'd try that with those kids of yours?"

Joey ignored her comment. "You should hear Mari. She's more excited than I've seen her in a long time."

He wasn't playing fair. No doubt, Mari was ecstatic at the thought of going somewhere without the children. Julie loved her brother and sister-in-law but found their literal interpretation of "go forth and multiply" somewhat embarrassing. Her friends could hardly believe they'd made her an aunt five times over with five-year-old Matthew, four-year-old Marcus, three-year-old Lucas, and fourteen-month-old twins John and Naomi.

"She needs this trip."

Julie noted the concern in his tone. "She's not. . ."

"She's fine," Joey reassured quickly. "Back in her full-time roles of mother and pastor's wife, but she's lost her sparkle."

A breast cancer scare on top of her mother's death would depress any woman. "She's been through a lot. You need to take some of the load off with the kids."

Joey sighed. "I try but Mari says her job is to keep me free to handle my pastoral duties."

"What about putting them in day care during the week? I'd be happy to pay the fees."

"Use of the church day care is one of the benefits of the position, but Mari says she's a stay-at-home mother for a reason. She refuses to put the kids in day care for more than a few hours at a time."

Julie admired her sister-in-law's ability to organize her family and home. The model homemaker, Mari ran their home like a well-oiled machine. Not only did she cook fabulous meals, she kept a spotless home, and they had five well-behaved children. And she managed to work tirelessly with Joey in the church.

Maybe that's what really made her nervous. Julie knew that if she said yes, Mari would find that her efforts to train her sister-in-law in the fine art of homemaking had failed. No doubt, the place would be in total chaos within hours of their departure.

"Noah's willing to help."

The mention of his name caused a stab of pain in Julie's heart. She didn't think she could bear seeing Noah daily. *That would be worse than the kids,* Julie thought.

"I understand, Julie."

Maybe Joey did understand that the idea of caring for his kids all on her own terrified her, but he had no idea how she felt about Noah Loughlin. The overwhelming sense of abandonment she'd felt when Noah relocated to South Carolina to accept the position of associate pastor at Cornerstone Church still bothered her.

Noah and Joey had met at seminary, and when he set them up on a blind date, claiming Noah was perfect for Julie, she decided to reserve her opinion. Instead, she found Noah to be handsome and personable and fell into "like" almost immediately.

When Joey's family moved away, Julie had leaned on Noah, and he'd helped make the separation bearable. Then in May, Noah's out-of-the-blue announcement that he'd taken the associate pastor position took the wind out of her sails.

Julie had never thought she'd miss Noah so much. Only after he'd left had she realized how much she loved him. But Noah had never indicated he wanted more than their casual relationship.

Still, she'd considered the idea of relocating to South Carolina a time or two before Joey had casually shared how popular Noah was with the women of the church.

Evidently, he'd moved on, and she decided she had to as well. Even now, Noah's presence played a major part in her relationship with her family. The thought of seeing him gave her reason to keep fifteen hundred miles between them most of the time. On the rare occasions when she traveled to South Carolina, she tried to avoid him as much as possible.

When Noah called, he acted as if nothing had changed, but Julie knew everything had changed for her. She refused to be involved with a man who couldn't be bothered to seek her opinion when it came to making decisions that affected them both.

"At least pray over it," Joey requested, bringing Julie back to their conversation. "If you can't see a way to do this for us, we'll understand."

Sure they would, Julie thought with a grimace. For the rest of her life they would have long faces and sad stories about how they would have visited the Holy Land that time if things had worked out for them. "I assume Noah's already agreed to take over at church?"

"He's looking forward to this opportunity."

He would be, Julie thought. "You mean he doesn't rate a free trip?"

"The church didn't give us the trip," Joey explained. "Friends found they couldn't go and gifted us with their nonrefundable tickets. You'll find having Noah around will be a great help. The children adore him."

"Maybe you should ask him to babysit while you're away."

"Mari insists on family."

"Just my luck," she mumbled under her breath.

"Did you say something?"

Julie coughed. "Okay, Joey, you win. I'll see what I can work out."

"You already said you were coming for a couple of weeks. And we'll be home to spend Christmas Day with the kids. I promise not to say anything about the expensive gifts you buy, either."

That almost made it worthwhile. Julie couldn't understand why Joey could never accept her gifts in the spirit they were intended. "What about the kids' Santa?"

"Mari plans to do the shopping before we leave."

Obviously, no stone would be unturned once the wheels were in motion. "I'll let you know. Tell everyone hello for me."

"I will. Julie," he called when she started to hang up, "I don't mean to pressure you. Asking you to care for five kids is a major favor."

You're telling me, Julie thought. "Joey, I love you, Mari, and those kids with all my heart. You know I wouldn't refuse anything any of you asked that's within my power to give, don't you?"

"I hoped that would be the case," he admitted, his big laugh making her homesick. "We love you, too."

～

Noah could see his arrival had disturbed Joe's deep concentration. "You were lost in thought," he commented as he sat in the visitor chair.

Joe grimaced. "Suffering from guilt pangs. I suspect I just coerced Julie into babysitting for us while we're away."

Noah doubted that. Julie never stopped looking for ways to repay her brother for what he'd done for her. She'd see this as a prime opportunity. "I doubt you coerced her."

"We know we're taking advantage, but I don't know where else to turn. Mari needs this break."

"Julie does know I plan to help in every way I can?" When Joe nodded, Noah asked, "You don't think she would refuse because I'm here, do you?"

Noah felt his friend's scrutiny.

"She's already planned two weeks' vacation over the Christmas holiday. Why would you think that, anyway?"

Noah's gaze zeroed in on Julie's image in the photo sitting on the credenza behind Joe's desk. Her blemish-free complexion and chocolate brown eyes gave her a youthful, innocent beauty that struck Noah in the pit of his stomach. He missed her so much.

Taller than the average woman, she stood somewhere around five-foot-ten and longed to shed those final twenty pounds that would take her to a size six. She frequently finger-combed her thick, shoulder-length brunette hair back from her forehead.

"She's become very good at avoiding me," he admitted glumly. "I haven't talked to her in a couple of weeks. I keep getting her voice mail."

Joe frowned. "Why would she ignore you?"

Noah leaned back in the chair and crossed his legs. "I wish I knew. I thought everything was moving along smoothly. I believed Julie—actually, I've started seeking God's guidance in regards to asking her to marry me."

"You're that serious?" Joe sounded surprised.

"I am. I don't know how Julie feels, though. I believed we were both serious, but now that she's barely speaking to me, I don't know what to think. She's been distant since the move. You think that's the reason?"

"Probably," Joe said. "My sister puts on a brave front, but she's afraid. I had a real struggle leaving her behind. I've been her guardian since our parents died. At least I had them during the hard times. Now she doesn't have anyone."

"She still has you."

"Not as accessible," Joe declared. "I asked her to come here, but she says it's our time to be a family without her breathing down our necks. I have no idea why she feels that way. Mari and I love her a great deal."

Joe's thoughts intrigued Noah. Maybe her brother could give him some indication as to why things had changed. "Do you really think she's afraid?"

"I hear it in her voice at times," Joe admitted. "Sort of a little-girl sadness, almost as if she's close to tears. But I don't see it when she's visiting. She seemed fine when the twins were born and when she came to help after Mari's surgery. She doesn't say much about us moving away anymore."

"I wish she'd tell me what's on her mind," Noah said.

Joe's hearty laughter echoed around the room. "In your dreams, buddy. Women believe the men they love should be capable of reading their minds. I've learned to listen carefully to what Mari says so I don't end up in an argument."

"Julie won't tell me anything," Noah declared. "When I told her God called me to Cornerstone, she told me to do what I had to do. What kind of comment is that?"

"Women's logic?"

"I'd hoped she'd be as happy for me as I was for her when she got her promotion at work."

"Had you expressed any intent toward her?" Joe asked curiously.

"No. I felt God was telling me to give her time. She's young and I don't want to rush her into marriage too soon."

"It's a good idea to take your time and seek God's guidance in choosing your helpmate," Joe advised. "Even if I do know Julie has excellent values and morals and is a generous and loving woman. Of course, I admit to a slight prejudice. Would you like me to pray with you?"

"Please."

The two men bowed their heads, seeking God's guidance in the matters of the heart.

After Joe finished praying, Noah thanked him and the conversation turned to the business of hospital visitations.

⤳

Two weeks alone with five children? The very idea terrified Julie. Helping out with parents nearby was one thing, but handling things alone would be an entirely different matter.

What if one of them got hurt or became ill? What if she became sick? Every possible negative scenario played through her head.

Stop it. You're a capable woman—able to handle any and every thing thrown at you and more. Well, not everything. She hadn't dealt with Noah's desertion.

The thought gave her a moment's pause. Was his presence the real reason she didn't want to go? Seeing him daily while knowing how she felt about him would be difficult enough. Knowing she would have to walk away again and never have him in her life made it nearly impossible. Could she withstand the pain it was sure to cause?

Joey had said Mari needed the trip. Was there something he wasn't telling her? She didn't think so. No doubt, there were aspects of their lives they didn't share with her, but they'd always shared the major problems like Mari's cancer.

Her brother's determination to give his wife this vacation surprised Julie. While Joey wasn't as clueless as some men were when it came to women, he'd never struck her as the romantic type. Julie agreed that Mari would benefit from the trip. In fact, she would be the first to say Mari deserved a vacation.

She opened the calendar on her PDA. She'd already requested off the week before and the week after Christmas. How would her boss react to her adding another week? *No time like the present to find out,* Julie decided as she picked up the phone and requested a few minutes of his time.

She left Kevin's office fifteen minutes later with her plans approved. As it turned out, he had already planned to give everyone an extended holiday break.

Julie liked her boss. After graduating at seventeen, she had gone off to college with the intention of getting her bachelor's degree as soon as possible. She'd chosen computer engineering, and during her college years, her instructor's high praises of her abilities had led her to Kevin Moore.

He'd offered her a part-time job and she'd worked hard to help him design the business software programs. When she graduated, the position became full-time.

Her brother and sister-in-law sold Julie and Joey's parents' house after Joey accepted the Cornerstone position. Julie had used part of her share of the money for a down payment on her condominium and invested the remainder in Kevin's firm. The investment had been a wise one, and with her generous salary, Julie lived a debt-free life with considerable savings in the bank.

Julie couldn't help but wonder what role Joey's prayers had played in Kevin's decision. The Lord worked in mysterious ways.

Once she completed the projects on her desk, her calendar would be clear until after New Year's Day. Julie decided not to mention that third week to Joey. If the situation overwhelmed her, she might decide to head for home as soon as Joey and Mari returned. Julie had no doubt she could appreciate the peace and quiet of her condo after a hectic two weeks in their home.

Back at her desk, she picked up her cell phone and spoke "Joey's office" into the auto dialer. "You'd tell me if Mari were sick again, wouldn't you?" she asked when he answered the phone.

"It's nothing like that," he said without hesitation. "Mari's depressed. Grieving for her mother and thinking about her own mortality. The cancer scare made her give serious consideration to what would happen to our family if one or the other of us weren't around."

"You think that's why she's insisting on family staying with the kids?"

"Could be. She asked me the other night if I thought you'd agree to guardianship if something happened to us."

"You mean raise the kids?" she asked with a squeak of fear in her voice.

"Don't panic, Julie. It's not going to happen."

"But it could."

"If God sees fit to take us from this earth, I know you'd willingly accept the responsibility. No matter how frightened you might be, you'd provide the children with the love and guidance they need. I assured Mari I didn't doubt it for a minute."

Her brother's confidence in her shook Julie to the core. She'd never once considered the possibility of raising his children. As far as she was concerned, Joey and Mari would still be around when their great-grandchildren were born.

"That's the sort of melancholy I'm hoping a vacation will alleviate," Joey told her. "Having you here taking care of the kids will reassure her considerably."

"Okay, Joey, I'll be there for Christmas," Julie agreed, despite her reservations.

"I can't thank you enough, Julie. We'll call tonight to finalize the plans. Mari will be so happy."

Julie could tell Mari wasn't the only one. Joey sounded excited, too. "I'd say you owe me a big one, but it's no more than you've done for me."

"Because I love you," Joey said.

"Because I love you back," Julie responded in their usual exchange. "Tell Mari to list where she gets her endless supply of patience. I'll need to order a double batch."

"That one's easy, Jules. It comes from God."

"Then you'd better start praying now."

"We both should," Joey suggested.

Chapter 2

Julie refilled her coffee cup and leaned against the counter beside Mari. "Are you excited?"

"Yes and no," her sister-in-law admitted. "I've dreamed of going, but I'm torn over leaving the children. I know you'll take good care of them, but I worry people will think I'm a bad mother."

"We both know that's not true," Julie said, her thoughts going, back to the scare of the summer when Mari found the lump. Julie had come to stay with them for two weeks then, helping care for the children and forcing Mari to take it easy after the surgery.

Even that had been a struggle. If she laid down for a nap, more often than not one of the kids slept with her. Despite the protests of her husband and sister-in-law, Mari always rose early to prepare meals and stayed up late doing chores. Nothing stood in the way of Mari spending quality time with her children.

"I'm not as worried about the older boys as I am the twins. I'd take them along, but they'd be the only children," she said, bringing Julie back to the present.

"Exactly the reason they need to stay here with me. I'm looking forward to spending time with the twins. I promise to cuddle them as much as you would. And I'll call right away if there's any emergency."

"You're wonderful to do this for us," Mari said, tears clouding her bright blue eyes. "Not only did I find the love of my life when I married Joe, I got the sister I always wanted."

Julie opened her arms to Mari and they embraced. "I don't want you worrying. Think of it this way—you'll both be better parents after a little break. I plan to keep them so busy they won't have time to miss you. Well, maybe just a little," she teased at Mari's playful frown.

"Naomi, no," Mari called, going over to stop the child's efforts to escape the high chair.

Julie caught a glimpse of Joey and Noah as they carried the suitcases out the front door to load them in the church van.

Noah looks more like a cover model than a minister, Julie thought. Standing over six feet tall, he wore his executive suit with a flair that most men could never achieve. His olive-toned skin gave the impression of a permanent tan and suited his short black hair and gorgeous doe-brown eyes. He laughed at something Joey said and stole Julie's breath away.

14

"I bet he packs the church," she said softly. "I mean. . ." Julie's voice trailed off and she looked at Mari. "I'm sure Joey does, too."

Her sister-in-law chuckled. "Neither of them does badly. Julie, Noah told Joe he thinks you're avoiding him."

She focused on the bottom of her coffee cup. "Why would he think that?"

Mari stepped closer and wrapped her arm around Julie's shoulders. "Joe and I don't want to interfere. We want you to be happy. Do you love Noah?"

Julie glanced at the front door, afraid the two men would return in the middle of their conversation. "I don't know what I feel. Or what Noah feels for that matter. I just know I don't want a long-distance relationship."

"If you care for him, why would it matter?"

Julie knew she couldn't tell Mari the truth. After Noah had left, she'd decided she'd spent far too much of her life without the people she loved. While Joey had worked hard to take care of her after their parents' deaths, he hadn't been her father and mother.

Just about the time she'd begun to feel settled with him and Mari, she'd graduated from high school and started college. They had two children and one on the way when she graduated. Julie had insisted they remain in the family home and had gotten an apartment. She'd seen her family on a regular basis and felt content. When Luke arrived, she'd bonded with the infant. Then they moved to South Carolina.

Julie remembered the day Joey called to ask her to stop by the house so they could share their news.

"The beach, Joey?"

He'd laughed at her disparaging question. "The Grand Strand, Jules. Sixty miles of sandy shore, blue skies, and water."

"You sound excited."

"We are. You know Mari and I have been praying for God to lead us where we can do the most good. I'm confident Cornerstone Church in Myrtle Beach, South Carolina, is exactly that place.

"Mari and I looked on the Internet and found it's listed as the best family beach. The kids are going to love the area. They have amusement parks, miniature golf courses, and plenty of family entertainment shows."

"A nice place to visit, maybe, but who'd want to live there?"

"We do. Warm hospitality, small-town feel, with a population of twenty thousand."

Julie had glanced at the literature he'd handed her. "That swells to over 350,000 during the summer season. Come on, Joey, it's named after a shrub."

"Give it up, Jules. We're going. We'd hoped you'd consider coming with us."

"You mean move and live there?" When Joey nodded, she'd said, "No way. My life is here. My job, the condo, Noah."

He'd raised his hand. "Okay. It's just a thought. I've looked after you so long

I suppose I'm suffering from separation anxiety."

"Then don't go."

"We have to, Jules. This is what God wants us to do."

She'd found herself hoping they'd experience a change of heart, but when Joey asked if she wanted to keep the house, she knew they were serious.

When Noah followed them, Julie knew without a doubt that she couldn't handle another loss.

"I'm not into long-distance relationships," she told Mari. "I need to see the man in my life more than once or twice a year."

"Will having him around be too much for you?"

Mari's concern posed yet another problem. If Julie admitted the truth, her sister-in-law would refuse to go on the trip. "We'll be okay."

Julie hoped that would be the case. She planned to spend as little time in Noah's company as possible. Of course, she already had her doubts that would happen. She'd come downstairs this morning to find him waiting in the kitchen. He'd kissed her without hesitation. Surely he didn't think they'd pick up where they left off when he'd abandoned her.

After Joey and his family had moved, she and Noah had seen each other nearly every day. He knew exactly how much she missed her family and yet he'd chosen to follow them rather than stay with her.

Granted, she knew Noah had to follow God's leading, but the least he could have done was show a bit of hesitation over leaving her. He'd been so joyous about his job opportunity that Julie wondered about his eagerness to escape her.

"This isn't the end, Julie Joy," Noah had said that last night as they held hands over the dinner table. "It's a beginning."

His cryptic words puzzled her. How could it not be the end? Maybe she would have followed him to South Carolina if he'd asked, but he hadn't. Instead, she remained behind to deal with her love for him, and that had been no little task.

Julie recalled their conversation earlier in the week. She'd been on her way out when the phone rang. Her mind had been on her errands and she'd grabbed the phone without checking the caller ID.

"Hello, Julie."

"Hi, Noah. I'm on my way out the door to complete my errands before I fly out the day after tomorrow."

"Why don't you want to talk to me anymore?"

"Don't be ridiculous," she'd told him, more than a little aware he'd hit the bull's-eye with his guess.

"I don't think I am. This is the first time we've talked in two weeks. I miss hearing your voice."

"I've been busy getting everything organized."

"Joe told me you're coming. I can't wait to see you."

Had he honestly thought her so gullible that she'd believe him without reservation? "I'm sure you'll be far too busy in your role of associate pastor."

"Are you saying you don't want to see me?"

"We'll see each other, Noah."

"But do you *want* to see me?" he'd persisted.

What had he expected her to say? That she looked forward to as well as dreaded seeing him? That she feared one glimpse might undo her determination to move on with her life without him? "Sure I do."

"You could sound a bit more enthusiastic. It seems like forever since you were here."

"Nearly six months. Right after you accepted the position."

Ironically, not quite two weeks after Noah moved, Joey called to ask for her help. Julie had traveled to South Carolina only to find she and Noah were too busy to spend time together.

"I have so much to tell you. I want to hear everything you've been doing, too. I can't wait for you to meet our church family."

"I've already met most of them. Mari keeps me current."

"You must talk to her fairly often."

"Once a week or so."

"Why don't we talk that often? You call Joe and Mari but you can't find time in your busy schedule to talk to your boyfriend?"

How could she have told Noah she was far too angry with him for idle chitchat? Too afraid to hear how quickly he'd moved on in his new life without her? "We play lots of phone tag, Noah."

"Because you're never around to take my calls. I miss you so much at times that I dial your number just to hear your voice."

Julie had choked up at his words. If only she could have believed that. "Can we decide who's at fault later? I really do need to run my errands."

"Okay, Julie, if that's what you want."

His tone set her on edge. "What I want is to stay warm and cozy in my house, but I have to find Christmas gifts for the kids."

"Why can't you buy the gifts here?"

Julie sighed at his obvious inexperience. "Because it takes away the surprise element when they see what I buy for them. Besides, it's easier to shop alone. I'm going to have the packages shipped. I can't imagine getting on a plane with all this stuff."

"How much stuff?"

"There's a pile of boxes in my living room," Julie told him. "I am buying for seven. . .uh, eight people."

"You can send everything to the church. I'll sign for the packages."

"Thanks, but most of the stuff won't arrive until after I'm there anyway."

"What else can I do to help?" he'd asked. "Pick you up at the airport?"

She'd already had this discussion with Joey. Julie planned to rent a larger passenger van and drive herself to the house. "I've got a passenger van reserved at the airport. We're going to cover Mari's list after I get there."

"Sounds like you don't need me."

What could she have said? She didn't want to need him. "It's going to be hectic. My plane doesn't take off until around noon Sunday and I have two layovers."

"Take care, then. I'll be praying for a safe journey."

They had not spoken again until this morning. Julie had caught them up on the community they'd called home for years and her work. She'd listened to their news, and Julie realized that in just a few minutes, Joey and Mari would share their last-minute instructions before Noah drove them to the airport.

"It's cold out there," Joey said, blowing on his hands as they came through the kitchen door.

"You think that's cold?" Julie asked. "You should visit me more often. Your blood is thinning out."

Joey placed his chilled hands against her neck and she squealed and moved away.

Noah followed Joey, his cheeks rosy red. The boys congregated around his legs, vying for his attention. "Mari and Joe are happy you're taking care of my partners here."

Julie picked up three-year-old Luke, who'd fallen after Matthew and Marc pushed him out of the way. "We're going to take care of each other, aren't we, guys?"

The three boys nodded.

Noah rested his hands on Matt's and Marc's shoulders. "Feel free to call on me anytime. I've gotten to know these guys over the past few months."

Mari opened the cabinet door and took down two mugs. "Since Noah's covering for Joe, he won't be able to go home to his family for Christmas."

"That's a shame," Julie said. She believed in family holidays. No matter how busy her schedule was, she always made time to spend Christmas with her family.

Noah cupped his hands about the mug Mari handed him and sipped the hot coffee. "I don't mind. Joe and Mari deserve a vacation."

"He's joining us for Christmas dinner," Mari announced, passing Joey a cup of coffee. "I wrote notes about the plans for dinner, what to buy at the grocery store, what to take out of the freezer and when."

Julie smiled at that. "Perfect. Lists are my life. I can handle anything as long as I have a good set of instructions to follow."

Mari's loving smile filled Julie to overflowing with good feelings. "I know you'll do fine. Joe and I can't tell you how much we appreciate this."

"Consider it a cheap Christmas present," she joked.

"Oh, you," Mari said, tapping Julie's arm. "I'd better check upstairs one last time. I always feel I'm forgetting something."

"Leave something behind," Joe told her with a grin. "There's no room in the van."

After Mari left, Joey and Noah talked church business and Julie watched John feed himself. He abandoned his spoon and ate the cereal with his fingers. Fighting back the desire to assist, she noted his mother had given it to him dry and put his milk in a sippy cup.

When he indicated he was finished, Julie wiped his mouth and took him out of the high chair. She set him on his feet and watched him toddle into the living room where the rest of his siblings played.

Being in Joey and Mari's home was almost like being in her parents' home. The table they'd dined around had been in the senior Dennises' home for most of her life. The same furniture her parents had chosen for their living room sat in Joey's living room.

Joey had insisted that she take some pieces for herself. Julie had kept her bedroom suite and a corner curio that now contained her own and her mother's pottery collections. She also had a set of bone china that had belonged to her great-grandmother. She'd insisted they needed the rest of the furniture more than she did.

After depositing the dishes in the sink and wiping off the high chair tray, she glanced at her watch. "It's almost time, Joey."

He stood and walked around the table, his hands gently massaging her shoulders. "I'm glad you're here, Julie. Perhaps the kids and Noah can get you into church a couple of Sundays."

Julie caught Joey's gaze and shook her head. Their ongoing argument about her failure to attend church regularly happened every time they spoke on the phone or saw each other. Joey just didn't understand the demands of her career. It wasn't that she had forgotten her religion. She just didn't have the time or desire to attend church.

"I'm sure Noah doesn't want to hear this." Embarrassed that Joey had dragged him into their argument, she glanced at Noah and said, "Joey still thinks of me as a child."

Her brother frowned. "I know how easy it is to get away from God and church, Julie. You promised you'd go back."

"Drop it, Joey." He wasn't responsible for her any longer. Though she appreciated the way he'd taken care of her since their parents died, Julie wanted him to admit she was a responsible adult.

One of the children cried out, and Julie went into the living room to check on them. Joey and Noah followed.

"You should have arrived earlier and attended services with us yesterday."

His criticism stung. She'd been dead tired when she pulled into their driveway around eight o'clock last night. "I restructured my entire life to be here. Isn't that enough?" she demanded.

Joey remained steadfast in his determination to get his point across. "You can never give me a good enough reason for not attending church."

Mari came downstairs and handed her carry-on bag to her husband. "Joe, please," she requested softly, touching his arm. "Julie understands your concerns. It's between her and God."

"All I'm asking is that she attend church."

"And she will," Mari said patiently. "Julie knows what she needs to do."

"That's right, Joey. I'm an adult capable of making my own decisions. And for the record, I didn't come earlier because we had our company Christmas party Saturday night and I was expected to attend." Fuming, Julie took a couple of steps away from the group, still muttering her arguments. "I rush around all week to be with my friends so I can come up here and keep his kids and that's the thanks I get."

Mari came over and hugged her. "We do appreciate this, Julie. More than we can tell you. You two need to kiss and make up. I don't want this vacation spoiled because my two favorite people are angry with each other."

"I'm not angry with her."

"I'm not angry with him," Julie said at the same time. She walked over and hugged her brother. "I promise to go to church while I'm here."

"I suppose that's better than nothing," he agreed reluctantly.

"Good," Mari said, wrapping her arms around both of them. "We'd better talk to the kids one last time before we go."

Julie's heartbeat kicked into overdrive. They were about to grant her wish to be treated like an adult. Once her brother and sister-in-law said good-bye to their kids, she would be in charge of five small children. What was she doing here? Why had she agreed to their plan?

Having a few friends over for a small party was her biggest Christmas achievement. How would she turn the next ten days into a joyous occasion for her niece and nephews? At least John and Naomi were too little to warp with her failure.

"Boys, we want to talk to you," Mari said.

They are so cute, Julie thought as they assembled to hear what their parents had to say. Matthew, the oldest, was destined to be a lady-killer with those big blue eyes and jet black hair. At four, Marc was the quiet one. He came and stood within the circle of his mother's arms, not really listening as Joey outlined what they expected of them. Three-year-old Luke was the independent one. He sat on the floor, making truck noises and pushing ruts into the carpet with his dump truck. John toddled over to the toy box and proceeded to throw things out. His twin, Naomi, watched a television commercial.

"Aunt Julie will be your mommy until Christmas. I expect you to listen to her and behave," Joey said firmly. The older boys nodded while Luke continued to play. "Do you understand, Luke?"

The little boy nodded solemnly and said, "Auntie Hulie Christmas mommy."

The adults smiled at each other. Julie swung Luke up and playfully nuzzled his neck. "You're so sweet. I could eat you up with a spoon."

Luke squealed. "No eat, Auntie Hulie." She put him down and he went back to playing.

"You may wish you could before we get home," Joey warned. "Luke is our, ah, determined child. You have to be firm with him."

Joey pulled his oldest son into his arms. "Matt, you're the oldest. You help Auntie Julie. You guys know your mother and I will not tolerate bad behavior." He glanced at his sister. "Aunt Julie will punish you if you misbehave."

Julie panicked. That wasn't part of the deal. She couldn't discipline these children. "I never. . . I can't. . ."

"Yes, you can," Joey told her firmly. "You're the adult in charge." He spoke to the children once more. "We expect all of you to be very good while we're away. Do you understand?"

Matt nodded. Marc stuck his thumb in his mouth and fixed solemn blue eyes on his dad. Was that a tear creeping down his face?

Joey and Mari hugged and kissed the children one by one, with each "I love you" followed by another reminder to be on their best behavior.

"You're going to have the best Christmas ever," Joey reassured as he hugged Julie one last time. "By the time we get home, you'll be ready to settle down and raise a few of your own."

"Or run screaming into never-never land," she contradicted as she hugged Mari. "Don't worry. We'll be fine."

"You will. Thanks, Julie. You're a lifesaver."

Together the group huddled in the doorway, Marc and Luke hugging her legs while she and Matt waved good-bye. *Any moment now, pandemonium will break loose*, Julie thought, steeling herself for tears.

She experienced a moment's pause when they all went back inside after the van drove away. "Oh well, maybe this isn't going to be so bad after all," Julie said as she closed the door behind her and followed them.

Now where was that list? She found it on the kitchen counter. Back in the living room, she counted heads and settled on the sofa. Mari had kept her promise, listing everything in detail. At least she didn't have to worry about getting any of them off to school early in the morning. His November birthday had kept Matt out of school this year.

Busy with their packing and arrangements, Joey and Mari had not put up the Christmas tree. According to the list, they always got one from the tree farm. *That sounds interesting*, Julie thought. The closest she ever got to tree scent was the times she used pine cleaner in her house.

After she folded over three of the sheets, Julie realized that even though there was a lot to do, she could handle everything she'd read thus far. One day at a time. She laid the pages on the end table and asked, "So what do you guys want to do today?"

"Pway with me," Luke said, coming over to drive his truck along the chair arms and across her legs.

"I like this truck," she said, lifting the sturdy, large metal toy as he pressed it into her leg. "Is it a dump truck?"

"Big twuck," Luke insisted.

"It certainly is a big dump truck."

Luke shook his head stubbornly. "Not dump twuck."

Okay, so maybe she wasn't up-to-date on her toys, but it certainly looked like every dump truck she'd ever seen.

Julie opted to sit on the floor with Luke as he ran his vehicle around the carpet. Naomi toddled over with a book and sat down in her lap. She read to the little girl, listening to Naomi chatter in her limited vocabulary. Evidently, Mari read to her children often.

She found having the child in her lap a comforting experience. When she'd arrived the day before, Julie had expected the children to be shy around her because she hadn't seen them since June. They'd immediately showered her with hugs and big sloppy kisses.

Mari had fixed her a sandwich while the older boys fought over who was going to sit next to her. Joey had resolved the situation by telling them they'd have to take turns over the next two weeks. He'd sent them off to play afterward so the adults could talk. Julie had slept on a daybed in the nursery that night.

"Joe and I want you to sleep in our room while we're away," Mari had said as she tucked the babies in for the night.

"This will be fine."

"You'll be more comfortable in a real bed. Besides, I packed all my clothes so you'd have dresser space," Mari had said with a big grin. "At least that's what I'm telling Joe."

Julie had laughed and Mari joined in. She'd move her things into their room before the twins' bedtime tonight.

John came to join Naomi, and one sniff alerted Julie to the need for action before he could sit down. She lifted the twins in her arms and started toward the stairs.

"No!" Luke screamed. "Pway, Auntie Hulie."

His outburst surprised Julie. "Why don't you help me take care of John and Naomi first?"

"Don't want to. Want to pway."

"Play with Marc."

"Want to pway with you," Luke said, his expression crumpling.

"Okay, find me a truck, and we'll play when I return."

How does Mari handle it? Julie wondered as she changed the babies. She cast a doubtful eye on the way she'd pinned on the diapers. First thing she planned to do was splurge and buy some disposables. They would save her time and be much easier than the cloth ones Mari used. She'd even purchase extras for when they returned.

Julie emerged from the nursery with a twin under each arm.

Luke waited on the bottom stair, holding two trucks. "Come pway, Auntie Hulie," he whined.

Julie sat down to play with the three youngest, but within moments it was clear the twins were hungry. "Luke, I have to feed Naomi and John first. Why don't you join us for a glass of milk?"

"Don't want to," came his mutinous reply.

Doesn't he know any other words? Julie wondered as she settled the twins in their high chairs.

She pulled the milk carton from the fridge and searched the cabinets for their sippy cups. She found them in the sink, awaiting washup. Another item for her list.

By the time lunch was over, Julie was more than ready for a diversion. The boys didn't want to play together, and when they did, they generally fought over one toy. It took some doing, but by two o'clock, Julie had them dressed and secured in the van.

After driving to the superstore she'd visited with Mari and finding a parking space, she ordered the boys to stay in their seats. Julie removed the double stroller from the back and came around to take care of the babies, then allowed the boys to step out of the van.

She pulled Marc's hand up onto the stroller handle and then did the same with Luke. "You boys stay right here in front of me. Matt, take Marc's other hand." Julie locked the van, then they crossed the walkway and entered the store.

"No wandering off," Julie instructed once they were inside. "Stay where I can see you."

She read the overhead signs and avoided the toy aisle. Finding the disposable diapers posed no problem, but choosing the right size was a different matter. After reading numerous labels, she piled three packages into the stroller basket. No sense in running out at the most unlikely of times. She picked up several other items she thought would make her stay easier, including a half dozen extra sippy cups.

"Okay, guys, time to go."

Julie had never felt more obvious than when they moved through the store toward the cash register, catching the attention of more than one shopper.

A rack of sweaters caught her eye, and she stopped to sort through them, thinking Mari might enjoy the velvety knits. A squeal caught her attention, reminding her how quickly she'd forgotten the children's existence. Julie glanced around, spotting Matt and Marc playing hide-and-seek in the racks. Where was Luke?

"Luke?" she called, repeating his name when he didn't appear.

"Where is your brother?" she asked Matt.

He stopped running to look around and shrugged. Julie felt the blood rushing to her head. How would she explain losing one of the children on her first afternoon? Where could he be? She'd taken her eyes off him for just a second. *Lord, please help me find him. Please.*

"Luke? Where are you? Answer me."

Her cell phone rang and Julie feared it might be Joey or Mari calling with last-minute instructions. She considered ignoring the ring but desperation won out. "Hello," she called.

"Hi, Julie. It's Noah. Mari asked me to remind you to pick up Marc's prescription. I forgot to call when I got back from the airport."

"I've lost Luke," she cried as she searched the area for the missing child.

"Calm down, honey. When did you see him last?"

"He was right here when I stopped to look at a sweater. Matt and Marc were running around the racks and. . ." Julie gulped back the hot tears that burned her throat. "It couldn't have been more than a minute."

"Take a deep breath. Was Luke running with them?"

"No. I don't know. What if someone took him?"

"Go to the service desk now and ask for help. They'll know what to do."

Julie scanned the area. "I don't see it, Noah. Where is he? He was right here."

"Do you see a store clerk?"

She urged the group a few steps farther, cringing when Marc whined that he was hungry. She didn't doubt it after the way he'd played with his lunch. Feeding him was the least of her worries right now. "No McDonald's until we find your brother."

Luke crawled from underneath the clothes rack. "Pway on swide!" he exclaimed, clapping his hands in glee.

"Daniel Lucas Dennis, you scared me to death!" Julie yelled. "I thought someone had taken you."

His face puckered. "Pway hide-seek, Auntie Hulie."

She dropped the phone into the stroller and lifted him into her arms. "Honey, Auntie Julie's sorry she screamed at you, but you have to answer when I call your name. We don't play hide-and-seek in stores."

"He does that all the time," Matt announced.

"Why didn't you say so?" Julie snapped, feeling instant remorse. They were only children. Matt didn't understand how terrified she'd been.

Naomi chose that moment to hurl the cell phone, and Julie dove for it, barely keeping it from hitting the floor. She laid it on her purse in the upper section of the stroller and moved into the checkout line. "Tell you what, guys, let's pay for these things and we'll visit the drive-thru on the way home."

No way was she letting them out of the van again until they returned home.

Julie urged them forward. Her cheeks flamed beet red when she heard someone calling her name and realized she'd left Noah hanging on the phone. She lifted it to her ear. "You heard?"

"You used his full name. Luke must really be in trouble."

"Talk about conflicting emotions. Does it count that I hugged him after I yelled?"

"Remember what Joe said. You have to be firm with Luke. You have everything under control."

"Just barely. I hope I can keep it together until I get home. I'm not letting them out of the van again until then."

"But Luke wants to pway," Noah reminded, using the small boy's word.

"Not today."

"Better prepare yourself for a tantrum."

"I hope not. I don't think I could handle that on top of his disappearance."

"Respond in love, Julie. Don't do or say anything in anger that you'll regret later."

Was he talking about the kids or them? "When Joey told them I'd discipline them, I didn't realize how serious he was."

"Why would you think that? You've spent time around them in the past. Didn't you discipline them then? Or did you think they'd be angels for you?"

She glanced up to find the clerk watching the boys pile candy on the counter. "I have to go. I'm in the checkout line. Put those back, Luke."

"Don't get upset, Julie."

"Today's been enough to make me rethink the possibility of children in my future," Julie told him as she unloaded her purchases onto the counter, all the while keeping the three boys in her line of vision.

"No way. You'll make a wonderful mother. We'll talk when you get home. Don't forget the prescription."

"Does the pharmacy have a drive-thru?"

Noah laughed. "You're serious about not letting them out of the van again, aren't you?"

"Very."

"I'll run by the drugstore," he volunteered.

"Thanks, Noah. I'll buy you a burger for dinner."

"Make that two. I skipped lunch."

"We should be home within the hour."

"See you around six."

Later, while seated around the dinner table eating their takeout, Julie found herself relaxing a bit. Luke had not misbehaved. He had whined a bit but accepted her one sharp no. Julie suspected he realized he'd pushed her to the end of her rope already.

"I don't think he understands how frightening his disappearing like that was," Julie told Noah after the older boys finished and left the room.

"Luke is willful, stubborn, independent, and cute," Noah said. "Reminds me of someone else I know."

"Stop flirting, Noah."

"Why? Does it bother you? You never minded before."

Naomi tossed her sippy cup off the high chair. Noah caught it before it hit the floor and set it on the table. "You didn't answer, Julie Joy."

Very few people knew her full name. Her mother had been so delighted to have a daughter that she'd given her the middle name of Joy. Joey used it now and again and Noah loved to call her by her full name.

"I don't know. Can we have this discussion later?" she asked when John began to cry.

"Definitely. I need to know where I stand with you."

Julie removed the toddler from his chair and then Naomi from hers. "Come on, kids. Bath time."

"How about I keep an eye on the older boys while you bathe the twins?"

"Okay."

Upstairs, she put Naomi in her crib and took John to the bathroom. The idea of bathing both of them at once made her uncomfortable. Two slippery toddlers would be more than she could handle. Once John was in the tub, Julie found herself so preoccupied with thoughts of Noah waiting to see where he stood with her that she poured baby oil in her palm instead of shampoo. *What a mess that would have been,* she thought as she rinsed her hand in the bathwater.

She dried John and dressed him in his nightclothes before putting him in his crib. She wound the toy on the side of his crib and soft music filled the room. Julie lowered the lights before she took Naomi into the bathroom.

How would she keep from telling Noah how upset she was with him? There was no way she'd admit her true feelings. She tucked Naomi in for the night and went to the top of the stairs to call Marc and Luke. Soon all the kids were in pajamas and settled in bed. "Can Noah read our bedtime story?"

Julie called him from the top of the stairs. This house needed an intercom system. "The boys want you to read to them," she said when Noah came into view.

"I'd love to."

They had already picked out the book they wanted him to read. She watched for a couple of minutes and whispered, "I'll be downstairs."

Julie stopped by the nursery to check the babies and found them asleep. She retrieved the hamper from the bathroom and put a load of towels in the washer before going into the kitchen. It surprised her that Noah had picked up the debris from dinner and cleaned the kitchen. He'd even taken out the garbage.

While she waited on the laundry, Julie used her PDA to check her e-mail. "Are they asleep?" she asked when Noah returned.

He joined her on the sofa. "All tucked in, story read, and prayers said. Luke prayed that Auntie Hulie wouldn't be mad at him anymore."

Her heart clenched in her chest. She started to stand. "I should talk to him."

Noah caught her hand and shook his head. "He's asleep. Besides, he needs to understand it's dangerous to disappear like that. He knows you were afraid for him. He learned a lesson today."

Julie dropped back down on the sofa. "Why did I agree to this?"

"You're doing fine," Noah said, taking her hand in his. "You can't let the kids get to you. I know Luke's disappearance frightened you, but it worked out. Mari's technique is to divide and conquer. She never takes all the kids anywhere without assistance. If Joe's working, she waits until he comes home and takes a couple with her and leaves the others with him."

Julie slid her PDA back inside her purse and settled back on the sofa. "That's impossible since I'm only one person."

"I'll be your backup."

"Once I convinced myself I could handle this, I jumped in feet first. I don't mind the babysitting part, but I don't want to be the enforcer."

"No one does. But it's part of the job. Children need the love and guidance adults provide."

"It's hard."

He tucked a strand of hair behind her ear. "Just remember you're doing a good thing. Joe and Mari are getting a badly needed break and you're spending quality time with five kids who love you very much."

"I melt every time Luke calls me Auntie Hulie," she told him with a broad grin. "It's so hard to stay angry with him."

"Don't think Luke doesn't know it. He can wrap his mom and dad around his finger, too."

"I've seen you cave in, as well."

"Yep, they're great kids. Wish I had half a dozen just like them."

Julie shook her head. "Not me. Anything more than a couple requires great patience, and I can't claim an excess of that."

"Okay, do yourself a favor. Lean back and forget the kids. They're in bed for the night. You're free for eight hours."

"More like four. One or the other of them will be awake and needing something by then."

"Relax and don't think about that right now," Noah encouraged, sliding his arm around her shoulders. "Just rest and talk to me."

The dreaded talk. She tensed.

"Something's changed, Julie Joy. I noticed it when you were here this summer. I thought it might have to do with what was going on with Mari. But you've been distant for months now."

"Everything's changed, Noah," she blurted.

Puzzlement filled his expression. "In what way?"

Julie reached for a pillow that lay on the floor. "Seeing you. Talking face-to-face. We spent so much time together in the past that we never had these uncomfortable pauses. I feel them now."

"I don't feel any differently. I can't tell you how much I looked forward to having you here. I've missed you so much."

He obviously didn't have a clue. "Your choice, Noah. You know how I feel about long-distance relationships. You were the one who moved away. Frankly, telephone calls and e-mails aren't my idea of courtship."

"But I thought you understood that I had to follow God's leading."

"Why couldn't He leave you where you were? Joey and Mari followed His leading. Isn't it enough that my family followed His call?" Julie demanded.

"I had no choice. I want to work with Joey here at Cornerstone. I need the experience, and he's given me a new perspective which will help when I get a church of my own."

The overwhelming hopelessness that had filled her for months made itself felt. "That's all that matters, isn't it, Noah? Getting your own church."

He shook his head. "No. It's about a future of serving the Lord in the best way I know how."

She couldn't bear the closeness another moment. Julie stood and walked a few steps away. "I thought you were beginning to care about me."

"I was. I do," Noah insisted as he came to his feet.

"Then why is it I feel like I'm at the bottom of the heap in this relationship?"

"I care for you, Julie, but there's an order in my life and God will always come first. Isaiah 30:18 says, 'The Lord longs to be gracious to you; he rises to show you compassion. For the Lord is a God of justice. Blessed are all who wait for him !.' "

"What does that mean?" she demanded, exasperated that he'd quoted scripture rather than giving her the straightforward answer she wanted.

"It means we wait on God's timing, not our own. No matter where we might think our relationship is headed, it won't go anywhere without God shedding His grace on us."

"And exactly how does He develop this relationship?" Julie demanded with a scowl of protest. "How can He bless us when we can't even be together because He sent you so far away?"

Noah held her arms and looked her straight in the eye. "Distance is not the problem. God wants to bless you, Julie, but He wants you to exalt and serve Him. Why have you stopped?"

Joey had done his job. Noah had jumped on the bandwagon. She wanted all of them off her case. "I haven't," she denied. "I still believe."

"But you're not interested in serving?"

"I told you I'm busy," she said, refusing to look at him.

A steadfast look of determination crossed Noah's face as he lifted her chin and said, "We all are. Did you ever think that maybe Jesus Christ was too busy to die on the cross for us? For me, there's never enough opportunity to show my gratitude. I need to be in church every time the doors open. And when I'm not there, I should be using my free time to read His Word, pray, and witness to the lost."

"But you do those things anyway. That's your job."

Noah shook his head. "It's more than a job. It's every Christian's calling. When I accepted His name, I committed to become Jesus' disciple. And that means I go wherever He sends me. Never doubt that I wanted to stay with you in Denver, but I couldn't."

Julie spotted some toys the boys had left pushed under the chair. She picked them up and dumped them into the toy baskets. She glanced at Noah. "You've made friends here. Aren't there women who interest you?"

A frown creased his forehead. "Don't you think I'd tell you if that were the case?"

Julie shrugged. "Maybe you didn't know how."

"You don't have a very good impression of me if you think that. When I commit to anything, I'm in it for the long run. I can't be serious about you if I'm dating other women. Do you want to date other men? Is that what you're trying to tell me?"

"No. I miss you, Noah," Julie said softly, staring down at the stuffed animal she held.

"I miss you, too, but it's not forever. Once we work through this, our relationship will be stronger."

"How is that possible? I live in Colorado. You live in South Carolina. I see you once or twice a year. That's no way to build a relationship."

"Miles don't matter when you love someone, Julie Joy."

"Noah? I—"

"Don't panic." He advanced and reached for her hand. "Stop running from me. I care for you a great deal and I'm pretty certain I love you."

Julie pulled away. "How can you say that—after the way you abandoned me? You didn't give me any consideration in the matter."

"I did. I do."

"No. You didn't. You walked away from me—from us. I won't risk giving my heart to another person who can't be there when I need them."

Noah appeared shocked by her words. "I had no idea you felt this way."

"Okay, so now you know. What are you going to do about it?" she challenged.

"I'm going to pray for God's guidance—ask what He wants me to do."

Julie frowned. "You've already prayed, Noah. He told you to come here."

"Following God's will doesn't mean you only get one desire of your heart, Julie. He blesses you in all areas of your life."

"I think it's time we called it a night," Julie said, not bothering to respond to that. "The kids get up early."

"I need to know one thing. Do you care for me enough to ask for God's direction in respect to our relationship?"

Julie remained silent as she led the way to the front door. She lifted his jacket and held it out to him.

"Please pray about this, Julie," Noah beseeched as he took the coat. "I don't want to lose you."

"I have prayed, Noah, and I suspect God's told us we're better off apart."

Chapter 3

Parenting was no easy task.

Julie fell into bed, feeling more tired than if she'd worked round the clock. The minutes passed and she found she couldn't sleep. As if the children weren't enough strain, this emotional tug-of-war with Noah had drained her. She'd been honest with him tonight.

What did she want of him? Would she follow him whenever and wherever God dictated? She honestly didn't know that she could. He'd asked her to pray. She had prayed for peace of mind since the day Noah left her. She didn't want to think about it anymore tonight.

Julie fluffed the pillows and located Mari's list on the nightstand where she'd placed it earlier. The number-one item was the tree. If they were going to the tree farm, she would definitely take the twins to the church day care so she could keep Luke close at all times.

How easily he'd disappeared. Almost in the blink of an eye. Goose bumps rose up on her arms. For a moment, the panic she'd felt upon realizing Luke had gone missing paralyzed her. There would be no recurrence of today's incident. Not on her watch.

Julie barely remembered falling asleep before the sound of John's crying woke her. She went into the nursery and took him from the room before he woke Naomi.

"What's wrong, sweetie? Do you miss your mommy?" She filled his sippy cup and settled in the rocker downstairs to cuddle him. Julie hummed softly until he went back to sleep. After returning John to his crib, she headed for the bedroom.

"Auntie Julie, wake up," Matt called, patting her shoulder. She looked up into three sets of eager eyes. The twins weren't there. No doubt they couldn't escape the confines of their cribs. "We're hungry."

"Give me a minute to wash the sand out of my eyes."

Luke jumped onto the bed and peered into her face. "How did you get sand in your eyes, Auntie Hulie?"

She held his cheeks and kissed him on the nose. "You ask too many questions, Lukie." She tickled him and he giggled, screaming for her to stop. Soon the other boys piled on the bed, demanding the same.

Julie glanced at the clock and wiggled out of the heap. They were really roughhousing on the bed when she came out of the bathroom. "Okay, guys,

I don't think your mom would appreciate you jumping on her bed. Let's get the twins and go downstairs."

Julie had planned a healthy breakfast as she showered. Once she had them all in the kitchen, they frowned at every suggestion. Finally, she took cereal from the cabinet and milk from the fridge. The kids seemed satisfied with this so she decided not to sweat the small stuff.

"We're going to pick out our Christmas tree today," she told them as she rinsed juice glasses and placed them in the dishwasher. "Let's get dressed." She instructed the boys to brush their teeth.

They made a great deal of noise as they ran up the stairs.

"Your brothers are too loud," she told Naomi as she removed her from the high chair. The toddler grinned at her.

It took a good hour and a half to get everyone ready. A little less time than the previous day, but Julie wondered how Mari would handle it once the boys started school. She'd have to rise before the sun. On second thought, with her sister-in-law's organizational skills, the change wouldn't cause a blip in their daily schedule.

After delivering the babies to the church nursery, she loaded the boys into the van and checked their seat belts. This would be fun. She remembered the trees of her childhood, the rich scent of fresh evergreen wafting through the house. Strangely enough, as an adult she'd opted to go the artificial tree route, finding it simpler to create the perfect tree that way.

She loved decorating. Every year she searched the after-Christmas sales to choose the theme for next year's tree. She had boxes of decorations and everyone always said what a great job she'd done with her home.

Not only would this year's tree be live, she'd planned a major surprise for the kids. While running errands last week, she'd splurged and purchased every cartoon character ornament and light set she could find. She'd even packed them in a box and brought them on the plane with her. Julie smiled in anticipation of their delight.

She checked the map Mari had drawn. It should be just down the road on the right. According to her notes, the owner of the tree farm was a member of the congregation who donated the trees for the church and parsonage each year.

After parking, Julie turned to face the boys. "Okay, guys, here's the deal. I don't want you running off and getting lost, so you have to promise to stay with me. Understand?"

"Yes, Auntie Julie," Matt said, nodding his head.

"Luke, you hold my hand."

The child immediately obeyed her request, and Julie relished the comfort of his tiny hand in hers.

They hadn't been there ten minutes before Julie came to the realization that you didn't allow small boys to pick out trees.

half hour wrestling the overgrown tree into the stand. Julie still wasn't too sure the tree that brushed the ceiling and took up an entire corner would remain standing on its own.

Her nephews liked the cartoon character lights but had demanded their decorations. Matt had led her to the ornament box in the hall closet. She wasn't surprised to find a variety of standard Sunday-school-issue ornaments.

"What is this?" she'd asked, pulling a foil-wrapped paper cup from the box.

"Don't you know a Christmas bell when you see one?" Noah asked when Julie twirled the bell by the string.

"Obviously not."

"That's mine, Auntie Julie," Matt had said, taking it from her hand. "Let's put it right here in front."

"But, Matt, I bought all these great ornaments for the tree. Don't you want to use them?"

"I like my bell."

"Okay." She'd reluctantly pushed aside the new items, and they'd hung all the decorations in the box.

Tree decorating hadn't held the boys' interest for long, and they'd charged around the room, falling over boxes. When Luke stepped into a box of ornaments, Julie yelled, "Stop running or you're all going to bed now!"

Noting her frustration, Noah had stepped in and said, "Hey, guys, want to show Aunt Julie what you're doing in the Christmas play?"

Though they'd pushed and shoved in the fight for the limelight, he'd quickly organized them.

Matt spoke his few words of dialogue and had constantly looked to Noah for prompting. Marc and Luke had non-speaking roles, though she couldn't imagine how they planned to keep the two of them still long enough to produce a play.

Now that the children had been bathed and were in bed, Julie and Noah sank into the living room chairs. She leaned back and stared at the evergreen gracing the corner of the room. "Did you notice anything about this tree?"

"You mean beyond its monstrous size?"

"Most of the ornaments are below the three-foot level."

"Little-boy height," he said with a broad grin.

"Exactly." Julie pushed herself up out of the chair. "Oh well, I might as well finish decorating the green monster."

Noah stood and reached for the box of ornaments Julie had rescued from Luke's sneakered feet earlier. He used the ribbons she had tied on to hang them higher in the tree. "You were disappointed by the kids' reactions to your decorations."

He was too astute by far. "I'd hoped to please them. I should have known it wouldn't be easy. One thing I'll say about my nephews and niece is that they have minds of their own. And I'm proud they want to honor tradition even if I'm a bit disappointed I can't give them the perfect tree this year."

"Is perfection really that important?"

Julie held up the glass cartoon ornament for which she'd paid a hefty price. "I just thought the kids would love these."

"They do. But they like their ornaments, too. Don't you have ornaments that make it onto the tree every year no matter what theme you choose?"

Julie nodded, staring glumly at the tree. How different it was from what she'd planned. Noah had cut off a considerable amount just to get it into the house. Then finding a good side took some doing. At least the boys loved the musical lights, but she suspected she would hate them before the holidays were over.

"There are children in this world who have never seen cartoon lights," Noah commented. "Some never see a Christmas tree. Above everything else, Joe and Mari's children know the true meaning of Christmas. The extraneous trappings can never be as important as the true gift of Jesus.

"Besides, this poor pitiful tree might never have had anyone to love it if you and the kids hadn't come along. You, with your big tender heart and great love for those boys."

"Good point. Even this tree deserves love. Let's just pray I can keep it standing through the holidays."

"So how was your second day with the kids?"

"Busy." Julie shifted ornaments higher up on the opposite side of the tree. "What about you? How's your sermon going? Joey told me you were looking forward to filling in for him."

"I do appreciate the opportunity to preach. Of course, Joe is a tough act to follow. The congregation at Cornerstone loves him a great deal. He preaches to a full house every Sunday."

"I'm sure you'll do well," Julie told him. "Lots of people come to church for Christmas services."

Noah smiled wryly. "I suppose I should be thankful for that, but I'd rather people came to hear the message God wants me to share with them."

She adjusted the drape of the light strand over the branches. "They will. Give them time. You have years to serve God to your fullest."

"I'm ready now."

Julie turned to face him. "Then why follow Joey? Why not find a church of your own? A place where you don't have to live up to someone else's track record?"

"I need experience. Most churches consider me unproven material."

His response puzzled Julie. "Seems they wouldn't pass judgment until they'd heard you preach."

Noah picked up the tree topper, glanced at the tree, and back at Julie. "You have those clippers handy? We need to shave off some branches if you plan to use this."

"I'll be right back."

When she returned with the clippers, Noah climbed up the stairs and pulled the treetop closer. After trimming up the branches and stuffing them in the garbage bag Julie provided, he slid the glass character into place.

"Can you trim this tree all the way down?"

Noah shook his head. "It would be easier to slip out tomorrow and get a new tree. Think the boys would notice?"

"Probably. So explain why you're unproven material."

"In your case, age has nothing to do with your ability. You're an up-and-coming computer whiz kid. When they consider my age, I lack maturity, and being single doesn't help."

"That's a plus about my job. No husband required."

"I've always been fascinated by your work. I wouldn't have a clue where to begin."

"Experience." Though she enjoyed her work as a software engineer, Julie rarely discussed it with noncomputer people. Her tendency to get technical often resulted in glazed expressions. "So you like the area?"

"Different accent. Hospitable people. Actually, it's a great place to live. I could see myself here for a while."

Julie fiddled with the ribbon she held, tying it into a bow. Secretly, she admitted she liked the area, too. Back in the summer, Mari had insisted that she and Joe play tourist, and Julie had enjoyed herself a great deal. They'd laughed as they crammed as much into one action-packed day as possible. They'd walked along the beach, played a game of miniature golf, and gone to the Pavilion amusement park. Then they'd stuffed themselves on fresh seafood, and she'd begun to understand why so many people planned their vacations at the beach.

Still, she couldn't see herself living in Myrtle Beach. "I miss them all so much," Julie said. "I was heartbroken when the ministry called Joey and Mari away from Denver. I miss doing the aunt thing with the older kids, and I barely know the twins."

Noah flashed Julie a sympathetic smile. "You and Joe grew closer after your parents died, and now you live so far apart."

Her thoughts drifted back to the day Joey had called her friend's house to say her father was dead and her mother was in the emergency room. Her dad had taken her mom for a drive in his pride and joy—the old MG he'd rebuilt. A deer had darted onto the highway, and in his effort to avoid it, Joseph Dennis Sr. had rolled the car. The impact killed him. Her mother sustained a substantial amount of internal damage. Joey arrived minutes after the doctor pronounced Lillian Dennis dead.

At eleven, her parents' deaths destroyed her life. She'd always been their little princess, and then they were gone. Julie had grieved a great deal for the loving parents who had been ripped from her.

Joey constantly reassured her that everything would be okay. The accident happened in May, just one week before the school year ended. Fear of the changes she'd have to make haunted Julie, but her twenty-four-year-old brother changed his life to make sure nothing changed for her.

He gave up his apartment and came home. Julie slept in her bed, lived in the house she'd always lived in, and attended the school she'd always attended. She'd been fourteen when Joey and Mari married.

Once again, Julie had feared change, but Mari had loved and cared for her in the same way Joey had. Mari had worked with Joey, and when the time had come for Julie to go off to college, they'd helped with the costs.

"Yeah, Joey gave up everything for me."

"Seems so strange to hear you call him Joey."

"He tells me it's childish, but he's always been Joey to me."

"What about me, Julie? Do you miss me, too?"

Before she could answer, Luke surprised them both when he joined them at the tree. He found the control switch that started music playing and then rubbed his eyes. "Nay-Nay's crying."

"Oh! I didn't hear her," Julie cried, thinking she should have added a baby monitor to the shopping list. "She and John aren't sleeping well. Probably missing their parents."

Noah swung the child into his arms. "Come on, buddy. I'll tuck you in while Aunt Julie takes care of your sister."

Julie took Naomi from the crib and changed her. Noah walked out of the boys' bedroom just as she stepped into the hall with the child.

"Can I hold her?"

Julie handed Naomi to Noah. "I'll get her milk."

Noah and Naomi were sitting in the rocker recliner when she returned. She passed him the cup and returned to hanging ornaments on the branches.

She glanced at Noah a few minutes later and found him studying the sleeping baby. "I can't get over how perfect they are," he admitted with a sheepish grin. "You'd better take her. I need to get out of here so you can get to bed."

"Thanks for your help, Noah."

"Thanks for the tree party. I enjoyed myself." He lifted his coat off the coatrack and slid it on. "Oh, don't forget the final play practice Saturday at four. We'll probably run through it a couple of times since the play is Sunday night. There's a little party for the kids afterward."

"We'll be there. Are all the kids like Joey's? They seem a bit. . .um. . . reluctant."

"They'll do fine. Kids are born hams."

"Anything I can do to help?" Julie asked.

Noah winked. "Taking good care of my star performers is plenty."

Chapter 4

After an early delivery arrived the next day, Julie bundled the kids up and headed outside midmorning to work on the exterior decorations. The boys ran to play on the swing set as the twins watched from their stroller. She had brought all the boxes out onto the patio earlier to make things easier.

While people who lived in the area might consider it a cold day, Julie found it almost balmy in comparison to the December Colorado weather she'd lived with all her life. One of her friends had e-mailed her last night to tell her they had six inches of snow on the ground.

"What are you doing?" Noah asked.

Julie whirled to face him, clutching her chest. "Give a person a little warning next time."

"I saw you toting all these boxes and wondered what you were getting ready to do."

"Part of the shipment arrived today. My yard decorations."

"What sort of decorations?"

Was it her imagination or did he sound suspicious?

"I have tons of stuff," she said, stripping the tape from the box top to remove the inflatable cartoon character. "I can hardly wait for the kids to see it all lit up tonight!"

He grew silent and Julie glanced up at him. "Something wrong?"

Noah looked uncomfortable. "Hmm, Julie, this is the church parsonage. The congregation. . . Well, you know. . . Some of them might. . . What I'm trying to say. . ."

"Spit it out, Noah," Julie said impatiently. "You think the Cornerstone members won't appreciate the cartoon characters or outside lights on the church parsonage?"

He shrugged helplessly. "Some are concerned with appearances. They might find the decorations out of keeping with the true meaning of Christmas."

"Do they realize there are five kids in this house who are as entitled to rejoice as the next person?"

"Well, yes they do, but—"

"But nothing." Julie didn't bother to hide her exasperation. "The fact that their daddy is the minister and their home is the parsonage shouldn't prohibit them from having fun. And given the amount of money this church brings in from the day care, you'd think the membership could accept a few decorations for the kids. Tell me, if I drove by their homes, wouldn't I find similar yard decorations?"

"Probably. I just don't want repercussions for Joe when he comes back."

"He can handle them." Julie pulled the instruction sheet out of the box. "He said I could do whatever I wanted."

"Surely you realize he expects you to exercise restraint."

"So, I promise not to drain the electric company, but I do intend to string some lights and put up my decorations. If it makes you feel better, I have a Bethlehem Star for the porch and plan to put Joe and Mari's lighted nativity in the front yard."

"I'm sure that will be appreciated."

"So why don't you make yourself useful and help me figure this thing out?"

"Sorry, no can do," Noah said as he backed away. "That would make me an accomplice, and I'm already in enough hot water as it is."

"Because of this?"

"No," Noah said. "A member took exception to the topic for the Sunday morning sermon."

"Didn't you say you planned to preach on loving your neighbor?" Noah nodded. "That's ridiculous. It's what Jesus says in the Bible, not the gospel according to Noah."

"These ladies have feuded for years. It never occurred to me that they would feel I directed the sermon at them. They weren't even on my mind."

"Joey says he tells them he's only a messenger for God."

"I doubt that would work for these ladies," Noah said. "And what do I tell the director of music? He accused me of trying to do his job when I named a couple of songs to go along with Sunday's sermon."

"Joey doesn't request specific music?"

"Not exactly. Rob pointed out that Joe recommends songs. I didn't think he would be offended."

"It's ridiculous that people get so out of sorts over little things. Particularly Christians."

"Sinners saved by grace, Julie. Christians are no different from everyone else. Our feelings get hurt, we feel insulted, and we get angry when injustices occur. And we seek repentance and try to do better."

"Whose side are you on anyway?"

Noah grinned at her. "I'm on the side of right. Joe is always advising me to proceed slowly and cautiously."

"This church needs to open itself to change."

"Churches are about balance, Julie. No one group can control the situation. Philippians 2:2 says, 'Make my joy complete by being like-minded, having the same love, being one in spirit and purpose.' I'd be remiss in my duties if I didn't ask forgiveness from those I've offended just as I've asked you not to go overboard."

Julie hated feeling controlled. Rebellion surged within her. "Consider me forewarned."

"They'll probably send me to talk to you later," Noah responded.

"The messenger for their dirty work, huh?"

"It would be my pleasure to visit with you and the kids."

Julie surrendered. "Okay, Noah, just for you, so you don't get in hot water with the congregation, I'll keep it as low-key as possible. I can put most of the kids' stuff in the backyard where they can see it from the kitchen and family room. I'd planned to anyway so the day care kids could see it from the playground."

"Thanks, Julie Joy."

"Anytime." She started to the house and whirled back toward Noah. "I do have a singing welcome Santa for the porch. You think I'd better put him in the foyer?"

"Probably best so he doesn't conflict with the nativity," Noah said, grinning when Julie made a face at him.

Julie recognized that her desire to defy Noah and decorate the yard as she pleased stemmed from her anger, but deep inside she knew he was right. Joey would have restrained her if he'd been there. It was so much harder to accept from Noah because she'd once considered him her soul mate. They'd shared so many fun times, and now he seemed determined to control her.

By the time the inflated character rose to its ten-foot glory, lunchtime had arrived. Julie fought the temptation to stick the kids in the van and go for meals. Instead, she made toasted cheese sandwiches and soup.

Afterward, she cleaned the kitchen and put Naomi and John down for their naps. Matt and Marc went off to play, and Luke wandered around the house in search of his favorite truck. When he couldn't find it, he came to her for help. They found it at the bottom of one of the toy baskets.

Julie pulled the box containing the singing welcome Santa into the living room. Once she removed all the wrappings, she found it was only two feet tall. Surely something held it in place. She settled on the sofa with the instructions and tried to figure out why her life-sized Santa was so short.

"What doing, Auntie Hulie?"

She looked up at Luke. "Reading instructions."

Luke leaned on the Santa's head and Julie heard it click. He cried out when the Santa sprang to its full height, knocking him backward. His weight must have released whatever held it in place.

Julie jumped to her feet and picked the child up. "Luke? Are you okay?"

Seeing the way he looked at the Santa before he walked out of the room, Julie doubted Luke would have much use for the decoration. Oh well, if she made Santa sing, maybe Luke would change his mind.

She reached for the instruction sheet again. After figuring out how to make Santa sing and placing him at the end of the staircase in the vestibule, Julie pulled the next box over and began assembling the reindeer. Somewhere there was a sleigh with a waving Santa to be unpacked.

Her thoughts returned to Noah. Day three and they'd eaten, decorated, and cared for the kids together, and yet she still felt so distant from him. She didn't want to need Noah Loughlin. He expected her to understand and accept her place in his life without question or regard to herself. Julie considered that selfish.

Maybe Noah believed he could gain experience here at Cornerstone, but Julie felt he could have done so closer to home. Closer to her. She couldn't help but feel he'd put distance between them on purpose. She suspected her age had motivated him to give her time. Whatever the case, she didn't plan to give him the opportunity to hurt her again. If he needed distance, he could have all he wanted.

The doorbell rang. As she passed within range of the motion detector, the Santa began to twist at the waist and sing. Julie smiled and opened the door. "Noah?"

"I'm on my lunch break. I thought I'd stop by and make sure everything's okay."

"You don't need to check on us so often," Julie told him, turning back toward the living room.

He followed her. "I wanted to make sure you understood about the decorating."

"I remember a time when you would have pitched in and helped. You're different."

"Not really. I still enjoy the things we did together, the time we spent with each other. Those are my fondest memories."

Memories. She'd become a fond memory. Not exactly where she wanted to be. The silence grew more awkward and Julie asked, "You want a sandwich?"

"I wouldn't mind."

"We had toasted cheese for lunch. I think there might be some ham if you prefer a hot ham and cheese."

"Sounds great."

He followed her into the kitchen and sat at the table when she refused his help. "I remember sharing more than one of these with you," he said when she handed him the plate.

"Quick and easy. What do you want to drink?" She listed his options and he chose milk.

He took a bite of the sandwich. "Tell me about Mac and Bo. How are they doing?"

Julie poured a glass of milk and pushed the refrigerator door closed. She set it on the table and shrugged. "I rarely see them. We're all busy."

"You're too busy for friends?" Noah asked.

"They were always more your friends than mine."

"They liked you, Julie."

"I liked them, too. It's a struggle to see everyone," Julie defended.

"You were in the same Sunday school class."

"Don't go there, Noah. We'll only argue."

He pushed the plate away, leaving half the sandwich uneaten. "Is there anything we can discuss without arguing? I'm trying to understand, Julie, but you're determined to make it more difficult every time I see you."

"So why don't you just stay away?" she snapped as she grabbed a cloth and wiped down the counter.

He stood and placed his hands on her shoulders, turning her to face him. "Because I care about you."

Joey's words about Noah's popularity with the single women at Cornerstone came to mind. "I find that difficult to believe."

Anger changed his expression. "You know what, Julie? I don't think you care how I respond to that. You've already made up your mind. Believe what you want."

He stormed out of the kitchen and headed for the front door. Julie followed.

The Santa burst to life, directing Noah to have himself a Merry Christmas.

"Oh, shut up!" Noah yelled as he jerked the door closed.

Chapter 5

The remainder of the decorations went up and the follow-up visit never occurred. Even though Julie resented not being able to go all-out for the kids, she accepted proving a point would only antagonize the membership, and she really didn't want to do that.

She'd opted for a religious theme in the front and hid the lights and cartoon characters in the backyard. It bothered Julie that people saw evil in innocence, but right now learning to be a temporary mother kept her fully occupied.

The main thing she'd already learned was nothing went as expected when you had five children. Just getting them up, fed, and dressed exhausted her but by no means diminished their incredible energy levels.

Julie spent her days running here and there, asking questions they couldn't answer, and searching the lists for guidance from Mari. She'd be lost without her sister-in-law's information.

On Wednesday she'd braved the mall to have the children's pictures taken with Santa. Marc took an intense dislike to the jolly one, and Julie talked him into posing by Santa's knee rather than sitting on his lap. All the framed photos sat on the fireplace mantel along with the children's stockings.

By Friday she'd become friends with the deliveryman who'd stopped by every morning to leave yet another box. With the last of the decorations in place, she'd been able to concentrate on her gift-wrapping after the children were in bed.

Today was the final play practice. "Matt, where is your costume?" she asked when she couldn't find the information anywhere.

He shrugged and said, "I don't know."

She breathed deeply and reminded herself he was only five. It didn't matter that he could name every cartoon character in the video they'd watched earlier. Things like costumes weren't as important. "You've got play practice this afternoon. Why don't we go over your lines?"

Matt continued to connect and stack plastic blocks as he recited his lines a couple of times. Julie had to prompt him both times and felt certain he wouldn't recall them Sunday night.

One of the many plans she'd carried through on before flying out of Denver was to purchase a video camera. She decided now would be a perfect time to videotape the boys and let them see their performances.

"Marc. Luke. Come here," she called.

Her breath stopped when both boys brushed past the tree as they raced into the room. "Don't run in the house," she instructed. "If I get my new video camera, will you guys show me what you do in the play?"

When Matt nodded, Marc and Luke did the same.

"I'll be right back." John stood on the sofa beside her. Julie grabbed him around the middle and rested him on her hip. He grinned at her and she asked, "Are you Aunt Julie's boy?"

"Me am!" Luke cried, racing after Julie and throwing his arms about her legs.

She caught herself just before falling against the wall. She'd never get used to the boy's ambushes. "Yes, you are," she agreed, patting him on the back. "Play with your brothers until I get back."

Julie had studied the operation manual during her flight and felt confident she could operate the camera—especially after her fellow passenger had recognized the video camera and shared some operating tips. She picked up the small black case and started downstairs.

She would leave the camera with Joey and Mari. Of course Joey would say no, but she'd already thought of a way around his refusal. After all, if he planned to raise her nephews and niece across the country, the least he could do was send her videos. Movies would be much better than pictures. And, he'd promised not to say anything about the expensive gifts. She'd see if he could keep his word.

She settled John on the sofa and placed the camera case at the opposite end. Removing the camera, she adjusted the viewfinder so she could see all the boys. John launched himself forward, eager to check out the new toy. Julie grabbed him just before he fell off the sofa and settled him in her lap. Filming while moving the busy fingers of a child intent on maneuvering the camera into his mouth took some doing. "Look, John," she said, indicating the viewfinder. "See your brothers?"

Onscreen, the boys jumped and shrieked, waving at the camera. The baby bounced up and down and responded in gibberish. Julie likened them to rubber balls, always on the go. Not that she was so old, but watching them tired her out. John lunged for the camera again and Julie sighed. She felt guilty for wishing he'd taken a nap with Naomi, who slept in the playpen despite the turmoil in the room.

"We're going to make a movie to show Mommy and Daddy. Everybody's going to be in it. See, John wants to be a star," she said, struggling to pull the camera from the toddler's hold. "Who wants to talk first?"

"Me do!" Luke said, waving his arm as he jumped up and down. The entire room vibrated, and Julie held her breath when the tree wobbled behind him.

"Luke, calm down. What did you want to say?"

He ran over to the tree and hit the switch that set the lights to flashing and songs to playing. "Moosic," he said, pointing to the tree as he started to dance.

Not to be outdone, Matt came over and pressed his face against the camera lens. "And I picked out the tree, didn't I, Auntie Julie?"

Julie stifled her laughter and agreed, "You sure did. Do you want to say something to Mommy and Daddy, Marc?"

He hung his head and remained silent, nearly breaking her heart when he began to cry.

Julie turned the camera off and laid it in the case as she placed John on the floor. She moved to where Marc stood and knelt beside him, wrapping the child in a hug. "What's wrong, sweetie?"

"I want Mommy and Daddy to come home."

"They'll be here soon and they'll tell you all about their special trip. I bet they bring you a great souvenir."

"What's a souvenir?" he asked with a tiny sniff.

"A special reminder of places we visit. Would you be my helper today?" she asked, hoping the camera would divert his attention from his missing parents.

When he nodded, Julie took his hand and led him over to the sofa. After settling John at her feet with a stuffed animal, she pulled Marc's tiny body closer and picked up the camera. "Look right here. Do you see Matt and Luke?"

He nodded.

"Okay, guys, are we ready?"

The phone rang, and Julie wished for a cordless phone or an answering machine. She made a mental note to provide either or both before she left for home as she placed the camera on the floor and ran to the kitchen.

"Hello, Julie."

"Noah. Hi."

"You sound out of breath. Playing with the kids?"

"Dashing for the phone."

"Sorry. I wanted to touch base and remind you about practice."

Except for a glimpse of him Wednesday night at church, she hadn't seen Noah since he'd stormed out of the house on Tuesday. He'd called a couple of times but remained suspiciously absent. Neither of them had brought up the argument. Maybe he'd decided he was better off without her. "I didn't forget. We're having rehearsal right now. I bought a video camera and we're making a tape for Joey and Mari. I think seeing themselves perform will help the boys."

He didn't respond.

"Don't you think it's a good idea? Noah?"

"How are they doing?"

"Matt and Luke are real characters. I don't think Marc is showbiz material."

"It's a church production. They'll do fine."

"A little extra rehearsal can't hurt."

"Don't push them, Julie. They're just kids. If they become overwhelmed, they won't do anything."

"Oh, come on, Noah."

"I'm serious. I know you mean well, but please don't *make* them practice. Do something fun instead. Make sure they eat lunch and get the little ones to take a nap. That helps more than all the rehearsals in the world. See you this afternoon."

"What does he know?" Julie asked aloud after replacing the receiver. He wasn't a parent, either. Besides, it was on the list. Item number 36—"Go over Matt's lines with him." Mari had even written them in for her. And if that was what Mari wanted, that's what she'd get. No matter what Noah Loughlin said.

She returned to the living room to find Luke holding the camera upside down while Matt pretended to be a bear.

"Luke!" she yelled, grabbing the camera just before he let go. "This is not a toy, guys. If you want to look at it, ask. Otherwise, don't touch."

When Luke's lower lip wobbled at her stern words, Julie felt remorse. "Come here. You can help me and Marc film Matt showing your parents how he's turned into a bear." She sat on the floor next to John.

Matt started to growl and soon Luke abandoned her to join in. Marc decided he wanted to be in on the fun as well. Their antics were so funny that Julie burst into giggles. The harder she laughed, the worse they became, pushing each other away to stand before the camera. Luke cried out when Matt knocked him down. "Okay, guys, stop."

When she swiped tears from her eyes, John patted her face and said, "Cry?"

"It's okay, sweetie," Julie said, winking at the toddler. "Your brothers are funny bears. Matt, say your lines one more time and we'll watch the tape before lunch."

They weren't bored in the least, Julie thought as the jumble of little boys surrounding her on the sofa giggled at their own antics.

"You think your mom and dad are going to be surprised to find you've turned into wild animals?"

"Bears," Luke cried, growling again as he curled his fingers like claws.

The others followed suit.

"Let's make lunch." The boys followed her into the kitchen, and Julie soon had the meal on the table. So what if it was hot dogs and chips? They liked them. John nodded in his chair, jerking awake each time one of the boys shouted. Julie put him down for a nap and suggested Luke rest as well.

He crawled onto the sofa with the remote control. As he watched and rewound the tape repeatedly, Julie addressed Christmas cards.

When the grandfather clock gonged three o'clock, she put them away and said, "Luke, it's time to get ready for church."

"Don't want to."

"Well, you have to," Julie said, taking the remote and turning off the television.

"They need you in the play."

"Don't want to," Luke repeated, jumping up and running from the room. She heard Joey's office door down the hall slam.

What do I do now? Julie wondered when five minutes passed with no sign of Luke. She couldn't help but speculate how Joey and Mari dealt with their child's temperamental times.

She went to find the other kids, thinking she'd take care of Luke last. Julie soon had them ready to go, but Luke hadn't come out of hiding. She needed advice on this one. Perhaps Noah could give her some clues as to how Joey and Mari handled the situation. Julie dialed the church office. Soon Noah was on the line. "Does Luke have to practice today?"

"It's the final run-through before the performance tomorrow night."

"He doesn't want to."

"Because you rehearsed him?"

"What are you saying? That it's my fault?"

"It's not my fault, either," Noah said.

"I'm sorry, but he said he doesn't want to," Julie stressed. "At least that's what he said when I turned the video off and told him it was time to go."

"What was he watching?"

"We made a video. He's watched it a couple of dozen times. How do Mari and Joey handle him when he's like this?"

"Can I speak to him?"

Julie pulled the long phone cord over to yell down the hall. "Luke, Pastor Noah wants to talk to you.

"At least he came out of the room," she told Noah when the door opened. She leaned against the counter and waited while Luke took the receiver and responded to Noah's comments with head nods.

"Answer him. He can't hear your head rattle."

He's consistent, Julie decided when the child said he didn't want to go three times in a row. Luke held the phone out to her and wandered off again.

"See what I mean?"

"Joe doesn't give in to Luke's stubborn streak. You shouldn't, either. Even if he's not in the play, you have to bring him. If nothing else, perhaps he'll see the others and decide he doesn't want to be left out."

He has a point there, Julie thought. "I'll stress that his parents will be very disappointed and see what happens."

"Hang in there, Julie," Noah urged. "Joe wouldn't allow him to drop out, either."

His encouragement helped. Joey was right. Noah had been a major help. Even when she resented his advice, Julie knew he was only trying to help. She hung up the phone and went to find Luke. Taking his hand, she said, "Come with me. I have something to show you."

In his parents' bedroom, Julie sat on the bed and pulled Luke into her lap. Picking up the list, she pointed to where his mother wrote about the play. "Don't you think your mom will be disappointed when she hears you didn't participate?"

He twisted against her, trying to get down. "Don't want to," Luke muttered again.

Julie restrained him and looked into his face. "Why?"

"Don't want to," he said again.

Noah had said Joey wouldn't let Luke win, but how had he emerged the victor in this battle of wills? She had no idea what had prompted the child to change his mind.

Julie released him. She returned the list to the nightstand and said, "Fine, but you have to go to church with us. You can't stay home alone. Get your coat."

With barely seconds to spare, Julie shepherded her charges across the churchyard. She didn't feel victorious in her dealings with Luke. The child had refused to leave the house until she'd located his favorite shirt. Since she had no idea which shirt that might be and Mari hadn't covered that information on the list, Julie had no idea what to do. Matt had saved the day when he pulled the bright blue knit shirt from the drawer.

Once inside the church, Julie guided Luke into the pew and held John and Naomi on her lap. She smiled at the woman who came over and introduced herself as Kimberly Elliott.

"I'm the church's drama queen," she said, waving her arms flamboyantly as she gave a little bow.

Julie laughed and snaked a hand over Naomi's head to shake hands. "I'm Julie Dennis. Pastor Dennis is my brother. I don't think we met when I was here this summer."

"I was on vacation." Kimberly touched both babies' cheeks and then spoke to Luke, who hid behind the pew. "Pastor Noah told me you weren't going to be in the play. Too bad," she said sadly. "You did a great job as the shepherd boy. Guess I'll have to find someone else for my surprise."

" 'Prise?" Luke said, jumping up.

Kimberly nodded. "I have a real baby lamb. Guess I'd better find someone to take your place. Nice having you with us, Julie. 'Bye, kids."

Apparently Luke didn't care for the idea of giving up his role when there were live props involved, and soon he was on his way to the front of the church. Julie breathed a sigh of relief. John wanted to walk the length of the pew, and when she tried to settle him down, he started to cry.

Noah came over to sit at the other end of the pew.

"I'm hopeless at this," she said when her efforts to calm the child failed.

Noah flashed Julie a reassuring smile as he picked John up. "You're doing a great job."

"I doubt Joey and Mari would think so. I've done nothing but feed them junk food—hot dogs and chips, burgers and fries, chicken tenders, cold cereal, pizza—and now they're getting away with murder because I can't discipline them. I even have a church play dropout." She didn't even want to think about having lost Luke at the store.

"They trust you with the kids. They know you love them and will see to it they're cared for properly."

Julie noticed the looks in their direction and felt terribly embarrassed. "I should take them home. Could you bring the boys home after practice?"

"I suppose," he said. "They're having a cast party afterward. I'd hoped you'd stick around for that."

Naomi started to cry. Helplessly, Julie looked from one crying child to the other.

"Why don't we walk with them a bit?" Noah suggested. "They get tired of sitting still."

"Don't you need to help out here?"

"They can spare me."

She followed him into the fellowship area. Noah put John on the floor and let him go, keeping watch on the toddler as he wandered across the big room. When Julie did the same for Naomi, the little girl followed her brother.

Volunteers worked busily setting up for the party. A huge tree stood on the corner of the stage area, all dressed in white.

"Beautiful tree," Julie said, aware of the wistfulness in her tone.

Noah picked up a couple of cups from the table and filled them with punch. "The church ladies made all the decorations. We're having a White Christmas celebration next Wednesday night. They've planned a variety of activities to appeal to all ages. I hope you'll come."

She flashed him a look of disbelief. "You think I'm brave enough to bring these kids to something like that?"

Noah grinned and nodded his head. "Sure. Chances are you'd be on your own before the evening begins. People here love the kids. By the way, you can put the babies in the nursery Sunday night."

"Oh good, I wanted to. . ." She stopped talking and ran over to release John's hold from the tablecloth he seemed determined to pull to the floor. She guided him back to where they sat. "I thought I'd tape the play for Joey and Mari."

"Actually, the church has a videographer."

Julie's attention perked up. "Really? I didn't know that."

"Cornerstone has an active music ministry. They also film Joey's sermons and deliver them to the homebound. There's been talk of a local television program but that hasn't gone anywhere."

"Joey never mentioned that."

"He'll do it if that's God's plan, but he's not eager to be on camera."

Her brother, the television star. She would have to razz Joey about that.

Actually, she knew he had the charisma to be a television evangelist.

"Who's playing Santa for the Christmas party?"

"We don't do Santa at church," Noah said, waving at a teenage girl who entered through the side door. "I tell the Christmas story instead."

"That's probably best. By the way, where are the costumes? Matt didn't have a clue."

"Here at the church. They use the same ones every year."

"I wish I could have been here earlier. A live nativity would have been fun for the kids," Julie said, her enthusiasm growing.

"You're doing it again," Noah said softly.

"What?" she asked curiously.

"Taking control of the situation. Julie, this congregation has done the same Christmas program for years. I imagine some of the grandparents probably did this play when they were children."

"Well, then it's long past time for a change."

"I hope you don't plan to rock the boat the entire time you're here."

"Rock the boat?" she repeated, unable to control the mutinous frown on her face. "Well, blame it on whoever gave Joey the trip. If they hadn't sent my brother away, I wouldn't be here to interfere."

"You're not interfering," Noah said quickly. "You're a pastor's sister. You know about church politics."

"No, I don't do politics."

"This congregation does things the way their ancestors did them."

"Do the youth stay?"

"Joe said the congregation was primarily senior citizens when he arrived. Most of their children had moved their families on to more progressive churches."

No wonder they wanted Joey as pastor. He and Mari filled a pew, not to mention a Sunday school class. "That's exactly why they should be open to change. To make those kids want to grow up, marry, and raise their families in the church they've attended all their lives."

"The good news is those families are returning and others are joining. The number of children alone has increased tenfold since Joe took the job here."

Something else her brother hadn't told her. He'd never been one to toot his own horn, but Julie considered that quite an accomplishment.

"Joe gives full credit for that to the Lord," Noah told her. "He says all we can do is plant the seed and wait on God for the harvest. I look forward to having a church, to seeing how God uses me, but I have to accept that I'm just getting started in God's business."

"Isn't Joey's vacation your opportunity to shine?"

Noah reached down and lifted John onto his foot to give him a horsey ride. "Now isn't the time. Joe's worked hard here, and I don't want him coming home to troubles I've caused."

She'd heard that one before. "But what about those people you told me about? The ones who are upset with you?"

"We're good. I explained that I didn't mean any harm and asked their forgiveness. Hopefully, Joe won't come home to a request for my resignation," he added with a smile.

"You think they would go that far?" Julie asked, horrified.

"No," he said quickly. "My job is secure."

Julie couldn't help but wonder what Noah would do if his job were terminated. Would he return to Denver? Or would he go elsewhere? She restrained her curiosity and changed the subject. "I've been trying to come up with something for the kids on Christmas Eve. What do you think about Santa dropping off my gifts to them?"

"It might be a little confusing. Santa coming on Christmas Eve and again on Christmas morning."

He had a point. "I thought about having a birthday party for Jesus at the house on Christmas Eve."

Noah studied her for a few moments. "You're always thinking, aren't you?"

"I just want things to be special for them this year."

"So they don't forget Aunt Julie?"

A frown pinched her forehead. "You're really down on me today. I don't want them sad over the Christmas holiday because they miss their parents."

One of the ladies asked if it was okay to give Naomi a cookie. Julie said yes. John laughed as Noah swung him on his foot.

"They don't look particularly depressed to me."

"You wouldn't understand."

"Try me," he challenged.

Julie didn't say anything for several seconds, and then the truth poured out of her. "Joey gave up a lot for me over the years. I owe him, and he's never let me do anything to repay him. I can't fail on this one little thing he's asked of me."

"Did it occur to you that Joey did what God led him to do? He loves you, Julie, and his joy comes in seeing you grow in God and prosper."

"Still, I could have done more over the years. Like this trip, I didn't know they wanted to visit the Holy Land. I wish he'd let me do something without having to force it down his throat."

"Looks like he did. Don't you think these two weeks mean more to Joe than any monetary gift you've ever given them? Your willingness to give up your time this summer and again, now, proves your love beyond measure."

His comment shocked Julie. Taking time off for her family seemed more of a gift for her. "I never considered it as anything more than being there for the family I love."

Like a strike from a bolt of lightning from above, Julie realized that same sense of love had driven Joey to care for her after their parents' deaths.

Noah set his foot on the floor and offered a hand to help John stand. "It's not wrong to want people you love to have nice things, and it's great that you can provide them, but even if you were broke and sleeping on their couch, Joe and Mari would love you."

John toddled off to play peekaboo with one of the adults. Noah appeared amused when Naomi came over and plopped down on his foot. He grabbed her hands and lifted her into the air. "Why don't you just go with the flow and stop trying to organize? These little guys don't know the meaning of the word. Enjoy spending time with the kids. Give them the gift of yourself."

Julie sensed an underlying reason for Noah's direction. "What experience taught you that?"

"It's obvious, huh?" When she nodded, he said, "Don't forget I have a brother with type A personality. He has a wife, two children, and all the plans in the world. Toby nearly worked himself to death until he got the wake-up call a couple of years ago."

Julie shook her head. She smiled when Naomi mimicked her action. "I'm not like that. I just like organization."

Noah's knowing look disputed her claim. "Just so long as you aren't into denial."

"Very funny. I know my limitations."

"I'm not convinced."

One of the women stepped from the kitchen and called that practice would be over in five minutes.

Noah set Naomi on her feet and stood. "Time for announcements. You coming?"

She sighed. "The twins won't sit still. I'll stay here with them."

"I'll be happy to keep an eye on them for you, Miss Dennis."

The volunteer was the young woman who'd entered the fellowship hall a few minutes before. Dubious, Julie looked at the teenager. She was barely sixteen.

"Good idea, Robin," Noah said, grabbing Julie's hand. "Don't worry. She babysits often for Joe and Mari."

"Okay, just long enough to hear the announcements," Julie told the girl as Noah dragged her from the room. "I'll be right back."

"Take your time. I won't let them out of my sight."

"I really shouldn't take advantage of her like that," Julie said as Noah rushed her to the sanctuary. "She's helping prepare for the party."

"We'll be back before you can say all five kids' full names ten times," Noah said with a laugh.

Chapter 6

After announcements, the cast members poured into the fellowship hall. Making sure her brood stayed out of trouble kept Julie busy. The volunteers had organized games and food. The masterpiece of the dessert table was the cake decorated to resemble a nativity.

"Who did that?" she asked Noah.

He studied it for a few minutes. "I'd say Natalie Porter. Avery will be upset."

"Why?" she whispered.

"They have a standing rivalry. Avery owns the bakery and Natalie makes specialty cakes in her home."

"So why didn't he make one, too?"

Noah shrugged. "Probably no one asked him. He doesn't have her flair for the original. You should get a slice of that cake. What Natalie does with cakes could be a sin."

Noah was right about the children. Matt, Marc, and Luke sat with families of their friends. One of Robin's friends had joined her and they begged to watch the twins. "Okay, but come and get me the moment they get to be too much."

"I thought you were joking when you said I'd be alone," Julie told Noah.

"Mari never hesitates when anyone expresses an interest in spending time with the kids."

Maybe that's how she keeps sane, Julie thought.

After going through the line, they joined Kimberly Elliott at her table.

"How did practice go?" Julie asked as Noah held her chair for her.

"The lamb jumped out of Luke's arms," Kimberly said with a laugh. "They were all chasing the poor thing. It took another ten minutes to get them going again after that. I'm glad Luke decided to participate."

"He couldn't refuse. You had him from the moment you said there was a baby lamb."

"Quite possibly the most stupid thing I've ever done," Kimberly said. "I may have to tie it to Luke tomorrow night so it can't run away."

They all laughed.

"Excuse me, ladies," Noah said. "I'll be right back."

"I told Noah the kids would enjoy a live nativity."

"I wish," Kimberly said softly and then looked embarrassed.

"He told me the play never changes."

54

The woman nodded, lowering her voice as she spoke. "I'd so love to produce different dramas for Christmas and Easter, but I don't think the idea would go over well."

"You won't know if you don't try," Julie said.

The woman appeared thoughtful. "I've been working on an Easter play for some time now. Maybe I'll approach Pastor Dennis when he gets home and ask his opinion."

"Do that. I'm certain Joey would be open to the idea." Julie dug her fork into the dessert. "Noah said this cake could be a sin," she said, taking another bite.

"Isn't it, though? Natalie makes excellent cakes."

Noah sat down. "What are you ladies talking about?"

"Julie thinks I should ask Pastor Dennis about the play I've written for Easter," Kimberly said.

Noah glanced at Julie.

"You think it's a bad idea?" Kimberly asked hesitantly.

"Not at all," he said with an easy smile. "I had no idea you'd written a program."

"I've written lots of stuff. Even have some Christmas and Easter programs published."

"I'm impressed. You've been hiding your light under a bushel."

Kimberly flashed him a shy smile. "It's my hope to one day see one of the programs at Cornerstone."

"Then by all means, ask Pastor Dennis for guidance," Noah said. "I'd love to see your production. I'm sure the congregation will be impressed to hear we have an author in our congregation."

Kimberly glanced at her watch. "It's five thirty."

"Guess that's my cue to get ready for my part," he said, winking at them before he headed to the office.

"Noah is a nice guy," Kimberly said, her gaze following him across the room. "Mari mentioned that you and he dated. You make a nice couple."

Were they a couple? Once she'd gotten past her resentment, it had been easy to slip back into the idea of a relationship. But in a few days she'd return home and he'd stay here. Julie couldn't help but wonder if Kimberly's interest was more than passing curiosity.

Noah reappeared dressed as Simeon. The kids giggled when their youthful assistant minister emerged as an elderly man. He took a seat on the stage and called to the children to gather round him on the floor. Instead of the usual spiel about good boys and girls, he launched into the story of the first Christmas. Julie found it refreshing that Cornerstone didn't celebrate the commercial aspect of the holiday.

That's what I forgot, Julie thought. Buying gifts for the kids would not demonstrate the most important part of the Christmas experience. She had seen an angel tree at the mall. Maybe they could pick out a name and buy gifts for needy kids.

After Noah passed out bags of goodies to the kids, he left the stage and came to stand by her side. "So how did I do?"

"Great," she said, glancing down at Luke and Marc to find them busily dumping their bags onto the floor. She knelt to pick up the stuff. "Wait until we get home."

"Mine," Luke said when she inadvertently put his gift into Marc's bag.

One of the mothers approached and spoke to the boys. She reached out to shake Julie's hand. "Hello, Miss Dennis. I'm Merline Jenkins. I thought perhaps Matt could come over one day next week and play with my Jeremy."

What should I do? Julie wondered. She glanced over her shoulder at Noah.

"Mari and Merline often trade off playdates," he said.

Julie wondered if she could talk the woman into taking all the boys for a few hours. "I'll check the schedule and let you know what date is good."

"Wonderful. Maybe having someone to play with will take Jeremy's mind off Christmas. He keeps asking how many more days."

"I wouldn't be so sure of that," Julie said. "Matt's just as excited."

When they started getting the kids into their jackets, Noah asked, "Can I walk you home?"

"If you want." Julie zipped John's coat closed and handed him to Noah before picking up Naomi off the makeshift bed. She wrapped the sleeping child's coat about her and said, "Come on, guys. Time to go."

At the house, Noah unlocked the door and they moved into the living room. The boys flung coats right and left, while John came to Noah for assistance. Julie laid Naomi on the sofa by her side. John toddled over to the toy box.

Noah settled back in the armchair. "I see the tree is still standing."

His words reminded Julie of her plan to secure it to the wall. Luke had almost knocked it over earlier in the day while playing with the switch that activated the lights. She closed her eyes and held her breath every time the boys raced about the room. She really needed to find some string. "Don't breathe hard or it'll fall," Julie cautioned.

As if to prove her point, Marc ran into the room and sent it to rocking. "Luke's a bad boy, Auntie Julie."

Though there were times Julie felt hard pressed not to agree with him, she said, "Don't be a tattletale, Marc. Go play."

When the child ran out, Noah laughed and said, "Seems to be holding up well to me."

"It's a Christmas miracle."

They laughed again.

"That was nice of Mrs. Jenkins to invite Matt over. Of course I don't know how Mari stands adding another child to the group on a regular basis."

"Mari takes it all in stride. She's a great mom."

Julie agreed wholeheartedly. "I'm tempted to offer Mrs. Jenkins all three of the older boys," she said. "I need to finish my shopping but don't dare take them with me after what happened last time."

"Take them to the church day care."

Somehow it didn't seem right to burden others with her responsibilities. "I couldn't."

"Come on, Julie," Noah encouraged. "Give yourself a break."

"Maybe for a couple of hours," Julie relented. "I never realized how hard being a mother is."

"It's harder when you jump into a ready-made family," Noah said. "Having babies one at a time lets you ease into the situation and gain experience as you go."

"You inspired an idea today."

Noah groaned. "Figures. I tell you to take a break and you're inspired to do something else."

"No, it was your Christmas story. I got to thinking about how I've shown the kids a materialistic side of Christmas and thought maybe I'd take them all to the angel tree in the mall and let them choose a name and help me buy the presents. What do you think?"

Noah appeared to give the matter some thought. "How would you explain Santa not coming to those kids' homes?"

"I hadn't thought that far ahead. I suppose it might be confusing for them to grasp the concept. I could tell them Santa picks the stuff up at the mall."

"And put the elves out of business?" he teased.

"Okay, what if I say we're buying special gifts for special kids?"

"Too special for Santa?" He shook his head. "Joe often talks to them about kids who don't have as much as they do. He wants the kids to understand Christmas is about Jesus' birth. They could put money into the Salvation Army buckets."

"What about church families? Anyone need anything?"

"The congregation looks out for them. This side of you fascinates me."

"What do you mean?" Julie asked, puzzled by his comment.

"Your need to give."

"Even if I don't get to church as often as I should, I do thank God for the blessings He gives me daily. I know my successes belong to Him. I just don't have time to get out there and do all I'd like to do."

"I'll keep my ears open just in case. People come into the church office fairly regularly this time of year."

A couple of minutes passed before Noah said, "I need to apologize. I behaved badly Tuesday. Apparently I haven't made my intentions clear."

"I wasn't making accusations, Noah. I can certainly understand that we weren't in the same place in our relationship. It's only natural that you'd want to find a spirit-filled woman to help with your ministry. Kimberly Elliott is very nice."

Bewildered, Noah exclaimed, "I'm not looking for another woman!"

"Then why would Joey say you're popular with the women here at Cornerstone?"

"I don't know. Maybe he was teasing you."

Something clicked in her head. "Or trying to make me jealous?"

"I doubt that. Joe didn't realize how serious I was about you until I told him."

"Noah, what did you do?" Julie asked suspiciously.

"He sort of asked my intentions."

Just what she needed—her overprotective brother involved in her romantic relationship. "What did you say?" she demanded, not bothering to disguise her exasperation.

"That I felt you were avoiding me."

Julie squirmed uncomfortably. Noah wasn't wrong there. She hadn't wanted to talk with him until she got her emotions under control for fear she'd tell him exactly how she felt. Now he seemed determined to bring their problems to the surface.

"This is between us, Noah. And Joey did tell me the women really liked you." She felt herself losing control. Julie didn't want to have this conversation—not now, not ever.

His scowl threw her off guard. "What are you talking about? Can't I talk with another woman without being seriously interested in her? Joe does it all the time. I don't see Mari getting all out of sorts."

"Because Mari is more secure in her place in Joey's life," Julie said pointedly.

"You feel insecure about me? I thought you knew how much I cared."

"I'm not a mind reader."

Noah's mouth dropped open. "I showed you all the time."

"You treated me like a casual date, Noah Loughlin. If we'd been serious, you would have consulted me before making your final decision. We would have discussed the options rather than you driving off to South Carolina without looking back."

"I did this for us. You resent the decision I made?" When she hesitated, he said, "Tell me, Julie."

"When you announced you were coming to Cornerstone, I felt like I didn't matter. I hate it when Joey treats me like a child, and I liked it even less when you did the same."

"I didn't." His helpless little-boy look didn't help.

Julie struggled to keep her irritation under control. "Be honest, Noah. You believed I was too young and felt you could go off, gain experience, and come back to pick up where we left off. You expected me to wait for you but didn't bother to ask if I would."

"You are young."

"You're only four years older than me. What makes you so much wiser?"

Noah looked more surprised with every revelation.

"Obviously nothing from your viewpoint. I never intended to pick up where we left off. If you'd noticed from all my efforts, I've been trying to keep our relationship going."

Julie did a one-handed sweep through her hair, moving it out of her face. "You certainly have a different idea of what that involves than I do."

"Okay, let's discuss this after the fact. How would you have expected me to deal with my options?"

His efforts to make her see reason frustrated Julie. "Will you watch the twins while I check on the boys?"

Noah agreed and she ran upstairs. The older boys were playing in their room while Luke was driving his truck along the upstairs hallway.

She returned downstairs to find Naomi had awakened from her nap and had joined John on the floor. The party food had filled Julie, but she knew the babies were probably ready to eat.

Noah followed her into the kitchen. "Are you going to answer me?"

"The twins need dinner and I need coffee."

After filling the twins' sippy cups, Julie started a fresh pot of coffee. Noah sat at the kitchen table after asking if he could help. She took toddler food from the cabinet and prepared plates for the twins. Then she took the cake plate Maggie had brought over yesterday and slid it onto the table.

"You should have told me," Julie said as she handed him a small plate, "then asked my opinion on the matter. We could have listed pros and cons and determined whether it was the most advantageous option."

Noah eyed her curiously. "You don't see the value of me working here at Cornerstone with Joe?"

Julie served herself a piece of cake and took a bite before sipping her coffee. "Not particularly. You're standing in his shadow. Not forming your own."

"I wasn't ready to pastor a church. Look at the mistakes I've made here this week."

"Trial and error, Noah. That's how we determine what works."

"In your field maybe. Churches have long-standing traditions that can't be discounted because I think my ideas work better."

"Sounds restrictive to me."

"But necessary for a cohesive church. There are enough destructive elements at work already without a pastor tearing his congregation apart. You're a freethinker, Julie. I admire that about you, but I have to be more methodical. I sought God's guidance in my decision."

"It's too late to change the situation now."

"Tell me what you want me to do, Julie."

"Does it really matter? You'd still have to seek God's guidance, and since He led you here in the first place, I hardly think He's going to send you home to Denver. You start praying about a transfer and you could end up in Alaska."

Noah's lips curved at Julie's musing. "Have you ever considered living in Alaska?"

"No, and I don't plan to, either."

"You need to open your mind to the possibilities, Julie Joy. God can use you anywhere in the world."

"Or He can leave me exactly where I am."

"Has it occurred to you that He's led you here twice in six months?"

"Well, yes, but not to stay."

"And yet you've spent at least two weeks both times."

"What's your point, Noah?"

He cupped the mug in his palms and met her gaze with one of determination. "I was wrong not to discuss this move with you. You're partly right in assuming I struggled with your age—but only because I don't want to rush you. I've been praying about us, Julie. Seeking God's guidance as to whether you're the one He intends for me. I know now that you are, and I don't want to lose you. Please don't let distance become the barrier that destroys us. We can make it work. I know we can."

"You'd better tell me how. I don't share your vision."

The twins protested their restriction in the high chairs. Julie released them and set them on their feet. They toddled toward the living room, and she followed.

"What if the promotion opportunity had been yours?" Noah asked as he followed on her heels. "What would you have done?"

She whirled around. "I would have told you and asked your opinion. That much I do know."

Noah's look was one of remorse. "I've enjoyed spending time with you these past few days, Julie. I miss you far more than you know, but I understand your anger. I admit, my failure to seek your opinion doesn't exactly support my statement that I have serious feelings for you. What can I do to convince you?"

Julie couldn't begin to explain how abandoned she'd felt after he'd left. How afraid. What could she do? Pick up where they left off and accept long-distance calls as a relationship until God led Noah to take another church? Who knew where he'd end up in the future? "I believe you realize you hurt me with your actions, but we still have a problem."

The conversation trailed off with the boys' arrival. Matt and Luke crawled up on the chair arms on each side of Noah, while Marc chose to join John on the floor.

Julie's gaze moved from person to person. How like a family they seemed, the two little boys in earnest conversation with Noah, and Marc, Naomi, and John playing at their feet. The homey warmth of the room contributed to the illusion. Mari and Joey might not have the most expensive furnishings in the world, but they had a nice home—a home that never lacked in love.

At Luke's request, Julie popped in the boys' video for Noah. He laughed heartily at their antics.

"You guys really know how to put on a show," he told them a few minutes later when he reached for his jacket. "I need to get home and put the final touches on my sermon."

Julie walked him to the door. "Are you nervous?"

"A little. It's in God's hands. You are going to be there, aren't you?"

"I told Joey I'd take the kids to church."

He kissed her cheek. "See you in the morning. Say a prayer for me."

"I will."

Noah paused and grasped her hands tightly in his. "I need to make you a promise, Julie Joy. If you forgive me, I'll never make another life-altering decision without consulting you first. I never left you behind. I've kept you in my heart. And I did look back." He squeezed her hands one last time and released them. "I am serious about my intentions. Meanwhile, we both need to seek God's guidance for our lives."

Later, Julie knelt by the bed to honor Noah's request. She prayed his sermon would reach the people God intended.

Unknowingly, he had stirred her to thinking of how she had pushed God lower on her list. She prayed for forgiveness, vowing to do better in the future. Concluding the prayer with an earnest request for God's continued guidance concerning her and Noah's relationship, she climbed beneath the covers.

As she lay there considering the revelations of the conversation, Julie thought about how communication breakdowns destroyed so many relationships. She didn't want to be a statistic, but she honestly didn't know any way to resolve their problem. Noah might be willing to wait, but she was ready to move on with her future. She loved him, but she couldn't share the truth with Noah yet. Telling him of her love would only make her more vulnerable.

Chapter 7

The following morning, Julie scrambled out of bed late, confronted with the chore of getting the children fed, dressed, and to church on time. *Joey would never forgive me if they missed church on my first Sunday,* Julie thought as she rushed to shower.

Nothing was where it should be, and with five minutes to go, they scrambled around in search of Naomi's patent leather shoes. At least Joey and Mari would be around next Sunday to help.

As organized as her sister-in-law was, she probably laid everything out the night before. Julie should have checked, but come to think of it, she hadn't seen the list since the day before when she and Luke had been dealing with the play situation.

"Auntie Julie, hurry!" Matt screamed.

She ran to the bathroom to find the toilet overflowing. Julie jerked clean towels off the racks and spread them about to catch the water. "What caused this?"

Matt shrugged and shook his head. Marc looked like he had something to say. "Marc?"

"Luke's a bad boy."

"Not!" Luke said, shoving Marc.

"Are, too!" Marc yelled, pushing back. Luke fell on the tile floor and started to cry.

"Boys, stop." Julie picked Luke up and made sure he hadn't fallen in the water. She held their shoulders to keep them apart. "Why is Luke bad?"

"He put Nay-Nay's shoe down there."

Julie groaned when Marc pointed to the toilet bowl. All eyes focused on Luke. The boy dropped his head.

Facing the monumental question of how to handle this, Julie simply didn't know what to do. She knew his parents would not allow Luke to escape punishment. But right now she knew dealing with the emergency was more important. Maybe Mari had listed a plumber's name.

She stepped into the bedroom and came right back to ask, "Have any of you seen the papers your mommy left for me?"

Marc nodded and pointed to the toilet.

"Luke, you didn't!" Julie cried, fighting the strong urge to spank the child. "Why?"

"Mommy said I had to be in the pway."

"Was this what you were trying to tell me last night, Marc?"

The child nodded. Tears welled up in her eyes as Julie prayed for patience. Why hadn't she listened to Marc when he'd tried to tell her about Luke's behavior?

She felt like she was in a rowboat left adrift in the middle of the ocean without oars. Every fact she needed to survive the next week was gone. Literally, down the toilet.

"What you did was wrong, Luke," Julie told him sternly. "You've destroyed important items that didn't belong to you and you've caused a problem with the house."

Glancing around to make sure the water had stopped, Julie decided to take the older kids to church and come back to clean up the mess.

After getting the boys to the right Sunday school classrooms, she started back down the stairs, carrying John and a shoeless Naomi in her arms.

"You're not staying?"

Julie turned to find Noah standing in the hallway outside the church office. Her breath caught in her throat at the sight of him in his navy suit.

She'd been looking forward to hearing him preach. Julie very much wanted to hear his message for the congregation.

"Oh, Noah, I'm in big trouble. Luke flushed Mari's list down the toilet."

Noah's eyes widened. "You're kidding. Why would he do that? When?"

"Remember last night when Marc told me Luke was a bad boy?" Noah nodded. "Guess he figured if there's no list, he wouldn't have to do anything. I needed that information to prepare for Christmas Day. I'm totally out of my element here. That list had the menu, the whereabouts of the kids' Christmas presents, even the people Mari and Joe wanted to invite to dinner. He flushed Naomi's shoe, too."

"What did her shoe do to him?"

"Who knows? He probably tripped over it or something. There's water all over the bathroom floor. I have to call a plumber and have no idea who to contact."

"The church's plumber is also a member," Noah said as he walked over to where she stood. "I'm sure he'll take care of the situation this afternoon."

"Well, that takes care of the toilet, but what about the list?" she asked, tears trailing down her face.

Noah thumbed them away and took John in his arms. "Stop now or you'll have them crying, too. The list is gone, Julie. You'll do the best you can. You can handle this with God's help. You know you can."

Julie felt her heartbeat quicken. Noah ministered because he cared for people, because of his ability to comfort, reassure, and help them believe everything would be okay if they just trusted God.

"Let's put the babies in the nursery. We'll check the house and then come back for services."

"You're not dressed for plumbing problems, and Naomi doesn't have any shoes," she protested.

"I don't plan to make the repair, Julie. Just turn the water off. And haven't you noticed that Naomi spends most of her time barefoot? Luke probably figured she didn't need shoes, anyway."

⚒

Julie slipped into the pew with Matt, Marc, and Luke just moments before the choir began to sing. She'd never been so exhausted. Getting herself out of the house every morning was challenge enough, but adding five small people and a bathroom disaster to the mix almost made it a near impossibility. It had taken a great deal of effort, but the children were in church. A smile tugged at her mouth. Joey would be proud.

She'd tossed the wet towels into the bathtub after determining the water had stopped. The doorbell had rung and Noah had opened the door to Robin's friend, who had come in search of Julie. Evidently, Luke had been overcome by remorse and had cried for Auntie Hulie until they'd located her.

Moments later, they stood in the hallway outside his classroom. His sobs and "I torry, Auntie Hulie" tugged at Julie's heart. She held him close and whispered about destroying other people's possessions.

Once he'd calmed down, she took him back into the classroom. Julie had watched the kids shower their teacher with Christmas gifts, embarrassed that she hadn't thought to buy gifts for the children's teachers. Of course, Mari could have had that on the list. She'd never know.

After their Sunday school lesson, they'd worked on a craft project. When Julie offered to help, Natalie Porter had quickly accepted.

"I don't mind the lessons, but I don't like crafts at all."

Surprised, Julie had exclaimed, "Really? After that cake you made for the cast party, I figured you'd try anything. I've never seen anything so incredible."

Natalie grinned as she continued to place red pipe cleaners on the table. "Thanks. Too bad the kids can't craft with cake decorations. We could really make progress if that were the case."

"That reminds me. I'd love to order a couple of cakes for Christmas. Are you booked up?"

"Pretty much. I promised Mari two cakes already. Do you think you'll need more?"

Julie shook her head. "I didn't realize she'd ordered them. Luke flushed my lifeline down the toilet last night. Mari had listed everything for me. Now it's gone."

Natalie glanced at Luke and back at her. "What will you do?"

Julie shrugged. "The best I can."

"Let me know if I can help," Natalie said as she assisted a child with glue.

Julie appreciated the woman's offer. "You can join us for dinner if you don't have other plans."

"I have friends coming down for the holiday. Thanks for asking, though."

"Bring them along."

"I'll let you know," Natalie had promised.

Emulating the adults around them, the boys pulled hymnals from the back of the pew. Julie smiled when Luke held his upside down and sang the traditional Christmas hymn along with the choir. When the song ended, all three boys sat and laid the books on the seat beside them. No doubt they understood bad behavior would not be tolerated in the sanctuary.

The choir sang and then there was another congregational song. The music director announced a solo and young Robin moved to the microphone. Her solo about the gift God gave His people at Christmas moved Julie to tears.

Noah rose and stepped to the pulpit. "If you would open your Bibles to the book of James, chapter 1, verse 17 and read with me. 'Every good gift and every perfect gift is from above, coming down from the Father of the heavenly lights, who does not change like shifting shadows.'

"The holiday season is upon us. A time for visiting with family and friends. Hustle, bustle, and good cheer. Shopping, decorating homes, writing cards, planning dinners, and making far more plans than we think we'll ever complete. A time for worries about whether our gifts will be liked, whether we've forgotten to buy a gift, or just simply because we have no idea what to buy. I see some of you agreeing with me.

"All those things are activities of the season, not reasons. There's only one real reason we celebrate Christmas and that's the birth of Jesus Christ. Listen to this scripture again."

Noah reread the verse, emphasizing the words to make his point. "There's only one true, perfect gift and that's Jesus Christ. Those who know Him as their Savior know exactly what I mean. Those who don't, continue to search for the missing element in their lives. The reason for their unhappiness, their discontent, their unease."

Julie glanced over her shoulder to see how people were responding to Noah. They appeared to be listening, nodding with every point he made. Noah danced on her toes with every word he spoke. She had busied herself with activities almost to the point that she'd opted to skip services this morning.

"How easy is it to know the Lord as your Savior? It requires a decision. A willingness to say 'I am a sinner.' A willingness to repent of those sins. A willingness to throw out the old and accept the new. A willingness to accept the gift of love.

"In a few days some of you will make resolutions for the New Year. The one life-changing resolution anyone can make is to commit his or her life to God.

" 'That's too easy,' you say," Noah said, stepping around the pulpit to the open stage area. " 'I'd never keep such a resolution.'

"It's not a commitment you make and then forget about in mid-January when the other resolutions fall by the wayside. It's a vow of change. A vow to do away with the old. To become new again. Reborn.

"If you're searching for the perfect gift for yourself, the 'one-size-fits-all, never-has-to-be-returned perfect gift,' choose salvation.

"Choose a Friend who walks with you even when you're alone. A Friend who never forsakes you. Brothers and sisters in Christ who welcome you into the fold with love.

"Do this and once you take that meaningful step, I promise that you'll never be sorry you did."

The service proceeded to the conclusion and an announcement about the children's play that night. During the closing prayer, Noah moved to the door to greet people as they left.

She and the boys picked up the twins from the nursery then walked across the yard to the house. As she changed the twins into playclothes, Julie considered the day as better for having attended Sunday services. Noah's sermon had been right on target. God had given the only true gift.

A few minutes later, Noah brought the plumber over. The older boys watched as the man removed the shoe, but the papers were gone. Julie suspected his stern warning about "things that don't belong in the toilet"—which he'd diplomatically directed toward her—had impacted Luke more than anything she might say on the subject ever would.

When the plumber left, Julie invited Noah to join them for lunch. He'd sat in Joey's chair and entertained the kids while she prepared and served the meal. Afterward, he'd helped clear the table and told her he had to run over to the hospital to visit a church member. "I'll see all of you at church tonight."

"Thanks, Noah."

He'd kissed her cheek and whispered, "Don't look so blue, Julie. God will provide."

After he had gone, Julie touched her cheek and prayed that God would indeed show her the way.

Chapter 8

After she tucked the children in for a nap, Julie lay on her bed, struggling to recall the bits and pieces of Mari's list that she had read. Why hadn't she put it in a safer place? Probably because it had survived the week before Luke decided to destroy his mother's missive.

Tomorrow she'd start working on the menu. She felt certain Mari's list involved lots of cooking but opted to simplify. Julie decided to order a few items to make the day easier for all concerned. Mari wouldn't feel like cooking after the long flight home.

Julie had barely caught her breath before the boys had to be back at church Sunday evening. The twins toddled off to play when Julie put them down in the church nursery.

"Too bad you have to miss the play," she told Maggie.

"I won't." She pointed to the television monitor on the wall.

"With all these babies?"

"I see enough to know what's going on. Sometimes they're so taken by something on the screen that they actually stop to watch."

"Thanks for taking care of Naomi and John."

"It's my pleasure."

Julie came back up the hallway to find everyone busy getting the children into costume. "Can I help?"

Kimberly shoved a hanger into her hand. "Help Matt into this and start praying none of them forget their parts," she said with a broad smile. "It's in God's hands now."

Julie settled into the front row seat beside Noah a couple of minutes before showtime.

"Everything under control?" he asked, taking her hand in his and giving it a gentle squeeze.

She nodded. Someone had been busy since this morning; the stage sets had turned Cornerstone Church into Bethlehem. She could almost imagine herself there. "Joey and Mari didn't have to travel to see the Holy Land," she whispered.

"It is impressive. Kimberly doesn't do anything halfway."

Julie glanced at him. "You like her, don't you?"

"As a sister in Christ."

"I like Kimberly. She's a fun person. Shh," she said as the lights dimmed.

A short time later, it was over. The play had been a success. Julie couldn't have been more proud if they'd been her own children and felt as though her buttons would bust when people complimented the boys on their performances. Her lack of faith shamed her when she considered she had believed they wouldn't be able to pull it off.

The beautiful story never failed to touch her, from the incredible step of faith of both Mary and Joseph in accepting God's plan for them to the humble beginnings of their Lord—the joy and celebration of the wondrous birth of a Savior sent to die for the sins of the world.

Seeing the children reenact the Christmas story gave the holiday such sweetness Julie found it difficult to restrain the tears. Joey and Mari would be so proud of their boys.

The lamb had provided them with the biggest laugh of the evening. It managed to escape Luke's hold again, and the entire group of children had chased after the poor thing. Finally, Luke grabbed the animal, and when the other kids left the stage, he'd remained, holding the lamb and smiling at the crowd. Marc had come out to lead him off.

Noah invited them out for ice cream to celebrate.

"Are you sure you want to do this?" Julie asked as they picked the babies up from the nursery.

"More than you know. I often join Joe and Mari for a Sunday meal. She's always kind enough to invite this bachelor to enjoy her fine cooking."

"Within the confines of their home. We could pick up something from the grocery store."

Noah shook his head. "We have to go to the ice cream parlor. They have the best flavors."

Julie gave in. "Okay, you asked for it."

He helped secure the children in the van. Julie figured the boys must be tired when they didn't make a lot of noise during the ride. Generally, the volume deafened her. "I meant to tell you I enjoyed your sermon this morning."

"Thanks. Hearing you say that means a lot."

His comment confused her. She wasn't a sermon expert, but his words had been succinct and to the point and at times she felt as though he'd directed the message at her. Had her propensity for gift-giving inspired him? "You were very convincing. I certainly can see the merit of feeling salvation is a special gift."

"I pray that anyone in church this morning who doesn't know the Lord will do the same."

"Amen," Julie agreed. She followed his directions to the ice cream shop she visited many times the past summer.

"Turn left at the next light," Noah told her.

She drove into the lot and parked near the door. "We can still buy ice cream and take it home."

"What fun is that? We need sprinkles and gummy worms and all sorts of stuff to really make it good."

Julie found his response amusing. "You're a kid at heart."

Inside the small ice cream parlor, they ordered bowls of vanilla ice cream and allowed each boy to choose his own toppings. Julie opted for a dish of plain vanilla with the intention of sharing with the twins.

They held hands while Noah blessed the food. The older boys sat inside the booth, with her and Noah on the ends. The twins sat between them in high chairs. She spooned ice cream into Naomi's mouth, and when John reached for the spoon, Noah fed him ice cream. He passed napkins to the boys, and the analogy Joey had once made of a family as a team came to mind. Noah had certainly been a team player during her stay.

"I'm looking forward to taking you to the cantata next Friday night."

She hesitated and Naomi grabbed the spoon, dumping the ice cream onto her shirt. Julie concentrated on wiping the child's clothing.

"You will go, won't you?" Noah asked somewhat doubtfully.

"I'm not comfortable leaving the kids," Julie told him as she fed Naomi more ice cream. "Can't we take them along?"

Noah had mentioned the idea while they were keeping the twins occupied in the fellowship hall the day before. She hadn't committed because she didn't feel right about leaving the responsibility of five children to someone else.

"The idea is to give you time away from them," Noah argued. "I doubt you'd enjoy the program if they were claiming your attention."

"I don't know. Joey said Mari wanted family to care for the kids."

"And you have. I'm sure they expected that I'd invite you out on a date at least one night while you're here."

"Maggie did say she'd babysit, but I don't want her to miss the cantata."

"She's seen it," Noah offered as he fed John a spoonful of ice cream. The toddler promptly put his hand in his mouth then rubbed ice cream on his head. "This is an encore performance. Everyone else saw the program when they did it Sunday before last," he explained as he dabbed John's hair with his napkin.

"I'll see what I can do," Julie said. "Now that I'm no longer following Mari's instructions for the holidays, I have to do my own planning."

The boys talked about the lamb as they finished their sundaes. Noah took them to the bathroom to wash their hands while Julie picked up the trash. Noah carried John and held the door while the boys filed out, followed by Julie and Naomi. She hit the button to unlock the van doors. Noah slid the door back and the boys climbed in.

Once they were all buckled in and on the way home, Julie said, "I wanted to ask about the Good Shepherd window fund. What is that?"

"Joe wants to replace that large window behind the pulpit with a stained glass window depicting the Good Shepherd and His flock. The membership has dedicated about half the money."

"Could I offer the rest in Joey's honor?"

Noah hesitated. "I'm not sure how he'd feel about that. The intent is that the window be dedicated to the Lord."

His attitude bothered Julie. Every time she brought up the subject of donations to the church, Noah discouraged her. "And how would me giving the other half of the funds affect that? You make it sound as though I'm offering tainted money. I earn every dime I spend."

"That's not what I meant. Joe's goal is to beautify God's house. From what Joe told me, the congregation jumped on board with the idea from day one. He gave me the impression they want to provide the funding."

"It's a donation, Noah. Not a demand for a plaque bearing Joey's name."

"I'll ask and get back to you. How's that?"

"Obviously it's the way it's going to be. I just wanted to donate to my big brother's church. Why does everything have to be such a big deal?"

"I haven't developed Joe's savvy when it comes to church politics, but I don't want him dealing with problems we've caused when he gets home."

It wasn't the first time she'd heard that phrase. She had a good idea why Noah had said it at least a half dozen times. "Joey asked you to keep me under control, didn't he?"

His guilty expression told her she'd been right on target.

"I'm trying to be the voice of reason."

"I'm perfectly capable of making decisions without the guidance of you two guys." She didn't say another word as she pulled into the turn lane and waited for the light.

"Julie, please. Don't get upset over this," Noah pleaded. "Joe asked me to help out."

"I wanna go home, Auntie Hulie."

They both glanced back at Luke.

"So do I." And she didn't mean Joey's home. She couldn't wait until her brother came home. She'd tell him exactly what she thought of his attempt to control her just before she got on her plane. Julie pulled into the church parking lot and stopped by Noah's vehicle. She left the van idling as she waited for him to get out.

"I'll help you get the kids inside," he offered.

"No thanks. I've got it under control."

"Julie?"

"Good night, Noah," she said, not bothering to disguise the coldness of her tone.

"I love you, Julie."

"You'll have to pardon me if I have my doubts."

He sighed and got out. She drove over to the parsonage and parked. When she opened the side door, the boys spilled out and headed for the house. Julie took the twins into her arms and glanced at the open door. She'd get it later.

She heard it shut as she unlocked the front door and glanced back to find Noah standing there. Turning her back on him, she went inside and locked up behind them, turning off the porch light.

After the kids were in bed, Julie lay down for a few minutes. She couldn't rest for thinking about what had happened with Noah tonight. How could she love someone who didn't accept her as an adult capable of making her own decisions? She wasn't looking for a replacement for her parents or her brother.

Her eyes drifted closed.

How did a cricket get into the bedroom? Julie wondered when she woke to the maddening chirp. It took a couple of moments for her sleep-boggled mind to recognize the ring of the phone. She grabbed it up, her voice coming out as if she'd swallowed a frog.

"Hi, Jules."

"Joey, do you know what time it is?"

"Need to set your clock?" he teased.

"No, but you could set yours," she said, reaching to turn on the lamp. "You're lucky you didn't wake the kids."

"I know it's early but we're leaving for our bus tour and Mari wanted to check in before we left. How was the play?"

"They did fine."

"Can't wait to hear all about it." Before she could say more, Joey spoke to someone in the background. "We're loading up. Mari says hello and to kiss the kids."

"Joey, we've got a problem," Julie began. The static crackle of the connection cut in before she could finish.

"Can't hear you, Jules. Gotta run. Love you."

"Love you, too," she whispered to the irritating buzz of the dial tone. She flipped the lamp off and lay back against the pillows with a sigh. She'd tried to tell him about the list. Maybe she could the next time he called. That is, if there was a next time before they arrived home.

Chapter 9

Monday morning dawned chilly and wet. After breakfast, her first action of the day was to discipline Luke for flushing the list and Naomi's shoe. After much consideration, she'd decided the only way to make him understand would be to take something he cared about a great deal from him. She opted for his favorite truck.

Luke cried and pleaded, but Julie placed the truck behind locked closet doors.

Later, she made sure all the kids were dressed and prepared to load them into the van. She had to buy stamps and get the remainder of her cards in the mail. She'd already left them far too long. At this rate, some of them wouldn't arrive until after New Year's Day.

The phone rang just as she was struggling to get Naomi into her sneakers. The child didn't want to wear them and kept curling her toes. Julie scooped her up and carried her into the kitchen to answer the phone.

"Hi, Julie. You have a minute?"

Surely he didn't want to discuss last night's argument. "More like ten seconds. What's up?"

"Computer problems."

She was no stranger to Cornerstone's antiquated equipment. She'd been telling Joey for months that it needed to be replaced. "What's it doing now?"

"Jean downloaded information from the Internet for one of the members, and weird stuff's happening."

"Sounds like she downloaded a bug. Have her run the antivirus program to check."

"What does it look like?"

Julie sighed. Unbelievable. With all the bad stuff out there, antivirus programs and firewalls were necessities. "I'll come over."

Julie helped the children with their coats and grabbed an umbrella for the walk over to the church. One thing for certain, Joey couldn't complain about a work commute. In the office, she instructed the kids to wait in the visitor chairs while she checked out the computer. As she suspected, there was no antivirus program.

"The good news is once this is repaired, we can use the backup to restore everything." At Jean's crestfallen look, Julie asked, "You backed up the files, right?"

"Not lately. Pastor Dennis will be upset. He told me to but I forgot."

Julie felt sorry for the woman. "We'll get it running again."

"Shouldn't we take it to the shop?" Jean asked.

Julie glanced at Noah. Obviously, the church secretary didn't know Pastor Dennis's sister worked with computers.

"No need. Julie's a certified expert, Jean. Do you have the time?" Noah asked. "With the kids and all, I mean."

"Bring it to the house later. I'll check it out after they go to bed. You'll need to pick up an antivirus program." She named the one she preferred.

"Thanks, Julie, you're a lifesaver," Noah told her. "I owe you one."

"Get my tables and chairs for Christmas Day and we'll call it even."

"Already done."

"Bet you had no idea it would be a full-time job when Joey asked you to help me out, did you?" Julie asked, reminding him of his promise to her brother.

Noah grinned at that. "I'm enjoying every minute. I keep waiting for the next shoe to drop."

"You mean flush," she countered at his pun. "We're on our way to the post office. You need anything mailed?" Noah and Jean shook their heads. "My friends will receive their cards after Christmas, but the PB and J smears will be a dead giveaway that getting them out hasn't been my top priority."

Julie felt her heart lift with Noah's laughter. She wanted to be angry with him. She really did, but she knew he'd agreed to Joey's request out of loyalty to her brother.

Noah removed his jacket from the coatrack. "I'll run to the office supply store and pick up that program. Then I can bring the computer over when you get home."

"Want to ride with us?" she invited. No sense in taking two cars when she was going to be in the vicinity anyway.

"Sure," he agreed. "Hold down the fort, Jean. God's army is marching forward to attack the church's computer virus."

"Find the last backup you did," Julie instructed before they headed out the door. "At least we can get that much restored."

They left the forlorn secretary in search of the programs Julie would need to get the computer operational. Even then, there was no guarantee the computer would work as it should. They really needed new equipment.

The rain had stopped, and the boys raced ahead of them at their usual speed while Julie and Noah followed at a more leisurely pace with the twins. "Joey called early this morning."

"Was he able to help with the list?" Noah asked as he waited for her to unlock the van.

"He woke me up. I never got the chance to tell him. By the time I got around to the problem, the connection broke up and they were loading the bus for their tour."

"So what do you do now?"

"Follow the advice of a wise friend."

"Oh?" Noah said, raising his brow in question. "Which advice was that?"

Julie punched his arm. "This friend suggested I pray about the situation, which I did, and I feel the prayer has been answered."

She secured Naomi in her car seat then repeated the task with John. She warned the children to keep their hands inside as she closed the door.

Noah reached to open the driver's door. "How did you reach that conclusion?"

"If I'd told them, they would worry. This way I worry enough for all of us and they continue to enjoy their vacation. Now I can do things my way and say the list went down the pipes. I can't feel bad about not doing as good a job as Mari if I don't know what's on that list."

Noah considered her words. "So you've adopted Luke's 'out of sight, out of mind' logic?"

"Don't tell him," Julie whispered, "but Luke did me a favor."

"You never needed the list, Julie. You've done a good job."

In that moment, she understood the importance of positive reinforcement from someone who cared. His arm resting on her shoulder, the earnestness of his expression, pushed her near to tears. Julie turned into his arms, her warm hug saying the words she couldn't.

The spontaneous hug surprised them both. She stepped back, laughing nervously. "I'm sorry. Being around the kids has me hyper."

"It's okay," Noah said, taking her hand in his. "A hug is one of the best experiences in the world."

"I know. The kids lavish them on me so freely that sometimes I feel overwhelmed by love."

Their gazes met and held for several seconds. The bond strengthened as Noah smiled and said, "Feel free to share the overflow anytime."

Julie climbed into the driver's seat and turned the key. She looked over her shoulder and started to back out of the driveway.

Noah pointed to the man standing at the front door. "Were you expecting someone?"

"Everyone stay put," Julie instructed. Out of habit, she shut off the engine and palmed the keys. "I'll be right back."

She ran across the yard and up onto the porch. "Hello. Can I help you?"

The way the stranger stood at an angle, shielding something from view, made Julie nervous. She felt silly when he tipped his hat in a gesture of politeness.

"I brought your cat. I know I'm early, but we're going out of town so it's now or never."

Julie gasped. He'd brought the children's Christmas gift a week early. How was she supposed to keep a kitten secret for that long?

"I took care of his shots and all."

Julie glanced up when Noah opened the door. She waved him back. "Okay, Mr. . . ?" For the life of her, she couldn't remember the man's name.

"Jones. Henry Jones. Sorry, ma'am, I delivered the others today. He's the last of the litter. Might be someone would take him off your hands."

Julie quickly took the kitten into her hands, enjoying the soft, furry feel of him. "Oh, we want him!" she exclaimed. "He's a surprise for the kids for Christmas. I need somewhere to keep him until then."

"Just put him in an empty room. He takes to the litter box really well."

An impossibility in this house, Julie thought. Oh well, she had no other choice. "Thanks for bringing him by, Mr. Jones. I'm sure the children will love him."

"Merry Christmas, Miss Dennis."

Julie unlocked the door and ran upstairs to Joe and Mari's bedroom. She pulled an old towel from the linen closet and placed it on the bathroom floor. She'd shut the kitten up in there and would take care of everything else later.

When the doorbell rang again, she secured the bathroom door and hurried downstairs to find Mr. Jones at the door holding a cardboard box. "Here's the rest of the stuff you'll need right away."

Thankfully, he'd anticipated the need for a litter box. There was also a bag of litter and a scoop. He'd also included some cat toys and a bag of food. It occurred to Julie that she'd just given herself another living thing to look after.

"Thanks again, Mr. Jones."

She hurried back upstairs and set up the items, closing the bathroom door behind her.

After locking up the house, Julie realized the rain had started up again. And of course her umbrella was in the van. She ran across the yard and climbed inside, swiping the rain out of her eyes.

"What did he want?" Noah asked curiously.

Julie buckled her seat belt and said, "Tell you later. Too many ears."

⌒

Noah sat with the kids in the van while she ran her errand at the post office. At the office supply store, Julie snagged a sales assistant and outlined what she wanted. She could probably get it cheaper but there was no time. Within minutes, she'd laid down plastic for three computers, software, and the necessary essentials. She even bought a phone with an answering machine and extra handsets that plugged into electrical outlets for Joey's house. No more running for the phone.

She got in the van, drove to package pickup, and jumped out to run around and open the back doors. She told the boys to move up a seat and folded down the backseat so they could stack the boxes.

Noah turned around to see what was happening. "What did you do, Julie?"

She answered him once she was behind the steering wheel again. "I took care of the problem."

"That's more than an antivirus program."

She flashed him a bright smile. "Isn't it wonderful? God provided two new computers for the church."

"God or you?"

"God used me. I've been telling Joey for months that the computer needed replacing. I got him a laptop so he can work from home when he needs to. And if the congregation doesn't want the donation, Joey can take both computers home with him. I don't think that will be the case. Once I get the old computer running again, we can set it up in your office." She flashed him a playful grimace. "I did buy you some additional memory and a couple of extra surprises." Julie turned up the heater to ward off the wet chill in the air. "Will we get snow?"

"Probably not," Noah said. "It might be interesting to see if it did snow. Jean tells me the city literally shuts down. Schools, businesses, even government offices close. She said they had a major snowfall on Christmas several years ago."

"I guess they're not prepared."

"Not much use for snowplows on the coast."

She glanced in the rearview mirror at the boys. "Matt, Marc, do you remember snow?"

They had been toddlers when they lived in Colorado. Both boys shook their heads. "Your dad used to take you guys and your mom on a sled and go down the hills really fast. Sometimes he'd crash and dump you all out. You always begged to do it again."

"Want snow," Luke announced.

"Maybe we'll have snow when your parents bring you to Denver to visit. We had so much fun making snowmen and snow angels. We even had snowball fights. I'm a good shot—always hit your dad right in the chest with those big wet snowballs."

The kids giggled, and Julie told Noah about watching a program where the man turned his lawn into a winter wonderland. Maybe she'd call around and see if anyone had the equipment. That would certainly be a surprise.

Soon they were home. The older kids went into the living room, while Julie and Noah carried the sleeping babies up to their cribs.

"What did the man want?" he asked as he laid John down.

"The kitten I bought the kids for Christmas arrived early. Mr. Jones is going out of town."

"You bought them a pet without getting their parents' permission?" Noah demanded.

Shocked by his bluntness, Julie said, "Joey sort of gave me blanket permission."

"You said *expensive* gifts. I'm sure he never considered you'd bring a pet into the family."

"Why not? Pets are good for kids."

Noah shook his head in disbelief. "Do you want me to take it to my apartment until Christmas Eve?"

"It's a him," Julie said, settling Naomi in the crib and removing her shoes. The baby flexed her toes and Julie smiled at the gesture. She felt the same way about shoes. "No. Thanks, though. I hid him in Joey and Mari's bathroom. Hopefully I can keep him there until Christmas morning."

"I wonder how a cat will fit in with Matt's hamster and that aquarium in the living room. I wouldn't even think about pets if I had five children."

Had she made a mistake? Maybe she should have asked first.

Noah covered John with a blanket. "Animals do help develop the kids' sense of responsibility. Matt loves that hamster. And they love to watch the fish eat."

"True," Julie said. "I have to keep the food hidden or they'll feed them until they pop. Luke's a bit heavy-handed when it comes to sprinkling the fish food."

"You don't allow him to shake it out of the container, do you?"

Julie found his question confusing. *How else did you feed fish?*

"Mari puts a pinch of food in his hand and holds him up so he can scatter it over the water."

"I suppose I should visit Joey and Mari more often."

"Good idea. I'd better run. Should I still bring the computer over later? Jean's right about that backup. Joe's not going to be happy. He worked hard to convince the congregation that a computer would save time for everyone. I think they agreed because he told them his sister would give free advice. I hope Jean hasn't lost the church tithe records. Or the budget stuff."

"It won't happen again," Julie promised. "This one has an automatic system backup. All she has to do is stick in a CD and it does the work."

"Are you going to stick around and teach us how to use it?"

"I'll make sure Jean understands before I leave."

"Thanks, Julie," he said, kissing her cheek before he darted down the stairs.

～

Noah showed up that evening around bath time. Luke seemed determined to take a bath with some special toy, and Julie left him searching with orders to stay out of the tub while she went downstairs to let Noah in.

One minute she was closing the door, and the next, a flash of yellow tabby shot past her. Julie groaned. Luke must have gone into his parents' bathroom. "Catch him!" she shrieked.

The child bounded down the stairs. "What that, Auntie Hulie?"

"Nothing," she said, hoping he would give up and go back to search for his bath toy.

No such luck. The child ran around the room, looking behind and under chairs in search of the scrambling ball of fur. "Me find!"

Julie looked to Noah for help.

The kitten chose that moment to make his escape. Luke followed. The animal ran up the Christmas tree, and she dashed after them, pushing Luke out of the way when the large tree toppled forward. The lights flickered and went out, ornaments smashing as they fell onto the floor.

"Julie?" Noah yelled, deep concern filling his voice.

Noah grabbed the kitten, handing it to Luke as he extricated Julie from underneath the tree. After she stood and he could see she was okay, Noah removed a cartoon ornament from her hair and started to laugh.

"Ho, ho, ho, Merry Christmas," she murmured sarcastically.

"I wish I had a video of that. You should have seen the look on your face when that tree fell. It was easily worth a small fortune."

"Matt, Marc, come see!" Luke bellowed at the top of his lungs as he hugged the quivering animal tightly.

Julie rescued the kitten, stroking him gently. He buried his claws into her arm when the boys bounded into the room. She'd probably have to pay for therapy. "Do they have pet psychologists?"

Noah started to laugh again.

"We got kitty!" Luke announced.

They converged around her to pet the animal while Noah attempted to set the tree back up. "I'll get something to wipe up the water," he said, disappearing into the kitchen to find a mop and bucket.

"Here, Matt, hold him gently while I help Noah clean up this mess. Don't go near the tree," she warned at the sight of their bare feet. She found a broom and dustpan and swept up the broken ornaments while Noah mopped up water.

"I take it you never secured it to the wall?"

"I'm going to see if Joey has any wire in the garage right now. Serves me right for procrastinating."

Noah started to laugh. "Julie, I'm sorry," he murmured, his mirth increasing until he bent over double. "It's so funny. That cat shot out from nowhere and ran up the tree. Luke was running around looking for him, and next thing I knew you were stretched out under that monstrous tree while that stupid Santa sang in the background."

The hilarity of the situation caught up with her and Julie joined in. Luke came over and wrapped his arms around her legs, gazing up at her with innocent eyes. "Lukie, you're going to kill me before this vacation is over," she said, setting Noah off in fresh laughter.

Chapter 10

"Want to go shopping tonight, Julie Joy?" Noah asked when he called about four thirty Tuesday afternoon.

He'd stuck around the previous evening to help get the kids and kitten settled in and attempted to put the tree back together while she worked on restoring the computer.

"How's it going?" he'd asked after connecting the tree to the stairs with the nylon fishing line they'd found in Joe's tackle box. He hadn't wanted to cut up his buddy's spool of line, but Julie had insisted.

"Joey won't need it again until next summer," she'd argued. "He can buy more."

After he'd finished with the tree, he pulled out a chair and sat down at the table.

"I can't believe Jean downloads anything without virus protection. She's lucky she didn't lose everything."

"She had no idea what could happen," Noah had defended. "Don't forget we don't have your computer expertise."

When it came to her work, Julie could handle everything—far different from the kids. While computers responded to her labors, the children resisted her efforts to fit them into little categories.

Luke's act of rebellion had pretty much taken care of her list-following tendencies. She would have to play this week by ear. Noah could hardly wait to see what happened.

She had hit a few more buttons then smiled her satisfaction. "One hundred percent virus free. Jean will need to re-create the last three months of tithe records, though. The accounting records seem to be all there."

"That's a relief."

He'd watched her strip open the packages she pulled from a shopping bag.

"These will help some. It won't be as fast as the new ones, but I think it'll serve your purposes. I'll work on the other two tomorrow night. I need to install the programs Jean gave me and transfer the data from this one."

And now, he'd suggested they go shopping instead. "You're joking, right?"

"No way. I have shopping to finish."

"You didn't wait to mail your gifts, did you?"

She knew him well. "No. I learned that lesson with Mom's birthday present. I mailed them the first of December. These gifts are for people here."

"Noah, I don't know. The kids—"

"Get back on the horse, Julie," he encouraged. "You can handle them. Besides, I'll be there to help."

"You promise?"

"You take Luke and the twins, and I'll handle Matt and Marc."

"What if I want Matt and Marc?"

"Okay, I'll take the twins and Luke."

There was a moment of silence. "On second thought, I'd just as soon keep an eye on Luke myself."

"So you'll go?"

"Yes. But only because I have shopping to finish as well. We can go after I feed the kids."

"But I'd planned to treat everyone to dinner."

"Too late. Dinner's already on the table. We're having hot dogs and baked beans if you'd care to join us."

"You made baked beans?"

"Actually, Mrs. Allene sent over a casserole. I think she's seeing too many takeout deliveries over here."

"I'm on my way."

"I'll set a place for you."

When he knocked on the back door, Julie waved him in. He washed up at the kitchen sink and sat in Joey's chair. She spooned a serving onto his plate and took her seat at the opposite end of the table.

After he blessed the food, Noah took a bite and said, "This is great. You're not eating the casserole?"

Julie grimaced at the suggestion. "Joey made beans a staple in our diet. I can barely tolerate them."

"You don't know what you're missing." He scooped up another big mouthful and savored them. She smiled when the boys did the same.

"Just consider it a bigger serving for you guys," she suggested.

Noah grinned. "Can't argue with that logic. Mrs. Allene's baked beans are the best I've ever eaten. They disappear so fast at the church dinners that I rarely get any."

"Does she have a secret family recipe or something?"

Noah shook his head. "I'm pretty sure it's in the church cookbook. Mari has a copy, I think. So how was your day?"

"We're falling into a routine. I get the children up, dressed, and fed. They play. I do chores and feed them lunch. They play. I do more chores. They play."

Noah laughed at her droll description. "That's quite a routine."

"I can't imagine how Mari has time for church work, friends, or anything else, for that matter. The kids take so much time."

Noah spooned more casserole onto his plate and added more to Matt's when he held his plate out. "Her friends are mothers, too. They visit while the children play. One day Mari and I were talking about getting everything done and she told me that routine doesn't have to be set in stone. She said that no matter how much she likes to keep a clean, orderly house, it's more important to spend quality time with the children. She says what goes undone today waits until tomorrow."

"But is that practical?"

"Sure it is. Think about it, Julie. If you don't do small loads of laundry today, you do larger ones tomorrow. If you don't run a partial load in the dishwasher, it's a full load tomorrow. The dust layer on the furniture is only slightly thicker."

"What about a working wife? Letting chores back up like that would make things difficult. Particularly with children."

"Froo, Auntie Hulie," Luke said, bringing his plate over to show her.

She took the plate, wiped his mouth, and excused him to wash up.

"I'd rather my wife not work while the children are small, but if she did, we'd find a way to make it work."

"I like my work. I mean. . .I want to work."

Noah found her response interesting. Did Julie see herself in his life? In the role of mother? "Then you will. It might make things more difficult but not insurmountable."

"That doesn't sound like a minister's point of view. Joey doesn't want Mari working. He feels her place is in the home."

"Don't you think they discussed it and then made the joint decision that she would stay home?" Noah asked.

"I suppose," Julie said with a shrug of her shoulders.

"They feel their lives run more smoothly because she's here taking care of their family and home."

"So you agree that's the best way?"

Her vagueness bothered him. "I didn't say that. It's a problem to overcome when it arises."

"Problem?"

"Situation," he corrected. "If you married me and we made a decision to have children, we'd come to a mutual decision on how to raise them. Who knows? Maybe I'd take a leave of absence and care for them."

"You'd do that?" Julie asked, obviously taken aback by his comment. "Even if the congregation frowned on it?"

"What kind of man would I be if I didn't put my family before the opinions of others?"

"They'd look down on me for forcing you to make that decision."

Noah fixed his gaze on her as he said, "Supporting each other in whatever we choose to do is what love is about."

"My job is probably more flexible," she said, shaking her head the moment the words left her lips. "Why are we having this conversation, anyway?"

Julie's abrupt turnabout didn't surprise Noah. He knew she was confused, and he wanted to clear that confusion from her mind.

One by one, the boys finished dinner and were excused. "Wash your hands and visit the bathroom," Julie told them. "We'll be leaving soon."

Noah started gathering plates and scraping them. "Why don't you take care of the kids while I clear this up and then we'll head out?"

The shopping excursion went well. Julie found that trading off responsibility with Noah made everything easier. If she wanted to look at something, he kept the children together, and she did the same when he shopped.

After finishing at the shopping center, they drove over to the Christian bookstore.

"I'm glad you had this idea," Julie told him as they waited for their gifts to be wrapped. "I'd all but decided to write checks and stuff them into Christmas envelopes. You really think these are okay for the Sunday school teachers?" she asked, studying the small daily devotionals they'd picked out.

"They're perfect."

After loading the kids, they piled the packages in the back.

"Anywhere else you need to go?" Noah asked.

"Home. The children are tired."

"Me, too," Noah agreed. "I only have a couple more gifts to buy. You never told me what you'd like."

"I have everything I need."

"Everything?" he repeated, his eyebrow lifting in doubt.

"I'll let you know if anything comes to mind."

"Just remember to allow others to experience the same joy of giving."

Life in the Dennis household settled to a dull roar over the next couple of days. On Wednesday, Matt went off for a playday with his friend, and Julie left the other children in day care for a few hours. She finished her shopping in record time.

She'd had a busy week. The church computer system was operational again. From her conversations with Jean, she knew the woman had been busy trying to put everything back together. Some information had been lost, but Jean had reconstructed the tithe records from the envelopes stored in the church office. She'd mentioned retyping some of Joey's sermon notes, but Julie suggested she wait until he returned and see if she should proceed.

Jean had faithfully backed up the system every day and admitted to loving the new, faster computer. No members of the congregation appeared to mind Julie's contribution.

The kitten had settled into the household, avoiding the children whenever possible. So far, she had fished Puff out of the aquarium twice. Hoping to curb the kitten's fishing tendencies, she'd visited the pet store to purchase a lighted cover for the huge container—but not before the two fish went missing.

The funniest thing was Puff's reaction to Matt's hamster. Secretly, Julie had dubbed the hamster Houdini. A master at escaping his cage, she had lost count of the number of times they had hunted for the hamster since she'd been at the house. Knowing the hamster was loose didn't exactly thrill her, either, but the kitten was terrified of the hamster and climbed to the highest points possible to hide.

Julie picked up kids' meals for everyone and headed for home. Merline was pulling up with Matt when she arrived. After lunch Julie decided to use Naomi and John's nap time to wrap gifts in the bedroom. She looked in on the older boys and found them playing.

The missing Christmas presents from Joey and Mari still troubled her. She felt clueless as to how to handle the situation. The temptation to pick up the phone and call Joey was strong, but the feeling he expected her to call kept Julie from dialing the emergency number. She wasn't ready to admit defeat yet. If the gifts didn't show up of their own accord, she supposed they could keep the children busy until Joey retrieved them Christmas morning. If only she'd studied Mari's list more thoroughly—but how could she have known it would disappear down the drain?

Christmas dinner plans were well under way. She'd placed orders for turkey and spiral-sliced ham. She'd visited the bakery for breads and pies and met Avery Baker. As Noah suggested, he'd tried to tempt her to order cakes, and when she admitted that Natalie Porter had donated two already, he'd provided a red velvet cake and fudge brownies. She'd asked about his plans for dinner and invited him to join them.

The guest list remained a puzzle. Finally, she'd asked Noah for a list of people who were alone for the holidays and invited them. So far, over half had phoned to say they'd love to come and asked what they could bring.

Julie told them to bring their specialty dish. There would be far too much food, but everyone could take plates home with them, and she felt certain there would be a few homebound church members who could benefit from a meal, as well.

She felt good about the plans. Christmas dinner would be served at four o'clock to give Joey and Mari time to spend with the kids and rest a bit before the guests arrived. After morning services, Julie planned to return home to organize things.

She placed several of the larger gifts in bags and topped them off with tissue paper. Julie liked the design on the paper she'd picked for the children. She finished the roll and tied on the ribbons before going to check on the boys. The twins were still asleep, and she found Matt and Marc playing in their bedroom. There was no sign of Luke.

The older boys only shrugged when she asked where he'd gone. Julie turned the house upside down. Her cries resounded across the backyard as she continued to search.

Noah raced across the church parking lot, pulling on his leather jacket. "What's wrong?"

"Luke," Julie said breathlessly. "I can't find him."

"When did you last see him?"

"He was playing with Puff in the bedroom about fifteen minutes ago."

"Then he hasn't gone far. What about Matt and Marc?"

"They don't know."

"Auntie Julie," Matt called from the back door. "Luke said Puff wanted to go for a walk."

Fear filled her as she looked at Noah. "Surely he didn't leave the house without permission."

Noah called the child's name again and again with no response. After another few minutes, he said, "We'd better call for help."

Julie dialed 911 and explained the situation. Within minutes, an officer arrived. He looked familiar, but she couldn't place where she'd seen him before.

"Pastor," he said with a nod of his head.

"Burt," Noah greeted him, reaching out to shake his hand. "I'm glad they sent you. You know Luke and he knows you. This is Pastor Joe's sister, Julie Dennis."

As the officer asked questions, the church lot began to fill with vehicles as volunteers arrived to aid in the search.

Julie lingered by the back door. "He can't have gone far," she insisted. "It's only been minutes."

"Come sit down," Noah urged, taking her arm and guiding her to a chair.

"If he's chasing the cat, there's no telling how far he's gone," the officer said. "We'll fan out and cover the area around the house."

"I'll get my coat," Julie said.

Burt shook his head. "I need you here, Miss Dennis. In case Luke finds his way back home on his own."

Fear planted its seed deep and wide in her mind as she considered the ramifications of not finding Luke. She hugged her arms against her body, fighting back the tears. "I managed to mess up the one thing Joey asked of me. I should have realized there's a reason they didn't have a dog or cat. If I hadn't bought that stupid kitten, Luke wouldn't be lost now."

"You can't say that for sure," Noah argued. "Luke could have disappeared for any reason. There are better ways to spend your time than blaming yourself for something you can't change."

"Like what?"

"Prayer for one thing. It can't hurt to send up a few on Luke's behalf. And the older boys need to be reassured."

She pressed her hands to her mouth. "I'm not fit to take care of children."

"Julie, stop," Noah demanded, pulling her close. "God is taking care of Luke. Don't doubt that."

Burt stepped closer and held out his hand. Julie took it and Noah's as he led them in prayer, seeking Luke's safety and Julie's comfort.

"We'll find him, Miss Dennis."

She offered Burt a weak smile. "Thanks for your help."

Time dragged by. When three o'clock passed with no sign of Luke or Puff, Julie paced the kitchen. "It will be dark soon and it's getting colder by the minute. I should be out there searching."

Her panic resulted in Noah reaching for her hand. "You should be here. When they find Luke, he's going to need your comfort. Let's pray again."

Naomi started to cry, and Julie went to comfort the baby. "She's so clingy. I think she knows something's wrong."

Julie relished the comfort of the toddler's delicate frame against her body. If only she could do the same for Luke.

Tears trailed down her cheeks. "Oh, Noah, I vowed Luke wouldn't get lost again while I was in charge. How will I ever tell Joey I lost his son twice? What if something terrible happens to him?"

"Nothing's going to happen. God is in control. Why don't I go check and see how things are going?"

Julie felt so alone after he'd gone.

God, please keep Luke safe, she pleaded silently as she rocked Naomi. *He's too little to know the dangers of the world.*

Matt came to stand by the chair. "Auntie Julie, can we have some milk?"

Glad for something to occupy her, Julie took them into the kitchen and filled glasses and cups and placed cookies on a plate.

After they started to eat, she stared out the window over the sink, seeking signs of the search. There was no one in sight. Noah still hadn't returned.

When the children finished their snack, Julie sat at the table with them and doodled along the edges of the menu for Christmas Day. They all needed something to do.

She set oranges in front of Matt and Marc with a bowl of cloves. "Help Aunt Julie," she told them, demonstrating how to push the spice into the oranges for the wassail she planned to make. Maybe their efforts wouldn't be as neat and perfect as they could have been, but the activity would help them all pass the agonizing time.

When the back door opened, Julie grabbed a towel and wiped her hands, demanding anxiously, "Noah, what did you find out?"

"They brought in tracking dogs. Do you have something Luke wore recently that they can use for scent?"

She ran upstairs and used his pillowcase to retrieve the pajamas he'd left underneath his pillow that morning, hoping the scent of oranges and spices wouldn't transfer from her hands to the garments. She handed them to the dog handler outside. The man waved the clothing under the dog's nose and spoke to the animal.

"Will it work?" she asked.

"We hope so, ma'am."

When the animal began to bark and strain at the leash, Julie broke down again. Where could he be? Injured or lost in the woods behind the house? Why hadn't she checked on them sooner?

Noah squeezed her hands. "It's going to be okay."

"Are there any signs he's out there?"

"They seem to be going around in circles. Burt found some small prints he feels are Luke's."

"He doesn't know the way back."

"Believe, Julie. Believe God will bring Luke home."

She grabbed a paper towel and rubbed her eyes. "I'm trying. Did I tell you Joey asked if I'd assume guardianship if something happened to him and Mari?"

"Would you?"

"What choice would I have? There's no chance I'd allow them to be separated."

"Is that the only reason?"

"No. I'd do it because they're my family and I love them."

The clock chimed the hour.

"But when I consider what a mess I've made in less than two weeks, I don't even want to think about what I'd do to them in a lifetime."

Noah patted her shoulder. "You've been a good parent. Let's keep things normal." He joined the boys at the table and helped with the oranges.

The atmosphere in the room seemed almost depressing. All the kids were abnormally quiet. She missed Luke's chatter.

Another few minutes passed and Julie started dinner. All Luke's favorites—just in case.

There was a knock at the door, and she recognized the officer from earlier. He removed his hat as he stepped inside. "Luke's been found, Miss Dennis."

"Thank You, God!" Julie shouted. "Where? Is he okay?"

"Fine. He and his kitten were fast asleep in a little valley not too far from here. Prepare yourself. He's rested and full of his adventure. Talking about how his cat escaped during their walk and he chased him."

An overwhelming distaste for the cat struck Julie. "You don't know a family who wants a kitten, do you?"

The man shook his head. "Can't say I do. Seems to me Luke deserves his pet after getting himself lost because of Puff."

His radio sounded and he responded. "They're bringing him to the house now."

"Thanks so much."

"Glad to help. The EMTs are here. They need to check Luke over just to be sure he's okay."

"Can they bring their equipment inside?"

The officer nodded and went back outside.

Julie turned into Noah's arms. "Thank God. I've never been so frightened."

"I could tell," Noah said as he curved the palms of his hands about her face and kissed her gently. "I love you, Julie Joy."

"I love you, too."

She pulled away and walked over to the storm door to wait. Her heart pounded when she saw the officer approach, holding Luke's hand. Puff hung underneath the child's arm as Luke talked excitedly. When they stepped inside, Julie dropped to her knees and hugged him close.

"Puff ran away, Auntie Hulie."

Julie hugged him tighter and cried softly.

He squirmed in her hold. "You're squishing me, Auntie Hulie."

She let go and reached for the kitten. "Give Puff to me. These gentlemen need to make sure you're okay."

Julie held the kitten against her chest and rubbed her hand over his fur as she waited for the EMTs to examine Luke. The child asked a million questions as they checked his vitals.

"He's fine, Miss Dennis. Nothing a good meal, a hot bath, and a good night's rest won't fix."

"Hungee, Auntie Hulie."

Julie almost smiled. At least getting lost hadn't hurt his appetite. "Dinner is nearly ready. Go wash up and tell your brothers."

After the room cleared, Julie burst into tears. Her shoulders trembled as she sobbed in relief. The sobs soon turned into hiccups.

"Oh, honey, everything's okay," Noah soothed, wrapping his arm around her shoulders.

"I was so afraid they wouldn't find him."

"I know, but he's home and none the worse for his adventure. That's a blessing."

Julie pulled back, wiped her cheek with one hand, then pushed the kitten at Noah. "Here. Take Puff. Put him in the cage in Mari and Joey's bathroom for now. I can't bear to look at him."

He cuddled the animal. "It's not his fault, Julie. He only did what animals do."

She didn't want to blame the kitten for Luke's disappearance. "It's my fault and I have to fix it. I should never have brought a kitten into this house." The noise of the boys whooping and hollering as they charged down the stairs reminded her she had work to do. She rubbed her eyes again. "I need to finish dinner."

"Don't make your decision out of fear. Why don't you sit and relax for a bit?"

"No," she said with a shake of her head. "I have to feed the children. Everything has to be normal."

Soon they were all gathered around the table, the scene as normal as every other night when they dined as a group. Luke went on and on about how Puff ran away until Julie felt she might scream.

"Luke, you know better than to leave the house without permission," she said finally. She could not allow him or the other boys to think this type of behavior would be accepted.

"Wif Puff, Auntie Hulie."

"Puff is not a responsible adult, Luke. You know you're not allowed to leave the house without permission," she said sternly.

Luke's expression crumpled, but Julie refused to give in. Protecting him was her job, and she wouldn't let this happen again. "You must understand how dangerous leaving the house alone can be. How do you think I'd feel if something happened to any of you? It would break my heart. And your mom's and dad's."

Noah attempted to intercede for the child. "I'm sure Luke is sorry he went out without permission."

"No, I don't think he understands," Julie argued with a firm shake of her head. "Luke, you will not leave the house again without an adult. Do you remember what your dad said? If you misbehave, he expects me to punish you. Do you understand?"

He sniffed and nodded his head.

"That goes for all of you. Does everyone understand what I'm telling you?" Julie's gaze shifted from child to child, and she waited for their response.

They all nodded.

"And, Luke, you cannot play with Puff again until I tell you it's okay. Understood?"

The child looked as though he wanted to cry. He nodded slowly.

"Why don't you take the kids into the living room?" Noah suggested. "I'll straighten up in here and bring you a cup of cocoa."

Julie felt as if she'd drop from sheer exhaustion. The older boys played at her feet while Naomi and John toddled about the room. Luke cuddled at her side.

"You know I love you, don't you?" she asked softly.

He nodded.

"Promise you won't go outside by yourself again?"

"Torry, Auntie Hulie."

She kissed the top of his head. "Me, too, Luke." *I should have taken better care of you today.*

Noah soon joined them, handing Julie the promised cup of cocoa.

The evening hours stretched on as they watched a Christmas special on television. "Okay, guys, time for bed," Julie announced. "I have a surprise planned for tomorrow," she blurted.

Four sets of eyes focused on her.

"What are you planning, Julie?" Noah asked.

She had arranged for them to have snow the next day. After calling for information, she'd hired a company to turn the backyard into a veritable snowy playground.

Not as good as a good old-fashioned snowfall, but the kids would enjoy the experience. Granted, the snow wouldn't last long as the outside temperatures warmed up, but the memories would last forever.

"Just wait and see."

"You make me afraid when you talk like that. I never know what to expect."

"Keep 'em guessing. That's my motto."

Noah lingered after the children's bedtime, and Julie couldn't decide whether he was concerned that anxiety might overcome her again or hoped she might spill the beans about the surprise.

When she started nodding off on the sofa, he stood and said, "Guess I'll head for home and prepare for the big surprise."

Julie's eyes felt so heavy as she struggled to her feet. "Good idea. Get plenty of rest. You're going to need your energy."

He pulled on his jacket. "Now I'm truly nervous."

"Don't worry," Julie reassured with a mischievous smile. "I have complete faith you can handle this."

Noah kissed her cheek. "You rest, too. It's been a stressful day."

"Definitely an incident I don't care to repeat. Only two more days until Joey and Mari return. Thank the Lord."

"Thank the Lord, indeed," Noah said, clasping her hand in his. "I'm grateful He provided this time for us to be together."

"Thanks for being here for me," Julie told him. "Especially today."

"Where else would I be?"

In her mind, the span of miles between them seemed an almost insurmountable issue, but in his presence Julie experienced overwhelming love for him. How could she make this work?

She waved good-bye and locked up the house for the night. Upstairs, she checked on the kids before heading off to bed. When she opened the bathroom door, Puff meowed in objection to being locked up all evening.

Julie opened the cage and picked him up, stroking his soft fur as she walked back into the bedroom. "I'm sorry I did this to you," she whispered. His body rumbled against her. "Noah's right. It's not your fault."

When Julie put Puff on the floor, he immediately sank his claws into Mari's comforter and climbed up to curl into a ball at the foot of the bed.

She had a strong suspicion Joey was going to kill her for this one. How could a decision that had seemed so simple at the time be so wrong? When she'd seen the advertisement for kittens in the newspaper, it never occurred to her that having one would be anything more than a good experience for the children. Now she understood the burden she'd placed on her family and had no idea how to change the situation.

Chapter 11

The following morning, Noah zipped his leather jacket closed and blew on his hands as he waited on the steps of the Dennis home. "Cold out here!" Noah exclaimed when Julie opened the door.

"Oh, come on, Noah. Spring in Denver is colder than this."

"What's that noise?"

"Come see," Julie invited.

Noah followed her to the kitchen and glanced out the window. He could hardly believe his eyes. "Snow?"

"Surprise!" she said, laughing at his confused expression. "There's more than one snowball out there with your name on it. I'm so happy the temperature dropped last night. The snow will last longer."

A good night's rest had obviously helped. Noah shook his head and said, "There's no end to what money can buy."

Julie punched his shoulder. "Even I know better than that. And you know as well as I do that this manmade stuff is nothing compared to the real thing. Money has its limitations.

"Everything is in God's hands. Money can't buy health or happiness. When the doctors diagnosed Mari, I'd have given every dime I had to keep her healthy for the sake of Joey and her children. I knew that would be God's choice. And I'm so thankful everything turned out for the best. When I got the news, I had this overwhelming feeling that if God needed to take anyone, it should be me. Mari had so many more reasons to live. So many people who needed her."

"Thank God it wasn't you," Noah said, the impact of her words making him ache.

"I've never been as relieved as when the doctors gave Mari the all clear. I love her so much," Julie admitted.

Noah wrapped his arms around Julie and hugged her fiercely. "And I love you."

About ten thirty, the children were playing in the living room when one of the men she'd hired knocked on the back door and said, "We're ready when you are, Miss Dennis."

"Thanks." She walked into the living room. "Let's get your coats, hats, and gloves. We're going outside to play."

"Don't want to," Luke told her as he continued to roll a tiny car around the rug.

"Come on, Luke," Julie pleaded. She wasn't in the mood for his rebellion today. "You'll like this surprise."

"Wanna pway car."

"Fine," she snapped. "You can nap on your bed while everyone plays in the snow."

"Sno." He jumped up and grabbed the coat Julie held. After two failed attempts to pull it on, she held it for him to slide his arms in and then turned him around to zip the coat closed.

"My do," Luke objected, pushing her hands away.

While she admired his attempts at self-sufficiency, Julie longed for the days when baby Luke had allowed her to do things for him. She handed him his hat. "Put this on. I'm going to get John and Naomi. Don't leave the house," she warned.

When she released them into the enclosed backyard a few minutes later, the boys went wild with excitement. They were everywhere, kicking through the snow the men had mounded here and there. Matt, Marc, and Luke laughed uproariously when Julie nailed Noah with a snowball right away. When he came after her, she started to run and slipped. Noah rubbed a handful of snow in her face.

Julie accepted his hand and stood. She brushed her clothes off, and when he walked away, she quickly formed a snowball. "Noah!" she called.

He looked up and the snowball splattered against his chest. He grabbed two handfuls of snow and squeezed them into a weapon of his own. As he approached, Julie pulled Matt in front of her as a shield. "You wouldn't hit an innocent child with that, would you?"

"Spoilsport."

He handed the snowball to Matt, who immediately turned and tossed it at Julie.

She grabbed a handful of snow and reached for the child. "Joseph Matthew Dennis, you're going to be sorry!"

Over in the churchyard, the kids had stopped playing and congregated at the fence to watch. "Let them come play," Julie told Noah.

He hesitated for a few moments before he pulled a cell phone from his pocket. Julie waited expectantly as he spoke to the center director. "Okay, thanks, Mrs. Hill. I'll let Miss Dennis know."

"Are they coming?"

"She says most of the kids aren't dressed warmly enough to play in snow. She's afraid they'll get sick if they get their clothes wet. Plus they only have a few more minutes of recess."

Julie felt saddened by his news, but realistically she knew the center director was right.

The machine continued to turn water into snow while the boys pushed a large snowball around the yard, stopping at the gate to the fence. While Noah finished the huge snowman, Julie went inside for a colorful scarf and a carrot for his nose.

"You think the congregation will say something about us placing this snowman near the church?"

"I doubt he'll last long enough for them to complain."

About fifteen minutes later, Luke came over and wrapped his arms around her legs. "Cold, Auntie Hulie."

She gathered the shivering child into her arms and squeezed him. "Time to take this party inside before everyone gets sick," she called to Noah.

"I have to get back to work, too. Thanks for the memories, Julie Joy," he added. "Only you would have thought of making your own snow day."

"I enjoyed myself."

"What time should I pick you up tonight? The cantata starts at seven. I thought we might go out to dinner before. What about five?"

"I'll check with Maggie and see when she's available."

"Call me."

After the children had warmed up, Julie sat on the sofa with them all around her. "Did you enjoy the snow?"

"I remember snow at our old house." Matt jumped from the couch and ran across the room to tug a photo album off the bookcase shelf. He thumbed through the pages. "See?"

Julie studied the photo of Joey, Mari, Julie, Matt, and Marc hugged up to a gigantic snowman. "I'd forgotten that. You guys were so little."

"Where me, Aunt Hulie?"

"You weren't born yet, Luke."

"What borned?"

Oh no, she thought. She didn't plan to touch that one.

"You weren't there," Matt told him.

Out of the mouths of babes. Why hadn't she thought of that? She turned the pages, enjoying the journey into the past.

"Daddy likes this picture," Matt volunteered, flipping the page open to a photo of Julie and Joey with their parents. "He says that's Grandpa and Grandma Dennis."

The picture, which had been taken the winter before their parents' deaths, brought tears to Julie's eyes. Joey had been home for Christmas when that huge snowfall had come. "Mom liked to make figures out of the snow. Our snow couple had children and a dog. Mom wanted to build them a house, but Daddy said she'd used up all the snow."

The boys giggled and Julie regretted that they'd missed the opportunity to know their father's parents. They were such loving and giving people. They would have loved Joey's children so much. At least they'd had a close relationship with Mari's mother. She wondered if they missed their grandmother Edy as much as their mother did.

"Well, guys, I have to get busy. Lots of work to do before Sunday. I need you to entertain yourselves for a while."

Luke raced for the stairs.

"Where are you going?"

"Find Puff."

Dread shot through Julie. "Have you forgotten what I told you about Puff, Luke?"

He came over and leaned against her leg. "No forget." She ran her fingers through his hair. "Pway with twuck, Auntie Hulie?"

That seemed a good alternative to playing with the kitten. She opened the closet and took down his favorite. At least it wouldn't entice him out of the house. "We'll work on your gifts for your parents after I finish in the kitchen."

Julie had visited the craft store to pick out items for the boys to make stepping-stones for their parents. She'd gotten Joey and Mari a mosaic bench for the backyard and figured they'd enjoy the stones while they sat and watched the children play. Later, she'd prepare the concrete and put it in the pans so they could decorate them with the various stones they'd chosen.

In the kitchen, she dialed Maggie's number and waited for the ring. Noah had overcome Julie's objection to leaving the children by having Maggie insist on babysitting. "Hi, it's Julie. Are we still on for tonight?"

"I'm looking forward to it. What time?"

"Noah wants to go to dinner around five. Is that too early?"

"Not at all!" Maggie exclaimed. "I love spending as much time as possible with the children."

Julie kept busy all afternoon, not giving herself time to think about spending the evening with Noah. She hesitated to call it a date. It had been months since they'd shared anything more than a phone call. She felt comfortable with him after having spent so many hours of the past two weeks in his company, but she knew Noah wanted to know where they were going as a couple, and she didn't have a clue.

Chapter 12

Julie slipped her diamond stud earrings on before she ran downstairs to open the door to Maggie Gregory.

"You look nice."

She looked down at the sparkly red Christmas sweater she'd paired with a black skirt and boots. When she'd packed for the trip, she'd almost left it behind but had second thoughts. It was too pretty not to wear. "Too bright for church?"

"Not at all. The color is perfect for Christmas."

"Thanks for doing this for me. Who's keeping the nursery tonight?"

"Whoever's next in rotation. We take turns so no one gets burned out. If you don't mind, I'd like to take the children over to visit Mrs. Allene. She hasn't been feeling well, but she wants to give them their gifts."

Julie felt bad that she hadn't checked on the elderly neighbor. The woman had been so kind to Julie during her stay.

They walked into the living room to find toys spread everywhere.

"You guys know the rules," Julie said. "Put everything away but one toy. Now please."

The boys picked them up, dumping them into the baskets where Mari stored them. Julie admired the way her sister-in-law had trained the boys to pick up after themselves. They even tried to make their beds and put their dirty clothes in the hamper.

"Is it okay to take them over to Mrs. Allene's?" Maggie asked again.

"Of course. I should have checked on Mrs. Allene. Let me get her gift from us."

Julie had wrapped the gift just yesterday and knew exactly where she'd placed it underneath the tree.

"She knows you're busy with the children."

"Are you sure she's up to the commotion? And be sure to keep an eye on Luke," she warned.

Maggie patted Julie's arm. "Don't worry."

She tried not to but it was difficult. The woman was probably far better equipped to care for them, but they were Julie's responsibility. "My cell number is on the pad by the phone. It's long-distance, but call if you need me." She dropped into the armchair. "I'm so used to taking care of them, I'll probably try to spoon-feed Noah."

They both burst into laughter. The doorbell rang and Julie chuckled again when she let Noah in.

"What's so funny?"

"Nothing," she told him, winking at Maggie as they stepped into the living room. "Where are we eating?"

Julie wasn't familiar with the restaurant Noah named.

"Try their salmon. It's fantastic," Maggie suggested. "I'm not expecting you back until late. Have fun."

"Not too late," Julie told her. "There's a lot to be done tomorrow."

"Just concentrate on having fun tonight, Julie," Noah told her. "You can worry about the rest tomorrow."

Noah helped Julie with her coat and took her arm as they walked out to his car. He opened the door, and the small interior seemed cramped after traveling in the van. "I'm glad you agreed to come tonight."

"I'm looking forward to the cantata." Julie found herself enjoying the outside decorations as they drove through the neighborhood. She really should take the children sightseeing. "I love Christmas. Everything is so sparkly and beautiful."

"Like you. You look great, Julie. But then you always look beautiful to me."

Warmth flooded her face. Noah had always been generous with his flattery. She knew she wasn't anything special, but it was nice to hear someone liked her appearance.

"I can't tell you how happy I am that we have this time alone."

The dashboard lights provided Julie with enough glow to study Noah's profile. "We've had time together."

"The kids were always just a short distance away. Your mind was on them more than on us."

"I can't help that," she defended.

Noah glanced at her. "I'm not criticizing you, Julie. I only ask that you forget about them for a few hours and just let it be us together."

Us. Was she prepared for "us" time? Over the past few days, her anger toward Noah had slowly evaporated, leaving behind the realization that nothing had changed. When she left South Carolina in a few days, she'd leave a major part of her heart behind.

Her love for Noah and her family would make going back to Denver even more difficult, but she'd deal with it again, alone, just as she'd done before. Well, not exactly alone. She would stand firm in her intention to return to church and give God a portion of her time. Tonight, she'd give Noah her undivided attention.

"I wish I could have taken you to see the Christmas entertainment available in the various theaters," Noah said as he helped her from the car.

"This is fine. I'm looking forward to the cantata."

The restaurant he'd chosen was cozy and romantic. A white cloth draped their table. Candles provided the subdued lighting. The waiter handed them their menus and after learning they weren't interested in wine, asked what they'd care to drink. Noah surprised Julie by requesting sweet iced tea.

"It's the beverage of choice at the church," he said at her questioning glance. "I've grown to love the stuff since I moved here."

Mari must give it to the kids, too. She'd wondered about that when she asked Matt if he wanted juice or milk and he'd said tea. Julie hadn't developed a taste for the beverage and opted for water with lemon at most meals. She had stuck with juice and water for the children, as well. *No kids allowed,* she chastised silently. "Tell me what's good."

Noah pointed out the items he'd enjoyed on previous visits. "Let's order different entrées and share."

She nodded agreement. They'd done that often when dining out.

"Do you still go to our restaurant?" Noah asked.

Julie shook her head. She didn't go anyplace that reminded her of them.

"I always loved their spaghetti. No one can make it like Jose."

Julie laughed with him. It never failed to amuse them that their favorite Italian restaurant had a chef named Jose. She recalled the time Noah had asked to meet him. It turned out Jose was the son of an Italian mother and Spanish father and had learned to cook the foods of two cultures.

"Did you repaint the condo yet?"

Julie had threatened to repaint the place about a thousand times since she'd met him, but she'd never gotten beyond paint charts. "I'll probably hire someone to do it soon."

"I can't believe you're still living with that mauve paint in the living room. You hated it."

She despised the color. It went okay with her white furniture, but she preferred more earthy tones. "It defeats the purpose if I paint it before I get new carpet."

"I thought you were going to redo the hardwood floors."

"When I have time."

"It does have a way of getting away from us, doesn't it? I can hardly believe I've already been here six months."

Julie didn't have any problem believing it. That's exactly how long she'd put her life on hold. She hadn't redone the condo simply because there was no one around to appreciate it but her, and she spent so much time at work that she'd convinced herself it would be a waste of time. She hadn't worked nearly as many hours when her family and Noah were around.

"Ready to order?" their waiter inquired after placing their drinks and a basket of bread on the table.

Julie glanced at Noah and back at the menu. "I'll have the Cajun grilled salmon," she said.

"Sounds good. I'll get a seafood combo. That way you can sample the variety they have here on the coast."

Noah passed her the basket after the waiter left to place their order. "Try these. They're called hush puppies. It's fried corn bread. Try one."

Julie recalled them from her visit this summer and had found them to be tasty.

The moonlight glimmered off the ocean just outside the restaurant. Even in the darkness, the vast amount of water on the horizon fascinated Julie. "Looks different at night. I've had a hard time adapting to the humidity here."

"Be glad you're visiting in winter. The summer heat leaves me breathless at times. I miss the mountains."

Julie nodded. Making comparisons between the two states was something she found herself doing often. The South Carolina sky seemed so much paler than the sapphire blue of the Colorado skies. Here, flat land stretched out as far as the eye could see. In Denver the mountain ranges were always in the western horizon. She looked forward to going home. "My vacation has gone so quickly. I can't believe tomorrow is Christmas Eve. The New Year will be here before we know it."

"Plan to make any resolutions?"

Julie sipped her water and set the glass back on the table. "To get to church more often. Maybe this will be the year to redecorate the condo."

"Or sell it and move here."

His comment surprised Julie. "I'm sure Joey doesn't want his pesky baby sister around interfering with his life. Having me miles away is probably the best thing that's ever happened to him."

"Why would you think that?" Noah asked, his intensity startling her.

Julie fiddled with her silverware. "He gave up too much for me already. I wouldn't dream of intruding on his family."

The waiter set their salads on the table. Julie placed her napkin in her lap and poured the honey mustard dressing over the greens.

"You're Joe's family, too, Julie. He'd never resent you."

"I'm his sister, Noah. That's not the same as a wife and children. He has plenty going on in his life without having me underfoot. Joey did his time. He deserves a break."

"You know it's not like that," he objected. "Even when you live in the same community, you don't see each other that often. You have your work and different friends and a place of your own to keep you occupied."

"I already have that in Denver," she pointed out.

Her response clearly exasperated Noah. "And I'm trying to say I want you in my life. You've already said you don't do long-distance. So where does that leave us?"

"In different places."

"Why are you so closed minded about this?" Noah demanded.

Julie laid her fork on the salad plate. "I'm being realistic. Your life isn't your own. You belong to God. What happens when you get a church of your own? Do you expect me to pull up roots and follow you to another new area? Be separated from Joey and Mari and the kids again?"

"I would if you were my wife. I love you, Julie."

"You loved me so much you walked away from us, Noah. Pardon me if I'm not able to trust that it wouldn't happen again if God called you. You're anticipating a future that can take you anywhere. I didn't ask you to change your life on a whim. Don't ask that of me, either."

"I want to share that future with you. Home is not the building, Julie. It's the place where you're happiest with the people you love. We could be happy if you'd just open your mind to sharing your life with me regardless of where we are. I realize I made a big mistake when I didn't discuss my intentions with you before I left. I didn't do it to put you out of my life. I did it so I'd have a future to offer you."

The waiter arrived with their entrées, and the conversation paused as they sampled their foods.

"Try this," Noah offered, spearing a shrimp with his fork and holding it out to her.

"That's good," she agreed. "Want to try my salmon?"

They sampled each other's food until they were full. When the waiter asked if they cared for dessert, both quickly refused. "I'll have to remember that seafood sampler next time I come here."

"So you're planning on there being a next time?"

When Noah tried to pick up where they'd left off, Julie glanced at her watch and said, "You'd better finish your coffee. It's already after six, and we need to get to the church a few minutes early to get good seats."

❧

"What's the answer, Lord?" Noah asked later that night as he rested in his recliner, searching his Bible for answers.

He believed he'd stated his intentions fairly clearly to Julie. He wanted to marry her. How would they ever progress if she wasn't willing to even consider the possibilities?

After dinner they'd driven to Cornerstone and found seats. He'd enjoyed hearing the cantata again. Noah felt confident Julie had enjoyed herself, as well. He'd seen tears in her eyes during the more moving songs, and she'd commented on how good the program had been several times when he'd walked her home.

Then when they'd arrived at her front door, she'd thanked him for a wonderful evening and said good night. He'd intended to plead his cause further. Maybe even give her the ring that burned a hole in his pocket.

Noah wished Joe were here now. He could use his friend's counsel. Joe understood Julie. Perhaps he could tell him how to reach her.

"I don't want to let her go again, Lord," he spoke aloud. "I believe You have guided her back into my life for this purpose, and I'm ready to accept the role of husband and provider. How do I make her understand?"

"Wait."

"How long?" Noah asked.

His gaze dropped to the Bible. Isaiah 42:16 leapt off the page at him: "I will lead the blind by ways they have not known, along unfamiliar paths I will guide them; I will turn the darkness into light before them and make the rough places smooth. These are the things I will do; I will not forsake them."

"Thank You, Lord," he whispered. God knew the answer. Noah only had to wait on His timing.

When Noah had asked if he could come in, Julie knew he wanted to continue their discussion. She'd explained that it was late and she had lots to do the next day. Her entrance set off the singing Santa. "That thing is getting on my nerves," she grumbled as she stopped to hang her coat and bag on the rack.

"I shut him off until after the kids went to bed," Maggie admitted. "They kept setting him off."

"I'll be happy to leave him here with Joey and Mari. Don't be surprised when he shows up in a yard sale."

"Did you enjoy yourself?" Maggie asked.

"I did," she answered with a broad smile and a nod. "The cantata was wonderful. Thanks for making it possible. How were the kids?"

"Pretty good. I took them to see Mrs. Allene. She gave them gifts and fed them ice cream and cookies."

Julie winced. She didn't envy Maggie—five kids on a sugar high. "I'm sure they enjoyed themselves."

"Mrs. Allene did, too. She loves those children."

From what Mari had told her, their neighbor had been widowed several years earlier. "What about her family? Doesn't she have children? Grandchildren?"

"A son. Dillon. He's an engineer somewhere overseas."

"He doesn't visit her?"

"Not often," Maggie said, shaking her head in dismay. "It's sad. I don't think he even realizes his mother won't be around forever. Her health has declined so much this past year, but I know she hasn't told him."

Julie curled up in the armchair and pulled a chenille afghan over her legs. "Why don't you call him?"

"It's not my place. I love Mrs. Allene like my own mother. I'd never do anything to upset her."

She felt confused. Their parents had never minded telling Joey when he was overdue for a visit. "Why would suggesting her son visit upset her?"

"She says he's busy. She puts his needs before her own."

Julie remembered that much about her parents. No matter what she and Joey did, they had stood by them. Joey had stood by her as well. "Maybe Joey could give him a call. Sometimes men understand each other better."

"I'll see how things go. If she doesn't get better soon, I'll make the call myself. I couldn't bear it if she left this world without seeing him again."

"You're close to her, aren't you?"

"When I rented my house, Mrs. Allene came over and welcomed me to the neighborhood. She invited me to visit Cornerstone. Thanks to her, I found my church home. She's been a true friend and I love her dearly. Now tell me about your date."

"It was nice."

"That's such a mundane word for a beautiful couple. Noah obviously cares a great deal for you."

"He says he loves me."

"You don't believe him?"

Julie fingered the fringe on the afghan. "He loves God more."

"As he should. Putting God first in your life is top priority."

Julie felt overwhelming selfishness as she tried to make Maggie understand. "But he walked away from us."

"Did he ask you to come with him?"

"Noah never committed to anything. After he left and I realized how much I loved him, I considered following him here."

"Why didn't you?"

"Joey said Noah was popular with the ladies at Cornerstone."

"We all like him, but I wouldn't say he's pursued anyone romantically," Maggie offered.

"I know that now, but I took Joey's statement to mean Noah had moved on with his life."

"Why would Pastor Joe make such a statement?"

"I intend to ask him when he gets home. But there's more to the story than that. When Noah received the job offer, he made his decision without even asking my opinion. If he truly loved me, he would have cared what I thought. I believe he feels I'm too young. But I'm old enough to know my own mind. I stopped being a child the day my parents were killed."

"So you want to marry Noah?"

Julie blew out a stream of air and dragged her hand through her hair. "I love him but I don't know that I can give up everything that's important to me to follow him as he serves the Lord."

"You can if God asks it of you." That wasn't the advice Julie wanted to hear. "Loving someone makes you want the best for them. And when you love them enough, there's nothing they can ask of you that you'd refuse. Your brother and

Noah have a very important calling. They need women they can depend on to support them in an arduous task."

"Joey certainly has that in Mari. I could never be half the woman she is."

"God doesn't want you to be like Mari, Julie. He made you unique."

"That He did," Julie agreed. "I'm a one-of-a-kind, break-the-mold-and-throw-it-away sort of woman."

Maggie laughed. "I'd say you need to search deep within yourself and determine how much you care for Noah. If you love him as much as I think you do, you'll figure out a way to put God first in your life and in your relationship. Otherwise, you're destined to live an empty life. Believe me, I know how that can be. Careers and friends don't replace the need to have a special person in your life."

"You never married?"

Maggie shook her head. "I kept telling myself 'one day,' but life got away from me. I'm fifty years old."

"That's not too old," Julie protested.

"I'm pretty set in my ways. I doubt I'd ever find anyone who'd have me at this point in my life."

"I don't believe that for a minute. You're a wonderful person, Maggie Gregory, and any man would be blessed to have you for his wife."

The woman's cheeks colored. "Thanks, Julie. I'd better be getting home. I have a twelve-hour shift at the hospital tomorrow."

"On Christmas Eve?"

"Sickness never takes a day off. I work tomorrow and I'm off until the following Wednesday."

"Will you join us for dinner on Christmas Day?"

"I plan to come over for a while. I thought I might take a plate over to Mrs. Allene and stay with her for a bit."

"We can get a wheelchair and bring her over for dinner if she's up to it," Julie suggested.

"We'll see," Maggie said as she prepared to leave. "Pray about you and Noah. God will lead you if you let Him."

Julie scrambled to her feet and followed Maggie to the front door. The Santa started singing, and she quickly turned him off before he woke the kids. Maggie laughed at her quick reaction.

"Thanks for tonight, Maggie—and for the advice. I promise to pray about my situation if you'll do the same. I think God has a Mr. Right out there for you, too."

"We'll see. Thanks again for letting me spend time with the kids tonight."

"Joey and Mari are blessed with their family," Julie replied, feeling melancholy as she considered not seeing the children again for months. "I'm going to miss them so much."

"Then perhaps you should consider making some life changes to accommodate all the people you love so much."

Perhaps I should, Julie agreed as she locked up for the night and headed upstairs.

Chapter 13

Julie set the alarm clock with the intention of rising early and getting a few chores out of the way before the children woke, but when it went off, she slapped the SNOOZE button and closed her eyes again. After three times, she rolled out of bed and headed for the shower.

Tilting her head back beneath the spray, Julie rinsed the shampoo from her hair and considered the restless night she'd spent. Thoughts of her date with Noah and then Maggie's words had made sleep impossible. Would she really have an empty life if she opted not to change? Surely not.

Last night hadn't been the night to lose sleep. She had far too much to finish today. Christmas Eve. Julie could hardly believe the end was in sight. Tonight she had planned a party to commemorate Jesus' birthday. At first, she'd invited Noah, and Matt's friend, Jeremy, but the list had grown steadily into a good-sized party.

Between tonight's party and Christmas dinner, Julie accepted it would be a hectic day. After getting the children dressed and fed, Julie loaded them into the van and started picking up the things she'd ordered. *Too bad the day care is closed on Saturdays,* she thought after the third stop.

The boys squabbled in the back until her head throbbed in earnest. Matt seemed determined to make Luke cry. "Leave him alone, Matt."

"He's touching me, Auntie Julie."

"Don't touch him, Luke."

"My twuck, Auntie Hulie."

"Give him his truck."

She swung the van into a parking lot and got out to separate Matt and Luke. "You know better, Joseph Matthew," she said sternly.

"He wouldn't share."

"You should have brought your own toy."

She checked her list and started the van, driving to the store where she'd ordered the turkey and hams. Thankfully, that was her last stop.

Back at the house, she fed the children lunch. "I need to get organized for the party tonight," she said in her no-nonsense tone. "If you can't play together, you'll have to take a nap. I don't have time to referee."

Once she started cleaning the house, the children seemed determined to test her. The twins woke after a short nap, whiny and demanding her attention. The older boys fought until she put them all in a time-out. The only way she'd get anything accomplished would be to hire a babysitter. Julie grabbed the phone and dialed Noah's number. "Do you have Robin's number?"

"Good afternoon to you, too."

"I'm sorry. I have tons to get done, and the children refuse to behave."

"Want me to come over?"

Julie didn't hesitate to agree. Her load was too heavy to shoulder alone. "Yes, please. I need two interruption-free hours to finish."

"I have a couple of things to pick up and then I'll be over."

"Could you pick up some cranberries? The grocery store was out, and I wanted to make a cranberry salad for tomorrow. The boys were fighting and I completely forgot about them."

"No problem. See you soon."

Julie couldn't believe the children's behavioral turnaround once Noah made his appearance. He took them out to play while she worked inside. She lingered at the window, watching him laugh as the children raced around him.

"Destined to live an empty life." Maggie's words struck home. Julie considered the fear of loss she'd dealt with when her family and then Noah had moved away. Could she deal with that emotion each time Noah's job required them to move on?

She saw Luke battling the blow-up figure. Julie took a step toward the door but stopped when she saw Noah lead the child away. She returned to washing the vegetables.

"Empty life." Her life these past two weeks had been full. Did she want to go back to a life devoid of family? Noah's declaration of intent certainly offered promise for their future.

"Just as My Son's birth offered hope for a dying world."

One tiny baby boy, born to die for a world of sinners He loved, had made such a difference. The thought made her concerns seem petty and shallow.

What was she really afraid of? Noah loved her. She loved him. Perhaps her inadequacies in terms of being a good minister's wife? Noah deserved someone like Mari. Someone who could help him carry through on his promises to God. Not a stubborn, opinionated woman subject to assumption and anger.

Julie arranged the veggies on the tray and covered them with plastic wrap. She was placing them in the fridge when the doorbell rang. She hurried to answer.

Natalie stood there holding a large cake box. "Hi," she said, pushing it into Julie's hands. She laughed at the Santa's movements as he sang. "Be right back." She ran back to her car and returned with a second box and a basket. "Merry Christmas. I brought you some of my specialty candies for the party. And some cookies for the children. Where are they?" she asked, glancing around the room.

"Noah has them outside. They were driving me crazy."

"Nice guy," Natalie said as she carried the treats into the kitchen for Julie.

"He is," Julie agreed. "Would you care for coffee or some eggnog?"

"I have to run. I need to finish my deliveries and get to the airport. My friends are flying in tonight."

They placed the items on the kitchen table and Julie walked back through the living room with her. "Come by later if you get a chance."

"We'll try."

"Thanks for everything, Natalie."

"You're welcome. It's been great having you here, Julie. I hope to see more of you in the future."

They hugged, and Natalie hooted with laughter when the Santa started singing again. "That thing is a riot. Merry Christmas."

Julie repeated the greeting and closed the door. She took her coat and hat off the coatrack and headed outside. Noah had the twins in their swings and alternated pushing them. He smiled when she stepped up alongside and began to push John's swing.

"Finished?"

"Finally. Looks like they've run off some of their excess energy."

"Would you like to go out for an early dinner?"

"Where did you have in mind?"

He named a chain restaurant Julie enjoyed. She released John's seat belt and removed him from the swing. "Sounds good. Come on, guys. Let's get ready for dinner."

They arrived to find the restaurant filled with holiday revelers. Tables crowded with family and friends visiting and exchanging gifts.

"Thanks again for your help," Julie told Noah once they were all seated. "I was close to the end of my rope."

"You were frazzled," Noah agreed. "Too much planning stressed you out."

"Probably. I shouldn't have done the party tonight. Tomorrow will be hectic enough."

"At least the party won't last long. After everyone leaves, you can put the kids to bed and put your feet up."

"Don't tease me," Julie joked. "I haven't relaxed in two weeks. No reason to think I'd start tonight. Now tomorrow night is a different story."

That night as the house filled to capacity, Julie found herself enjoying this group of strangers. The guests devoured eggnog, cocoa, sodas, cookies, birthday cake, and assorted snacks. Then they gathered around the piano to sing carols.

When Noah suggested they take their show on the road, her guests bundled up and walked over to the church. They stood out front, caroling and passing out candy canes to the sightseers who drove by to view the nativity. A few parked and joined in the festivities.

Robin had offered to stay at the house with the twins, and Julie took the older boys with her. They'd raced around with their friends and after half an hour, complained about the cold. She finally called good night to Noah and the others.

After she'd closed the door behind Robin, Julie breathed a sigh of relief. Soon the kids would be in bed, and tomorrow she'd be free.

When the phone rang around eight thirty, Julie decided one of the guests had forgotten something.

"Miss Dennis, this is Geneva Simpson. I called to ask when you'll be picking up the children's gifts. Mari has them stored in my attic."

Julie almost whooped with joy. "Oh, thank you, Mrs. Simpson!" She explained the catastrophe with the list, adding, "I had no idea where to look."

The woman laughed. "That Luke is a character."

"What time do you go to bed?" Julie asked. "I need to get someone to stay with the kids while I run out to your place."

"I can have my husband bring their things over after the children are in bed," Mrs. Simpson volunteered.

"I'd be eternally grateful."

"We're glad to help."

Julie felt overjoyed. "What are you doing for dinner tomorrow?"

"Chester and I will eat at home."

"Come eat with us. We're celebrating Jesus' birthday in fellowship. Several church members have agreed to come."

"We got your invitation, but we didn't want to be a burden."

If she only knew what a blessing she's just become, Julie thought. "I can't tell you the weight you've lifted from my shoulders. Please say you'll come."

The woman agreed and promised to have her husband bring the gifts after nine thirty. Julie's heart and steps lightened as she ran upstairs to settle the boys in bed. They were restless, anticipating the morning, and it took longer than usual for them to fall asleep.

After reading them the Christmas story, Julie turned off the lights and sat with them in the glow of the night-light. After much tossing and turning, Matt and Marc gave in to their exhaustion and drifted off. She sat on the edge of Luke's bed. "Want me to lie down with you for a while?"

He bounced on the bed, making room for her, and Julie cuddled him beside her. "Are you excited about Mommy and Daddy coming home tomorrow?" she whispered. His head bobbed up and down as she fingered his soft hair. "I know they'll be happy to see you, too. Will you miss Aunt Julie?" Luke nodded again and a knot formed in her throat. "I'm going to miss you guys so much when I go home."

"Why you go, Auntie Hulie?"

She wanted to cry. "Because my home is there."

"You stay with me."

"And where would I sleep?" she asked.

"Sweep with me."

Julie smiled at his generosity, though she couldn't imagine the two of them in the twin bed. "I love you, Luke."

Amazingly enough, all five of the children had fallen asleep by the time the headlights indicating the arrival of their personal Santa flashed on the house.

Julie ran downstairs to help Mr. Simpson. "You truly are Santa," she exclaimed as they piled boxes about the room.

"The missus and I added a few things," he said. "We never had any little ones of our own. We love these children so much."

"They are a lovable bunch," Julie agreed. "I know Joey and Mari appreciate your help. Providing for five children can't be easy."

Her gift to the family had been a computer and several programs intended to help the children's educational potential. She'd even added high-speed Internet access for the year. If they decided to homeschool Matt, the computer would prove helpful. Besides, they could e-mail her to save on telephone calls.

Still, her expensive gift wasn't comparable to those of this one couple who had probably used a bit of their pension income to provide for her brother's children.

"I'm glad you and your wife are joining us tomorrow."

"Geneva said we'd be coming. Can I help you with anything else?" he asked as he rolled a third bicycle into the room.

"You've helped more than you realize," Julie said, smiling brightly as she thanked him again. She wished him a good night and closed the door. Her spirits sank a bit as she approached the gift piles. Why hadn't she checked before Mr. Simpson left? Without hesitation, she went to the phone. "Noah, help."

"Julie, what's wrong? The kids?"

"They're fine. We got a blessing of sorts. Mr. Simpson just delivered their gifts, but nothing's assembled."

"Think Mari covered that on her list?"

"Probably. What am I going to do? I can build a computer from the ground up, but even with a complete set of instructions, I know nothing about toy assembly."

"I'm on my way. Maybe you should put on a pot of coffee."

"Thanks, Noah."

❧

Noah arrived a few minutes later, and Julie led the way to the unassembled red wagon that lay on the living room floor.

Julie plopped down on the floor and tried to fit two pieces together, groaning when they fell apart. "Why didn't Joey take care of this before he left? He promised Mari would handle everything."

"How do you know they didn't?" Noah challenged. "Maybe part of the plan was to ask someone to put this stuff together before tonight."

Julie passed the wagon instructions to him. He checked off the various parts to make sure they had everything they needed. "Where's the toolbox?"

"I'll get it," she offered, jumping up off the floor.

"You can run but you can't hide," Noah teased at her eagerness. "Don't forget the coffee."

Julie grumbled a lot to begin with, but as things began to fall into place, she felt a great sense of accomplishment. Her role in the children's Christmas had expanded beyond her gift-buying tendencies.

"Tap that spot gently, Julie," Noah requested as he held the handle in place.

"Like this?" she asked, blinking away tears when she managed to pound her finger. Noah howled with laughter.

Holding her throbbing finger protectively, Julie shushed him and said, "It's not funny."

"I'm sorry. Give it to me."

She held out her hand.

"The hammer, Julie," he suggested, his grin still in place when he took a moment to kiss her battered finger.

One tap and the piece slid into place. "There, that's finished," he said, using the handle to push the wagon away. "What's next?"

"At least the bikes are assembled."

"I don't recall Joe mentioning bikes for the boys," Noah commented.

"You don't think the Simpsons bought them, do you?"

Noah shrugged. "Probably. Matt and Marc often sit with them during services."

"But it's too much."

"God rewards the faithful," he told her. "I don't know how the kids can sleep. I always remember being too excited. Every year, I kept trying to peek to see if Santa had come. What about you? I bet you were worse than me."

Julie nodded. "I put out cookies and milk and begged to sleep on the sofa. Then I fell asleep before Santa arrived and woke up in my bed. I always believed he carried me upstairs before he left."

"I'm going to miss you," he began.

"Me, too," Julie said as she unpacked a box containing a small racetrack. "Even though I'm home, I suffer homesickness until work overwhelms me and I don't have time to miss everyone."

"Stay."

Her head jerked up. "I have my job. My condo."

"Sell the condo. Find a job here. You did a great job with the office computer. I'm sure you could find work."

The possibility of freelancing had occurred to her more than once.

"Once Joey and Mari come home, there's no reason for me to stay. They have each other and the children. They don't need me getting in the way."

"I need you." Noah dropped down on one knee before her. "I've prayed about us for a long time. And I'm confident God has shown me you're the one."

"I'm not," she objected, pulling back from him. "I'm too opinionated to be a pastor's wife. You'd never get a church with my big mouth getting you into trouble."

Noah laughed. "Maybe in time we'll both learn to temper our tongues and seek God's guidance before we speak. That doesn't mean I want to wait to make you my wife. I'm ready to settle down. To be blessed with a wife and children."

"I wouldn't want more than a couple of children," Julie objected.

"And maybe God will see fit to give you that exact number. He knows the plans He has for you. But if He gives you a dozen, you could handle them, Julie Joy. Children are a gift."

"I need time, Noah. I can't make this decision right now. It would be more emotional than logical."

He took her hands in his, his loving gaze meeting hers. "Love is an emotional attachment, Julie. It's having your heart, mind, and soul agree that you can't live happily without the person you love. Take all the time you need. I'll wait for your answer because I love you."

"When Joey said you were popular with the ladies, I thought. . . Well, I believed he meant romantically. I was heartbroken that you could forget me so easily when I loved you so much."

"Why didn't you ask? I never had eyes for anyone but you, Julie Joy. I never issued or accepted a dinner invitation or did anything to lead any one of them to believe I was interested.

"You think I walked away and didn't look back? It felt like I drove the entire way to South Carolina looking over my shoulder. But I had the hope that one day we would live happily ever after. To tell the truth, I don't know that I could have left you if it hadn't been for being close to Joe and Mari and hearing how you were doing."

"I didn't date either, Noah. I wrapped myself in my work to the point that I ate, slept, and breathed computers. I didn't want to go anywhere or do anything that reminded me of you."

He stopped working on the track. "That's why you stopped going to church?"

Julie picked up the cardboard pieces that dotted the floor. "It wasn't fun anymore. Sure I knew people, but everyone I'd connected with had left the church."

"God didn't."

"I know that now. If I'd trusted Him, I'd have gotten my answer sooner. Now I'm praying and seeking His guidance for my life. There's something I need to share with you."

Fear crossed Noah's expression.

"The real reason I'm hesitant to say yes is because I'm afraid I can't handle the pain."

"What pain?"

"The desertion, Noah. Having Joey and his family move away tore a chunk of my heart out. And when you followed, I felt devastated. And when I think about how our life together would force me to accept constant separation from the people I love. . . Well, I'm not sure I could handle that."

"I can't promise you won't ever leave people you love behind, Julie. But I can promise no one will ever love you more than I do. I've grown from our separation, too." Noah laid down the parts and concentrated on making her understand. "When Joey first suggested I cover for him, I thought, 'Here's my opportunity to prove myself invaluable to Cornerstone.' Instead, I haven't done anything I wouldn't have done if he'd been here. Well, one thing," Noah corrected. "I got to spend more time with his beautiful sister."

Julie felt her skin warm. "Thank you. I guess you spent so much time shadowing me and making sure I didn't cause trouble that you didn't have time to make your mark."

"I trusted you to do right, Julie. I never doubted you. All I did was voice my concern, and you cared enough to protect me as well as Joe."

"That's my problem. I don't know how to handle this life. I can't imagine being closely examined by a congregation."

"I can," Noah said softly. "Look at what you've done. I've seen nothing but your willingness to share with others."

"Oh, that's nothing," Julie said.

"It is something," Noah objected. "You took time off to care for the kids. You invited people to share Christmas dinner. You encouraged others to use their God-given talents. Those are all things a pastor's wife would do. You're a fine Christian woman, Julie Joy Dennis."

"I've had good role models. Attending church has helped me realize what I've been missing. I'm moving God to the top of my priority list."

He held out his arms and they hugged. "I can't tell you how thankful I am to hear that, but I hope you'll consider changing your place of residence."

Julie wanted to say yes—to make a new life with him. But could she be the woman he needed her to be? "I love you, Noah."

"Enough to marry me?"

"Oh, look at the time!" Julie cried when the clock chimed the hour. "You're a lifesaver, Noah, but you're going to be exhausted tomorrow. I mean today," she said upon seeing the hands had crept past three. "Merry Christmas."

"I'll be okay. It's not the first all-nighter I've pulled. You didn't answer my question, Julie."

"I don't have an answer."

"I told you I'd wait and I will, but remember families are their own circle of love. Friends complement that circle, but it starts with the family. You and I would be the start of that family, and wherever we are, we'd always have each other to depend on. You've been on my heart and mind every day we've been apart. We'd better get this job completed before the kids come downstairs."

They finished assembling the small race car track, and Noah spent several minutes watching the cars whiz around it.

Around four, Julie heard Naomi's cries on the baby monitor she'd purchased. She suggested Noah take a break and went to care for the baby. She returned to the living room to find him fast asleep in the recliner.

"Bless his heart," she whispered to Naomi. After the baby fell asleep, Julie laid her on the sofa and returned to the assembly.

"Why didn't you wake me?" Noah asked when he woke about an hour later.

"You needed to rest. You have to preach this morning. I'm nearly done here."

He allowed his gaze to drift about the room. "So this is what Christmas Eve is like for a parent. Spending the wee hours making sure everything is taken care of."

Julie tucked Naomi's baby doll into the toddler-sized stroller. "Joey worked his way through college doing assembly work. Called himself Mr. Fix-It."

"I didn't know that."

"Stick with me, Noah. I can tell you all sorts of stuff about Pastor Joey."

"I'm not going anywhere," Noah said pointedly. The clock chimed six. "Speaking of Pastor Joey, I'd better head for the airport."

"Are you sure you're okay to drive?"

"I can get through the day on that nap."

She walked him to the door. "You were right," Julie admitted. "The list didn't matter. Everything turned out fine."

"We can do all things through God who strengthens us."

"You sound like a pastor," Julie teased.

"Good," he said with a satisfied smile. He cupped her face and kissed her gently.

"Noah," she called as he started out the door, "thanks for everything. Be careful."

After he left, Julie took Naomi upstairs. She came back down to add her gifts to the rest and finished organizing the room. The nativity scene sat on top of the console television, and Julie smiled as she thought of the kids' reactions to her attempt to put baby Jesus in the arrangement when they had placed it there almost two weeks ago.

"Not before Christmas," Matt had insisted until she put the figurine back in the box and stored it away.

Julie left the tree lights burning and lay down on the sofa. What an experience it had been. She would miss the kids, but most of all she would miss Noah. What a friend he'd been in her hours of need. Despite his own full schedule, he'd never refused her assistance.

Noah had proposed. Excitement filled her at the possibility of becoming his wife. Her hopes plummeted just as quickly. Marrying Noah would bring so many changes to her life.

I'll miss everyone so much. Julie felt weepy at the thought of leaving everyone she loved behind.

"Father God," she prayed. "Thank You for my family. Please return Joey and Mari safely to their children. Help me strive to be a better witness for You. The gift You gave the world over two thousand years ago is truly the most wonderful gift of all.

"And, God, give me the right answer to Noah's proposal. I accept that with Your help I can be the right wife for him, but the human side of me argues the point. Give me a clear answer as to what You would have me do.

"And as always, thank You for loving and caring for me as only a loving Father can. Amen."

Chapter 14

"Wake up, Jules. Santa's brought what you wanted most for Christmas."

She stretched and offered up a sleepy smile. "And what might that be?"

Joey extended his arms and grinned. "Your beloved brother and sister-in-law, of course."

So much for her plans to be dressed and have a breakfast feast prepared. She snuggled against the sofa pillow and murmured, "Good, now you can worry about those little menaces you left with me."

"Were they that bad?" Mari asked, appearing concerned.

Julie tilted her head toward Joey. "They're his kids. What do you think?"

"I told Joey it was too much to ask of you."

Julie captured Mari's hand. "I had the time of my life. Did you enjoy your trip?"

"Oh yes. We have so much to tell you," Mari added, looking more animated that she had in some time. She glanced at the Christmas tree and back at Julie. "It's huge."

Julie pushed her feet to the floor and sat up. "There's a story behind that."

"And that lump of ice near the fence?" Joey asked.

"There's a story. . ." Julie and Noah said together, breaking into laughter.

"In fact, Julie could write a storybook," Noah said.

"I assume we still have five kids?" Joey teased.

No thanks to Luke's efforts to lose himself, Julie thought. But that was another story. "Five kids, two less fish, one hamster, and a kitten. Puff ate the fish, by the way. He's upstairs with the boys now. I meant for him to be a surprise, but Luke let the cat out of the bag."

"Bathroom," Noah corrected.

Julie bared her teeth at him. "Mr. Jones went out of town and brought the kitten by early. I hid him in your bathroom, but Luke wanted his bath toys and let him out."

"Then Puff, as he's now known, ran up the Christmas tree and toppled it on Julie," Noah added.

"Oh!" Mari cried, touching her hand to her chest. "Were you hurt?"

Julie tapped Noah's arm and whispered sternly, "You weren't supposed to tell that part." She looked at Mari and said, "Nothing but my pride. The tree's tied to the stairs so no one else will get attacked by that giant."

Joey laughed loudly and Mari shushed him.

"And whose bright idea was it to get a cat?" Joey inquired.

"You did give me carte blanche."

Her brother's incredulous look was a clear indicator of his thoughts on the matter. "So you got a cat?"

"Admittedly, not the smartest decision I ever made. I'm willing to do whatever it takes to rectify the situation. I can try to find him a new home before I leave. And if that doesn't work, I'll take him back to Denver with me."

"The children would be devastated if you took Puff away now," Mari said. "Besides, I've always wanted a kitty."

"He's a handful," Julie warned. "I didn't tell the boys he ate their fish."

"I suppose it's a trade-off of sorts. One new cat, two less fish," Joey said with a shrug. "So what's the story on the tree?"

Julie eyed the monster in the corner with more than a little disdain. "Matt picked it out. He insisted his mom would let him have this tree. You should have seen Mr. Simpson's face when they loaded it on the van."

"I wish we had a picture," Joey said.

Mari looked puzzled. "Matt knows I never let them choose the tree."

"They've taken me on a wild ride with all the things they claimed you'd allow."

"What about the list? I thought I'd covered everything."

Julie glanced at Noah and then back at her family members. "Luke flushed the list Saturday night. He threw Naomi's shoe in on Sunday morning to hold it down."

"He did *what*?" Joey demanded.

"He had his reasons," Julie defended. After all, he was only three. What did he know about adult fears? "We survived and that's all that matters."

Mari appeared near tears. "I missed my babies so much. I need to see them."

Joey watched his wife race up the stairs before turning back to Julie. "She got so homesick, I thought we were going to have to turn around and come back. Then after a few days with no calls, she started to enjoy herself."

"There were a couple of times I thought I'd have to call."

Noah squeezed Julie's hand. "She did a great job, Joe."

"I don't doubt it for a minute." He looked around the room. "Jules, I'm seeing all sorts of new contraptions about my house."

"Remember your promise. There's not one thing here that doesn't benefit the entire family. Noah did his best to keep me under control."

Joey glanced at his friend. "She guessed?"

Noah nodded. "About the tenth time I said I didn't want you coming back to problems we'd caused. Just accept the gifts in the spirit they were intended, Joe," Noah advised. "Julie's made the best of a challenging situation."

Noah's comment captured her brother's attention. His gaze fixed on her. "Not too bad, I hope?"

"Let's just say you're indebted to Noah for life," Julie warned.

"What about you?" Noah asked with a loving smile. "Don't you owe me, too?"

Julie pointed at her brother. "You did the favor for him." Then she grinned. "Actually, I couldn't have survived this without you."

"We make a good team."

Julie nodded agreement, forgetting about Joey as she and Noah shared the moment. "The best. You're going to be an excellent father one day."

"You'll make an excellent mom."

"I hate to interrupt this mutual admiration society meeting, and I can't really say what kind of parents you two will be until after I check with my kids, but Mari and I are obliged to you both. We needed the vacation."

"And now I need one," Julie said, bursting into laughter when she glanced at Noah. "Maybe I'll stick around for another week so you can wait on me hand and foot."

"Yeah, right," Joey said. "Stick around and I'll take Mari on another vacation."

"No way, brother dear. You've had your time. We'd better sort these presents before the children come downstairs."

Julie explained how the gifts had only been located late last night. "If anything's missing, we'll have to handle it later."

They had just finished when Matt appeared at the top of the stairs holding Luke's hand. The sound of lively little boys racing down the stairs echoed throughout the house.

"Marc, Santa came!" Matt bellowed as they burst into the room.

The room became a hub of activity as the boys scouted out the gifts.

"Boys, calm down," Mari instructed when Marc brushed past her on the stairs. She carried the twins. "Daddy has to read the Christmas story first."

"Wait," Julie ordered. "I want to get this on video."

She picked up the camera from the end table. The scene before her stole Julie's breath away as she looked at the image on the small screen. Just like when they were children and their parents carried out their traditions on Christmas morning, her brother's family now did the same.

Joey sat on the sofa with Mari at his side, Naomi in her lap, and John squeezed between them. The older boys sat on the floor at his feet. He held the Dennis family Bible open to the story of Jesus' birth. Tears filled her eyes.

Noah came to sit on the chair arm next to her. "Go ahead," she directed after adjusting the camera to record this Christmas morning.

The beauty of the story filled their hearts as Joey read of that wondrous birth so long ago.

"Luke, it's your year to put the baby Jesus in the manger," Mari said.

No one seemed the least bit concerned that he was going to handle the tiny porcelain nativity piece.

"Where is Jesus, Auntie Hulie?" Luke asked.

Julie passed the camera to Noah and went to rummage in the closet where she'd stored the box. She handed it to Luke, and once she saw his cautious handling of the figurine, she understood. Carefully, he made his way to the arrangement and laid baby Jesus into place.

"Let's pray," Joey said as he stood. "Heavenly Father, we come to You on this blessed Christmas morn to say thank You. Thank You for giving us Your Son, our precious Lord Jesus. Thank You for the love that surrounds us."

Julie glanced at Noah when he took her hand. She smiled softly and bowed her head again.

"Thank You for each and every member of my family and for our dear friend, Noah. Thank You for the bounty of gifts. We know that no earthly gift can ever match the wonder of what You've done for us. Please help us to be worthy of Your gift. Mari and I thank You for each of our precious children and for Your daily watch over them. As parents, we fully understand the sacrifice You made for us by allowing Your Son to die on the cross for our sins. And thank You for being here for Julie in her time of need—for giving her the strength to carry on in a momentous task. In Jesus' name, we pray. Amen."

A chorus of amens filled the room. The adults smiled when Luke jumped up and shouted, "T'ank You, God." The child turned to hug his father, and Joey swung him up into his arms. "So, how did Auntie Julie do as a mommy?" he asked.

"Auntie Hulie bestest Christmas mommy ever," Luke announced.

Her brother's love reached across the room to engulf Julie. "I knew she would be."

"You might change your mind when you know the entire story," she offered dubiously. Joey and Mari would probably never ask her to babysit again once they heard what had happened to Luke.

"They're safe and happy, Julie. That's all that matters. Hey, guys, let's see what you got for Christmas."

The children dashed for the tree. Joey and Mari joined them, making certain each child had a package to open.

Teary-eyed, Julie glanced at Noah.

"He's right, you know," Noah agreed. "No matter what happened, you kept going. You never gave up."

"At times, I wanted to," Julie admitted softly. "That's when I called on God and He sent you over to help out."

Noah kissed her hand. "I couldn't stay away." He took a tiny gift-wrapped box from his pocket. "You never did say what you wanted for Christmas." ·

She stripped away the paper and snapped the box open.

The lights of the tree twinkled in the lovely solitaire diamond. Julie gasped and placed one hand over her mouth.

"I want you to understand the depth of my commitment. I want to marry you, Julie Joy Dennis. I want you with me wherever we are. I want a family with you. I need you to stand by me in the pulpit as I minister to my flock."

"Oh, Noah, that's the part that scares me most. A minister's wife needs to have a calling as well. What if I let you down?"

"Are you a Christian, Julie?"

"You know I am."

"Then you have a calling. You're a disciple for our Lord Jesus Christ. You already give everything within you to those you love, and I love you just like that. I called my mom this morning and asked her to pray that you would accept. Please say yes."

"Are you sure? Do you realize what you're taking on?"

Noah's smile broadened as he nodded slowly.

"Yes then, Noah. I don't ever want to leave you again."

He hugged her tightly and removed the ring from the box then slid it onto her finger.

"Hey, you guys forgot the most important piece of decoration," Joey called, smiling as he held mistletoe over Mari's head and kissed her soundly.

Noah held out his hand. "May we borrow that, Joe?"

Julie leaned toward Noah and their lips met in the sweetest kiss they'd ever shared.

"Merry Christmas, Christmas mommy," Noah whispered.

Chapter 15

New Year's Eve

As the music segued into the bridal march, Noah's gaze fixed expectantly on the sanctuary door and he tugged at his suddenly too-tight collar. Julie stood there in her mother's gown, looking even more beautiful, if that were possible. In a few minutes, she would become his wife. Noah could hardly believe the progression of events that had taken place since she'd accepted his ring.

After Christmas dinner, they'd slipped away and driven to the beach to stroll along the nearly deserted white sandy shore. They'd held hands and laughed a lot as they discussed the events of the previous few days.

Noah couldn't have been more shocked when Julie suggested they get married on New Year's Eve. He'd stopped walking and asked, "You're kidding, right?"

She'd looked offended. "I wouldn't joke about something this important."

"But. . . There are so many decisions to be made."

"And we'll make them," Julie promised. "Together. With God's help. He has already answered so many prayers for me. I'm ready to be here with you. Not halfway across the country."

"You can't just up and relocate without preparation," Noah objected.

"I am prepared," Julie said quickly.

Her response had puzzled him. "But surely you've dreamed about your wedding day."

"I have," Julie agreed with a confident nod. "I know exactly what I want."

"Your church?"

She shook her head. "Since I'm marrying Cornerstone's associate pastor and I expect my brother to be at our wedding, it would hardly be fair to the congregation to drag you both away. We can get married at your church. Joey can give me away and conduct the ceremony. Mari and the kids will be my attendants."

"What about a dress?" Noah threw out. "That takes forever."

"I always planned to wear my mother's dress. It's stored in Joey's attic."

"It'll need alterations."

Julie shook her head and smiled brightly. "Fits perfectly. I got my height from Mom."

"What about decorations?"

"The church is already beautifully decorated for Christmas. All I need to do is add a few flowers and it'll be perfect."

"Photographer? They have to be scheduled months in advance."

Julie had refused to be deterred. "There's probably someone at the church. If not, we'll throw some of those disposable cameras around and ask our guests to take our photos."

Noah suspected she'd enjoyed systematically eliminating his every reservation. "What about the reception?"

"We'll have it catered. Surely the congregation won't mind if we provide all the food for the Watch Night service as well."

Noah led her over to a set of wooden steps leading down to the beach. They sat and he'd supported her against his chest, his arm resting about her shoulders. "Julie, you need to slow down. What will Joe think? He requires engaged couples to be counseled prior to marriage."

She'd shrugged. "So he can counsel us. Shouldn't take long considering he knows us so well."

"He may feel he's too close to the situation," Noah said. "Why the big rush?"

Julie tilted her head back against his shoulder and looked into his eyes. "Because I want next year to be the first of the happiest years of my life, and one way I can do that is by marrying the man I love. Do you have any idea how miserable I've been without you? I don't want to spend months planning an event that keeps us separated even longer. If we marry this week, I can go back to Denver to work out my notice, list my condo for sale, pack, and move here before the end of January."

"But we'll still be apart."

"Only for a short time. And then I'll be here as your wife, living with you in our own home, and planning for our future."

The wind off the ocean had picked up, and Noah pulled her closer when she shivered. "You could move here anyway. I'm sure Joe would love to have you staying with them."

"I don't want to be a guest in Joe's home," Julie told him. "I want to be your wife."

Despite his uncertainties, Noah hadn't wanted to refuse her. "Can we pray about this?"

"Certainly. But I prayed even before you placed this ring on my finger this morning. I've loved you for a long time, Noah Loughlin. Long enough to believe we can have a good, solid marriage."

"You didn't feel that way two weeks ago."

Julie sighed deeply. "I did. Definitely angry because you left me behind without letting me know how you felt, but I loved you then. I'd hoped you'd propose, and if you'd asked, I'd have moved here, too."

"You know I felt I needed to make preparations for the future. I'm still thinking we should consider where we'll be in another year or two."

"You want to wait that long to marry me?" she asked, disappointment in her voice.

"I only want what's fair. I'm asking you to give up a lot to be my wife."

"Isn't that the way of every marriage? My dad once told Joey that the secret of a good marriage is both people giving one hundred and fifty percent and expecting nothing in return."

"That's good advice." Noah stood and held out a hand to her. "You're cold. We'd better get back to Joe's. They'll be wondering what happened to us."

Julie smiled at him. "Let's talk to him about the wedding."

Noah shrugged. "Okay, but he's going to agree that it's too soon."

Back at the house, they'd parked and waved at the boys playing with their bikes in the backyard before they went inside. Mari cuddled a sleeping Naomi as she visited with Maggie.

"Where's Joey?" Julie asked softly.

"In the office."

She smiled at her sister-in-law and took Noah's hand, pulling him down the hallway. Julie tapped on the open door. "Do you have a minute?"

He looked up from the computer on his desk. "Sure. You caught me playing with your laptop. I wouldn't mind having one of these."

"It's yours," Julie told him.

"I can't take your computer."

"I bought it for you, Joey. I got a new computer for the church, too."

Joey had looked puzzled. "But you gave me that check for the window. Are you sure you can afford all this?"

"Consider the check my tithes for when I missed church."

"It's very generous of you. It means the church can probably dedicate the Good Shepherd window at Easter."

"Wonderful. I'll look forward to being there to see it."

"You're coming again at Easter?"

"That's what we need to talk to you about, Joe," Noah said, glancing at her. "Julie wants to get married at Cornerstone on New Year's Eve."

Again, Joey looked surprised. "There's plenty of time, Julie."

"No, Joey, there's not. I've spent months of my life angry with God for taking you, Mari, and the kids and then Noah away from me. I buried myself in work, hoping the pain would go away.

"It didn't. I brought that same anger here when I came to stay with the kids, and God opened my eyes to the truth. I'm standing in the way of my own happiness. God put it right there before my eyes, but I allowed stubborn pride to blind me. I love Noah and it's important that we spend every moment we have left making each other happy."

"That's an impossibility," Joey told her. "Not every moment."

"Is it?" Julie challenged. "Haven't you always told me nothing is impossible with God?"

Joey couldn't argue with that. "What do you think, Noah?"

"You already know I'd say 'I do' this moment if I could. Julie has ruled out every objection I offered. Tell him your plans," Noah encouraged.

As she'd outlined everything for her brother, Noah couldn't help but feel her excitement. "So you could marry us at seven o'clock with the reception following and still have Watch Night services afterward."

"It could work," Joey had agreed.

"It will," Julie assured. "All I need is for you guys to take the boys for tuxedo fittings. Mari can pick out her dress and something for Naomi, and I'll take Mom's dress to the cleaner. If it needs alteration, I'm sure Mari will help. We can be ready with time to spare."

"I'll need to run this by the church board."

"What about counseling?" Noah reminded.

Joe nodded. "It's a requirement."

Julie spoke up. "It's not that I mind the counseling sessions, but I thought they were to make sure the couples are ready for marriage."

"Among other things," Joe agreed. "I want you both to understand the seriousness of the step you're taking."

"Do you trust Noah?" Julie asked.

Joe glanced at him and said, "With my life."

"And your sister? You introduced us. I've known Noah almost as long as you have. I love him with my heart and soul, and I want to be with him as his wife as soon as possible. I don't want to spend months planning a major production while living in Colorado. Not when I can be here with the people I love. The only doubts I have relate to the kind of minister's wife I'll be, but I'm willing to give it my all."

Her brother had smiled at them. "We'll set aside some time this week, and if you both feel this is right after counseling, I don't see any reason why you can't be married New Year's Eve." Joe stood and held out his hand. "Looks like you'll be getting a tax write-off, buddy."

"Hey, that's the woman of his dreams," Julie said with a laugh.

The days passed in a whirlwind of activity, and as promised, Julie had carried out her plans with time to spare.

Noah suspected Joe's in-depth relationship sessions regarding compatibility, expectations, personalities, communication, conflict resolution, long-term goals, and even intimacy had surprised her. But he'd recognized her sincerity from the questions she asked and the responses she gave.

At the last session, Joe hugged Julie and said, "I wish I could tell you marriage is the easiest thing you'll ever do, but that wouldn't be true. You'll work harder than you've ever worked, but when you celebrate sixty or seventy years together, you'll have no regrets."

Joe had reached out to shake his hand before pulling him into a hug. "Welcome to the family, Noah."

He'd found himself becoming more eager with each passing hour. His parents and family had flown in two days ago. They loved Julie and expressed no doubts as they pitched in to help finalize the plans. His mother had even managed a rehearsal dinner the previous evening.

A couple of Julie's girlfriends had flown in that morning and now sat in a pew on the bride's side of the church as her honorary attendants.

Julie carried a bouquet of the red roses she'd chosen to blend perfectly with the Christmas decorations. Candles flickered in the low light.

She stopped at his side, and when Julie smiled at him, Noah felt at peace. As they had practiced, Joe placed her hand in his and stepped into the pulpit.

"Dearly beloved." The words echoed in the hushed silence of the sanctuary. A few minutes later, everyone laughed when Julie said, "I do" and Luke said, "I do, too."

After the service, the photographer finished his work and they moved to the fellowship hall to greet their guests. Before they realized it, Joe announced it was time to gather in the sanctuary for Watch Night service.

"Do you want to leave?" Noah asked.

"Let's stay and welcome in the New Year with our church family."

"Come with me," Noah said, leading her to the balcony and their own private world.

They enjoyed the program, particularly the music, and with the New Year only minutes away, Noah lifted her hand to his lips. Her rings sparkled in the light as he whispered, "Look what happened all because you agreed to take care of the kids."

Julie's soft laughter was that of delight. "I was afraid I couldn't handle them. And now I'm thinking I wouldn't mind being a real Christmas mommy."

Noah grinned at her admission.

The New Year's countdown started and they joined in.

"Three. Two. One. Happy New Year, Mrs. Loughlin!" Noah exclaimed, pulling her into his arms.

Joy sparkled in her eyes as Julie glanced heavenward and whispered, "Thank You, Jesus."

EXCEPT FOR GRACE

Dedication

To all God's disciples who helped me find my way.
And to Jesus Christ for loving me enough to die for my sins.

Chapter 1

"You want me to build what?"

"A cross," Kimberly Elliott repeated, focusing on the way his voice had risen with his question. "An old, rugged cross for my Easter program."

Wyatt Alexander ran his hand along the cabinet front he'd been sanding when she let herself into his workroom. "I don't do stuff like that. I build furniture and cabinets."

Kim refused to take no for an answer. This program was too important to her and to Cornerstone Community Church. "Beth says you're the best carpenter she knows."

That got his attention.

"She has to say that. She's my sister."

Kim didn't feel that was the case with Beth. When she had asked her about a carpenter, Beth immediately recommended her brother and proceeded to point out his pieces in her home. Kim recognized Wyatt Alexander's work as quality. "Not every sister holds her brother in such high regard."

He removed his safety glasses, appearing uneasy with the discussion. "Beth's a good sister."

Never having had a sibling, Kim wasn't certain whether his discomfort had more to do with her request or having to say something nice about his kid sister.

She changed tactics and flashed him her most beguiling smile. "I know it's early to be thinking about Easter; but there's so much to do, and I wanted to get this out of the way first thing."

Kim found Wyatt difficult to read. He continued to run his hand over the furniture, frowning slightly before he reached for sandpaper and smoothed it over the piece.

"You have measurements?"

Kim tried not to show her excitement. "It's for a boy about this tall," she explained eagerly, holding her hand about chest high.

She heard his quick intake of breath before he asked, "A boy?"

She nodded. "He'll need a foot stand and pegs to hold on to when he stretches out his arms. The end result should probably be somewhere between six and seven feet tall."

"You have a boy playing Jesus?" Wyatt asked again, sounding incredulous.

"It's a children's play," Kim explained.

"At Cornerstone?" He sounded doubtful.

"How did you know?"

"You're my sister's friend, and since she attends Cornerstone, I figured you must, too. So how did you convince them to let you break tradition?"

She knew from his question that Wyatt was more than a little familiar with the church. She didn't recall seeing him there, though. "I asked."

He nodded, a half smile touching his mouth. "Yeah, I can see where you might have worn them down."

His mockery might have offended Kim if she didn't want his help so badly. Then again he wasn't the first to recognize her persistent nature.

Wyatt continued, "I suppose I could turn a couple of landscape timbers into a cross. There's probably enough scrap lumber around here to build a footrest."

"What are landscape timbers?"

"Those long wooden poles people put around their flower beds. Don't tell me you've never seen them."

She shrugged. "I live in a condo at the beach. The ocean is my yard."

Wyatt sighed heavily. "If you ask at the hardware store, they'll help you find them. Buy two eight-footers and bring them over. I'll work your cross into my schedule."

Kim could have hugged him. Producing this play was one of the most important things in the world to her. "Thanks for your help. I'll be sure to put your name on the program."

"I'd just as soon you didn't." When Kim looked at him, he said, "I don't want people thinking they can ask me to build anything under the sun. You're the exception."

She wondered why but dared not ask. "God appreciates your help."

His grim look expressed his true feelings. "I doubt God cares one way or the other. I'm only agreeing because you're my sister's friend and I owe her."

His feeling that God didn't care stabbed Kim in the heart. She knew how much God loved every one of His children. If only she could make him understand. The feeling she shouldn't antagonize him further was strong. "How much will this cost us?"

"Since I have no idea what the going cost for cross construction is, let's just say this one's on me. You provide the material. I'll provide the manpower."

Kim found his prickly personality difficult to interpret. Not sure if he was joking or not, she decided to play it light. "I think we can afford that. Thanks again. I'll let you get back to work."

He didn't bother to respond when she called good-bye. She exited the crowded and vacant front office, admiring the antique wooden door as she turned the old brass knob. Outside in the parking area, the hound that had greeted her earlier with his ominous bark all but shoved his head beneath her hand. Kim caressed his floppy ears and spoke softly to the animal, glancing back at the metal building that housed Alexander Woodworking.

Her gaze stopped on the carved wooden sign that read, MEETINGS BY APPOINTMENT OR CHANCE. She'd surely opted for chance when she showed up without calling first.

Steering her car back down the lane, Kim recalled Beth's warning that Wyatt's shop was a few miles out of the way. Earlier she had suggested her friend come along, but Beth had plans and said Kim would do fine on her own. She'd taken the afternoon off and followed the directions Beth had written on the notepaper, driving past the road twice before spotting the small sign hanging beneath his mailbox. Just as Beth had described, she found the workshop located behind the house. How he'd managed to find something so rural right outside the city limits of Myrtle Beach, South Carolina, was beyond her.

Beth had told her very little about her brother. Kim knew he had to be a few years older than she was, but she couldn't determine how many. The picture she'd seen at Beth's must have been taken years before. Wyatt Alexander looked very different in real life.

His facial features were actually more striking than handsome. A film of dust from the sanding coated his collar-length thick hair, but she could tell it was dark. He wore it combed back, exposing a wide forehead, high cheekbones, and a chiseled profile. His sea blue eyes reminded her of the ocean during a storm.

He stood about six feet tall, and his wardrobe consisted of worn jeans and a long-sleeved denim shirt. No doubt about it, Wyatt Alexander had a commanding presence.

Kim wondered if all his clients felt so awkward in his presence or if only she had. From the moment she'd introduced herself, the feeling he didn't want her there had dominated their discussion. Still, a part of her refused to feel anything less than jubilant. She needed a cross, and he had promised to build it for her. That was all that mattered.

⌇

What had he just agreed to do? Wyatt brushed his hand through his hair and knocked loose some of the sanding dust. He needed to remember to lock that door. And fix the front bell.

He'd been startled when he'd glanced up and spotted Kimberly Elliott standing there. She was a tiny thing, not much more than five feet or so, and he doubted she weighed a hundred pounds. She wore her black hair cut short and straight, and those huge green eyes didn't miss a thing.

Why had Beth sent that woman his way? She had to know he wasn't the least bit interested in building a cross. But he also knew his sister worried about his salvation. Other than his parents, he figured she was the only one. God had very little use for an old sinner like him.

129

He should have said no. But he loved Beth and owed her a great debt. If she wanted him to build a cross for her friend, there was no reason why he couldn't. Maybe it would give Beth a bit of comfort to see the cross standing in the church and know he'd built it with his own two hands.

He pushed the safety goggles back on and reached for the sander. He'd do a good job on the cross to impress his sister. Maybe even his parents. Wyatt's lips curved into a cynical smile as he considered whether or not he should let Kimberly Elliott put his name on the program. Maybe that would show the people at Cornerstone he wasn't all bad. No doubt the tongues would start wagging again the moment they learned the source of their cross.

Would knowing that the troubled Alexander boy had built it make it intolerable for the congregation? Many years ago he'd learned to live with their judgmental ways. Did Kimberly Elliott have any idea what she'd gotten herself into by asking for his help?

Chapter 2

The bell over the antique mall door jangled, and Kim glanced up from the notes she'd been working on between customers. Pastor Joe had suggested a drama team committee meeting, and she wanted to be prepared.

Her smile broadened at the sight of her pastor's wife who was also her friend. "Mari. Hi. I was just thinking about calling you."

"And here I've saved you all that effort of dialing the phone," she teased.

Two years earlier, after the heartbreak of her last failed relationship and learning her parents wanted to retire early and travel, Kim had returned home to the beach. She hadn't regretted her decision. Renewing relationships with people from her past, coming back to her home church, and making friends with people like Mari Dennis made her happier than she'd been in a long time.

Kim laughed. "If only all my plans worked out so smoothly. Where are the kids?"

"At home with their dad. He volunteered to watch them when I said I planned to come here to look for a gift. Mumbled something about five bulls in a china shop."

No doubt he understood the premise of turning five small children loose in a store as crowded with stuff as Eclectics. Not that they were bad. In fact, the Dennises had some of the best-behaved children Kim knew.

"He's working at home today anyway. He's using that new laptop Julie gave him to write his sermon."

The pastor's sister, Julie, had burst into their lives like a breath of fresh air two weeks before the Christmas holiday. She'd come to care for the Dennises' five children while their parents toured the Holy Land. Kim had met Julie when she brought the older boys to play practice. She liked the young woman immensely and had been happy when Julie and Noah Loughlin, their associate pastor, solved their differences and married on New Year's Eve. Soon Julie would join their congregation, and Kim looked forward to her being there.

"How is she?"

Mari picked up a collector's plate from the counter and looked it over before replacing it carefully. "I hope not as lovesick as Noah. She sent him home after their honeymoon with a promise to follow him here as soon as she packs up and sells her place in Denver. He's been moping around ever since. You should have seen his face when I mentioned finding a birthday gift for her this morning.

131

I hope he realizes she'll never let him forget if he doesn't remember her birthday this year."

"But he won't forget, thanks to you. You're really in your Good Samaritan mode today. So do you think Julie might like an extra large lion?" Kim chuckled.

The huge garden statuary had stood outside in front of their antique mall ever since her dad had acquired it years ago. Her mother couldn't believe he'd bought it, but over the years it had become a location marker for their store. Directions to Eclectics always included the phrase "*with the lion in the parking lot.*"

"I don't think she has a use for a large stone lion. Besides, how would anyone find you if you sold that thing?"

"True," Kim acknowledged. "Are you looking for anything in particular?"

"She collects pottery."

Kim shook her head. "Don't have any. I have the card of a local potter who does beautiful work. On the expensive side, though."

Mari sighed. "I'll just wander around and see what I find." She started to walk away and stopped. "What were you going to call me about? Wait—let me guess. The Easter play?" When Kim nodded, she grinned and asked, "How did I know?"

"How could you not? Have I talked about anything else since Pastor Joe told me?"

"You deserve to be excited. Julie was beside herself when Noah told her. She's so glad you asked."

Kim had the pastor's sister to thank for her success. She didn't know whether she would have asked about putting on the play if Julie hadn't encouraged her to try. "I'm pretty excited myself. When Pastor Joe asked me to stop by the office, I just knew he was going to tell me no."

Mari shook her head. "I read the play, Kim. There's no way they could have refused you."

"I want everything to be perfect."

Mari nodded. "And it will be. You have many people dedicated to your success. We believe your play is the beginning of change for Cornerstone."

"Not without struggle, I'm sure. Pastor Joe told me a couple of older board members weren't happy with the decision at first."

"But the others were in full agreement," Mari pointed out, "and soon they all came around. People don't always respond well to change in the beginning, but eventually they understand it's essential to accomplishing the church's goals."

"I know, but I wouldn't want my play to cause problems in the church."

Mari smiled. "Joe and the board members prayed. You prayed. I prayed. This is what God wants."

Kim fiddled with a stack of business cards, arranging them neatly in the holder. "Can you help? I know you have your hands full with the kids, but I could use your talents."

"What did you have in mind?"

"Costumes?"

Mari shrugged. "What sort of budget do we have?"

"The church gave me a couple of hundred dollars, but I plan to supplement that with my own funds."

"There's no need to break the bank," Mari cautioned. "We can look for bargains at the fabric stores. Lots of fabric is wide enough that it probably wouldn't take more than a yard for each child."

"Thanks, Mari."

"I'm as excited as you are. I know the message will be even more poignant with the children performing the roles."

"I want Matt as a disciple. He already has the perfect name for the role. Too bad Mark, Luke, and John are too little."

Mari looked doubtful. "I'm afraid Matt's a bit young."

"He can handle it."

Mari wasn't convinced. "We saw the video of the Christmas play. Our boys wreaked havoc in that program."

"Luke did steal the show," Kim agreed. "But it was my fault for giving him a live lamb as a prop. I plan to keep Matt's role simple. One speaking line and some walk-on scenes."

"If you're sure. By the way, Julie says to tell you she has a million ideas and can't wait to get here to help."

Kim giggled. "You gotta love that woman. Noah says she takes planning to new heights."

"I don't know what she has in mind, but knowing Julie as I do, she'll jump right in. I'd better see what I can find. Joe will be wondering what happened to me."

"Take your time," Kim said. "It'll make him appreciate how hard you really work."

Mari walked away with a smile, and Kim thought back to the day she'd approached Pastor Joe with the Easter play she'd had published. He had been very complimentary and congratulated her on her writing success. He'd asked to read the play before he presented it to the board. She'd come prepared and handed over copies of the program before leaving the church office.

Kim had experienced a sinking feeling in the pit of her stomach the following morning when she'd answered the phone and recognized the pastor's voice. She just knew he wanted to let her down gently. But the news had been good. She still couldn't believe they were allowing her to produce *Except for Grace*.

"Can you stop by the office?" Pastor Joe had said.

"Sure. Any time in particular?"

"I'll be here all day."

"See you around lunchtime then."

The butterflies in her stomach hadn't allowed her to consider food. Kim had driven to the church and gone straight to the office. Joe Dennis had greeted her and invited her to have a seat.

"First, I wanted to say I'm humbled by what I read. You definitely have talent."

"Thanks, Pastor Joe."

"I'm serious, Kim. Your play is incredible. The renewal I felt was too tremendous for words. I immediately asked Mari to read it, and when she agreed I contacted the board to ask them to consider the matter. Since then, the two board members who read it promptly recommended it to the others. It's excellent. I mean. . ." Pastor Joe had paused then said, "Well, the story moved me to renew my faith."

His words had sent a chill down her spine. She'd felt the same way as the words appeared on her computer screen, almost seeming to write themselves.

"Two members hesitated at first, but then the entire board voted unanimously to allow you to produce your play for Easter. They even suggested we advertise."

Kim had gawked. "You're kidding."

Pastor Joe had shaken his head. "No, I'm not. After I described how it renewed my spiritual foundation, they all wanted copies. I've received so many positive comments. I hope you don't mind."

"What? Hearing my work complimented?" Kim had asked with a trill of laughter. "Bring it on. I think I can handle all you can give and more." Her careless repartee had struck Kim as prideful, and she'd felt instant remorse. "I'm sorry. That was facetious, and you're serious."

"I understand, Kim. I know you're excited."

She had nodded slowly, feeling her eyes moisten. "I've prayed over it. Several times, in fact. I so wanted Cornerstone to do something of mine. But I was afraid to ask. If it hadn't been for Julie. . ."

Pastor Joe's expression had grown curious. "What does my sister have to do with this?"

"She encouraged me to come to you with the play."

He had smiled. "Thank the Lord she did. I have a feeling about this program. It's going to be quite an Easter celebration around here this year. Did you hear the Good Shepherd window will be dedicated on Easter morning?"

"That's wonderful!" Kim had exclaimed. "I can't wait to see it in place."

"God is truly blessing Cornerstone this year."

Overwhelmed, Kim hadn't been able to speak and only nodded. Silently she had prayed God would indeed use her as one of His disciples.

Mari drew her back to the present when she laid some items on the counter.

Kim smiled at her. "Did you find something for Julie?"

"No, but I found plenty for myself."

Eclectics was exactly what the name implied, a mixture of just about anything a person could want. The store itself covered nearly an acre and contained furniture—antique and used, books, records, jewelry, bric-a-brac, glass, dishes, rugs, and yard ornaments. She bought some items outright, then worked with the owners on commission for other things.

Mari had chosen a carved wooden box, a tiny pink glass rooster, and a couple of books. As Kim wrote up the paperwork and wrapped the items, they talked about getting together soon.

"I could use a girls' night out," Mari said. "It's hard to believe it's only been three weeks since we got back from vacation. I want to show you our photos."

"I can't wait to see them. Will Julie be here in time for our night out?"

"She told Noah she's packing the condo now. They had some good news, too. When she turned in her two weeks' notice, her boss said she's too valuable to lose. He wants her to continue her computer troubleshooting work from here and travel to Denver as needed. I think Noah and Julie are both very happy she won't have to look for work."

"That is good news. I'm so eager for her to get here. If she hadn't encouraged me, I'd never have had the nerve to approach Pastor Joe. I kept thinking I shouldn't rock the boat."

"I'm looking forward to having her here, too," Mari said. "She's the sister I never had. Joe's a bit worried that she's going to shake things up at Cornerstone."

"I'm sure she'll fit right in."

Mari glanced at the antique clock on the counter. "I need to run. I'll be in touch to make plans."

"Talk to you soon. Tell Pastor Joe and the children hello for me."

"I will," Mari said, waving good-bye as she walked out the door.

Chapter 3

After work Kim drove straight to the hardware store to buy the landscape timbers. The salesperson directed her to an outside display. As she studied the long poles, she could see why Wyatt thought they'd make a good cross. She picked through the lot, choosing the more battered pieces. It took a bit of finagling to load them into her sedan, and then she set off for Wyatt's.

She parked and got out. Where was the dog? She walked over to find a CLOSED sign on the door. Great. What was she supposed to do with the two eight-foot poles sticking out of her trunk? Kim thought she heard the whine of power tools inside and tried to look in the window. *Could he be here? Only one way to find out.*

She knocked on the door. When there was no answer, she knocked again and shouted his name loudly.

She should have called first. Walking back to the car, Kim considered what to do. Maybe she could leave the timbers by the building if she could get them out of the car. She started to untie the cord.

"I'm closed."

Kim whirled around. "Hi."

Wyatt seemed a bit surprised by her presence. "What are you doing here?"

"I brought the timbers. I wanted to make sure you had them when you're ready to start work."

He used his pocketknife to cut the cord and pulled the poles from the trunk. "Good thing your seats fold down, or you'd never have gotten these in here."

Wyatt hefted one onto his shoulder and carried it to the building.

"I thought you'd gone home for the day."

When he returned for the other one, Kim followed him inside. She noticed the floor was covered with wood shavings from the piece on the workbench. "What are you working on?"

"A fireplace surround for a house in Charleston. I have a lot to do. They want it next week."

Kim studied the workmanship of the piece. "This is gorgeous."

"I'm trying to replicate some unusual trim in the house. It's kind of tricky."

She traced her finger along the smooth wood then walked over to study the carving on an armoire. She glanced at him. "You did this?"

"It's all my work."

136

"I'm impressed. I can see why Beth says you're the best."

He didn't say anything as he picked up the carving tool and continued the project he'd been working on.

"I'm excited about the cross. I know you'll do a fantastic job."

Wyatt grunted.

"I've been working on my to-do list today," Kim said. "I still can't believe they're going to let me do the play." Again he didn't speak. "Did you ever attend Cornerstone?" she asked.

"When I was younger."

His answer encouraged Kim to ask another question. "Why not now? Beth and your parents are there all the time."

Wyatt dropped the carving tool on the counter and faced her. "Look. I'm busy here. And as for Cornerstone, that's none of your business. I'll get to the cross as soon as I can. I'll let Beth know when it's ready."

Kim reached into her coat pocket. "Here's the store card. You can reach me there during the day."

"I'll call you."

Kim quickly said good-bye. "I'll lock up after myself."

When only the scent of her perfume lingered, Wyatt wondered why he'd let her stay as long as he had. Why hadn't he told her he was busy instead of listening to her prattle? Maybe because he found Kimberly Elliott interesting, even entertaining at times. She was the first woman he'd ever met who could talk a mile a minute without stopping for breath.

And if he told the truth, she wasn't bad to look at either; but his sister's little friend was out of his league. All that was left for him was his shop and life as he knew it. He'd secured his fate all those years ago when he'd decided to drink and drive.

After leaving Wyatt's, Kim hurried through her grocery shopping and headed home. She wanted to work on her planning but knew she had to do laundry if she intended to shower and wear clean clothes. She'd used the last towel in the linen closet that morning.

Maybe she could work on the notes over dinner. She'd picked up some frozen microwave meals. Not that she minded cooking, but preparing a meal for one seemed senseless.

After she put the laundry in the dryer, Kim went into the kitchen and placed her dinner in the microwave. She prepared a small salad and poured some flavored bottled water into a glass before settling in at the table with a legal pad and pen.

She made notes as she ate, listing the character parts she could recall. She'd need to do a more detailed list later that included the walk-ons. For now, the key player would be Jesus.

It definitely required someone who would carry through with the commitment, someone capable of learning the lines. And since a child would play the role, she needed supportive parents who would guarantee the child's presence at practice.

Kim listed the boys who fell in the ten-, eleven-, and twelve-year-old age range. She marked through several of them immediately, knowing they'd never be willing to devote so much time to the play.

Chase. She smiled as she jotted down the name. Perfect. The twelve-year-old was tall for his age, well mannered, and one of the few children she knew who respected his elders. She'd seen his interaction with Beth enough to know that. And having an aunt who was active in church would help ensure he carried through on his commitment.

She grabbed the cordless phone and dialed Beth's number. "Hi, have I interrupted your dinner?"

"I picked up burgers. Chase is studying for a math exam. How was work?"

"Slow. Mari stopped by. She's going to help sew costumes for the play."

"I'm so happy they said yes," Beth said. "When you mentioned you were going to talk to Pastor Dennis, I figured they were so anchored to tradition they'd never consider anything but the cantata."

"I thought the same," Kim admitted. "When Pastor Joe called me to the office and said yes, I nearly fainted. I've been singing God's praises ever since."

"I'm thrilled," Beth told her. "That play deserves to be seen."

"Thanks. That's why I'm calling. Do you think Chase would take on the role of Jesus? I know it's a major commitment, but I'd help him any way I can. We'd only practice once a week up until a couple of weeks before Good Friday, and then we'd probably have a few extra rehearsals. What do you think?"

"Why don't you come over and ask him?"

"But he's studying," Kim said.

"He's due a break. I just fixed a snack for him."

Beth and Chase lived in the condominium next door to hers. For now, it was just Beth and Chase. Beth's husband of three years, Gerald Erikson, was overseas in the military.

"I'll be right there."

Kim turned off the dryer and grabbed her keys before leaving the house. Multistoried, their second-floor condominiums opened onto a breezeway that fronted the parking lot. She stepped around the divider wall and rang the doorbell, smiling at Chase when he appeared in the doorway.

The boy's broad smile reminded her of someone. "Hey, Miss Kim."

Probably Beth, Kim thought as she stepped inside. "Hey, Chase. How's the studying going?"

"Pretty good. It's math. I'm good at that," he said with an air of confidence.

Kim knew the child had won math and science awards at school. "Did your aunt Beth tell you I was coming over?"

He shook his head. "I answered the door on my way to the kitchen."

The condos were designed with two bedrooms and a bathroom near the entry door. A hallway led to the galley kitchen and combination dining/living room, with the master bedroom and bath off to the side. Balconies fronted the building, looking out onto the beach.

Kim indicated he should lead the way. "I hear there's a snack waiting. Don't let me keep you."

They found Beth in the living room, crocheting as she watched television. "Your snack's on the counter, Chase. There's a cup of cocoa for you, too, Kim."

She picked up the cup and went to sit down next to Beth. "What are you making?"

"A tablecloth." Beth spread out the work she'd done. The pineapple design was detailed.

"It's beautiful. Granny tried to teach me. I couldn't catch on."

"God gave you other talents. Speaking of which"—Beth tilted her head toward Chase—"did you ask him yet?"

"Let him eat first."

"I'm so excited for you," Beth said. "And for Cornerstone. It'll be a wonderful first for everyone."

Kim felt the heat creep up her cheeks. The opportunity thrilled her, but the praise of her work took some getting used to. "I just pray I can carry it through to give God the glory."

"You know you can. Didn't God give you the talent and the idea?"

"He did. To tell you the truth, I'm more thrilled by Cornerstone saying yes than I was when the editor bought the program."

Beth looked doubtful. "I seem to recall you bouncing off the walls for several days after getting that news."

"That was pretty exciting, too," she admitted with a grin.

"And now you get to see it performed."

"I finished studying my math," Chase announced. "Can I watch television?"

Beth glanced at the clock. "Until eight thirty. Then you need to take your shower and get into bed. You want to be rested tomorrow."

"Yes, ma'am."

"Before you go, Miss Kim has something to ask you."

The feeling she'd seen that expression before hit her again when he looked at her. "This year Cornerstone has agreed to produce the Easter play I wrote. The main character in the play is Jesus, and I wondered if you'd consider taking on the role." When the boy didn't say anything right away, Kim added, "I don't want to pressure you, but it would mean a great deal to me and the church."

"But soccer practice starts soon." He looked at Beth. "You promised I could play if I kept my grades up."

"We'd only practice one night a week in the beginning," Kim promised. "I'll work with you on memorizing the lines and such."

"Can I think about it?"

"Of course. I want you to pray about your decision, Chase." She glanced at Beth and back at the boy. "The main thing is, this is our chance to do something good for Jesus. People who don't know Him as their Savior will attend the play, and I'm praying the message will touch their hearts and help them realize they need Jesus in their lives."

The boy nodded. "I'll let you know."

Kim smiled at him. "That's all I can ask."

After Chase left the room, Kim looked at Beth. "Think I can compete with soccer practice?"

"Maybe. Chase has a strong sense of service to God. He's the child who always wants to do good no matter what his friends say."

"Thank the Lord for that. You're certainly blessed."

Her friend nodded. "So tell me about Wyatt," Beth said. "I imagine he was surprised to see you."

Kim considered that an understatement. "He wasn't very enthusiastic about my request. At first he said no, but then he agreed to build a cross using landscape timbers and some scrap from his business."

"Did you tell him I sent you?"

"And that you said he's the best carpenter you know," Kim added. "He said you had to say that because you're his sister. Is he always so gruff?"

Beth laughed. "Wyatt can be difficult at times. When did you see him?"

"Yesterday and again today. He told me to bring over the landscape timbers, and I figured the sooner the better. I took them after work. The building was locked up tight, but he opened the door just before I was about to leave."

"He puts in lots of hours," Beth said. "He's always deep into some project or another. I can't say the last time he attended a family gathering."

"He was working on a very detailed fireplace surround today. Said it has to be completed by next week."

"He's a true artisan. I just wish he had more of a life."

Kim sipped her cocoa. "This is good." The wind rattled the chimes on the deck. "Sounds like there's another weather change on the way."

"The winds are blowing in colder air. The weather report says the high will be in the thirties tomorrow."

Kim pulled her sweater closer at the thought of another chilly day at the beach. "I think I antagonized Wyatt when I asked why he doesn't attend Cornerstone. He told me it was none of my business."

Beth winced and concentrated on pulling more string from the ball. "He used to go. Back when he was married to Karen. It's a tragic story." Sadness etched lines in Beth's expression. "Wyatt's turning away from God has been a burden on my heart for years." She lowered her voice as she spoke. "That and the fact that he's separated himself from Chase."

Kim felt as if Beth had handed her yet another piece of the puzzle, but she had no idea where it went.

"I'm not sure he ever truly believed," Beth continued.

"But he attended church," Kim said.

"Because our parents forced him to go. I suppose Daddy thought if he could get him there God would do the rest. Wyatt told me once he wanted no part of Daddy's religion. It's difficult to believe in a forgiving God when your Christian role model is your harshest judge." Beth sighed heavily. "And even tougher being young and foolish and having your face rubbed in your every mistake, particularly when your father is the one doing the rubbing. I thought things had improved after Wyatt married Karen and Chase was born. Wyatt seemed to settle down."

A vague image teased Kim's thoughts—that of a withdrawn older boy who always seemed unhappy. Everything fell into place. How could she have forgotten him? All those years ago Wyatt Alexander had become the example of "what not to do with your life" for more than one parent at Cornerstone. She'd been twelve to his sixteen, and, despite her parents' efforts to shelter her, rumors of Wyatt's exploits had circulated throughout the church youth. Kim remembered that he hung out with a tough crowd and drank, and then he'd gotten his girlfriend pregnant. She recalled the baby being born about the time she'd gone off to college.

"What changed him?" Why was she so curious about Wyatt Alexander?

Beth glanced toward the bedroom, listening for the sound of Chase's television before she continued. "Wyatt and Karen went to a party one night when Chase was just under two. They had too much to drink, and there was an accident on the way home. Not their fault—a large truck tire shredded on the interstate, and Wyatt rolled the car. Karen was thrown from the vehicle and died instantly. The car ended up against a concrete piling, and Wyatt was pinned inside. They had to use the Jaws of Life to cut him free."

"That's awful."

Beth nodded. "After the truth came out about their drinking, Daddy really came down hard on Wyatt. Told him he wasn't fit to be a father. Wyatt agreed. He left Chase with them. I always believed he'd come to his senses and take Chase home, but he didn't. Our parents aren't young people, and as their health worsened, taking care of Chase became more difficult for them. I agreed to become his guardian. When Gerald and I started dating, he didn't mind, and we agreed to remain as Chase's guardians after we were married. He loves Chase, too."

"He's a lovable child," Kim agreed. "But I don't understand how Wyatt could abandon his son."

"Wyatt was badly injured in the accident. I know people don't understand, but he's doing what he thinks best for Chase. I have to respect that, but Chase knows Wyatt is his father."

"Why not just let you adopt him and never tell the child?"

"I wouldn't want that. And neither would Chase. He may not understand his father, but he's entitled to know the truth about his family. I'm praying that one day he and Wyatt can form a father-son bond and put the past behind them. Meanwhile I'll ensure he has a safe, loving home."

"What about when you and Gerald decide to have children of your own? Won't Chase feel out of place?"

Beth shook her head. "If Wyatt doesn't make a decision soon, I'll ask to formally adopt Chase." The television clicked off, and she glanced at the clock. "It's his bedtime."

Kim stood. "Let me go so you can get him settled for the night."

Beth took the mug and set it in the sink. They hugged and walked toward the door. Beth stopped by Chase's room and said, "Miss Kim is leaving."

He came to stand in the door. "Night, Miss Kim."

She touched his cheek. "Night, honey. Sleep well."

When she opened the door to leave, he called her name. She looked at him. "About the play. . ." he began. "I'd like to play Jesus."

"Think about it a day or so," she encouraged him. "I don't have to know right away."

"But what you said about helping those people. You mean like my dad, right?"

Kim glanced at Beth then reached to hug Chase. "God works in His own time, and I can't say who the play will help. It could be a complete stranger. Or it could be no one."

"But it could be my dad," he said. "I want to help, Miss Kim."

"You will. You have a good heart, Chase Alexander. Let's talk about this at church on Sunday, and if you still feel you want to take the role, I'd love to have you portray Jesus." He nodded. "Pray about it. It's a major commitment."

"I will," he declared solemnly.

Kim winked at him. "And I'll pray that you ace that math test tomorrow."

He smiled, and she knew exactly where she'd seen that smile before—lurking in the corners of Wyatt Alexander's mouth.

Chapter 4

Pastor Joe rapped on the podium, and the chattering stopped as heads turned to where the pastor stood. "We appreciate everyone coming to this meeting. We thought it would be a good idea to meet and determine where everyone can help with the Easter program.

"First thing, though, I have a prayer request from Mrs. Allene Rogers. As most of you are aware, Mrs. Allene has been ill for some time now. The doctors officially diagnosed her with cancer this morning." Several gasps echoed about the room. "I know all of us will keep her in our prayers. I don't want to put a damper on our Easter celebration plans, but it's important we pray now."

After they lifted their heads, Pastor Joe turned the meeting over to Kim.

She smiled as she moved to the podium. "Thank you so much for being here. It means a lot to me. Tonight I'd like to share a list of needs and see where everyone's interests lie. First of all, we'll need some stones."

"I'd like to make them," Avery Baker said.

"Sounds like fun," Natalie Porter said.

Kim saw the resentment in Avery's eyes when he looked at Natalie. The standing rivalry between the two was old news at the church.

Avery Baker owned the local bakery. Natalie Porter had come to the area a couple of years before when a heart attack forced her to step away from the hectic lifestyle she'd lived in New York. Since her arrival, Natalie had made a name for herself with the delicious creative cakes she made in her home, and Avery refused to see her as anything but the competition.

"Okay if I put you both down for that project?" Kim asked, not surprised by Avery's grudging nod.

"Great. For now we need sufficient kids at practice to fill the roles. Chase Alexander is the most important since he's agreed to play Jesus. The disciple roles are still in limbo. I may have to use some of the older girls."

"Wouldn't this have been easier with adults?" Geneva Simpson asked.

"Certainly," Kim answered. "But I have two main reasons for a children's performance. The first is that I'm praying a little child will lead them. The parents of a number of our children do not attend services. It says a lot that Cornerstone's children's outreach program is so strong, but I'm praying their parents will come for the play and want to come back.

"My second reason is that I feel it's important the children play a role in the Easter celebration. The adult choir has the cantata on Palm Sunday, but there's very little for the children and youth beyond the egg hunt. We all know the statistics regarding children and how important it is to involve them in church while they're young."

Several members of the group nodded, and Kim continued. "I have a list of what we need volunteers to do. The church budgeted two hundred dollars, and Mari has been searching the fabric stores for inexpensive material. Wyatt Alexander has agreed to build our cross for the cost of materials only."

The puzzled expressions on the older members' faces took Kim by surprise. "I'm sure he'll do an excellent job. He does beautiful work at his woodworking business."

"Where does he attend church?" Pastor Joe asked.

Kim swallowed hard. "Nowhere actually. Beth Erikson and I were talking about carpenters, and she told me her brother's the best. I didn't want to leave our cross to the last minute, so I approached Wyatt, and he agreed."

"Good idea," Pastor Joe said with a smile and a nod. "God needs more workers, and perhaps we can encourage Mr. Alexander to attend the program."

"Ah, pastor, he's Wilbur and Kay Alexander's son," Burris Simmons volunteered. "There's some history there."

"We all have history, Burris. I look forward to thanking Mr. Alexander for his help."

Kim suspected the Alexanders had talked with Pastor Joe about their son. "Actually he doesn't want any recognition."

Pastor Joe's nod indicated his understanding. "Go ahead, Kim."

"I was thinking we need a platform for the pulpit area. To raise the children high enough to be seen."

"I'll ask for lumber donations at prayer meeting tomorrow night," the pastor said, jotting a note on his pad.

Kim smiled her thanks. "We won't have stage curtains, so everything will need to be set up before the scenes unfold. I have pewter trays and goblets at the store, so unless they sell before Easter, I'll provide those. If they sell, I'll replace them with something else."

She read from the list. "We need fabric and trim and seamstresses. Costumes for disciples, crowds, soldiers, angels—and a white robe for Jesus."

Mari raised her hand. Kim called on her.

"I devised a rough pattern for some of the regular costumes last night. I had a flat full-sized white sheet and got two costumes out of one sheet. We can dye them in various colors and use a macramé cord around their waists for belts."

"Excellent idea," Kim said. "That's the sort of creativity we need. I'm sure I have a couple of flat sheets I never use. Only the key characters' costumes need to be fancy. Shoes can be any kind of sandal. We need greenery for the garden. And the stones. Preferably a lightweight version."

Mari raised her hand again. "I picked up a pattern for those fancier costumes today."

"So we need to come up with a final number of participants?"

Mari nodded. "And then later we can have a work night to finalize the costumes and props."

Kim added that to her list and continued with her notes. "I can't begin to tell you all how important it is to work with the children whose parents don't attend. We'll be seeking a major commitment from each child and will need to do our part to help them carry through."

"That means the bus will need to pick up children on practice nights," Noah said.

"I thought we might plan practice nights to coordinate with children's church over in the fellowship hall. Closer to the actual performance we'd need to bring them in more regularly, but we can deal with that later."

"What about music and sound effects?" Rob, their music minister, asked.

"We need soft music to play between scenes. And sound effects like thunder and driving nails."

"And a crowing rooster," he said. "I have a sound effects CD."

Kim scribbled another note. "Some children have beautiful voices, and I'd like to incorporate their talent into the play. I'm sure we all remember Missy Reynolds's rendition of 'Away in a Manger' at Christmas. It would be a shame not to utilize that talent. My plan is to include every child who wants to be a part of *Except for Grace*. It will mean adding roles as we go, but if a child wants to be in the play, I feel he or she should be.

"I also thought we might have refreshments afterward. Nothing fancy—cake and punch, nuts, that sort of thing."

Natalie raised her hand. "I'll donate a cake."

"Me, too," Avery said. "And some cookies."

Kim jotted their names in her notes. "Wonderful. Have I forgotten anything?"

"What about using a grapevine to make the crown of thorns?" someone suggested.

Another hand shot up. "I have that machine that puts studs and eyelets in fabric. We can use that for the soldiers' costumes."

The ideas flew back and forth for several minutes, and Kim wrote rapidly, not wanting to miss anything. Not only did she plan to involve the children, but she also wanted the adults to feel they were part of the process.

"We've made some definite progress. Oh, angel wings. We need angel wings."

Everyone laughed at her last-minute addition.

"I'll be responsible for those," Natalie said. "How many angels?"

"At least three. Does that include the costume?"

"Sure," Natalie agreed. "Does white satin with gold cording sound okay?"

"Perfect," Kim declared, scribbling Natalie's name on her sheet. "At the risk of repeating myself, I can't tell you all how much I appreciate your help."

"I think I speak for everyone when I say how delighted we are to have this opportunity," Pastor Joe agreed. "All our volunteers will need to report to Kim. Let her know if you have donations."

"I'll ask the senior ladies' sewing guild about the costumes," Mari offered. "I'm sure they'd love to participate."

Kim nodded. "I plan to check back with everyone, and you have my number at the store and at home if you need to contact me. I'm honored that Cornerstone has shown such faith in me. I intend to give it my all."

After the meeting the group members chatted among themselves. Kim looked around when Maggie touched her arm and smiled at her friend. "I'll do everything I can to help, but I can't commit completely because of my schedule and Mrs. Allene."

"I understand," Kim told her. Mrs. Allene had brought Maggie Gregory into their midst about ten years before when Maggie moved into Mrs. Allene's rental property. Since Kim's return to the beach, their friendship had developed, and she considered Maggie one of her best friends. "I'm so sorry about Mrs. Allene. Didn't they have any idea?"

Maggie shook her head. "I went to the doctor's office with her. The doctor seemed as shocked as we were."

"Did they say how bad it is?"

"He said maybe six months if she agrees to treatment. Why didn't I make her go sooner?"

"You didn't know," Kim said, hoping to offer her some comfort.

"I'm a registered nurse. I knew something was wrong, but I let her convince me it was only the aches and pains of old age."

"Who will take care of her? Will she have to go into a home?"

"I'm considering requesting a leave of absence."

"Will the hospital allow you to do that?"

"I've worked for them for years and taken very little time off. I would think they'd give me this leave."

Kim nodded, thinking how selfless Maggie's action was.

"Mrs. Allene does have a son. I've been trying to get her to call him. She said she would once she knew what was wrong. Will you go over with me after the meeting and see if we can convince her to make the call?"

"Sure," Kim agreed readily.

"I'm glad you asked Wyatt to build the cross. He built my television armoire. I found his shop one day and couldn't resist."

"Your armoire is gorgeous." She hesitated then let out a breath. "Wyatt Alexander is a very complex man."

"What are you thinking, Kim?"

"Nothing."

"Please tell me you're not attracted to him."

Kim looked away. "You know I promised not to get involved with another man who would hurt me in the end."

"I'm not sure you can help yourself. You heard Burris. The man has issues."

"I didn't need him to tell me that. I knew that from talking to Wyatt."

"Be careful, Kim. You know your heart."

"And I remember the vow I made to God. I will not end up the loser in yet another relationship. This is ridiculous. I've met the man twice."

"I can tell by the look on your face that there's already more to this than meets the eye."

"Beth confided a bit of their past to me—most I'd forgotten."

"I know some of his history, too, having moved here soon after his wife died." Maggie frowned.

"I told you there's nothing to it," Kim said, trying to assure her friend—and herself. "Let's finish up here and go over to see Mrs. Allene."

Chapter 5

After their visit to Mrs. Allene's, Kim drove home, parked in her space, and took the elevator to her second-story unit. The chill of the night encouraged her to walk faster along the open walkway. She rounded the corner to her doorway and screamed when she nearly ran into a man.

"Hello, Kim."

"Wyatt? Did you come to visit Beth and Chase?"

"They're not home."

Kim had phoned Beth earlier to tell her about the drama committee meeting. "She went to check on your mom. She's not feeling well."

Wyatt's brows drew together slightly as he handed Kim an envelope. "Would you give her this for me?"

"Sure. Did you want to come in for a soda or something and wait a few minutes to see if they come home?"

"No, it's late. I need to be getting home."

"We had a meeting tonight about the play," Kim said before he could walk away. "Everyone is pleased you're building the cross."

"It's nothing."

"It most certainly is!" Kim exclaimed. "The cross is precious. Jesus died there for us."

Wyatt held up his hands and took a step back. "Whoa. Maybe making that cross is beyond my capabilities."

"I don't think so. Our Lord was a carpenter as well."

Wyatt shrugged. "You had a late meeting," he said, abruptly changing the subject.

"Not really. Maggie and I went over to see Allene Rogers and try to talk her into calling her son. She's been diagnosed with cancer, and it's bad. She told us to mind our own business."

"I remember Mrs. Rogers. She was my Sunday school teacher years ago. Nice lady."

"Did you know her son?"

"Dillon Rogers is older, closer to my parents' age. I was a kid when he left for overseas."

Kim pushed her purse back up on her shoulder and longed for her gloves in the nippy night air. "I wish someone could make her understand she needs to let him know."

148

"Obviously she has her reasons. I think you should honor her request and stay out of the situation."

"Her son needs to be here for her," Kim said. "Family is important. How would you feel if something like this happened to your parents and they didn't tell you?"

"I'd think they had their reasons."

She couldn't believe he could be so coldhearted. "I don't think that would be the case at all."

"Stop trying to figure me out, Kim."

"I'm not. I just don't believe you'd turn your back on your parents in their time of need."

"Take it from me, Kim. Not everyone wants to be saved. I'm comfortable in my skin, and I am what I am. I don't need a crusader."

"But you'd be so much happier if you—"

"Let it go," Wyatt interrupted forcefully as he started down the landing to the elevator. "You have no idea what's better for me. No idea at all."

"I know Chase is your son." She clamped her hand over her mouth as the words slipped out.

"Why doesn't that surprise me?" he asked, the question laced with sarcasm.

"Beth is my friend."

"Didn't you ever wonder why she hasn't discussed this with you before now? Maybe because you didn't remember her wayward brother and now she feels the need to explain me?"

"Beth's not like that. She just can't understand her older brother."

Wyatt shrugged again. "What's to understand? I'm doing the best I can."

"Chase needs to be part of your life. You're his father."

"I'm the man who killed his mother."

"But Beth said—"

"The accident wasn't my fault," he filled in. "I know, but if I hadn't been drinking that night, I wouldn't have been so careless. I wouldn't have rolled that car and killed Karen."

"Do you think you're the only person to blame yourself, Wyatt? We all have things we could have done differently."

"What did you do?" he demanded. "Choose the wrong nail polish color once in your life?"

"That's cruel."

"I'm a bad man, Kim. I abandoned my child after I killed his mother."

Bad man. His words flashed into Kim's head, reminding her of Maggie's warning and her own vow to God. Unable to help herself, she said, "Because you felt that was best for him."

"Obviously Beth didn't share the entire sordid story."

"She said you were badly injured."

"That's an understatement. I lost my foot in the accident. I didn't know if I'd ever walk again. Chase didn't deserve to be burdened with a crippled father."

"He's a very caring child. He wouldn't resent you."

"Thanks to Beth and my parents. I suppose God knows right. The path Karen and I were on would have destroyed him. What kind of life would he have had with two free spirits as parents?"

"Beth said you attended church when you were married."

"Do you want to know why we went to church?" The self-loathing in his tone spoke volumes. "So we could pick up Chase after he'd spent the weekend with my family while we partied. Showing up for preaching kept them off our backs and stopped their sermons about our lives of sin. We were so good at hiding things that on those Sundays when we were so hungover we couldn't attend church, my parents figured we had to be sick. We were masters of illusion until everything fell apart."

"But you've changed."

"Have I?" he asked with a slight smile of defiance. "Like I said, I don't need a savior. Stay out of my business."

～

Later that night Kim lay in bed, unable to sleep as she considered Maggie's shock when Mrs. Allene told them to mind their own business.

Outside Mrs. Allene's house, she'd seen tears in her friend's eyes. "She knows you have her best interests at heart. I'm sure she didn't mean to hurt you."

"I know, but I don't want her to wait too long. He's overseas, and I'm sure he'd need to get things in order and request a leave of absence from work."

"Pray about it, Maggie. I will, too. Mrs. Allene needs time to adjust to the news. Cancer is scary business."

Maggie nodded. "That's why she should be surrounded by people who love her."

"She will be. She has her extended family—you and all the members of Cornerstone. And, the truth be told, you've probably been there for her more than her son over the years."

Kim's thoughts turned then to her own shock when Wyatt warned her to stay out of his business. His words lingered, and his attitude still stung. She didn't need him warning her to stay clear of his bad-boy persona. She remembered again her promise to God.

Perhaps she'd gone too far in her efforts to make him see her side of the story. He resented her sudden involvement in his life, and Kim could understand why. She'd said things she'd never have said if she hadn't been so stirred up over Mrs. Allene and Maggie.

Learning Wyatt had lost a foot was disturbing. Beth hadn't mentioned that. It certainly made his almost-hermit nature more clear. No doubt he preferred keeping to himself rather than dealing with people's sympathy.

Kim closed her eyes and sought God in prayer, asking her heavenly Father to soften Wyatt's heart and open Mrs. Allene's eyes to the need to call her son. She prayed for Maggie and then asked God to forgive her for the attack on Wyatt. She owed Wyatt Alexander an apology.

Chapter 6

Business filled the next few days. When sales picked up, Kim suspected everyone had finished packing away their holiday decorations and wanted something new to brighten their homes.

Kim found herself exhausted by the time she arrived home each evening. She'd talked with her parents the day before, and they had promised to be home for Easter. Her mother was more excited than Kim. "Just imagine," her mom had said, "I'll be able to tell everyone my daughter, the playwright, is producing her program."

She laughed at her mother's statement. "That's a little grandiose for a church production, don't you think?"

"I've always been proud of your talent."

"I know." At times her mother's bragging embarrassed Kim.

"So bring me up-to-date on what's happening at the beach."

The news of Mrs. Allene's cancer stunned her mother.

"Give me her number. I'd like to call her."

Kim found the church directory and flipped to the *R*s. Mrs. Allene's smiling face flashed before her, and pain hit Kim at the thought of not having the elderly woman in her life. She recited the number. "We're praying for her."

"I'll certainly do the same. She's always been such a vibrant woman."

"I think this illness has affected her. I went with Maggie to talk to her, and she got really upset when we urged her to call her son home."

"Where is Dillon? Still in Saudi Arabia?"

"Somewhere like that," Kim replied. "I can understand her not wanting to be a burden to him, but I know how I'd feel if it were you or Daddy. She has so many decisions to make. It breaks my heart."

"You can't force her to do something she doesn't want to do, Kim."

"But don't you think he'd want her to call him?"

"I'm sure she will. Once she's ready. I'm sure she needs to get herself together first. Parents have to stay strong for their children."

Kim hadn't considered that. "I miss you and Daddy."

"We miss you, too, sweetie, but we're enjoying our stay in Sedona. You should see this place. RVs everywhere you look."

"Has Daddy played golf?"

"Are you kidding? I have to pry the clubs out of his hands every night."

Kim loved her mother's sense of humor. "Are you playing, too?"

"Only when he can't find someone else. And I never argue about being left behind."

Her mother had never cared for the game. At home in Myrtle Beach, Kim's father had played every opportunity he had, and with the number of courses in the area, that opportunity was around the corner all year long.

The only time her mother had objected to his golfing was when some of his business associates wanted to play on Sunday mornings. She'd insisted the Lord had blessed him far too much for him not to attend church.

Her father argued he could worship God just as well during a golf game while breathing the fresh air as he could on a hard pew in church. Her mother disagreed, so later on Sunday afternoon her dad would usually disappear for a few rounds.

"Why do you suppose he never pursued golf professionally?" Kim asked the question she'd often wondered about.

"Maybe out of fear he couldn't support a family. At least he's been able to take early retirement and golf to his heart's content. Enough of that. I called to talk about you. Congratulations again, Kimmie. I knew you could do it."

"God did it, Mom. Those words aren't mine. They're His. He deserves all the glory. I'm honored to serve as His vessel."

"That's my girl. Love you bunches."

"Love you, too, Mom. Give Daddy my love. And be sure to include the church in your prayers. It's going to take a major collaboration to carry this off."

"Honey, you know we'll be praying for you and the church. And I'll send you a little something to help with the budget."

"You don't have to," Kim told her. "I'm adding to what the church gave me."

"A bit more won't hurt."

Kim started to say good night and then asked, "Mom, do you remember Wyatt Alexander?"

"Wilbur and Kay Alexander's son?"

"Yes. What do you remember about him?"

"Kay's had the women of the church praying for him for years. Why do you ask?"

"I met him recently. He's building the cross for the play. He does beautiful cabinetry work. I'm thinking of asking him to redo my kitchen."

"Renovation is expensive. You should get a couple of quotes before you decide on a contractor," her mother advised.

"I know he'd do a good job."

"I'm sure he would, but cover all your bases. Good night, Kim."

She hung up and jumped when the phone rang again immediately. Perhaps her mother had forgotten something. "Mom?"

"Wyatt Alexander here. I called to tell you your cross is nearly finished. I thought maybe you could stop by and tell me whether it's what you wanted."

He sounded so dispassionate. Kim cautioned herself to restrain her excitement. "Sure. When?"

"Wednesday evening?"

"Right after work. We have play practice afterward, so I'll be able to tell the kids about the cross."

"See you Wednesday then."

"Definitely. And thanks, Wyatt."

"It's nothing."

She didn't argue the point, but Kim definitely felt it was a step in the right direction. Anyone who would build a cross for God's church couldn't be all bad.

Wednesday afternoon was slow, and for once she was able to get out on time. Kim felt a sense of trepidation as she drove to Wyatt's. Should she apologize? No doubt Wyatt didn't appreciate a stranger meddling in his business. Would he treat her as coldly tonight as he had that night?

She found herself thinking about him too much for her own comfort. Her inability to choose the right man had caused her numerous heartbreaks in the past. Her attraction to bad boys always resulted in her being the one who was hurt.

Kim found it embarrassing that the girlfriends she'd grown up with had married and had children while she kept messing up. She'd become rather adept at avoiding her matchmaking friends' attempts to set her up.

She hated to think her self-imposed title of drama queen ran over into her love life, but it did. Every relationship ended with major drama. She'd read the self-help books. She didn't consciously look for men her parents wouldn't approve of. She loved and respected them enough that she'd never do that. Nor was it a latent desire to show her wicked side by choosing men with charming, self-confident personalities who were totally unreliable.

Kim prayed for the right man but second-guessed herself, convinced she needed to show God's love to these men. And after the relationships ended, she fantasized about the could-have-beens. A friend had once told Kim her need to save the world spilled over into her relationships. Kim couldn't dispute that.

The last one had been the worst ever. He'd ended up in jail after using money he'd borrowed from her to scam a number of senior citizens, including a couple she'd introduced to him at the store. He'd had the nerve to write her, claiming it wasn't his fault. Just how gullible did he think she was?

She'd gone to talk with Pastor Joe, and he'd told her she would never be happy as long as the men didn't share her faith and similar moral views and outlooks on other matters that were important to her. That was the moment she vowed to God she would never choose another bad boy.

Maybe it was her love for Beth and Chase that made her want Wyatt Alexander to be different for them. Or maybe she feared he was the kind of man she could be attracted to. Whatever the case, she had a promise to keep.

Because of her tight schedule, Kim called in an order for pizza at her favorite place and picked it up on her way out. Maybe she could interest Wyatt in joining her for dinner. She parked in the space in front of his building, and his dog came running. Kim lifted the box higher to keep it from the dog and jumped when he threw back his head and howled. She hurried to the front door.

Wyatt had taped a note there telling her to come around to the side entrance. Kim followed the narrow walkway toward the sound of pounding. She stepped inside then stopped at the sight of Wyatt beating the cross with a chain. "What are you doing?"

He glanced up at her. "Giving it character. You wanted an old rugged cross."

She could see the dents in the wood and the way he'd chopped rather than sawed the ends. He'd even used rope to lash the poles together. Wyatt stood the cross up on the footing he'd created.

"Is that safe to stand on?"

When he nodded, she stepped onto the platform and rested against the cross. "Chase hits me about here. What do you think? Tall enough?"

"Chase?"

She noted Wyatt's pallor. "Yes, he's playing Jesus and doing a wonderful job."

He didn't say anything, and Kim figured she'd better change the subject. She stepped down from the platform, catching Wyatt's hand when it seemed a bit far to the concrete floor. She hoped Chase was more flexible. If not, she'd make another step for him.

Kim walked over to where she'd left the pizza box on his workbench. "You like pizza with the works?"

He joined her. "Sure."

She handed him a couple of napkins and held out the box. Wyatt picked up a slice of pizza and took a big bite. Kim paused to say grace before taking her first bite.

Since she saw no place to sit, she leaned against the workbench and ate her pizza. "I'm thinking of remodeling my kitchen. What do you think? Store-bought or custom-built cabinets?"

Wyatt frowned. "You really need to ask?"

She grinned. "I suppose not. Would you care to give me an estimate?"

"I don't need work. I have more than enough."

"I really need new cabinets. Mine are literally falling apart. The front came off my silverware drawer last night."

"I could fix that for you."

"I already tried wood glue and duct tape. I want a new kitchen with dark cherrywood cabinets, black granite countertops, and stainless steel appliances."

He looked impressed. "You've done some planning."

"Mostly dreaming," Kim said, lifting the pizza box and offering it to him.

"Eat all you want. I never eat more than a couple of slices. I want one of those revolving cabinets and a pantry. Maybe some drawers for pots. And drawers deep enough that stuff won't get stuck when I try to open them."

Wyatt half smiled at her comment. "That has more to do with the contents than the depth. There's no such thing as a bottomless drawer."

"True."

"You don't want to jump into this right now," he warned. "Renovation isn't the easiest experience at the best of times."

He had a point. She didn't need to be required to make any more decisions. "Maybe in April after the play is over?"

Wyatt wiped his hands on the napkin before going out front to the desk. Kim could see him through the open door and watched him dig around a few minutes before he came back with a kitchen-planning guide. "Use this to choose the cabinet designs. I can take the measurements later if you still want to do the remodel."

"Oh, I want to do this," Kim said confidently. "Once I make up my mind, there's no going back."

His dark eyebrows shot upward. "That can't make life easy for you."

"I believe people should stand by their commitments."

"When there's a commitment," Wyatt agreed. "In this case you expressed a desire to redo your kitchen, and I'm taking that to mean you want an estimate. There's no commitment until you sign a contract. Unless you're trying to make a point about something else?"

"No," Kim assured him quickly. "I can understand why you might think that. I owe you an apology for the other night. Mrs. Allene's situation had me upset, and I took it out on you. Your personal life is none of my concern."

"People often have reasons for their actions," Wyatt said. "You should never judge anyone until you know all the facts. And you can't possibly know the situation in my family."

Kim felt thoroughly chastened. "I can only promise to try to keep my nose out of your business. I love Beth and Chase a great deal. Their happiness is important to me. I hope you can accept that."

"No, I can't. Until a few days ago you were in the dark about my existence, and now you're feeling enlightened. Beth and I have an agreement, and you can rest assured my son lacks nothing."

"Just his father." The words popped out before she could stop them. "I'm sorry. I shouldn't have said that."

"No, you shouldn't have," Wyatt agreed. "I have to get back to work. Are you okay with the cross?"

"It's exactly what I wanted."

"I'll bring it over to the church when it's done. I need to stain it first."

"We can take care of that," Kim said.

"Thanks, but no. Every piece that comes from Alexander Woodworking is as detailed and precise as I can make it. I believe in doing the right thing when it comes to business."

Kim got the point. Score one for Wyatt. "I'll leave you to your work. Again, thanks for your efforts on behalf of Cornerstone."

"No problem." Wyatt turned back to his work.

Her appetite had disappeared. Feeling dismissed, Kim said, "I'll leave the pizza."

"Thanks for dinner."

She went out the side door. That hadn't gone well. Granted, she'd involved herself in something that was none of her business, but she'd done it out of love for her fellow man. She wasn't judging him. Was she? Maybe it did come across that way.

Chapter 7

January slipped into February, and Kim was happy with most aspects of their progress. While everything else was right on schedule, the children were proving to be the problem. Tonight was no different.

She had stressed to the main characters the importance of showing up for practice, but many nights she reassigned roles to another child with the proviso that the role belonged to the original child when he or she came back.

Most of the children wanted to be in the play so badly they were okay with the stand-in roles. Kim found herself reworking the script to add roles for the more dedicated children.

Mari pulled out a chair and sat down beside her. "I'm sure Jesus is pleased to see we have five new disciples tonight."

Kim nodded. "I have a vision of every child who has ever visited Cornerstone showing up the night of the play and my having to explain to their parents why they can't perform. I don't care, though. I'll fill every role regardless of whether I have to use boys or girls."

Mari smiled at Kim's determination. "And we're working on getting them dressed. You should see some of the costumes. Natalie glued feathers on her wings."

Kim glanced at her. "Really?"

Mari nodded. "We have some fancy costumes, including a crown for the king. One of the senior ladies made it from a piece of gold fabric and glued on the stones."

Their dedication touched Kim. "This is so incredible. I expected simple stuff. The children will be thrilled."

Mari nodded. "We know a shot of confidence can come from feeling well dressed."

Kim smiled at her. "We'd better get this practice underway." She stood and called, "Jesus is coming! Where is my crowd?"

Jesus walked into the room, surrounded by children shouting, "Jesus is coming!"

"Are you sure about Bryan?" Mari asked when the boy slipped in the side door.

"Playing Peter? There's something right about that, don't you think? I know he can be mischievous."

Mari flashed Kim a wide-eyed look of amazement.

"Okay," she admitted. "He's a major brat, but he can handle the role. Maybe it's not smart, but I felt led of God to do it."

"Did God lead you to pair Natalie and Avery on those stones?"

"Exactly," Kim said with a huge grin. "Think of the greater good. Avery needs to stop viewing Natalie as a competitor and start seeing her as a sister in Christ."

"And you're hoping he'll see this through working together with her for the church's greater good?"

"It's doubtful. Natalie's already referring to Avery as a control freak."

"That's not surprising," Mari murmured with a little laugh.

"You think I should separate them?"

"Of course not. We teach the children to love one another. This is Avery's and Natalie's opportunity to show Christian love for each other."

"Let's hope it works. Good thing those stones are made of papier-mâché."

Mari giggled. "Oh, Julie called today. She sold her condo and will be here next week."

"I'm sure Noah's happy about that."

"Ecstatic. He's missed her so much."

"Did they find a place yet? I heard a two-bedroom unit in my building is coming open soon."

"You might want to mention it to Noah. He's been looking but refuses to finalize anything until Julie gets here. I can't say I blame him. Joe got the parsonage, so it wasn't a question of where we wanted to live, but if I'd had to choose I'd have wanted something bigger and newer."

"Some churches give their pastors a housing allowance. I think it's a good idea. At least that way they have an investment for the future."

A cry alerted them to mischief. Kim looked at Mari before she walked over to where Bryan had shoved another child. "What's going on here?"

The boy looked so sweet sugar wouldn't melt in his mouth, and the smaller child looked frightened. Kim took Bryan's arm and walked with him into an empty classroom. "Why are you bullying the smaller children?"

Bryan looked down at his feet. Kim lifted his chin and looked directly into his eyes. "What does God think of bullies?"

"He doesn't like them," the boy mumbled.

"Then why would you do it, Bryan?"

"He gave Jeremy a sucker but wouldn't share with me."

"Are you going to abuse everyone who doesn't share with you?"

"No, ma'am."

"Good. I want you in the play, but I can't allow you to mistreat the other children. Do you understand?"

He nodded, and Kim patted his shoulder. Here again her attraction to bad boys had come through. She could see something in Bryan that few others saw.

He could do this. She knew he could. "How are your lines coming along?"

The child perked up. "I know them. Wanna hear?"

"I will as we go through the play. I think you owe Enrique an apology."

She escorted him back to the fellowship hall and waited for him to say he was sorry before leaving him with the other children.

Back in the fellowship hall, she noticed the cross standing near the door. Her gaze shifted around the room until she saw Wyatt sitting along the sidelines. He half smiled and lifted his hand in greeting.

Onstage Chase spoke his lines, and Wyatt's gaze moved to the boy.

Kim walked over to where he sat. "He's good, don't you think?"

"He appears to know what he's doing."

"Wish I could say the same for all of them," Kim commented as the narrator prompted the kids who forgot their lines in the Lord's Supper scene.

She groaned and covered her face. "This is the easiest line in the play, and they can't get it out."

He looked doubtful. "Why are you doing this?"

"To share the message."

"Isn't that the pastor's job?"

"Pastor Joe does an excellent job, but he needs help," Kim said.

"Seems like a lot of work for a program that lasts an hour or so."

Kim shrugged. "The choir practices every week for months before performing the cantata."

"Are they doing that for Easter?"

"Yes. The choir will perform on Palm Sunday night. Our play is on Good Friday night."

"Well, I brought your cross. I made an adjustment on the step height."

"You didn't have to do that," Kim said.

"It didn't take long. You want it on the stage?"

"Can you wait a few minutes?"

He nodded, and Kim rose from the chair as the children missed their marks again. "Time to direct."

~�ैⴰ~

Wyatt relaxed in the chair and glanced about the room. This was the first time he'd been near the church of his childhood in years. Nothing much had changed beyond the carpet and pew cushions. His parents had insisted he and Beth attend church. He hadn't minded so much when he was younger, but when he became a teen Wyatt resented being forced.

None of his friends went to Cornerstone, and he'd been stuck with lots of kids he didn't like. Of course, he hadn't gone out of his way to make himself popular either. He'd tolerated the situation for years, even after he and Karen were married. But after Karen's death he decided he was an adult and would do what he wanted.

His decision caused a rift between him and his father. Wilbur Alexander had very little tolerance for a son who refused to serve God. Wyatt wanted his father to accept his right to decide what he wanted to do with his life, but they still had their differences over the situation.

Occasionally Beth argued that his past was old news and it wasn't the same church he remembered, but Wyatt had trouble believing that.

Strangely enough he didn't feel the same level of discomfort tonight. Could it be because Kim made him feel welcome?

When the time for the cross came, Wyatt carried it up onto the stage area.

"That's perfect," Kim told him. "Now we need a stage to raise the children six or eight inches so the audience can see them better."

What did it take? Some measurements, lumber, nails, or screws. What made that so impossible?

"We have plenty of donated lumber but no carpenters," Kim explained.

He could walk away, too, but when Wyatt looked into Kim's eyes, he knew he couldn't say no. He found it very difficult to refuse her anything. "I can build one."

"Oh, that would be wonderful!" Kim exclaimed. "I so want them to be seen."

He couldn't help but wonder why her happiness gave him such great satisfaction.

The play demanded her attention again, and he sat down to watch. After practice was over and most of the kids had left with their parents, Wyatt asked Kim if she'd eaten.

"I came over here right after work to get prepared."

"How about joining me?"

She hesitated.

"We need to discuss the plans for the stage," he added. He wasn't playing fair, but he didn't necessarily feel she'd been playing fair when she mentioned the stage in the first place. He suspected Kim recognized him as a soft touch. Oddly enough he'd always been harder than nails for everyone else.

"What restaurant did you have in mind?"

"One that serves steak and potatoes?" At her dismayed look he grinned. "Nothing that heavy, I promise. I'd never sleep tonight."

"Me either. Perhaps a place that serves soup or salad with sandwiches?"

"You want to ride together or drive your car? I can bring you back here."

"I'll ride with you."

Mari came over with the boys to say good night.

"Mari Dennis, this is Wyatt Alexander. He built our cross." She looked at him and said, "Mari is our pastor's wife. These are her three oldest sons, Matthew, Mark, and Luke."

Mari reached to shake his hand. "The cross is spectacular."

"Nice to meet you, Mrs. Dennis," Wyatt said. "You, too, guys. As for the cross, Kim gives good instructions."

"I can't take credit," Kim denied quickly. "It's so much nicer than anything I imagined."

"I try."

"We're out of here," Mari said, grabbing the youngest boy's shoulders and guiding him toward the door. "See you Sunday, Kim. We'd love to see you, too, Mr. Alexander."

After the lights had been turned out and the church locked up, Kim settled in Wyatt's truck. They discussed restaurants and agreed on a place that met both their needs.

After ordering their food they sipped iced tea, and Wyatt used her pen to sketch out on a scrap of paper a plan for the stage.

"Just let me know when you want to get the measurements."

"What's the earliest we can clear the area?" he asked.

"Thursday morning, I suppose."

"The stage will need to be broken down afterward?"

"We'll have Saturday to put everything back together. Do you plan to build the stage in place or move it there later? I can ask Pastor Joe for volunteers to assist you."

"Get the volunteers, and we'll decide. If we don't have sufficient manpower, I can build it in place."

Their food arrived, and Kim concentrated on the broccoli and cheese soup she'd chosen. "This is delicious."

Wyatt took a bite of his burger. "I was hungrier than I realized."

Kim remembered the plans in her purse. She swallowed hastily, coughing when the soup went down the wrong way.

"Are you okay? Here," he said, lifting her glass from the table. "Take a sip of tea."

Kim coughed and spluttered for a moment longer, then said, "I'm okay. I wanted to show you my kitchen plans." She grabbed her oversized satchel and dug around until she located the planning sheet he'd given her.

"You won't need a kitchen if you choke to death."

She laughed and unfolded the pages. She smoothed them out and placed them in the center of the table, facing him. "What do you think?"

He picked up the sheet. "Looks like you've figured out what you want."

"I'm excited about redoing the kitchen," Kim said. "That planning guide made the choices so much easier."

"But you agree you need to wait until after the program to start work?"

Kim sighed. "Yes. Will you put me on your calendar for April?"

"I'll see what's pending. We can do some of the preliminary planning to help move the plans along. And I'm getting a new saw with a built-in computer."

"How does that work?" Kim spooned more soup into her mouth.

"You put specific measurements into the computer, and it directs the cutting of the boards. I figure it will pay for itself. Even experienced carpenters make mistakes."

"But not often," Kim countered.

Wyatt wiped his mouth. "Not if we can help ourselves. It cuts into the profit margin."

"How did you get into carpentry work?"

"I was hooked when I took a class in high school. Dad had the equipment sitting in his shop, and once I learned how to use it, I wanted to build stuff all the time. It became an expensive hobby."

"So you turned it into a way to make a living?"

Wyatt dropped his napkin onto the table and pushed his plate away. "Not at first. Dad works for a soda distributor, and he got me a delivery job. Karen and I had just married, and he insisted I needed something dependable. It's logical he'd feel that way. He's worked for the company for more than thirty years.

"Anyway, I went to work for them and did woodwork on my own time. Soon everyone in the family had more wooden bowls than they needed."

"You made Beth's fruit bowl, didn't you?" Kim asked. When he nodded, she said, "It's gorgeous. You should sell them. I'd buy one."

He chuckled. "I'll keep that in mind."

"So when did you start your company?"

"About three years ago. The distributing company required a clean driving record, so the accident and subsequent driving-under-the-influence charge put me out of work. Dad was furious. Not because I caused my wife's death but because I'd lost my job."

"You made a bad choice, Wyatt. I think you should forgive yourself."

"I wish I could. It makes me sick every time I think about how I deprived Chase of his mother. I don't deserve his love."

"So you think your guilt is sufficient reason to deprive him of both parents?"

"You don't understand."

"Maybe I don't," Kim agreed. "Let's not argue. Tell me about the business."

"I got a job with a cabinetmaker and spent the next few years learning the trade. About three years ago the owner decided to retire and offered me his equipment at a good price. I got a loan, and Alexander Woodworking was born. I put up that metal building behind the house and started work. I haven't looked back since."

"You work alone?"

"I have a couple of part-time people who help out. They're retired and like a few hours now and then. The cabinets pay the bills, but the specialty pieces are my favorites. My house is full of furniture I built."

"I'd love to see it."

"Anytime," he told her. The waiter asked if he wanted more tea, and Wyatt shook his head. "It's late. Guess we'd better let these people go home."

He took care of the bill and escorted her to his truck. "Maybe next time you can tell me about you," he said as he fastened his seat belt and started the vehicle.

"I don't consider myself anywhere near as interesting."

He looked at her, and their gazes caught. "Let me decide for myself."

"Only if you agree I can do the same."

He leaned closer and kissed her softly.

Kim pulled back. "Wyatt. . . I. . .we. . .why did you do that?"

"I wanted to."

Kim didn't know how to respond.

Chapter 8

Kim found her thoughts returning to Wyatt and the kiss more often than she liked. The feeling that he didn't give himself as much credit as he should remained foremost in her mind, though.

The accident that killed his wife had started a downhill spiral that had only become worse over the years. He'd suffered and grieved alone, staying away from Chase and his family because he didn't feel he deserved to be loved.

If only he realized God loved him despite his poor choices and welcomed the opportunity to share that love with him. Kim knew that except for that very same grace she would be in the same place as Wyatt.

The realization that she was more attracted to him than she should be struck Kim. She knew she was in danger of breaking the promise she'd made to God. She couldn't become involved with Wyatt Alexander. He wasn't a Christian. They didn't share the same faith. She would end up getting her heart broken.

As if worrying about Wyatt wasn't enough, Kim found each passing week brought a fresh feeling of panic. The issue of the kids' attendance still hadn't been resolved, and most of them needed a great deal of work on their lines. They had a couple of weeks before they needed to pick up the pace, and she hoped they could settle everything before the night of the play.

Julie arrived on Monday, and she, Maggie, Mari, and Kim decided to celebrate by doing lunch and some shopping on Saturday.

"Welcome to the beach," Kim said as she hugged Julie.

Kim had told Noah about the unit in her building, and the couple had taken a look. Julie liked the setup, especially the closeness to the beach, and it appeared Kim might soon have even more Cornerstone neighbors.

When they discussed restaurants, Kim mentioned the place she and Wyatt had visited. "They have excellent soup and salads. Wyatt said the burgers were good, too."

Mari glanced at her with raised brows. "That sounds suspiciously like a date."

"We were discussing plans for the stage at church. I took pizza over to his shop when I went to look at the cross, and I'm sure he felt the need to return the favor."

"You're not getting in over your head, are you?" Maggie asked.

When she didn't speak, Julie looked around the group. "Anyone care to fill me in on what's going on?"

"Do you want to tell her, Kim?" Maggie asked.

She shrugged. "If Julie's going to be one of my friends, she needs to know what a lousy judge of men I am."

"It's not your fault you have bad luck with relationships," Maggie said.

"Oh, come on," Kim said. "I make the choices. I'm a bad-boy magnet," she told Julie. "If there's a man out there destined to break a woman's heart, he comes at me like a heat-seeking missile."

"And you keep making the same mistake over and over?" Julie guessed. When Kim nodded, she said, "I suspect women typically choose the same type of men. It all has to do with traits that appeal to us. It's not an outward appearance thing either."

"So how do I lose this fascination for the wrong type of man? I promised I wouldn't become involved with another man who would break my heart, but I find myself thinking Wyatt Alexander doesn't give himself the credit he deserves."

"He's not a Christian," Mari reminded her. "That's your first warning. You can't hope to understand each other's needs if you're not on the same level spiritually."

"I know, but he's hurting," Kim said, sadness weighing heavily on her heart. "I'm certain his unhappiness stems from one bad decision he made years ago."

"You can't save him, Kim," Maggie said. "Leave that in God's more than capable hands. When He's ready for you to meet the right man, you'll be the first to know."

"Maggie's right about that," Julie offered. "I had some serious anger issues with Noah. I'd made up my mind we'd never work things out, but God interceded on my behalf—and look where we are now."

"God helped you improve your relationship with Him. Once that happened, you were able to have a loving relationship with Noah," Mari pointed out.

"I know Wyatt has to be the one to change his life, but he needs guidance."

"Not yours, Kim," Mari warned. "You're already borderline fascinated with the man. First thing you know, you'll be in love and heading for heartbreak."

"He kissed me."

"What did you say?" Maggie asked, her eyes wide.

"I was in shock, too. I asked why he did it, and he said he wanted to."

"What are you going to do?" Mari asked.

"I don't know. I've got too much on my plate right now to worry about relationships. I'm about ready to pull my hair out with this group of children. I've yet to get the disciples to say that one line right."

They discussed the play for a few minutes before the conversation eased into other topics. Kim took a sip of soft drink and set her glass on the table. "How is Mrs. Allene?"

"Not good. The chemo makes her nauseous."

"They've brought medicine so far, you'd think they could figure out how to keep it from making the patients so sick."

"I'm praying things will improve. It's heartbreaking to see her suffer so."

"Did she call her son?"

Maggie frowned slightly as she shook her head. "I'm staying out of it. I'll do what I can for Mrs. Allene. She's my friend, and I love her a great deal."

"I'm sure she'll call him soon," Kim said.

"Do you think Joey should contact him?" Julie asked.

The other three women looked at each other and shook their heads in unison.

"We've already asked, and Joe believes it is Mrs. Allene's decision," Mari said. "He says she'll call her son when she's ready."

"Wyatt says the same thing," Kim offered.

All three heads turned in her direction, and she held up her hands. "We talked that night after Maggie and I tried to convince Mrs. Allene to make the call. I thought he'd agree with us, but his advice was to stay out of her business."

"I don't get it," Julie said. "Our parents died so suddenly. I can't imagine that Joey would want anyone to give up an opportunity to spend time with their loved ones."

"Joe can't allow his personal feelings to come before Mrs. Allene's wishes," Mari said.

"Maybe it's a man-woman thing," Julie said.

"I'm surprised you told Wyatt," Maggie said.

"He remembered Mrs. Allene from his childhood Sunday school years."

"I'm finding myself more and more intrigued about this Wyatt guy," Julie admitted.

"He's cute," Mari told her. "I met him at play practice."

"I'm sure you'll see him around the church a time or two before the play. I'm hoping he'll attend the play as well."

"Who knows? You might be more of a draw than you realize," Julie said.

A couple of days later Wyatt called about getting measurements for the stage. They arranged to meet at the church around two, but she had to cancel.

She dialed his number. "Wyatt? It's Kim. I'm tied up here at the store. My salesclerk Ruby had to pick up her sick child at daycare. Pastor Joe says to come by the church office. He knows exactly what we want so it shouldn't be any problem. I'm truly sorry."

"Did you want me to come by later to get those kitchen measurements?"

"Call me after you finish at the church, and I should be able to let you know if we can make it work."

<hr />

That afternoon Wyatt parked by the church office and went inside. The secretary immediately called the pastor. He came out of his office and reached to shake Wyatt's hand. "Good to see you, Mr. Alexander."

"Call me Wyatt."

"Only if you'll call me Joe."

Wyatt wasn't exactly comfortable with that. "What if I call you Pastor Joe?"

"That'll do."

The two men worked together pulling measurements and discussing what needed to be done to make the stage work.

"Noah and I will help. Do you think you'll need more men?"

"I can probably get my helpers if we need them," Wyatt said, amazed that he'd just offered to provide laborers for a volunteer job. Oh well, it wouldn't hurt him to spend a few bucks for a good cause. Particularly since his son played such a key role in the performance.

"I'm sure Kim's told you how appreciative we are of your help."

He slipped the notepad and pencil into his pocket. "She has."

"I hear Beth says you're the best carpenter she knows."

Wyatt felt slightly embarrassed. "Definitely a kid-sister kind of statement, don't you think?"

Pastor Joe nodded. "My sister tells everyone I'm the best pastor she knows. It's going to cause her problems now that she's married to a pastor. I suppose I'll get demoted to second best."

The two men laughed and walked over to sit on the front pew.

"Why haven't I seen you here before?" Pastor Joe asked.

"I haven't attended Cornerstone since my wife was killed."

"Why?"

Wyatt didn't find himself uncomfortable with the pastor's question. "You know my parents." Pastor Joe acknowledged he did. "Well, their church philosophy was that as long as I lived in their house, they decided where and when I went to church. They weren't above coercion. My desire to participate in team sports or even hang out with my friends gave them means. On Sundays I couldn't leave the house unless I went to church first."

"You resented that?"

Wyatt nodded. "None of my friends attended Cornerstone, and I wanted to be with them. Of course, my friends didn't attend church anywhere. They were like me, sneaking around doing stuff they had no business doing. And every time the church doors opened, I had to show up, more than a little aware that I wasn't deceiving God with my presence."

"Did you feel guilty?"

He shrugged. "Maybe a little at first. Mostly I tuned the messages out and thought about my plans for the afternoon. Things like where we would hang out and who was bringing the beer."

"I think every parent hopes their children will develop a love for God. If they can't reach them, they pray someone else can. I know how I feel about my five children."

"I met three of them," Wyatt said.

Pastor Joe pulled his wallet from his pocket and showed Wyatt the family photo he carried with him. "The two little ones are twenty-month-old twins."

"Nice-looking family."

Pastor Joe nodded his agreement. "Mari is the love of my life. Nothing would be the same without her. I was working as an investment banker when we met. My parents had died, and I'd assumed guardianship of my teenage sister. Mari loved Julie and cared for her like her own sister.

"When I felt led to become a minister, I thought Mari would disagree. At that point we had three boys, Julie had just graduated from college, and I knew financial security would be an issue for Mari. To tell the truth, it was for me, too. I didn't see how I could support my family and do God's work. But He showed me the way.

"Sorry. I turned this onto me, but what I wanted to say was I was one of the fortunate ones. My parents raised us in a Christian home. When they were killed in a car accident, I knew God had His reasons even though they were far beyond my comprehension. I never resented going to church because I'd developed a love relationship with Him."

"A love relationship?"

Pastor Joe nodded. "The Bible says, 'Love the Lord thy God with all thine heart, and with all thy soul, and with all thy might.' People think I love God because I'm a minister, but it's more than that. The relationship goes beyond what I feel for my family or friends. God is first in my life."

"Why do you suppose I never developed that rapport?"

"Could be you resented your parents for controlling your life so much you refused to allow God to do the same."

"I wasn't ready to do God's work, but my parents didn't want to hear that. After high school I met Karen at the club where she worked. She'd come to the beach with the intention of partying for a while before she settled down.

"We hooked up, and when Chase was on the way, we married. Her parents lived in Florida, so she didn't have to worry about anyone forcing her to go to church."

"Our Chase?"

Wyatt nodded. "He's my son."

"How did your wife die?"

"In an accident," Wyatt told him. "We were happy, or I suppose we thought we were. Our lives had a comfortable sameness. We'd work all week, and on the weekends, we'd get my parents or Beth to babysit so we could party.

"We'd been to a party the night she died. Both of us had more to drink than we should have. A semi in front of us had a blowout. I was following too close and ended up flipping the car."

"It could have happened if you'd been sober."

"Killing Karen was bad enough, but I lost my foot, too. Because of one stupid decision, I deprived my son of his mother and stuck him with a crippled father. In fact, that night Chase hadn't felt well. He had a cold, and Karen wasn't sure we should leave him. I convinced her it was okay. If I'd listened, she'd still be alive today."

"You can 'what if' the situation to death, but the truth is that only God knows what the future holds. We make our mistakes when we try to guide God instead of allowing Him to guide us."

"You mean like leaving Chase with my family instead of raising him myself?"

"You made the decision based on the grief and pain you were feeling at the time. You loved your wife and son and believed you couldn't make a difference for her but were determined to make a difference for Chase."

"Beth's been good for him."

"Your sister is a good woman. She loves Chase. And I know she worries about your salvation."

"I wish she wouldn't."

"That's the way of Christians when it comes to the people we love, Wyatt. Praying for you isn't something we turn on and off at will. God lays a burden on our hearts for every lost lamb, regardless of whether you're our own flesh and blood or a stranger. When we take on the mantle of Christ, we become His disciples." He paused for a moment, reflected, then asked, "Wyatt, are you angry at God?"

Wyatt shook his head. "No. I just feel He has no need for an old sinner like me."

"Did you ever accept Him as your personal Savior?"

"I made a declaration and carried through with baptism at fourteen, even though I wasn't sincere. I did it to fool my parents and everyone else."

"But you didn't fool God."

"No. I was two-faced. One for the people at church, another for my friends. Neither group knew the other existed."

"What are you feeling now, Wyatt?"

"Honestly, I don't know. When Kim asked me to build a cross, I couldn't believe I agreed to do it. Then when she mentioned this stage I offered again. Believe me when I say I don't usually do anything for the church."

"Perhaps God has presented you with the opportunity of service. I'm sure He appreciates the way you've responded. Cornerstone has another project we could use your help with."

"What's that?"

"The church has a large stained glass window scheduled to arrive two weeks before Easter. We're planning a dedication service for Easter morning. We have to prepare the area for the window. It involves cutting out that wall and framing it up for a fixed window. I've been asking around, and our builders are tied up with construction projects. I'd hate to disappoint the congregation by not getting it in place."

"Let me check my schedule." As soon as he spoke the words, Wyatt wondered what possessed him to keep agreeing to help with Cornerstone's needs. "I'd better get going."

"God loves you, Wyatt. No matter what poor decisions you've made in the past, God has a plan for your future. He wants to bless you."

"Thanks, Pastor Joe. Maybe if we'd had a minister like you here at Cornerstone when I was growing up, I'd have that love relationship you speak of."

"Can we pray before you go?"

The pastor rested his hand on Wyatt's shoulder. "Our precious heavenly Father, we come to You, seeking understanding. We praise You for sending Wyatt to Cornerstone to help in Your work. Please guide his hands in the building of these projects, and may they be used to glorify You in the production of the Easter play.

"Lord, Wyatt has other needs. He's feeling regret because of past experiences. Help him understand that no matter what he's done, You died for him. Help him accept that forgiveness and grow in his love for You. And help him realize the ways of the world are not Your ways, and be with him as he begins his walk with You."

"You sound like it's a given I'll find Jesus," Wyatt said.

"I feel you already have. My question is, what are you going to do next?"

Wyatt stood. "I'd better go."

"Nice meeting you, Wyatt. I'm here at the church anytime you feel like talking."

"Thanks."

Back in his truck Wyatt reached for his cell phone and dialed Kim's number. "I'm just leaving the church. Can we meet another night?"

"Sure. Is everything okay?"

"Yeah. Fine. I met with Pastor Joe and got the measurements for the stage. It shouldn't be a problem."

"I'm glad he was able to help."

"He's a nice guy."

"The church has been blessed by his presence. You should hear him preach. He and Noah Loughlin are truly men of God."

"I'll follow up on those measurements soon."

"Sure. Take care."

Wyatt picked up a burger at a drive-thru and headed straight for his workshop.

His conversation with Joe Dennis played heavily on his mind. Particularly that statement about him finding Jesus. Pastor Joe struck him as very different from the ministers of his past. He felt tempted to attend one of the man's sermons. Somehow he doubted this man's spin on fire and brimstone would be similar to the sermons of his youth. Those pastors had convinced him he'd never make it to heaven.

All these years he'd resented his father and avoided God, but since that first day Kimberly Elliott set foot in his shop, he'd agreed not only to one project but now three. Even though he hadn't said yes to the Good Shepherd window, Wyatt had no doubt he would help.

But the real question for him was, why was he doing all this? Why was he agreeing to job after job for the church? Was Joe Dennis right? Was God directing his path?

Maybe it was time. He hadn't done such a great job on his own. He'd been impressed by more than Joe's personality. The pastor exhibited the sense of peace Wyatt had craved his entire life.

When he'd partied he had sought answers in beer, loud music, and other people, but he'd never found them. After he lost Karen, he kept to himself and concentrated on making his business successful. In his rare spare time, he hunted and fished and tried not to think about the pain of his losses.

Not a day went by that he didn't miss his son. He felt a stabbing pain in his heart every time he saw Chase with Beth. He'd avoided family get-togethers for that very reason. He knew his son was getting older and didn't understand why his father wanted nothing to do with him.

It wasn't that he didn't want his son—he just didn't want to confuse the boy any more than he already had. For ten years he'd turned over his parental rights to Beth. Was it fair to Chase to step back into his life now?

Joe Dennis had given him so much to think about today.

And even some things to pray about.

Chapter 9

As the days flew past, Kim felt the growing pressure to see things finalized. The groundhog's prediction of another six weeks of cold weather made part of her look forward to spring while another part told her spring would bring the play.

Wyatt had come over to get the measurements for the kitchen, and Kim sensed a change in him. He seemed happier. She wondered why. Maybe he'd taken on a big project for his business.

She'd expected to be uncomfortable around him, but he kept things all business.

He'd wowed her with a wooden bowl. "I think this is the color you wanted?"

Kim found the dark cherrywood absolutely perfect. "This is fantastic."

"I'll keep that stain in mind when I finish building the cabinets. I have a stone sample you may want to look at for a backsplash."

It surprised her that Wyatt had used his own time to find materials for her kitchen. "Sure. I'm debating. The glass tiles are gorgeous."

"Costly. What about stainless steel?"

"Cold. Tile can be cold, too, but I like it better. I want designer tiles."

"Did you look at the granite?"

"Mari and I rode over there a couple of weeks ago. I found one I really liked. The owner said he was pretty sure it would work with cherry cabinets. I'd appreciate your opinion if you have time."

"I need to go over there in a couple of days. I'll take a look. Have you considered flooring?"

"I don't have any idea what I want. I'd thought about wood, bamboo even, but I'm afraid I'll have too much wood."

"Is there such a thing as too much wood?" Wyatt teased, joining in when she burst into laughter.

"Wood, stone, and tile will definitely need something to soften it."

"Have you considered a kitchen designer?"

"I visited a couple of showrooms and noted things I liked. I'm going to get tile and floor contractors to do the work, but I need to coordinate everything to keep costs down. My budget won't stretch as far if I hire a consultant to do the work."

"Some companies offer the service free when you buy their products."

"But I'm not buying their product. You don't offer design services, do you?"

Wyatt shook his head. "I'm strictly a cabinetmaker."

"And I'm taking your advice and not worrying about this right now."

"Good idea."

"Pastor Joe told me you've agreed to help with the Good Shepherd window."

Wyatt nodded. "He mentioned it the day I went for the stage measurements. He called me a couple of days later, and I said yes."

"I can't wait to see it in place!" Kim exclaimed.

"I haven't seen the window, but Pastor Joe assures me it's a beautiful stained-glass piece."

"Mari said he's very impressed with you."

"I'm not impressive."

"Cut yourself some slack, Wyatt. Pastor Joe is a good judge of character."

"I'm definitely a character."

"I'd say you're hopeless, but you'd agree with me."

He nodded. "I would."

❧

The drama committee had scheduled a work night for the last Tuesday in February. Kim was eager to know where they stood in terms of costumes and props.

She drove over to the church to find people already at work. Mari worked with the women who had agreed to sew costumes. Two women cut out the garments while several others used portable machines on the long tables.

They chattered as they worked, quickly sewing together the sides of the garments before they hemmed the necks, sleeves, and bottoms. Other women pressed the pieces and placed them on hangers.

She walked over to where Mari had just hung another costume on the rack. "This looks like a production line."

"No one wanted to be left out. I figured the more the merrier."

Kim sorted through the costumes, finding robes with long vests in stripes and fabrics in keeping with the time Jesus and the disciples walked the earth.

"There's a room in back where we can store the costumes and props."

"Do we have enough fabric?"

"More than enough," Mari said. She indicated the clothes on the rack. "Most of the ladies who sewed those costumes paid for the material themselves."

"The program is thick with all these acknowledgments."

"Probably best to thank the entire congregation for their support and encouragement and leave it there. You don't want to take a chance on missing anyone."

"Good idea," Kim said.

Mari smiled. "Did you find parts for those other children?"

Kim nodded. "I think so. Where's Maggie?"

"Mrs. Allene took a turn for the worse this afternoon, and they admitted her to the hospital. Maggie said she called her son this weekend. She doesn't think Mrs. Allene told him how bad things are, though, since he only promised to come for a visit soon."

"I'd be furious if my parents did something like this to me," Kim declared.

"I'm sure your parents have their secrets, Kim."

"Did Natalie and Avery show up yet?"

Mari tilted her head to the opposite end of the room. "Avery's over there with his chicken wire and papier-mâché."

Kim glanced over to where Avery Baker worked, noting the black plastic garbage bag he wore to protect his clothing. "You think he'll get Natalie to wear one of those?"

"I seriously doubt it." One of the women called Mari over.

"Go ahead," Kim told her. "I'll grab a bite to eat and find a project."

They had agreed to a potluck, and Kim had gone in with Mari and Maggie to purchase a deli tray and some breads.

Kim smiled at Pastor Joe as she approached the food table. "Good turnout, don't you think?"

"Excellent," he agreed. "People like to be involved."

She slathered a bun with mustard before adding ham, lettuce, and tomato. She spooned potato and pasta salads onto her plate and scooped a serving of homemade banana pudding into a dessert bowl.

"Take this for me," Pastor Joe said, handing her his plate. "I'll get us something to drink."

She chose one of the tables along the side. Pastor Joe placed two cups of tea on the table and sat down. He said grace, and they started to eat. "Heard from Wyatt lately?"

Startled, Kim looked up. "We talked right after you told me he agreed to help with the window. He came over to measure my kitchen."

"You're not getting in over your head, are you?"

She could play dumb, but he'd see right through that. She'd discussed her last breakup with him when she promised before God not to fall into the same trap again.

Pastor Joe had warned her about the importance of carrying through on vows made to God, quoting Ecclesiastes 5:5.

She'd been emphatic that nothing would stand in the way of her achieving her goal to avoid bad boys. "I'm struggling," she admitted. "Every time I'm around Wyatt I see glimpses of a good, decent man, but then I remind myself he's not a Christian."

"And if he were?"

"I probably wouldn't be attracted to him," Kim said.

Pastor Joe's hoot of laughter drew some gazes in their direction. "You're something else, Kimberly Elliott."

"Seriously though, I see Wyatt as his own worst enemy. He's shared some stuff with me, mistakes he made in his youth that have colored his attitude toward life."

Pastor Joe nodded. "I agree. I suspect he shared some of that same history when we talked. But I sensed something happening with him. A change he finds surprising. He can't believe he keeps agreeing to help with these church projects."

Kim giggled. "No doubt he regrets the day he agreed to build the cross for me."

"I don't think so. Do you think he would have given such attention to detail if he didn't care?"

"His carpentry work is important to him. I don't think anything would come out of Wyatt's shop that isn't top-notch. That's the way he works."

"I wouldn't discourage you from friendship with Wyatt, Kim, but look out for yourself. Find a God-fearing, decent man and settle into a happy life. That's what God wants for you."

"I know. Believe me, there's nothing I want more than a man who loves God first, then me, and wants a family. And yet I continually sabotage myself. Why do I find lying cheaters so attractive?"

"That's a question you have to answer for yourself. Is it an attraction to the man himself or the belief that your love can make him a decent human being?" He held up his hand when she started to respond. "Don't answer that for me, Kim. Answer it truthfully for yourself."

"I already know the answer. They see the weakness in me. I lay my heart out there on a platter and take whatever they offer. I dare to believe they have a grain of goodness in them, and maybe for a moment or two they allow the good to shine through; but they always revert to their old ways.

"In their minds it's fair as long as they don't get caught. They figure what I don't know can't hurt me. They never think about the fact that every lie comes to light eventually."

"That's not the life your heavenly Father wants for you."

"Pray for my wayward heart," Kim requested softly.

"That heart is one of my favorite things about you."

"Then pray for God to give me strength, to send the right person to accept the love I need to give. And pray for Wyatt Alexander, that he can accept the love of his heavenly Father and turn his life around. Pray he forgives himself for making the wrong decisions and accepts that the gifts he's already been given are greater than the losses he's incurred."

"I already have. I've prayed for you both. Forgive yourself, too, Kim. Leave those bad decisions you made in those relationships in the past. Concentrate on the future joy God has planned for you."

" 'Delight thyself also in the Lord: and he shall give thee the desires of thine heart,' " Kim quoted.

"Exactly. We'd better finish up here," he added. "I suspect Mari thinks I've wasted enough time eating."

Kim winked at him and began gathering her trash. "I'll tell her it's my fault. That you were counseling one of your lost sheep."

"She'd never buy that. You're about as lost as the sun in the sky."

"During an eclipse?"

"Things are always darkest before the dawn," he countered. "Sometime when you have an opportunity I'd like to sit down with you and discuss writing. I have some ideas I'd like to put together, but I don't have a clue how to proceed."

"I'll tell you what I know, but bear in mind that my experience is limited to plays." She looked across the room. "I think I'll see if Natalie and Avery need help with those stones."

"I'll ask Mari what she wants me to do. She'll probably make me iron. She knows I hate ironing." He smiled and turned to go.

"Natalie, Avery," Kim said as she walked over to where they worked. The atmosphere felt so thick she could cut it with a knife. "Looks like these are coming along."

"They would be if Natalie would stop making suggestions," Avery snapped.

"I didn't realize you were a committee of one, Avery. All I said was that we needed to use different shades of gray to cast shadows on the stones."

"Then why don't you let me build them so you can color to your heart's content?"

"Don't be a jerk."

Anger filled his expression.

Kim laid her hands on their backs. "Come on, guys. We're setting an example for the kids here. Can't you put aside your differences for them?"

He glared at Natalie. "It's not my fault. I offered to make the stones, and then she horned in like she always does."

"If you didn't want my help, why didn't you just say so?"

"And have everyone look down on me?" he demanded. "They'd all be saying, 'Poor Natalie. That Avery is such a bad guy.' "

Natalie turned away. "It's useless. I can't work with him, Kim."

"Okay, tell you what. Let's leave Avery with the stones, and we'll build the tomb."

"Hey, I wanted to do that," he objected.

"You can't do everything," Kim told him. "We can all work together as a team, or I'll split the project and we'll work separately. You decide."

"Fine," he said sharply, apparently put out by her mandate. "We can work together."

"I thought so. I'm going to see how everyone else is doing, and then I'll be back. Don't make me separate you two," Kim warned, sounding like a parent chastising her unruly children.

She smiled at Avery's mutterings when he turned on Natalie. "I *figured* your friend would take your side."

"I can hear you, Avery."

The two of them fascinated her. They'd probably be good friends if Avery could get beyond seeing Natalie as his rival. Of course, Natalie wasn't the type to let Avery browbeat her.

The door opened, and Maggie stepped inside. Kim took a detour over to say hello. "Mari said you were with Mrs. Allene."

"I just left the hospital. They got her settled into a room, and she's sleeping."

"Is it bad?"

Tears clouded Maggie's eyes. "I don't think it will be long. I requested a leave of absence for personal reasons. The hospital agreed."

Kim hugged Maggie close, and they shared their grief at the thought of losing such a good friend. "What about her son?"

"I'm calling him," Maggie declared.

Kim stepped back and looked at her. "Are you sure?"

"Very. I will not let Mrs. Allene go to her grave without the comfort of her only child. I don't care what she says. It's not fair to her or her son. Dillon Rogers needs to be here for his mother."

"Do you have his number?"

"It's on her speed dial. I'm going over there to pack some items, and I'll get it then."

"You need help?"

"I'm good. I can't call myself her friend if I allow her to die alone. I have to do this."

"You don't need to justify the situation for me. I agree that it's the right thing to do."

Maggie looked around the room. "I'm sorry I can't help. Looks like a good turnout."

Kim lowered her voice. "I've been over refereeing Avery and Natalie. I told them I'd separate them if they couldn't play together."

Maggie giggled, and it did Kim's heart good. "Avery is so stubborn," Kim continued. "I don't know why Natalie offered to work with him."

"I think she hopes Avery will accept her one day," Maggie said. "She once told me there's more than enough business in this town for both of them."

"But Avery can't stand being second best. He sees Natalie's work and goes off the deep end every time. If she offers something, he has to offer something bigger or better. I believe Natalie is willing to be his friend, but his manly pride refuses to allow that. Let's pray the Lord opens his eyes. I asked Pastor Joe to pray for the same for me."

"What's up, Kim?"

"Wyatt Alexander. I'm starting to see his good traits over the bad."

"Don't forget your vow."

"I haven't. It just breaks my heart to see someone so unhappy and not be able to help."

Kim felt the gentle pressure of Maggie's hand against hers. "We can't make other people happy, Kim. They have to do it for themselves. Prayer works. Look what it's done for me."

Maggie hadn't always been a Christian. In fact, she'd come to know the Lord only within the last decade.

"I know," Kim said. "God makes a major difference in all of us when we give Him control. Of course, it's hard to give up that control."

"What exactly do you think you can do for Wyatt Alexander that his family hasn't?"

"Nothing." Kim knew that was true. If they couldn't reach him, what made her think she could? "Let's talk about this later," she suggested. "You need to take care of those things for Mrs. Allene. We can't solve the problem tonight, not even with our best effort."

"I'm praying, Kim."

She hugged Maggie. "Me, too. I'll try to stop by the hospital after work tomorrow to visit Mrs. Allene. Let me know if I can help in any way."

Maggie nodded. "I'm praying for your program, too, Kim. I know it's going to be wonderful."

Chapter 10

Wyatt had just come inside to fix himself a sandwich, when he heard a tap on the back door and Beth let herself in. "Beth? Where's Chase?"

"At his friend's. We need to talk."

"I just left the shop. You want a sandwich? Something to drink?"

"I'll take a soda."

He pointed to the fridge. "What brings you out here on a school night?"

"Gerald called tonight. He'll be home soon."

"That's great."

"I've missed him." Beth took out a few containers that needed to be thrown away and removed the soda bottle from the back of the shelf. She pulled out a stool and sat down at the island. "I wanted to talk to you about Chase."

"I'm listening." Wyatt took a bite of his sandwich.

"I want Chase to stay with you so Gerald and I can have some time alone."

"Mom would keep him."

His answer seemed to irritate his sister. "Sure she would, but in case you haven't looked lately, Mom isn't as young as she used to be. Chase is an active child. He has a number of activities that require someone to drive him back and forth. He needs you, Wyatt."

He laid the sandwich on the paper towel and looked at her. "What is this about, Beth?"

"It's about you being a father to your son."

"Did Kimberly Elliott put you up to this?"

Beth appeared startled. "Why would you think that?"

"It's not the first time my parenting has been questioned lately."

"I'm sorry, Wyatt, but she's my friend. We did talk the other night after she came here to ask you to build the cross. I wanted her to understand the decision you made."

"I wish you hadn't. She has a tendency to control the situation."

"No, she doesn't. Kim has a tendency to think with her heart rather than her head. If she's said anything to you, it's only because she feels Chase deserves better. That's why I'm here tonight. You know I love him like my own, but I can't help thinking we're not being fair to him."

"Chase is doing fine."

"He's a good kid, but he's nearly a teenager. Don't you remember how confusing those years were?"

"I had both parents and look how I turned out. You honestly think I'm ready to direct Chase's path?"

"It's been ten years, Wyatt. If we wait another ten, he could be married with kids of his own. I'm not joking. The opportunity for you to bond as father and son could be lost. I'm not getting any younger, and neither is Gerald. We're thinking about starting our own family. Kim asked how Chase would feel when that happened. And I honestly don't know."

Wyatt slammed his hand against the countertop. "I knew she had something to do with this."

"And I told you she doesn't."

"So what's this really about?" he asked frostily.

"Gerald is being reassigned to a base in Arizona. He wants us to live together, and I want that, too. So we've reached a decision. If I'm going to be Chase's mother, we'll have to make it legal. Gerald and I will adopt him, and he'll live with us in Arizona and be raised as our son."

The idea hit Wyatt like a kick in the stomach. Although he hadn't lived with his son since Chase was two, Wyatt had known the comfort of having him just a few minutes away. Could he bear not having him close? "And if I don't agree to adoption?"

"Then you step up to the plate and become the dad Chase deserves."

"You'd trust your heathen brother to raise your precious nephew?"

Beth frowned. "Don't pull that on me, Wyatt. For years I've worried and prayed for you, hoping you'd realize you're not at fault for Karen's death. What if you'd died instead of her? Do you think she would have asked me to raise Chase?"

Wyatt knew his wife would never have considered the idea of someone else parenting their son.

"I love you, and I love Chase," Beth said before he could answer. "I know you love him, too. I see the longing in your eyes when we're all together. Why don't you give him a chance to influence your life for a change? I think you'll be impressed by your son."

The thought scared him. "What if I agree to the adoption?"

"Is that what you want?" Beth asked softly. "To hear him call Gerald Dad? To see Chase once or twice a year? To be totally uninvolved in his life? If we adopt him, we won't accept child support. He'll be our son. Not yours."

He tried to hide his misery from her probing stare. "I want him to be happy, and I'm not sure I'm capable of making that happen. How do you think he's going to feel about being forced to leave the only home he's ever known and come here to live?

"I don't know anything about kids. I work all hours of the day and night. What about getting him to school and those activities you mentioned? Who's going to feed him and make sure his clothes are clean? Make sure he does his homework and gets to bed on time and doesn't watch stuff on television he has no business watching?"

"The brother my parents raised," Beth answered simply as she came to stand beside him, rubbing her hand across his shoulders. "You know how parenting works. You make decisions that may not be popular and live with the consequences. The rest is easy. You cook for yourself. You do laundry. You clean. And Chase does chores at my house. He knows how to help. Or you could hire a housekeeper." She punched his arm lightly. "And I'm positive Chase can tell you what you shouldn't be watching on television."

"You're a real comedian, Beth."

"But you admit you can handle the situation?"

Wyatt tossed his sandwich in the trash can. His sister's news had killed his appetite. "I don't know. Do you need an answer tonight?"

"We have some time before Gerald comes home. Why don't you think about it and let me know? You could start by spending time with Chase. Weekends. School nights."

He rubbed his hand over his face. "I didn't need this right now, Beth."

"Do you think another day would have made a difference, Wyatt?"

"Probably not."

"All I'm asking is that you accept your God-given right to parent the precious son you've been given. Karen would have been proud of Chase."

"I know. He's really something. Did I tell you I watched him at play practice the other day? He's learned most of his lines already. They only had to prompt him a time or two."

"He has an excellent memory. Just like you."

"Yeah, I never forget anything," he agreed, the deeper meaning of his statement evident to them both.

"It's time, Wyatt. Put the past behind you and step into a future with Chase. I promise to be with you as much as possible, but I want Chase to know his dad as I know him. You're a pretty special guy. Let yourself believe that and let him love you. You won't regret it."

Her words humbled him. He looked down at his hands. He could feel the moisture in his eyes when he looked up at her. "How did we get to this? At first it was a couple of years for me to get back on my *feet*. Then he was in school, and I was working those long hours. Then I didn't want to take him from the only home he's ever known. I excused myself from ten years of his life."

"Chase knows you love him, Wyatt. I've shared with him everything I know about you and Karen. I know he's wondered why he didn't live with you, and I've tried to make him understand. Did you know Chase prays for you every night? That one reason he wanted to be in the Easter program was because he hoped you would find God and be happy?"

"What made him think that?"

"Kim mentioned he could help people find Jesus Christ, and you were the person he thought of. And before you blame Kim for that, I want you to know he came up with the idea all on his own."

Wyatt knew it was past time. "Okay, Beth. Do we need to discuss this with Chase?"

She nodded. "I don't want him thinking I'm abandoning him. He needs to make the final decision."

"How about if we plan on Chase spending some time with me each week until Gerald gets home, and then he can move in for the duration of Gerald's leave? We'll look at the situation after that, and if he's unhappy, we'll decide what to do then."

Beth hugged her brother. "I think Chase will be happy spending time here. You can do all those manly things with him. He loves Ole Blue, and he's always been fascinated by that deer head over your fireplace. And you can tell him things about his mother I never could."

"It has been a long time since I was this uncertain about something."

"Your confidence level will grow with experience. Stop thinking everything to death. Experience the love of your son."

❧

The plans for the conversation with Chase proceeded quickly. On Friday night Wyatt went over to Beth's, and they ordered pizza.

When Beth brought up the subject of Chase spending time with his dad, Wyatt steeled himself for a definite no or even tears.

"I'd like that."

Chase's simple response blew him away. How could the child he'd all but abandoned those many years ago want anything to do with him? "Why, Chase?"

The boy's gangly body shifted with his shrug. "You're my dad. All my friends talk about the fun things they do with their dads, so I figure we'd have fun, too. Will you help me build a birdhouse for Miss Natalie?"

The word *help* registered in Wyatt's mind. His son hadn't asked him to build the house but to help. Chase's ability to be so generous in his love rocked Wyatt's world. "We can do that."

Chase smiled. "Can we go to church? Miss Natalie lets me help in her classroom sometimes. She makes neat stuff."

"We'll see."

"I really like church," the boy said.

"I know, Chase. Your aunt has told me."

"Can I watch my movie?" he asked his aunt.

"Yes. Can you watch it in your room? I'd like to talk to your dad."

"Sure. 'Bye, Dad. See you."

Wyatt's gaze followed the boy from the room. "I'm humbled by that kid."

"He knows that you love him, and now he's going to do something his friends are doing. He's not the rebel you were."

"I bet Mom and Dad love that."

"They love you, Wyatt. They don't always understand you, but they care about what happens to you and Chase. Be thankful Chase isn't like you were, or you'd have had him back in your life much sooner."

"Is that why you want me to step up for the teenage years?" Wyatt teased.

Beth laughed. "Smart, huh?" She glanced toward the bedroom door and lowered her voice. "He might hear us and think the wrong thing."

"He's going to be okay, Beth. You've done a wonderful job, and I promise to do everything in my power to justify that love you've instilled in him."

"What do you think about his spending next Friday night at your place? You could take him fishing. He's never been."

Wyatt's eyes widened. "He's never been fishing?"

"I don't do bait. I'll come to your place for a fish fry and bring him home with me for church."

"Sounds like you've worked this out to your benefit. Of course I certainly need to remedy the fishing situation. He's an Alexander man. He's got to love fishing."

"What if he's too softhearted?"

"There's only one way to find out." He called his son's name, and the boy came running.

"How would you like to spend next Friday night with me and go fishing on Saturday?"

Surprise flashed in Chase's expression. He smiled broadly and nodded.

"That's what we'll do then. Bring warm clothes. It's cold on the water this time of year."

"I don't have a pole."

"You can use one of mine, and we'll get you your own if you like fishing."

Chase flung his arms around his dad's neck and hugged him. "Wait until I tell Buddy. He's always talking about his dad."

Wyatt choked up.

"Finish your movie and get ready for bed," Beth directed. "And work on your fishing strategy. I'm expecting to eat lots of fish."

"We'll catch hundreds, won't we, Dad? We can do loaves and fishes like Jesus did."

"Fish can be difficult to catch sometimes," Wyatt warned, all the while hoping his son's first fishing experience would be a good one. "We'll have to take it one step at a time."

❧

With the arrival of March, Kim found herself with frazzled nerves. So many aspects of the play were in place, but the children's inability to commit to the performance drove her crazy.

They hadn't had one practice yet in which all the children with assigned roles were present. She'd reassigned and rearranged roles every week until she could hardly keep track of the changes. At least she could count on Chase Alexander.

She'd been a bit surprised the previous evening when Chase said his dad had brought him to practice. She'd meant to call Beth and ask if everything was okay, but time had slipped away from her.

Ever since Mrs. Allene had come home, she'd been running errands and picking up groceries to help Maggie. She also visited with Mrs. Allene as often as possible to give her friend a break.

Maggie had reached Dillon Rogers, and he'd promised to make arrangements to come home. Maggie had tried to impress upon him that things were pretty bad, but she didn't think he believed her. He'd kept arguing that his mother had told him not to worry.

"I couldn't believe he was being so thickheaded," Maggie told Kim. "Does he honestly think his mother would say, 'I hate to bother you, but I'm dying—and could you come home?'"

"At least he's coming."

"He'd better make it soon. The doctor doesn't think she'll last long."

Wyatt showed up a few minutes after practice, looking stressed.

"Wyatt? Where's Beth?"

"At home, I suppose."

"Hey, Dad."

Wyatt handed Chase the keys. "Wait for me in the truck. You can play the radio, but don't start the engine. I need to talk with Miss Kim."

The distinct impression he wasn't happy with her gave Kim pause. She hadn't seen or talked to him over the past few days. "I wondered if Beth was sick. Chase told me you brought him to practice."

"Stop beating around the bush," Wyatt snapped. "You want to know what's going on. Ask."

"I don't understand."

"Don't act so innocent. You got what you wanted, Kim. I'm fulfilling my fatherly duties. Chase is living with me part-time."

His hostility shocked her. "What are you talking about? I never—"

"Sure you did. And now that Gerald's about to return stateside, I can either accept responsibility for my son or they'll adopt Chase, and maybe I'll see him a couple of times a year."

Kim gasped. "They won't let you see him?"

Wyatt snorted. "It would hardly be practical. Beth is going to live on a military base in Arizona with Gerald."

"Beth's moving?"

"That's what I said."

"She didn't mention it."

Kim would miss having Beth next door, but she understood her friend missed her husband and wanted to be with him. She could tell the change frustrated Wyatt. She wanted to believe Wyatt wanted his son with him or he would never have agreed to Chase's living with him part-time. "So how's it going?"

The look he flashed her spoke volumes. "Just wonderful. Between carting him around to his school, sports, and church activities, I barely have time to do my work. At first it was just Friday night and Saturday, but before that weekend was up Beth decided she wanted him to stay with me more."

He wasn't being fair. It wasn't her fault Beth expected him to spend time with his son. He was just like the others. Confront him with a challenge and he had to find someone else to blame. Chase was his responsibility, not Beth's. "I'm sure things will settle down once you adjust to each other's schedules."

"My life will never be the same. Beth and her meddling friend have made sure of that."

"If you mean me, my name is Kimberly Elliott. I did not meddle in your business. Tell you what, Wyatt—why don't you go home and hide in your precious workshop? I'll make sure Chase gets to and from practice. I wouldn't want you to be inconvenienced because of me."

"Why don't I just take Chase home for good and see what that does for your little play?"

Kim couldn't believe he'd be so cruel. She knew without doubt that none of the other children in the church could do half as well as Chase. The part of her that wanted to throw down the gauntlet fought for dominance, but she restrained herself.

"Chase has worked very hard for this, Wyatt. Don't punish him or the church because you're angry with me."

"I'm not angry with you." Wyatt growled his frustration. "Well, maybe I'm taking it out on you. I'm ashamed and furious at myself for letting things get so bad. For years I've thought of myself. Sure, I love my son, but it was easy to believe he was better off with Beth. Now I have Chase, and Beth, and you, and even Cornerstone demanding stuff from me I'm not prepared to give."

"Are you talking about the stage?"

"No. The stage is finished. All I have to do is screw it together."

"Then what?" Kim asked. She wanted to understand his confusion, particularly the role he felt Cornerstone played.

"You all expect me to be something I'm not."

"You mean a loving father and good person?"

"That and other stuff. You make me think about being different, and I've been the same for so long I'm not sure I want to change."

"We all change, Wyatt."

"Have you?"

"I've made mistakes in my life," Kim admitted. "And I vowed I'd never make them again. I'm struggling, but I'm getting there."

"But how can you be struggling? You're a good Christian woman. Why would you worry about anything?"

"I want the same things as every woman, Wyatt. A husband, children, a happy home; but I keep making the wrong decisions, and I'm still alone."

"What sort of decisions?"

Kim felt uncomfortable with the question. "I'm attracted to the wrong men."

"What sort of men?" he asked curiously.

"Mostly lying cheaters who aren't looking for the same things I am."

"How do you meet these men? Surely not at church."

"Either I'm a magnet, or there's a sign somewhere on earth that says, 'If you want a stupid woman, find Kim Elliott.'" Her pathetic attempt at humor went unnoticed.

"What attracts you to these men?"

"My friends tell me I want to change them. I don't. I couldn't if I tried. But I do see good hearts in them, and maybe they don't intend to hurt me, but they can't help themselves any more than I can. Maybe they believe they're letting me down easy by making me think the worst."

"What do you want in a man?"

Kim shrugged. "Someone good and decent and capable of love, and he has to be a Christian."

"Why?"

"I want to raise my children with my husband."

"Not going to church doesn't mean he wouldn't be there for them."

"How can he guide them to do what's right if he's not willing to do right himself?"

"You don't have to go to church to be a good person."

"But good relationships require things in common with your spouse. The most important thing we'll share is a relationship with our Lord and Savior."

Wyatt just looked at her. Finally he said, "Chase is waiting."

Kim's gaze followed him as he made his escape down the aisle. He glanced back, and she waved good-bye.

"You're doing the right thing, Wyatt," she said softly as the door closed behind him. She glanced upward and whispered, "Thanks."

Chapter 11

Kim had just finished writing up a customer's purchase when the phone rang. "Eclectics. How may I help you?"

"Hi, it's Mari. I wanted to let you know Mrs. Allene died this morning."

Kim felt a knot grow in her throat. "How's Maggie doing?"

"She was with Mrs. Allene. She said she had pretty much slipped into a coma. She didn't think she suffered. She said Mrs. Allene drew one deep breath and passed from this world."

"Where is Maggie now?"

"At her house. She said Dillon Rogers went to the attorney's office to pick up the will. She tried to tell him Mrs. Allene had told her what she wanted for her funeral, but he wouldn't listen. He said they'd talk after he saw the will."

"Why is he being such a jerk?"

"He's grieving, too."

Kim had her own opinion about the man after what Maggie had told her. He'd flown in midmorning Tuesday, and from the moment he'd shown up at the house in his rental car, he'd treated Maggie like hired help rather than Mrs. Allene's friend.

"I asked Joe about tonight's practice, and he said we should go ahead," Mari said.

"You think everyone will be up to it?"

"We'll miss Mrs. Allene a great deal, but everyone has an investment in the play, too. I feel we should honor Mrs. Allene by forging ahead. Joe agrees."

"I'll be there. I'll probably take a few minutes this afternoon to run by and see Maggie. You want to go with me?"

"Joe and I are going over later this morning."

"What about food?"

"I'm sure the bereavement committee will want to take a meal over to Mr. Rogers tonight."

"You think he'll accept?"

"I pray he's not difficult about accepting the meals *or* the funeral arrangements. Mrs. Allene has been part of Cornerstone all her life. It would be very cruel of him not to allow us to be involved in the services. Joe plans to go over there after Mr. Rogers gets back from the lawyer's office."

"I can't believe he wouldn't listen to Maggie."

Later that afternoon Kim left the store in the hands of her assistant and went over to Maggie's. Kim noted her red eyes as she hugged her friend. "I'm sorry. I know how much you loved Mrs. Allene."

"I'll miss her."

"We all will. What can I do to help?"

"You've helped just by being here."

"You want to come over to the condo and spend the night? Or I could stay here if you want."

"I'm okay. Mari said you're having practice tonight."

"Do you think we shouldn't?"

"Of course not," Maggie declared. "Mrs. Allene was thrilled about the Easter program. She always asked how things were going before she got so sick."

Kim stayed with Maggie until it was almost time to leave for church. She called the store and learned Wyatt had phoned. She dialed the number he'd left. "Hi. Ruby said you called."

"I wondered if you could pick up Chase. I have to finish some cabinets for delivery tomorrow. I'll probably end up working all night."

"I'm at Maggie's. Mrs. Allene died this morning."

"I'm sorry to hear that. Are you having practice?"

"Pastor Joe thinks we should. I'll arrange to have Chase picked up if I can't do it myself. I'm pretty sure the van runs by your place."

"I'm sorry about this, Kim. I already feel like I'm letting Chase down, but I committed to this order before I knew he would be staying with me."

"It's not a problem, Wyatt," she reassured him. "We transport several children to and from church events."

"I'll pick him up if I can break away."

"Just keep working," Kim told him. "I'll make sure he gets home. Did he eat yet?"

Kim could have declared he growled. "No. I forgot."

She glanced at her watch. "Why don't you order a pizza? I'm sure he'd love that."

"Okay. Thanks, Kim."

After ending the call with Wyatt, she dialed the church office and asked that Chase's name be added to the van route for that evening. She returned to the living room to find Maggie paging through a magazine. She doubted her friend even saw the pages. "Wyatt called the store. He needs someone to pick up Chase."

Kim thought about the situation for a few minutes and decided to tell her friend. "Can I talk to you in confidence?"

"Sure. You know it'll never leave the walls of this house."

Kim didn't doubt that for a minute. Maggie was not a gossip. "Wyatt's angry with me. He thinks I had something to do with Beth's asking him to step up and be a father to Chase."

"Did you?"

Kim shook her head. "I may not agree with him missing ten years of his son's life, but I never suggested Beth force Wyatt to take over Chase's care."

"Do you know what's going on?"

"From what I can piece together, Beth's moving to Arizona to live with Gerald on the base. She told Wyatt they would adopt Chase and raise him as their son or he would have to accept his responsibility. Gerald's home on leave, so I haven't had a chance to talk with Beth yet. They're seeing how things work now. I don't want Wyatt to fail at this."

"I'm sure Wyatt doesn't want to fail either."

"He's been alone for so long."

"Be careful, Kim," Maggie cautioned.

"It's already too late. I know it can't work, but I'm involved up to my eyebrows in their lives."

"I came to Cornerstone right after his wife died," Maggie said. "I was still sorting faces and names, but I remember Mrs. Allene getting very upset when people judged Wyatt so harshly. Whenever the subject arose, she reminded them everyone makes mistakes."

"Do you think he's as bad as he tries to make me believe?" Kim asked.

"Could be he wants you to think the worst of him. A good Christian woman showing more than a passing interest in him and his son might be more than he can handle."

"I want what's best for Chase."

"And Wyatt?" Maggie asked.

Kim traced a pattern in the sofa fabric with her finger. "Yes, of course, Wyatt, too. He's so unhappy. He hides it well, but he blames himself for his wife's death."

"I'm sure it became a defining event in his life. Probably even the point where the rebellious boy became a man. He's certainly taken steps forward over the years."

"In everything but family and religion."

"Do you pray for him?"

Kim nodded. "Daily."

"Do you think Wyatt will ever accept Jesus as his Savior?"

"Beth told me Wyatt once said he tried to fool God, and He took his wife and his foot. I thought she meant he was angry with God, but she says not. He told me he doesn't need a Savior."

"But he built the cross and the stage."

"And he's going to frame out the Good Shepherd window," Kim said. "I suspect he's reached a point in his life where he might want to change and doesn't know how."

"He's got a strong witness in his parents and sister. Not to mention his son. I imagine Chase will see to it that his dad comes to church with him."

"If Wyatt can get his schedule under control. He knows Chase is supposed to be at church tonight, but he's tied up with a cabinet order that's due tomorrow. I believe he wants to be a good father but isn't sure what to do about it."

"What do you mean?"

"Like tonight—you should have heard him when I asked if Chase had eaten. He'd forgotten to feed him. I imagine Wyatt has existed on sandwiches, but Chase needs more. He's a growing boy."

"So how can we help?"

"I thought about freezing some dinners to help get them over the rough spots."

"You don't even cook for yourself," Maggie said.

"Because I don't like cooking for one," Kim reminded her.

Maggie nodded. "You want help?"

"Oh, Maggie, this isn't a good time for you."

"I loved Mrs. Allene, and I'll miss her—but one way to get over losses is to jump back into life. I figure I'll take several more days then call the hospital and have them put me back on the schedule. Meanwhile I can make a few meals to help out. Mrs. Allene gave me her macaroni-and-cheese casserole recipe. Not the one from the church cookbook. The family recipe."

"You're kidding!" Mrs. Allene's casserole had always been the congregation's first choice at church dinners.

"She made me promise to keep it secret. I think it would please her to know Chase and Wyatt were enjoying the casserole." They spent a few minutes planning menus. "I have a bag sealer, so we can put the food in those and seal them tight."

"What about a cookbook? You think that would help Wyatt?"

"If he had time to cook," Maggie said.

"Beth prepared Chase's snacks. Wonder what he's doing now?"

"I know Natalie would bake him a batch of cookies if you asked. She thinks Chase is a great kid."

"Maybe I will. I'm trying not to involve too many people. I don't want to upset Wyatt." Kim checked her watch. "I suppose I'd better head for church."

"You want company?"

"Sure. We can use all the help we can get."

"Let me comb my hair and grab my purse."

On the way out they discussed the house Maggie rented from Mrs. Allene. "I have no idea what Dillon Rogers will do. Probably sell everything and head overseas again."

"You don't think he'll rent you the house?"

Maggie shook her head. "He doesn't strike me as the type who is particularly interested in living at the beach. Although he did say it was good to be home."

"I can imagine a few things about the States are an improvement over a foreign country."

"I don't want to look for another place to live," Maggie said. "But it won't be the same without Mrs. Allene next door either. Mari said the same thing."

The elderly woman had lived between the church parsonage and the home Maggie rented.

"I'll help you look if you have to move."

"It's probably time I consider buying something. Mrs. Allene gave me a good rent because she was more concerned about someone taking care of the house than making a profit. Anything I find will be much higher. I might as well pay myself."

"Mom and Dad gave me a deal on the condo when I came back to manage the store. It was one of their rental units. I've enjoyed having a place where I can make changes when I want to."

"Did Julie and Noah buy the unit in your building?"

Kim shook her head. "Too expensive. The owner got multiple offers."

"I imagine Julie is tired of Noah's apartment."

❧

Practice went better than expected that night, and Kim praised the Lord. Mrs. Allene's death, along with questions about what Dillon Rogers would do, was on everyone's mind, but that didn't seem to hinder their progress.

When the kids loaded into the van for the trip home, Mr. Simmons asked Kim if she could take Chase home. "I had more kids than usual tonight, and it'll be late when I drop him off."

"I'll take him. I appreciate your picking him up."

"No problem. Great play."

Kim smiled at his encouragement. Everyone in the church seemed determined to offer the positive reinforcement she needed.

Maggie had walked up and stood beside her. "I heard. I'll walk home with Mari. It's possible I'll hear from Dillon Rogers tonight about the plans for Mrs. Allene's funeral. We'll talk tomorrow about what we discussed earlier."

Kim hugged Maggie and called to Chase. After they were in the car, she asked, "How do you like staying with your dad?"

"It's okay. He's kind of busy. He's gonna help me build Miss Natalie a birdhouse. She said she wanted one for her yard. One of those with the copper tops like Dad has."

"I'm sure both of you will enjoy that."

"Miss Kim, do you think my dad will come to the play?"

She pulled onto the highway. "I'm sure he'll try."

"Aunt Beth said she'd be there."

"A lot of people will be at the play. Does that frighten you?"

"Sort of. Aunt Beth says I need to ask God to give me strength. She says He'll relieve my fears."

"He will." Kim glanced at him. "I've asked Him to relieve mine, too."

"You're afraid?"

"Sure I am. I try not to worry though. I'm here for you, Chase. I appreciate what you're doing. The play wouldn't be a success without you."

"Aunt Beth says I shouldn't be prideful."

Kim smiled. "It's hard, isn't it? We want praise for a good job, but when you're working for Jesus it's not about praise. We're doing this to show our love for Him."

She parked in the yard, and they met Wyatt coming out of the house with a cup of coffee and a wedge of cold pizza.

Chase called hello to his father and ran inside. Kim wondered what the hurry was. "Did you finish?"

Wyatt shook his head. "I've got hours of staining to do. I need to make sure Chase gets to bed and then go back to work."

"Need an extra set of hands?" When he hesitated, she said, "I know my way around a can of stain."

"If you're sure. . ."

"I wouldn't offer if I weren't. If you'd like to get started, I'll fix Chase a snack and see that he takes his bath."

"I need to spend a few minutes with him," Wyatt told her. "I've been in the workshop all week. Beth's going to be furious. I promised we'd spend time together."

"I'm sure she understands you had prior commitments. Chase mentioned the birdhouse you're going to help him build. I think he has a crush on Natalie."

Wyatt nodded. "The minute these cabinets are hung, I'll gladly build all the birdhouses he wants."

"Not build," Kim said. "His objective is that you help him."

"I know. I hope he understands this work is what puts food on our table and keeps a roof over our heads. I suppose I'll have to cut back if Chase comes here to live full-time. Let me go speak to him."

Kim waited in the kitchen, sipping a cup of the strong coffee he had made and wondering about Wyatt's comment. Surely he wouldn't consider sending Chase away.

Wyatt returned about ten minutes later. "Chase said he'd take a shower after he watches his program. He's going to call the shop when he gets in bed."

"You have a phone out there?"

"Yeah, but we're using his walkie-talkies."

Kim grinned. "I bet he enjoys that."

"Seems to. I have so much to learn. I want to make him happy."

"He's a tween, Wyatt. He's about to undergo a total change."

He held the door open for her. "What's a *tween*?"

Her lack of experience with children had led Kim to read several books on child development to help her in working with the kids at church. "He's no longer a child, and he's not a teen, so they refer to them as *tweens*."

In the shop, he found her a smock, safety glasses, and gloves and directed her to the area where he'd set up the cabinets on sawhorses and boards. "Wouldn't it be easier to stain these once you get them in place?" Kim asked.

"I like to control my environment."

Kim nodded. "Okay, show me how you want it done."

After a short lesson on the Wyatt Alexander method of applying stain, she went to work. He watched for a minute and, after a satisfied nod, he himself began staining a cabinet door. "How was practice?"

"Better than I thought. I was afraid everyone would be depressed over Mrs. Allene's death, but they're determined the show must go on."

"Have the arrangements for her funeral been made yet?"

"I suppose her son will make them tomorrow. I pray he allows the church to be involved."

The walkie-talkie crackled to life, and Chase said good night. "Night, Chase. Love you."

"Love you, too, Dad. Night, Miss Kim."

Wyatt hit the button for Kim to say good night to Chase and returned the unit to the counter. "Dillon will have to do what he's comfortable with. She was his mother."

Kim didn't comment on the father-son exchange, but it pleased her that Wyatt told Chase he loved him. "Mrs. Allene told Maggie what she wanted, and he wouldn't even listen. He had to have a copy of the will. I don't think Mrs. Allene would have put her funeral plans in the will. She's been at Cornerstone all her life. The congregation needs the funeral as much as Dillon Rogers does."

"Why would you say that?"

"He hasn't been in his mother's life for years. The membership has been Allene Rogers's family, too. Look at Maggie. She loved Mrs. Allene enough to take a leave of absence from work and care for her."

He looked stunned. "Without pay?"

"Yes. Maggie and Mrs. Allene grew close when Maggie first moved to the area. Mrs. Allene invited her to church, and Maggie's been there ever since. We're afraid Dillon Rogers will handle things quickly and return overseas. Mrs. Allene deserves better."

"Is he her only family?"

"No. She has cousins and nieces and nephews here as well."

"He'll need to handle the estate before he leaves."

Kim concentrated on staining the cabinet door. After she finished she asked Wyatt's opinion.

"You do good work."

She grinned at him. "Told you."

"I'd tell you to start another one, but it's nearly ten thirty."

"I probably should get home and check with Maggie to see what plans have been made."

"I appreciate your help."

"Next time ask before the last minute." Kim peeled off the gloves and removed the safety glasses.

"I'll remember that, though I'm going on record as saying there won't be a next time. Chase needs more than a part-time dad. No more last-minute staining jobs. Thanks for bringing him home."

"My pleasure." She hung the smock on a nearby peg and picked up her car keys.

"Kim!" Wyatt called as she started to leave. "Let me know about the funeral."

"I will."

Wyatt's dog raced over when she left the building, barking at her and then pushing his head beneath her hand. Kim greeted him and rubbed his head before unlocking her car door.

What a day it had been. She'd never have thought she'd volunteer to help Wyatt in his workshop, but it hadn't been all bad. At least she'd seen a different side of him. And maybe he'd seen a different side of her.

Chapter 12

A nd then he accused me of taking advantage of an old lady," Maggie told Kim and Mari.

Mari had called the store the next morning and suggested they take Maggie out to lunch. She hadn't said much, but Kim suspected something was up.

"After Mari dropped me off, I barely got the lights on before he started pounding on the door. I thought maybe he wanted information for the funeral, but he started throwing out accusations right and left. I had no idea Mrs. Allene had changed her will to leave the rental property to me."

"Has he made any plans for the funeral?" Mari asked.

Maggie shook her head. "None that I'm aware of."

"Joe said he was going to call him today to see what he plans to do."

"Do you think he called yet?" Kim asked.

"I have no idea. He doesn't always share church business with me."

"I don't even care anymore," Maggie announced. "If Dillon Rogers doesn't have a funeral for her, I'm planning a memorial service myself. I won't allow him to hurt the church."

"What will you do about the house?" Kim asked.

Maggie frowned. "I'll worry about that after the funeral is over."

"You think he'll contest the will?"

"He threatened that last night. Then when he had me in tears, he couldn't escape soon enough. I don't think he's very comfortable with sobbing women."

Mari took a sip of her iced tea. "Most men aren't."

"Then they shouldn't make us cry," Kim pointed out.

"I tried to call you, but you weren't home," Maggie said.

"I hung around and helped Wyatt stain cabinets. He had a big order that's due today. I got home around eleven or so and figured it was too late to call."

"I think I finally cried myself to sleep around three." Even as she spoke, her eyes filled with tears.

"Oh, Maggie, I'm so sorry."

The woman rose quickly. "I need to run to the ladies' room. I'll be right back."

Unsure what to do, Kim looked at Mari. "How do we help her?"

"Prayer is the only recommendation I have. It's not fair to judge Dillon Rogers based on his treatment of Maggie."

"He's not being fair," Kim declared. "You know as well as I do that Maggie would never ask Mrs. Allene to change her will. In fact, we were talking about finding her another place to live the same day Mrs. Allene died. She had no idea what Dillon Rogers planned to do with the rental property."

The waitress arrived with their soup and salad. After she left, Mari said, "I'm sure he's shocked by the arrangements his mother made. Maggie's not family or anything."

"She was like a daughter to Mrs. Allene," Kim said.

Mari looked sad. "The idea of people fighting over worldly possessions is so depressing. I was an only child, too, but Mom had very few things to leave me. We sold a lot of it to pay her bills."

Kim reached over to squeeze Mari's hand. She kept forgetting Mari had lost her mother not so long ago. Her mother's death, coupled with Mari's own breast cancer diagnosis within such a short time span, had thrown their friend for a loop. Everyone had been heartbroken the previous summer when the pastor had announced his wife had cancer. Mari had been blessed with a miracle of physical healing, though, and then had fought her way out of the depression that tried to take control of her life. She'd seemed happier since their Christmas vacation, but she still experienced times of sadness.

"I know it was never Mrs. Allene's plan that Maggie suffer because of the situation. I hope Pastor Joe lets her son know everything Maggie has done for his mother."

"I don't," Maggie said, returning to her seat. "I did what I did out of love for Mrs. Allene, not so she'd leave me a house in her will. I've already decided to sign it back over to him."

"He doesn't understand," Mari said softly.

"Nor does he want to," Kim insisted.

"Don't let your distaste for bad boys color your attitude toward him," Maggie told Kim. "I have to forgive him just as Jesus expects."

Kim felt somewhat miffed by their comments. "I'm not particularly big on forgiving people who intentionally hurt others."

Maggie poured the dressing over her salad and unrolled her silverware. They said grace, and she took a bite before saying, "Hate the deed, not the person, Kim."

"What if you can't separate the person and the deed?"

"Then you need to get to know them better," Mari offered. "We make our initial decision on whether we'll like a person so quickly that we can miss out on special people if we don't take a second look."

"It's still not right," Kim insisted. Laying her fork on the salad plate, she dug around in her purse and pulled out her cell phone. She held it out to Mari. "Will you at least call Pastor Joe and see if he's talked to Dillon Rogers yet?"

"Only so you don't get indigestion," Mari said, smiling, as she punched in the numbers and hit SEND.

"Hi, Jean. Is Joe there? Okay. Thanks. . . . No. I'll talk to him when he gets home."

Mari closed the flip phone and pushed it across the table to Kim. "You'll be happy to know he's gone over to talk with Dillon Rogers."

"That's good, right?" Kim asked, looking at Maggie.

"We'll see. It all depends on what he decides."

The waitress topped off their glasses and asked if they wanted dessert.

Kim ordered a hot fudge brownie. Mari and Maggie opted to pass. "You know you'll want something when you see mine," Kim told them, grinning.

"True. Bring three forks," Maggie told the waitress.

Their laughter seemed to relieve the heaviness of their earlier conversation.

"Maggie's coming over to the house this afternoon to help with the costumes."

"I thought those were finished."

"They were until you added five more children."

Kim shrugged. "What's a director to do? If they come, they must be in the play."

"We can always use audience members," Mari suggested. "I don't think you can add another thing to the play without going back to Adam and Eve."

Kim giggled. "That sounds more like a miniseries. I've been thinking we need more practices. I wonder how Pastor Joe would feel about putting the stage in place the week of the play so we can practice in the sanctuary."

"Joe would work around us, but the congregation might not look favorably on having the church pieces removed for regular services."

"True. But I was thinking the children need to become familiar with the stage so they don't trip or fall."

"You should ask Joe. He's probably already anticipated this anyway."

After they sampled the dessert and talked for a few minutes longer, Kim grabbed her bag. "Well, ladies, business calls. Have fun."

"Want us to come by later and help you find those pewter pieces for the play?" Mari asked.

"I took care of that on Monday. I got nervous when someone asked how much the pieces were. I told them they would be on sale after Easter."

"You are a nut," Maggie said.

"That's *salesperson extraordinaire* to you."

Back at the store Kim found herself feeling a little out of sorts when she considered Maggie's chastisement of her attitude toward Dillon Rogers. Of course, Maggie had a point when she'd said, "Hate the deed." Her anger had to do with his mistreatment of her friend. She didn't know the man well enough to judge him.

The afternoon passed slowly. A few lookers came in and left with empty hands while others returned to purchase items they'd seen on previous trips.

Despite the activity, she was playing computer games when the phone rang around four o'clock.

"Busy?" Maggie asked.

"I wish. Did you and Mari finish the costumes?"

"Until you add more children."

"No more kids. I have to draw the line somewhere."

"Good idea. You've single-handedly turned fabric stores into the area's number-one business."

Kim laughed. "Not with those deals Mari's been getting. Are you feeling better?"

"Yes. Joe called home and told Mari the funeral is Saturday morning at the church. The visitation will be at the funeral home Friday night, and a luncheon for the family will be held following the service. Dillon doesn't want any visitation at the house, nor does he want anyone bringing food over."

"At least that's something. Has the bereavement committee started planning for the luncheon?"

"I put you down for ham. I'm making the macaroni-and-cheese casserole. I'm making extra for Chase and Wyatt."

"And I'll get extra ham. That goes well with mac and cheese."

"I need to run. Dillon asked for my help in identifying his mother's favorite dress."

"Is he treating you better?" Kim asked.

"I think Joe might have told him he should talk to me about the plans. Mrs. Allene had told Joe during one of his visits that I knew what she wanted."

"I'll talk to you tonight then."

Kim felt relieved for Maggie's sake. She knew her friend would have been heartbroken if Dillon Rogers had left her out of the arrangements.

She ran by the grocery store after work to pick up ham and a few more items. After she put away the food, Kim picked up the phone and dialed Wyatt's number. He answered on the third ring.

"Did you get the cabinets installed?"

"With minutes to spare. The contractor hinted he'd like to send more business my way. I said we'd talk."

That didn't strike her as cutting back, which was what Wyatt had said he would do. "I called to let you know Mrs. Allene's funeral is Saturday morning."

"Flowers or contributions?"

"I didn't even think to ask. I just got the time of the funeral late this afternoon."

"I'll check tomorrow's paper. I'm sure the obituary will say. Are you feeling better now that the plans have been made?"

Kim considered his question and told the truth. "I'm struggling with Dillon Rogers's treatment of Maggie."

"You mean about the funeral plans?"

"And the will," Kim said. "Mrs. Allene left Maggie the rental property she lives in. He didn't take that news well."

"I imagine not," Wyatt said. "Don't you think he's entitled to feel upset? His inheritance has been given to a stranger."

Kim wasn't happy Wyatt agreed with Dillon's behavior.

"Maggie wasn't a stranger. Mrs. Allene wanted Maggie to have the house. I don't believe he should question his mother's decision."

"He can't be sure Maggie didn't influence her."

"That's a terrible thing to say. How can you even suggest something like that?"

Wyatt sighed. "I've never met your friend, Kim. I can't tell you what she's like. Mrs. Allene's son can't either."

"You men are all alike. And you have met Maggie. She bought a piece of furniture from you."

Wyatt grunted his irritation. "Don't get upset because I don't agree with you about this. I'm entitled to my opinion, too."

"Not if that opinion is based on total disregard for my friend," Kim snapped back. "I'll have you know Maggie never expected one thing in return. Maggie showed Mrs. Allene Christian love. She's already said she'll sign the house back over to him before she'll argue the point."

"Then it won't be a problem."

"If Mrs. Allene wanted Maggie to have the house, she should have it," Kim persisted. "Oh, why am I arguing with you about this? You can't begin to understand how Maggie feels about the man's attacks on her."

"If anyone understands attacks, I should," Wyatt countered. "You pounce on me every time I disagree with something you say."

"I do not."

"Then why don't I feel the love right now?"

She couldn't win. "Forget it. I only called to tell you about the funeral."

"And I appreciate that," Wyatt said. "I also appreciated your help last night. I thought maybe Chase and I could stop by later and finalize the measurements for your kitchen if you have time."

"Are you sure you want to come into enemy territory?"

"I can handle it if you can. We'll be there around eight."

Wyatt and Chase showed up right on time.

"We brought something to sweeten you up," Wyatt said, handing her a white bakery bag. "Sorry. They were hot when we got them. We ate ours at the store."

She looked inside to find a couple of warm doughnuts. "Thanks." She turned to his son and asked, "Did you enjoy the doughnuts, Chase?"

"Yes, Miss Kim. Dad picked me up from school, and we worked on plans for the birdhouse. Dad says measurements are important. He said to measure twice. . . ." His voice trailed off, and he glanced at his father.

"Cut once," Wyatt prompted.

"Yeah, that's it. I'm going to help Dad with the measurements for your cabinets. He said I might be able to help build them in the shop."

"Good for you." She glanced at Wyatt. "Unless you need a third pair of hands, I'll leave you to your work."

"We'll shout if we do. Oh, do you have measurements on the new appliances you picked out?"

"They're in the folder on the counter. You'd better get busy. It's nearly Chase's bedtime."

"We probably should have waited until tomorrow night. He stays up an hour later on Friday and Saturday."

Kim ripped off a paper towel and grabbed the doughnuts on her way out of the kitchen.

Her awareness of the two males in her home was strong, but Kim forced herself to remain focused on the program she was watching. She refused to stand around watching Wyatt work.

Her glass of soda sat on the end table. She opened the bag and dug inside for her favorite, a plain glazed. Kim took a bite and savored the doughnut.

It seemed their earlier argument had rolled right off Wyatt's back. Why couldn't she forget as easily? The anger she felt at injustices was not what God intended for her. He wanted her to "forgive and forget" as Maggie had told her.

Finally Kim gave up on the program and walked over to the kitchen door. Chase chattered nonstop as he held the tape measure while his father read and jotted down measurements.

"We're nearly finished," Wyatt said when he noticed her.

"No rush. Do you think I'll be able to get the cabinets I wanted in here?"

"Maybe even a couple more." He tapped the pad on the counter. "I'll take these back to the shop and draw up a plan. Did you want them all the way to the ceiling or dropped so you can display items across the top?"

"Dropped. I have lots of stuff to display."

"You may have to have some of the ceiling redone once the soffit is removed."

Kim nodded, watching Chase as he tried to use the tape measure without his dad's assistance. "Your helper is waiting on you."

"Poor guy's done enough of that lately. I hope I can dedicate the time he deserves now that I have that last project out of the way."

He wrote the last number on the paper. "That's it, buddy. We're finished." He held up the folder. "Mind if I take this with me?"

"You think I should buy the appliances now?"

Wyatt shook his head. "I'd wait. They look to be fairly standard sized. If you can't get these specific units, you should be able to get others that fit.

Chase, let's get out of here so Miss Kim can call it a night."

"Thanks, Wyatt. You, too, Chase. Your dad is gaining an excellent assistant. Do you have a minute, Wyatt? I'd like to speak with you privately."

"Can I run next door and pick up my books?" Chase asked.

"I don't want you going into the condo without me." He glanced at Kim. "Beth and Gerald went on a short cruise."

Kim nodded. She had been watering Beth's plants while they were away.

"Finish rolling up the tape, and then we'll get your books."

They walked down the hall to her door. Kim shifted uncomfortably. "I'm sorry. I keep jumping to Maggie's defense, and she doesn't want me doing that. I guess she recognizes how weak I am when it comes to forgiving others."

Wyatt's expression was one of understanding. "I'm not your enemy, Kim. I only want you to consider both sides of the story. You know your friend, but you didn't even consider the fact that Mrs. Allene's son doesn't. His mother was an elderly, sick woman living alone. Those are prime targets for people who take advantage of others."

"But he judged Maggie without giving her an opportunity to defend herself. Don't you think Mrs. Allene mentioned her friend Maggie in the telephone calls and letters to her son?"

"Maybe, but could be he thought Maggie was his mother's age. Then when he arrived and found her to be much younger and a beneficiary in his mother's estate, I'm sure doubts arose in his mind."

His logic made sense. "I'm sorry I jumped on your case."

Their gazes locked as Wyatt reached to tuck a stray lock of hair behind her ear. "I admire your loyalty to your friends. I'd like to be numbered among that group."

"You are. I admire you for what you're doing, too, Wyatt. I know Chase's happiness means a lot to you."

The intimacy of their conversation struck Kim as Wyatt leaned forward. She placed her hand against his chest. "Don't. We can't do this."

He covered her hand with his. "Why not?"

"I made a vow to God. I won't make another mistake."

"What if it's not a mistake?"

Before she could respond, Chase came out of the kitchen, waving the tape. "I'm finished. Ready, Dad?"

Wyatt looked at Kim and nodded.

"See you at church, Miss Kim."

Kim hugged the child. "Thanks again."

"Got one of those for me?" Wyatt asked.

She hugged him and stepped away quickly.

What am I doing? Kim asked herself after closing and locking the door. Allowing Wyatt and Chase Alexander to get under her skin didn't bode well for her heart. Kim knew without a doubt she could never again accept a man who believed he didn't need God in his life.

If anyone needed God's grace it was Wyatt Alexander. He needed to accept that he was forgiven and get on with the major task of raising his son in a Christian home.

She could only pray that one day Wyatt would come to know the full extent of God's grace in his life and learn to depend on His Son rather than himself.

Chapter 13

The funeral for Allene Rogers became a celebration of her life. So many words of comfort were spoken not only to her son and other family members but also to the members of the congregation who had loved the woman and been loved in return.

Pastor Joe's sermon touched on the woman he'd known for a short time, and eulogies from those who had known her much longer were a true reflection of the woman's impact on so many lives over the years.

No one had been more surprised than Kim when Wyatt came into the church and sat down next to her on Saturday morning.

The service started out with the congregation singing "Amazing Grace," and as the words to the song filled her heart, Kim found her awareness of Wyatt standing next to her, singing from the same hymnal, nearly overwhelming.

Maggie stood on her other side, her voice cracking with emotion as she sang the words. Kim suffered for her, knowing how difficult this must be.

Mrs. Allene was interred next to her husband in the church cemetery. Afterward Wyatt invited Kim to lunch, but she told him she had to help with the funeral luncheon. She needed to distance herself from him.

"You can come, too, Wyatt," Maggie said. "There's more than enough food for anyone who wants to pay tribute to Mrs. Allene."

Thanks, Maggie, Kim thought as they walked into the fellowship hall. Pastor Joe and Dillon Rogers stood inside the door. They shook Dillon's hand and offered their sympathy.

"I'm so sorry about your loss, Mr. Rogers," Kim said.

She found his smile much like Mrs. Allene's. "Call me Dillon."

Wyatt shook his hand. "Your mom was quite a woman."

"Mom set a real example for me. Too bad I wasn't a good son when she needed me most."

Wyatt glanced at Kim. "I doubt she would have wanted it to be any different," he said when Kim didn't speak.

"I need to help get the food on the table," Kim said hastily. "I'm truly sorry about your mother. She will be missed."

Kim left Wyatt and Dillon talking and went to find Maggie. "He's kicking himself for not being there when his mother needed him."

"He shouldn't do that," Maggie said softly.

Kim looked at her. "Yes, he should. He should have come home sooner."

"Mrs. Allene didn't want that, Kim. I'm sure he would have come if she'd called when this started, but she didn't. Besides, who are we to judge Dillon Rogers? I saw Mrs. Allene often and had no idea how sick she was. If we're assigning blame, my name should be at the top of the list."

"That's not so," Kim pointed out. Why was Maggie trying to shoulder all the blame? It was true Mrs. Allene should have told her son the seriousness of her illness, but other family members should have looked out for her. "No one did more for Mrs. Allene than you."

"She was a dear friend. I'll miss her."

"You can't blame yourself for her death," Kim insisted.

Wyatt walked over to stand beside Kim. "She's right. No one had the ability to change the way things happened. God is in control."

Kim couldn't have been more surprised by Wyatt's words. "Exactly my point," she said, glancing at him. "She thinks she should have noticed sooner that Mrs. Allene was sick because she's a nurse."

"Sometimes we're blinded to the truth when it comes to those we love," Wyatt said. "Or they hide things from us so we don't suffer with them."

Maggie smiled and rested her hands on their arms. "I love you both for the comfort you're offering. I know I couldn't have changed the situation. God was ready to take Mrs. Allene to her glorious home going, and no amount of wishing on my part will change that. I wouldn't bring her back if I could. She's in a much better place. I pray she's already met my family and told them I know the Lord. That would make them so very happy."

Kim hugged Maggie close as the tears flowed.

"Come on, ladies," Wyatt said somewhat stiffly. "Your guests are waiting. We need to get this food out there."

Maggie sniffed and dabbed her nose with the delicate handkerchief she carried. "You're right. Mrs. Allene wouldn't want us crying our eyes out at the celebration of her life."

After Maggie walked away, Wyatt rested his arm around Kim's shoulders. "Are you okay?"

"Just sad for Maggie."

"But happy for Mrs. Allene?"

Kim nodded. "We always miss those people who impact our lives."

Wyatt looked deep into her eyes. "I know I'd miss you if you weren't around."

Kim felt herself growing warm. She turned quickly and grabbed the platter of sliced ham. "I'd better get this on the table."

Wyatt took it from her hands. "Let me carry that for you."

What is he doing? Kim wondered as he moved into the dining area. If she didn't know better, she'd say Wyatt Alexander was pursuing her. She needed to make sure he understood where they stood. She could never marry a man who didn't know the Lord. Marry? Kim frowned. Where had that come from? Wyatt was just being a good friend. Wasn't he?

～

As the days passed, Kim wondered if they would be prepared on time. No doubt the show would go on, but her confidence level seemed to take a nosedive with the weekly practices. Surely nothing had to be as difficult as it seemed.

Kim strongly suspected this was the very reason the church had never varied from tradition on their plays. The traditional plays were so much simpler.

But she refused to be defeated. A friend from church always said she needed to pray a little harder when things got her down. So Kim did exactly that.

Beth and Gerald had returned from their cruise, and Chase remained with his father. She knew Beth missed the child a great deal, but she felt optimistic that father and son would be okay.

Kim ran into Beth on the breezeway in front of their condos and stopped to catch up on the news. Gerald had left for the base in Arizona, and Beth decided not to take any action until she knew something more definite.

"Once we find a place there, I can rent the condo on a weekly basis and still have a place to stay when I come home for vacations," Beth told her.

"That's a good plan. I'm sure the money will come in handy once you start a family."

"Oh, Kim, does change ever frighten you?" Beth asked. "I want to be with Gerald, but moving across the country to a new area and leaving my family behind frightens me. How can I not be there for Wyatt and Chase?"

"Change frightens me, too," Kim agreed. "I know it's difficult, but I think they'll be okay. I've seen the two of them together several times lately, and they're getting along well."

"Chase tells me you've provided food for him and his dad. Is there something else on the horizon for Wyatt and Chase?"

"No. Those meals were mine and Maggie's way of helping Wyatt and Chase adjust. As you know, I promised God I would never involve myself with a non-Christian man again, and that's one promise I'm determined to keep."

"Is your heart listening to what your head is saying?"

"I'm struggling, Beth."

"I've noticed a change in him, Kim. If you'd asked me a few weeks ago I would have said you'd never see Wyatt in a church. Since I've been home I've seen him at Chase's practices, as I'm sure you have. He's not dropping him off either. He's sitting in the audience and watching. He's very proud of Chase's portrayal of Jesus."

"I hope for his sake that he can find the happiness God promises him."

"What about you? If Wyatt became a Christian, would you feel differently about him?"

"I care a great deal about Wyatt. I consider him a good friend."

"Just a friend?"

Kim found that question difficult to answer. She wanted to answer with an unequivocal yes, but Wyatt Alexander had begun to play much too large a role in her thoughts for that. She'd gone so far as to ask herself the same question Beth had asked, but her vow kept her from being tempted to give things a try. "That's all it can be," Kim said with a determined nod of her head.

"I admire your strength. Too many women become involved with men, believing they'll change them, only to find it never works."

"I've been right there with those women," Kim said. "Wyatt needs to accept God's forgiveness and forgive himself so he can move on with his life."

Kim knew Beth surely felt her confusion. A truly committed woman would put Wyatt out of her life. She wouldn't talk about keeping vows and regularly place herself in the path of temptation. Wyatt Alexander was beginning to mean too much to her, and Kim knew she had to take action soon or she'd be in over her head.

"I can't believe the play is this weekend. Where did the time go?" Beth asked, changing the subject.

"The older I get, the faster the years seem to go by. Are you coming to dress rehearsal Thursday night?"

Beth nodded. "I'm helping in the back, getting them into their costumes."

"The rehearsal will be the true indicator of what will happen. Pray the children understand how important this is."

"I have."

⤙⤚

As Kim expected, five of her key players didn't show up for the dress rehearsal. "Where are they? I specifically told each of them they needed to be here tonight."

"Maybe we need to assign volunteer staff to make sure the key players are here," Julie suggested.

"Oh, they'll be here for the play," Kim said. "It's almost as if they think they don't need the practice."

"Could be they have homework or family activities."

"They're probably home watching television or something."

"You're on edge tonight," Julie said.

"I'm terrified everything will fall apart."

"God won't let that happen, Kim. He gave you this play, and He'll use it for His glory."

"I hope so. For now, though, we'd better do something about the missing actors."

Kim reassigned the roles to willing volunteers, keeping a list in case she needed to do the same the following night.

She walked into the sanctuary to find Wyatt and the other men putting the stage in place. "I thought you were going to do that tomorrow."

"We thought rehearsal should be as true to the actual performance as we could make it," Pastor Joe said.

"We put the long, narrow table in the choir bay for the Lord's Supper scene and the cross in the baptismal," Noah told her. "I stood on it, and it seems sturdy enough."

"Avery and Natalie put their stone wall in place," Pastor Joe said, indicating the area with a nod of his head.

"Julie said you had the sanctuary looking like Bethlehem at Christmas," Noah pointed out. "This surely has to be Jerusalem."

"It's wonderful," Kim said. "A theatrical group couldn't have done better."

"And with God in the mix, it's going to be a soul-winning night."

"Pray with us, Pastor Joe," Kim said.

He led them in prayer, and then the group scattered to their various assignments. Noah would work the lights while their music minister controlled the music and sound effects.

"Are you staying?" Kim asked when Wyatt lingered at her side.

"I want to see how the stage holds up under the kids."

She thought of what Beth had said about Wyatt watching his son and figured Chase was the reason he wanted to hang around. "You can be our audience. Let me know if you have any suggestions to improve the performance."

Kim walked up front to address the group of children that had assembled in the front pews of the sanctuary. "Okay, kids. As far as we're concerned, tonight is the night of the performance. You need to be very careful with your costumes and props. We won't have time to replace anything that gets damaged.

"When we move to the back, you need to remember the audience will be able to hear you, so remain very quiet. I know that's asking a lot, but this is important. I also need silence so I can hear where we are with the lines and know when to move forward.

"Mr. Stevens is making a video of our performance tonight, and we'll watch it afterward while we eat our snack. Pastor Joe, would you like to share a few words of encouragement with the children?"

"I think we have a fine group of actors and actresses here, Miss Kim. I know they're going to do the Lord and Cornerstone proud. If you'll all bow your heads, we'll start with a word of prayer."

Afterward the children moved to the hallway behind the pulpit area. Over in the far corner was another small stage where the narrator would stand.

Onstage Mary, Joseph, and the baby Jesus were illuminated in the spotlight, and the star of the East shone in the background. Robin, their narrator, passed her microphone over to little Missy Reynolds, and the music started. Kim felt chill bumps when the child's voice soared with the words of "Away in a Manger."

She slipped into the back and turned on the baby monitor Mari had brought along. The other unit was on the narrator's podium.

The song ended, and Robin began to speak, sharing the passage of time from Jesus' birth until the beginning of His ministry.

"Jesus is coming! Jesus is coming!"

She knew from the chanting that the smaller children had just entered with Chase following them. Kim wanted so badly to step out and watch the program but knew it was more important she stay put. Tomorrow night's performance would require her to direct from behind closed doors.

Mari walked along with the children lined up in the back area, shushing the children as the volume increased.

Kim found herself holding her breath as scene after scene unfolded. Chill bumps raced along her arms as Robin shared stories of the grace their Lord and Savior bestowed on so many people.

They made it through most of the scenes with minor incidents. Before she knew it, the disciples filed through the choir room door and sat down at the table for the Last Supper.

When Chase spoke his line about one of them betraying him, another child gasped and cried, "Who?"

The sound of laughter came over the speaker.

Bryan, the boy who had bullied the children in an earlier practice, said, "Silly, you're supposed to ask, 'Is it me?' "

"Miss Kim says the line is, 'Is it I, Lord?' " another child corrected.

"She didn't."

"It's Judas," another child volunteered, and the argument started.

Kim stepped into the sanctuary and confronted the unruly children. "Why can't you get this one line right?" she demanded. " 'Is it I, Lord?' " she repeated. "What's so difficult about that?" One of the smaller children laughed, and she whirled about. "This isn't funny. It's very serious. Jesus is about to be betrayed."

The child looked as if she were about to cry.

Mari stepped into the sanctuary. "Kim, why don't you take a break now?"

Tears welled in Kim's eyes as embarrassment overwhelmed her. "I'm sorry." She ran out the door without looking back.

Kim went out to her car and sat down in the passenger seat. Once they started, the tears wouldn't stop. Here she was, a day away from the final program, with a group of kids who couldn't repeat one little line properly. She needed a miracle.

She heard a tap on the window and looked up into Wyatt's face. Kim felt even more embarrassed by his presence. He opened the door and passed her a handful of tissues. "Are you okay?"

She managed a teary response. "Obviously not. I just made an idiot of myself."

"They're kids, Kim. They'll give you everything they have to give, but when the urge to play strikes they forget everything else. They were trying to figure out what to say."

Kim sniffed. "That never should have happened. I have no right doing this."

"It's preperformance jitters. You want things so perfect that you got upset when things went wrong."

She flipped down the visor and lifted the mirror cover. "I'm a mess. Those poor kids will think I've lost my mind if I go back in there with raccoon eyes."

He lifted her chin and looked at her face. "You don't look so bad. Go to the ladies' room and freshen up. I'll let Mari know you're coming back."

"I'm so embarrassed," Kim said as she climbed out of the car.

Wyatt took her hand in his. "Everything will be fine. You shouldn't get so worked up though. It's not good for you."

"It definitely makes me look foolish."

Back in the sanctuary the performance stopped when Kim entered the room. She could sense everyone's eyes focused on her. "I'm sorry. I owe everyone here an apology, particularly those of you playing disciples. Please forgive me."

Pastor Joe stood and came over and placed his arm around her shoulders. "We know how stressed you are. Right, children?"

The chorus of yesses made her feel even guiltier. Had she forgotten the reason she had chosen the children? "I never meant for anyone to suffer because of my determination to succeed."

"We appreciate that determination, Miss Kim," Pastor Joe told her. "Your dedication to our success means God will reap the benefits. And we all agree we need to remember how serious this part of the story of Jesus' death is. Right, kids?"

Another roar of yesses resounded.

"Why don't we go over the scene again to reassure Miss Kim?" He guided her over to the pew, and she sat down. "And if anyone feels overwhelmed, just raise your hand, and we'll stop."

"Thanks, Pastor Joe." She looked at the children, sensing their apprehension and desire to make things right. "You're all doing an excellent job. I know the play will be a big success. Please don't hold my behavior against me. I had no right to act like a baby. I need a big pacifier."

The children laughed and moved back into place as the lights were adjusted.

Kim suspected it was more the other adults' coaching than her outburst that made the scene better. There was only one "Was it me, Lord?" in the bunch, and that came from a fill-in disciple. When Bryan said something to the child, an adult quickly interceded.

"Perfect!" Kim called to them as she rose from the pew. "Let's keep going."

They watched the video in the fellowship hall over snacks, and Kim realized things weren't as bad as they seemed. After the van had left to take the children home, the adults sat, discussing the play.

"I think that went well," Pastor Joe said.

"After I got myself under control," Kim agreed with a sad smile.

Wyatt sat next to her and reached over to squeeze her hand. "We all understand how important this is to you, Kim. You have a major investment in the play. When I build something, I'm always on edge until the buyer says it's exactly what he wants."

"I'm the same way about my sermons," Pastor Joe agreed.

"He is," Mari confirmed. "He goes over them time and time again, asking if something makes sense and if I understand where he's going with the message."

"Giving of ourselves is important," Maggie said. "Wanting the children to perform at their best isn't wrong."

"But yelling at them is," Kim countered. "I appreciate your understanding, but please don't make excuses for my behavior. I owe you all an apology. Not only did I scream at the children, but I did it in God's house. Two no-no's. I need to ask God's forgiveness."

"I'm sure He's already forgiven you," Mari told her. "All in all, I think the rehearsal went well. Don't you?"

"I'm pleased with how it progressed," Kim said. "I think the audience will be in awe of the children's performances. I know I am."

"Tomorrow is the day," Pastor Joe said. "The costumes and props are wonderful. Not to mention the sound effects. Those driving nails are the worst. And the thunder-and-lightning scene couldn't be more realistic. Let's pray that God will bless our program."

Everyone bowed their heads as Pastor Joe led them in prayer.

After the pastor's "amen," Wyatt said, "I guess I'd better go see if Chase managed to get out of his costume."

"Thanks," Kim said when he squeezed her shoulder. "I appreciate your kindness."

"We all have our moments, Kim. Doesn't mean we're bad people. Just given to human failings."

"Amen," Pastor Joe agreed.

Chapter 14

Good Friday dawned clear and sunny, and Kim couldn't help but hope the weather was a sign of God's blessing on their performance. She sat on the balcony, enjoying the serene blues and roar of the ocean as she drank her orange juice.

She went to the store for a couple of hours but took the remainder of the day off to finalize last-minute details.

She was at the condo when her parents arrived around three. "It's so good to have you both here," Kim declared as she hugged her mother and then her father.

"You're nervous," her mom said.

Kim smiled and nodded. "Very. This is it. Good or bad, the play is over tonight."

"And God will bless this work, Kim. His work. I know He will."

"He already has. There's time for you and Daddy to take a nap if you want. I have sandwich meats in the fridge. You know where everything is. Help yourself."

"But where are you going?" her mother asked.

"Back to church. I wanted to make sure you arrived safely."

"You're a good daughter." Her mother kissed her on the cheek.

As Kim sat in the sanctuary, viewing the scenery, the full wonder of how things had come together dawned on her. God truly was in control. Not only had He given her the idea for the play, but He'd given her the people to bring that idea to fruition.

Every costume sewn and every prop built were the result of a dedicated friend who desired success for God's work. Their efforts assured Kim she would see her play at its best. Even the children were determined to excel in their performances. That knowledge enveloped Kim in peace. God would make it happen.

"I knew you'd be here," Pastor Joe said.

She smiled at him. "I can't stay away." She picked up the realistic loaf of plastic bread she'd found earlier that day. "Take a look at this."

He turned it over in his hands and shook his head in amazement. "Not even the kids can destroy this. Of course, Chase is going to have a difficult time breaking it in two."

"I have a real loaf for that. I just thought this would look good on the table.

I bought some artificial grapes, too."

"You've handled every detail. I'm impressed."

"And I've seen a side of myself I'm not particularly thrilled with," Kim told him.

"Do you think you're the only person to lose control?"

"Well, no. But that doesn't make it all right."

"God is pleased with you, Kim. You may have hurt some people, but you returned and sought their forgiveness. That's what God expects us to do."

"But what if they don't want to come back because of that?"

"Has anyone indicated that? Have any parents called?"

"Well, no," she admitted.

"I know that God plans to bless Cornerstone greatly this weekend."

She was relieved to hear him say so, then followed his gaze to the wall draped in white fabric. "Is it in place?"

Pastor Joe nodded. "The plan is to drop that curtain at the sunrise service on Easter morning."

She let out a breath and smiled. "God is so good."

"His grace is more than sufficient," Pastor Joe agreed.

A few minutes later, her heart swelled with pride as the excited children began to enter the building. Just as she expected, every child with an assigned speaking role was present. Kim felt disappointed for the stand-ins but knew that was the way of performances.

She'd reward them in the future. Meanwhile, tonight they would become part of the crowds that surrounded Jesus.

Kim gulped when Wyatt and Chase entered the room, Wyatt looking very handsome in his dark suit. "Beth's picking up Gerald at the airport, and then she'll stop by for Mom and Dad."

"Gerald's flying in for the play?"

"For Easter actually, but he came a couple of days early so he could see Chase perform." He squeezed his son's shoulder and smiled down at him.

"You'd better get into your first costume," Kim said.

Chase nodded and walked over to where Mari distributed costumes and waited in line.

"Break a leg," Wyatt told her.

"I'm so nervous," she said, holding out a trembling hand to demonstrate.

Wyatt took it in his. "Worse than Chase, and he has big shoes to fill tonight."

"That he does. Let's pray for him," Kim suggested.

She could tell Wyatt was uncomfortable, but he bowed his head as she prayed for God to work His miracles tonight for all the children's success and particularly Chase.

After saying, "amen," Kim looked up, and Wyatt winked at her.

"Let me get out of here so you can prepare."

He walked over to where Chase stood and spoke to his son. The boy flashed him a broad smile.

After Wyatt left the room, her curiosity got the best of her, so she asked Chase, "What did your dad say?"

"That I'd do Jesus proud."

Kim felt humbled by Wyatt's words to his son.

"You already have," Kim assured. "You've done your best, and that's all anyone, including God, asks."

"Thanks, Miss Kim."

She hugged him and smiled.

Over the next few minutes, confusion and chaos reigned as the adults focused on preparing the children for their roles.

"If anyone needs to visit the bathroom, go now," Kim said. "Once we get started, we'll go straight through. No bathroom breaks or do-overs tonight."

Natalie laughed at Kim's comment as she helped an angel into her costume.

"Did you sew these by hand?" Kim asked, running her finger along the sequin-covered wing straps. "I couldn't believe it when Mari said you'd glued feathers to the wings."

"I had some extra time on my hands. And a couple of extra feather pillows," she added. "What do you think of the stones?"

"I'm impressed."

"By the stones?" she asked curiously. "Or the fact that Avery and I worked together on the project?"

"Both."

"You'll never know the sacrifices I made for your success."

"God's success," Kim corrected. "He loves you for every effort you've made on His behalf."

Pastor Joe rushed into the back. "It's standing room only out there. We're gathering chairs from the classrooms for the aisles."

Kim smiled at Wyatt as he followed the pastor. "You're going to lose your seat."

He shook his head. "Beth's saving me one in the front row."

"All that advertising must have paid off. I heard it on the Christian radio station today," Mari said from across the room.

Maggie finished tying the belts on the smaller children. "I imagine the nursery is full, too. I'd better go see if they need more help."

"I asked when I dropped off the twins," Mari said. "They had it covered."

The drama team rushed around, getting everyone dressed and lined up according to his or her role.

"Look at me, Miss Kim," Bryan said, holding out his arms to reveal the colorful costume. "I look like Peter in the storybook."

"You certainly do." The fact that he stood at least a head taller as he spoke about the costume told Kim she'd made a good choice.

Mari walked along the row, shushing the rowdier kids. They had no idea how their voices carried.

Kim's butterflies took over when she heard Pastor Joe speaking to the congregation and visitors.

"We'd like to take this opportunity to welcome everyone to tonight's performance. For those of you who are first-time visitors, welcome to Cornerstone Community Church. We know without a doubt that you will be blessed by the performance of *Except for Grace.*

"The play was written by our very own Kimberly Elliott. She's been a member of Cornerstone since she was as young as some of the children you'll see performing tonight. We're doubly blessed to have the children and youth who have dedicated their time over the past few months to make this program a success.

"And now a couple of housekeeping matters." He told the audience how a child's number from the nursery might pop up on the big screens to alert the parents they were needed and then gave directions to the bathrooms.

"And now," he said, the lights going down and a drumroll sounding, "Cornerstone Community Church presents *Except for Grace.*"

As the scenes unfolded, each child spoke his or her lines with such clarity that Kim knew God was directing them. The knot in her throat competed with the moisture in her eyes as she listened to Chase say his lines perfectly. She knew hearts were being touched in that audience tonight. Hers certainly was.

It seemed the hours of practice culminated in just a few minutes. Kim shivered as the play reached the part where Jesus died on the cross while thunder rolled and lightning illuminated the darkened room. The sound effect of the curtain being rent in two could be heard throughout the building.

Jesus' body was taken from the cross and moved to the stone tomb. Chase crawled from the tomb into the choir bay and came into the back to change into his white robe while the angel comforted the women at the tomb.

There was yet another audible gasp in the congregation when Chase reappeared high in the baptismal, his arms stretched out as he spoke Jesus' words from the Gospel of Matthew.

" 'Go ye therefore, and teach all nations, baptizing them in the name of the Father, and of the Son, and of the Holy Ghost: teaching them to observe all things whatsoever I have commanded you: and, lo, I am with you always, even unto the end of the world. Amen.' "

Applause filled the room, and the adults quickly organized the children and moved them on to the stage to take a bow.

"Let's give them all another hand," Pastor Joe exclaimed with a broad smile. "Kimberly Elliott, our author and director, and the cast of *Except for Grace.*"

They bowed again.

"Tonight we've been given a glimpse into the life of Jesus Christ, our Lord and Savior," he said. "At Christmas we consider the love God showed by sending His Son to the earth.

"Easter is grace. And except for God's grace, we'd all live in a dark world, lacking the love we've been given so generously. If you don't know Him already, Jesus Christ can be the greatest love of your life. Just as young Chase demonstrated on the cross tonight, Jesus stretched out His arms to show us exactly how much He loved us.

"His gift is nothing we can buy or earn with good deeds. It's freely given with great love, and all He asks in return is that we love and serve Him. He's a refuge when the burdens of the world become too heavy. Our friend and constant companion.

"The altar is open to anyone who feels the need to come forth and give his or her life to Jesus. If you don't know what to pray, members of our congregation are here to pray with you.

"It's a difficult walk, but it gets easier with that first step. With every head bowed and every eye closed, let's sing 'Amazing Grace.' If you don't know the words, just listen and be rewarded by this wonderful song."

Kim was the first person to kneel at the altar. She thanked God for His forgiveness and offered Him praise for the success of their efforts. Others soon joined her, and she knew joy untold when Wyatt knelt at her side. Chase came down from the stage and knelt by his father.

"Hey, Dad, can I lead you in the sinner's prayer?"

Wyatt hugged his son close and whispered, "I'd be honored."

Kim looked up, and Pastor Joe motioned her over and whispered, "Kneel and pray with anyone needing assistance." He motioned for Mari, Natalie, and other adults from the play to do the same.

Members of the choir stood in the audience and continued to sing as more church members stepped forward to pray with the unsaved surrounding the altar.

After at least a dozen people accepted Jesus Christ as their Savior, Pastor Joe held up his hand to stop the music. "You're all invited to join the cast for refreshments in the church fellowship hall. Just follow the hallway. Now I think we should give the cast and volunteers another round of applause."

After the applause died down, he said, "The sanctuary will remain open for any of you who would like to return and pray at the altar."

A jubilant group gathered in the fellowship hall.

The dessert table held the donations from Avery, Natalie, and other members of the congregation. As usual, Natalie had outdone herself, and several smaller cakes with photos from the play airbrushed on them sat on the table. She stood nearby with a knife in hand.

"They're too pretty to eat!" Kim cried when she started to serve.

"Don't worry. I took photos for you. Plus I have the photos I used on the cakes themselves. They're from the rehearsal."

Kim felt someone's hand on her shoulder and turned to find Beth standing there. "Wasn't Chase wonderful?"

The woman's eyes were bright with unshed tears. "He was perfect for the role. And then when Wyatt. . .I'm so happy."

Kim hugged her and whispered, "I thought I'd lose it when Chase came down in that white robe and knelt to pray with his father."

"I know," Beth said softly.

Kim glanced around the room. "Where are your parents?"

"Over there with Wyatt. I just wanted to tell you how much we enjoyed the play."

"Thanks for all your help."

Beth squeezed her hand and stepped aside for the next person to offer their congratulations. Kim made the rounds, speaking to the parents, saying how much she enjoyed their children, and inviting those who didn't attend the church to visit Cornerstone again.

She grabbed a plate of food and took a minute to rest her feet, when Wyatt came over to sit with her.

"Too bad the local paper doesn't do reviews," he commented. "The public would demand an encore performance."

Kim smiled at him. "The children did a wonderful job. Makes all my doubts seem so insignificant."

"I know it certainly affected me."

"I'm so happy for you, Wyatt. I know Chase is ecstatic."

"I feel good," he admitted. "It's something I should have done years ago when I convinced myself I didn't need a relationship with God. Now I know I do."

"We all do," Kim said. "We were created to worship. We may spend years searching, but God is all we need."

He nodded. "I'm looking forward to the future."

"Thanks for coming, Wyatt. The play wouldn't have been the same without your efforts."

"God has been at work in a number of lives lately. I'm thankful mine is one of them."

He hugged her and said good night.

⁓

Early Easter Sunday, Kim was seated in the sanctuary for the sunrise service, when Wyatt and Chase entered. Her parents, whose seats she was saving, were talking with friends a few pews back.

"Mind if we sit with you?"

She slid over to make room for them. "Not at all."

"You look beautiful. I like your Easter suit."

"I like yours, too."

"What, this old thing?" he asked, pulling on the lapels of the suit he wore.

Kim laughed. "Chase has already told me you two went shopping for new suits yesterday."

Wyatt grinned at his son. "You can dress him up, but you can't take him anywhere."

"You both look very handsome."

"Pastor Joe will be preaching to a full house today," Wyatt said, glancing around at the pews.

"Wonderful play, Kim." She smiled at the member who complimented her. Her fear that change would hurt the church proved itself unjustified as several more people gave their compliments before the pianist played the opening music. Her heart filled to overflowing when some of the older members took time to tell Wyatt how glad they were to see him at Cornerstone again.

When her parents returned to their seats, they greeted Wyatt and Chase. At her mother's questioning look, Kim shook her head and turned her attention to the pulpit.

As always, the message of Easter brought tears to her eyes.

"As some of you are aware, we started a beautification fund awhile back." Pastor Joe walked over and untied the string that held the curtain in place. "Today we dedicate the Good Shepherd window. May it represent the grace and love of Jesus Christ to all those who enter Cornerstone Community Church."

The fabric fluttered to the floor, exposing the Good Shepherd and His sheep in the stained glass window.

"It's beautiful," Kim whispered in awe.

"Isn't it, though?" Wyatt agreed.

After the service, Pastor Joe gave an altar call, inviting anyone who cared to join the church to come forward. Wyatt moved to the front of the church and spoke to the minister before taking a front row seat.

Afterward Pastor Joe invited the congregation to extend the right hand of fellowship to the new members.

Kim smiled as she shook his hand. "Welcome to Cornerstone, Wyatt."

"Thanks, Kim."

"Your salvation means a great deal to a number of people. I hate to welcome and run, but I need to get home and work on lunch. Maggie's joining us."

"We're going to Mom and Dad's." He squeezed her hand. "Thanks again, Kim."

"Happy Easter, Wyatt."

Chapter 15

So what do you think about Wyatt Alexander joining Cornerstone?" her mother asked as they worked together in the kitchen.

"I'm very happy for him and his family."

"Do you love him?"

"He's a friend."

Her mother appeared skeptical. "If you say so, but I suspect you're in deeper than you realize."

Kim lifted the pot lid and checked the green beans. Giving them a final stir, she poured them into a bowl. "I have no doubt Jesus can make a difference in Wyatt, but he has a long path ahead of him. I'm holding firm to my vow."

"I suspect you'll have your hands full, making him understand you're interested in him only as a friend."

"I gave God control of my love life, Mom. I have to await His answer."

The doorbell rang, and her mother squeezed Kim's hand in understanding before going to answer the door. Kim could hear her welcoming Maggie. They came into the kitchen and, after catching up, talked about the Elliotts' journeys in their RV.

"The places you've visited sound wonderful." Maggie looked at Kim. "We should leave them here to handle things and go see for ourselves."

Her mom laughed. "As long as Jimmy could play golf, he wouldn't complain."

Maggie sighed. "Maybe one day I can get away. But I have to go back to work next week."

Kim's mother slid her arm around Maggie's waist. "That was a wonderful thing you did for Mrs. Allene."

"I loved her a great deal."

She nodded. "Kim told me around the house. Have you worked through that yet?"

"Not really. We went to the lawyer's office the other day, and I offered to sign it back over to Dillon. The lawyer objected, though. He said Mrs. Allene said I'd do that, and she wanted me to have the house. Now I feel like I'm dishonoring her wishes by saying no."

"I agree. Allene knew what she wanted. You've been like a daughter to her these past few years."

"I never expected anything more than her friendship. She also listed several items from her house that she wanted me to have."

"Well, Dillon will have to come to grips with his mother's will. Although he inherited his mother's house, I doubt he plans to stick around. He hasn't lived here for years."

"Maybe he's considering an investment for his retirement years," Kim suggested as she pulled the ham from the oven.

"Mrs. Allene told me he's fairly well-to-do," Maggie said.

"So he doesn't even need the rental house," Kim said. "He probably sees his mother's actions as a slight to his being her only child. I can't believe he's still treating you this way," she added.

Maggie looked at Kim's mother. "Let's drop the subject before we get Kim stirred up."

"Doesn't take much for that," her mother said.

"Hey, no dissing the cook allowed."

They laughed. "What can we do to help?"

"Everything's ready."

Kim arranged the items along the island front, using it as a buffet. Her mom called her dad to the table.

"Maggie," Kim's dad said as he walked into the kitchen, opening his arms. "Good to see you."

"You, too, Mr. Jimmy. Retirement agrees with you."

"I can't complain. We've seen a lot of the states in our travels."

"And a lot of golf courses, I hear," Maggie teased.

"My fair share," he countered with a grin.

Everyone enjoyed the meal and reminisced about past Easters. "Did Cornerstone have its egg hunt this year?" her mother asked.

Kim nodded. "Mari said they had a good turnout."

"This has been a memorable Easter. Seeing our daughter's play performed so beautifully was such a blessing."

"Kimmie did good," her dad said.

"I can't take the credit. The play was nothing without the children and the adults who gave their all."

Her father lifted his tea glass. "Here's to Cornerstone's success."

"Here, here," Maggie said, tapping her glass against his.

"So when does your kitchen renovation start?" her mother asked.

"We talked about this month, but it depends on where Wyatt stands with the cabinets. He took measurements a few weeks ago. You won't know the place when we finish."

"Do you have the plans here?" her mother asked.

"Wyatt has my folder. I'm getting everything I've always wanted."

"Good thing it's a small kitchen," her dad said.

"I started a kitchen fund when I bought the condo."

"I'm eager to see the end result," Maggie said.

After the meal, they cleared the table and moved to the living room. The afternoon passed quickly, and soon Maggie said good-bye so Kim could have some time alone with her parents. They were leaving again on Wednesday.

"It was wonderful seeing you both," Maggie declared, giving them each a hug. "Have fun in Florida."

"There's room if you want to tag along," Kim's dad offered.

"Hey, you didn't invite me along!" Kim exclaimed.

"Someone has to keep the business running," her father said.

"He only invited me because he knows I play golf," Maggie teased.

Chapter 16

Kim found she missed the practices and deadlines and knew life would have been boring without the kitchen renovation. On Thursday Wyatt called to tell her to pack up the kitchen. He arrived with help on Saturday morning, and they gutted the room in a few hours, leaving nothing more than an empty shell.

"We're going to pick up the cabinets and start putting them in place. Did you order the appliances?"

Kim nodded. "They have them in stock. I need to call when we're ready for them."

"Good idea. I think maybe by next Monday. Did you decide on flooring yet?"

"I'm still waffling between hardwood and tile."

"The wood might be better since you're having granite countertops. Have you considered expanding it into the living room?"

"I'm thinking about it."

"You need to decide soon." He hesitated. "What are you doing next Saturday? I promised Chase an outing to the beach. Want to come with us?"

Kim thought about the invitation. Spring fever had struck, and she was ready to enjoy the sunshine, but she wasn't sure. "You and Chase would have more fun alone," she said instead.

"I can't swim with him."

Kim had forgotten about Wyatt's missing foot. "Sure. Okay. You can come here, and we can go down to the beach."

"Beth suggested that, too. She said we could come up to her condo to shower and change."

"Sounds like a plan. If you finish my kitchen, I'll fix us something to eat."

"Are you trying to tempt me to work faster?"

"Of course not," Kim said with a broad grin.

"Good. It won't work. Your kitchen is a work in progress. Besides, everybody knows we need junk food to make the day worthwhile."

"What time?"

"Is nine too early?"

"We'd probably need to go a bit later. The water will be cold without the sun."

Wyatt shrugged. "I haven't walked in the water for a long time."

"Wear shorts, and we'll give it a test run."

"I don't want people staring at my prosthesis."

"Everything gets easier with practice, Wyatt. After a couple of looks most people accept things and move on."

"Can you?" he asked.

"I don't know why not. Does Chase have a problem?"

"He's intrigued. I had to show him how the prosthesis worked when he came to stay with me. He seems okay with it now."

"So maybe I'll be intrigued, too," Kim said in an effort to lighten the discussion. "You'll have to show me how it works."

"I can do that."

❧

The Saturday of their outing dawned clear and bright. The weather report promised no rain, and Kim hoped it was right. She hated those surprise rains that left a person damp and out of sorts.

All week she'd told herself she was doing this only to help a friend. But she'd taken time to buy new clothes that included a one-piece swimsuit, a pair of capri pants, and a print shirt. She'd even bought a new pair of sneakers.

Wyatt had made progress in the kitchen. All the new cabinets were in place, and the countertop was scheduled for Monday. The hardwood floor and tile installations had been completed on Friday.

Of course, all sorts of details still needed to be handled, including plumbing and lighting. And she needed to finalize her paint choice.

When the doorbell rang, Kim quickly wrapped her sarong around her waist and slipped on her flip-flops. She grabbed her beach blanket and tote bag on the way out. "Ready?" she asked after opening the door.

Chase wore his swim trunks with a T-shirt, and Wyatt had on khaki shorts with a T-shirt and sandals. Kim caught herself glancing down at his artificial limb. "You'll do."

He seemed uncomfortable. "We'll see."

"Let's find a place on the beach before it fills up."

They rode the elevator and took the stairs down to the beach. Already people dotted the area. "How about here?" Kim asked, spreading the beach blanket. Chase and Wyatt nodded agreement.

"Ready to get wet, Chase?"

"Yeah," he responded enthusiastically.

"Hold on," she said, pulling a tube of sunscreen from her bag. "Put some of this on."

Kim had already applied her sunscreen, so she untied the sarong, kicked off her flip-flops, and said, "Race you to the water."

The two of them played in the waves for several minutes before Kim suggested they head back to the beach. Chase shook his hair, spraying water all over his dad. Wyatt grabbed his son and wrestled him to the blanket.

Kim grabbed a towel from her tote. "Here, Chase, dry your hair." He dried off a little, then started down the beach to study a jellyfish that had washed up on shore. She noticed Wyatt staring at her. "What?"

"I've never seen you without makeup. You look good."

"The beach is the only place I go without my war paint."

"You don't need it. You have beautiful eyes."

Kim could feel her cheeks grow warm. "Thanks. Did you hear from Beth yet?"

Wyatt nodded. "The move is definite. They've been assigned military housing."

"How is Chase adapting?" She spotted him wandering in the distance.

"I think he's okay. He's picked out paint for his room and wants me to build a bookcase and desk."

"Is he planning to help?"

"Do you doubt it?"

Chase had shown more than a passing interest in the work being done in her kitchen when he'd accompanied his father.

"He's been looking for plans online. He's even found the complicated plans to build secret compartments."

"Every kid needs a hiding place."

"He's got Ole Blue sleeping on a rug by his bed. I told him Blue was a yard dog, but he broke me down."

Kim laughed. "I bet that dog is in heaven with a kid in the picture."

"They get along well."

"Let's explore with him a bit," Kim suggested.

"You go ahead. I'll wait here."

Kim shook her head. "It's your day with your son. You can't sit on the beach and leave him to entertain himself. Nor can you expect me to entertain him."

"Okay," Wyatt growled, removing his sandals. "This will probably be a first for this beach. Prepare yourself for the finger-pointing and whispering."

"I'll ignore them if you will."

"Deal." They shook on it, and Wyatt retained his grasp of Kim's hand.

The two of them walked along the shore to where Chase danced in a shallow pool of water. "Hey, Dad!" he called. "Did you see that monster jellyfish back there?"

"Sure did. Be careful around them. They have quite a sting."

"You ever get stung?"

"I stepped on one in the water once."

"Hey, if you stepped on him with your fake foot, he couldn't hurt you," Chase said.

Kim looked at Wyatt and smiled. "That's one way of looking at it. You guys want to build a sandcastle? I have some buckets in my condo storage unit."

"Let's build something different," Wyatt suggested.

"Can we make a gator or a croc?" Chase asked eagerly. "I like gators best."

"You wouldn't if one of them got you in his teeth." Kim grabbed him about the waist.

"Oh, he's too tough to be good gator bait," Wyatt teased, ruffling his son's hair.

Chase grinned at his dad. "You're tougher than me."

The three of them were still on the beach at around one o'clock. Chase and Wyatt showed amazing talent with their sand gator and drew several interested onlookers.

Kim stood up and brushed the sand off her hands. "You guys ready for a shower and a snack?"

"Dad said we could get hot dogs."

"Well, let's get moving then. I'm ready for lunch."

Back at the condos they went their separate ways to shower and change. Wyatt exchanged his shorts for khaki slacks, but Kim didn't push the issue. A trip to the beach was a major accomplishment.

Wyatt and Chase took her to a little hot dog place they'd found and liked.

"Hope you like this place," Wyatt said as he held the door for Kim.

"I love a good hot dog."

After they received their food and slipped into a booth, they prayed, then attacked their food with the healthy appetite of people who had spent hours in the sun.

"Dad, can we play putt-putt this afternoon?"

"What do you think, Kim?"

She laughed. "My dad would love him."

They chose the largest place on King's Highway and spent the next couple of hours challenging each other. Afterward, they climbed into the truck and went to the arcade. There they crowded into a photo booth and made faces at the camera. Kim couldn't keep up with the men as they ate cotton candy, snow cones, and ice cream and downed mega cups of soda.

"You guys ready to call it a day?" Kim asked. "I need to check in at the store."

"Ah, do we have to?"

Wyatt placed his hand on his son's shoulder. "You heard Miss Kim. She has things to do. And I promised Aunt Beth we'd take your grandmother to the grocery store."

"I forgot."

"We'll do this again," Wyatt promised.

They walked back to the truck, and Wyatt drove Kim home.

Kim said, "You guys sure you don't want to finish my kitchen tonight?"

"Can we, Dad?"

"I'm teasing, Chase. We can't do anything else until we get the counter-tops in."

"What will you do for dinner?" the boy asked.

"My fridge is in the living room with my microwave. I have some food I can heat and eat."

"Can we remodel our kitchen, Dad?"

"Not now. We need to build your desk and bookcases."

"Can we work on those tonight?"

"I don't think so. After we visit your grandparents, we need to study our Sunday school lessons." He glanced at Kim. "Did I tell you I signed up for the new-Christians' class?"

"Don't they do those on Sunday mornings during Sunday school?"

Wyatt nodded. "I want to join the Bible study class, too."

Kim recalled that first fire in a new Christian. "That's a good idea."

He parked in his sister's parking space. "Wait here, Chase. I'm going to walk Miss Kim upstairs and get those wet clothes we left in Beth's condo."

They took the elevator up to the second floor.

"I really enjoyed myself today."

Wyatt propped himself against the side of the elevator. "I did, too. And there's no telling when Chase will run down. I have a feeling we're going to work on the birdhouse tonight."

She laughed, and Wyatt did, too. Kim found the sound pleasing. "He doesn't want the day to end."

"Neither do I," Wyatt admitted. "Thanks for making it special."

"I didn't do anything but have fun."

"I need someone to teach me how to do that."

The elevator door opened, and she stepped into the walkway. "Follow Chase's lead. He'll keep you young."

Wyatt stepped out, too. "No, seriously, I need you in my life, Kim." She turned and looked up at him. "I'm not saying this very well, but I care a great deal for you."

"I care for you, too, Wyatt. You and Chase."

"As friends? Or could it be more?"

Could it be more? Kim already knew the answer in her heart. Her feelings for Wyatt Alexander were strong, but she was afraid. Despite the feeling she should step out on faith, she couldn't help but wonder if she would be making a mistake.

"Only God knows what the future holds," she told him.

Chapter 17

Wyatt was in Kim's apartment when she arrived home Monday afternoon. She could see Chase doing his homework on the balcony.

"Whew." The scent of the stain filled her nostrils. "I'm surprised you have any sinuses left."

He grinned. "I took off the mask when I helped Chase get set up out there. I figured it's too smelly in here for him."

The balcony doors were open, and the ocean breezes helped a little.

"Did you fix him a snack?" Kim asked as she glanced through the mail.

"I picked him up from school, and we stopped on the way over here."

She moved closer to where he had touched up the stain on her new cabinets. "Oh, my counters," she cried, running her hand over the shiny black granite. "They're beautiful. I can't wait to see everything in place."

"The appliances arrive tomorrow. Did you set up a plumber to connect the ice maker, dishwasher, and sink?"

Kim nodded. "He's coming on Thursday."

"So you'll have a kitchen by the weekend. We should celebrate."

"I'll celebrate by putting my house back together."

"You can do that anytime. I'm offering a picnic at Brookgreen Gardens. Just the two of us. Chase is spending the day with Beth." He appeared excited by the idea.

"I do work, you know."

"Can't you get someone to cover for you?" he asked with a hint of disappointment in his tone.

"Why Brookgreen Gardens?"

Wyatt shrugged. "I thought about what you might enjoy. I considered the theaters but don't know what you've seen or want to see. Then I thought about the gardens and figured the fresh air and statuary would appeal to you."

"I haven't been to the gardens since I was a kid," she admitted.

"Say yes, Kim."

"The best I can offer is I'll let you know."

"Oh, come on. You know you want to."

Kim shook her head at his coaxing. "I think you're jumping the gun. My kitchen isn't completed." Her nose wrinkled as the fumes filled her head. "How much of that stuff are you planning to put on today?"

"Just this coat. Beth said you could sleep over at her place if it's too strong.

227

She's coming back to pack. That's one reason she wants Chase. He has to sort through his stuff and decide what's going to my house."

"So you've agreed to make it a permanent thing?"

"We're going to see what Chase thinks Friday night."

"I'm sure he'll want to stay with you."

Wyatt looked hopeful. "I've enjoyed having him around. I've missed out on so much of his life."

Kim prayed Chase would choose his father. She knew losing his son at this point would break Wyatt's heart. "I have a good feeling about you two," Kim said. "Decide what you want me to do while I change."

As she traded her work clothes for an old pair of jeans and a T-shirt, Kim thought about how much she'd enjoyed having Wyatt around lately. Coming home to him and Chase most afternoons had brightened her former quiet existence.

With her parents on the road, she missed having family nearby. Maggie had returned to work, and Mari was busy with her family. Julie and Noah were doing the newlywed thing, and Natalie was busy as well.

Maybe she would agree to go with him. She hadn't seen Brookgreen Gardens in years. And secretly Kim admitted it pleased her that Wyatt had thought about what she might enjoy.

Back in the kitchen Kim helped stain the island cabinets. They talked about a variety of topics, including the Bible study class Wyatt attended. The group was studying the book of Romans, and Kim had been reading along to keep up with his questions.

"You promise to think about Saturday?" he asked.

"Okay, I'll agree to the gardens if you let me provide the picnic."

"Sounds like a plan. Chase and I have enjoyed those dinners you and Maggie prepared."

⤜⤛

As they entered the gardens on Saturday, Kim admired the fighting stallion sculpture that welcomed them.

"Beautiful work," she commented.

Wyatt was in a good mood. Chase had chosen to live with his dad even though he wanted to visit his aunt regularly as well. Wyatt had no problem with that. It was the least he could do after all he'd put them through. He paid their admission and followed the signs to the picnic area where they spread the food on the table.

Wyatt said, "I think you must be blessed when it comes to good weather and outings. Last time we came we brought my grandmother, my aunt, and my cousins. It started to rain the minute they laid out the food, so we had to grab everything and jump back into the car to wait it out.

"Then things went from bad to worse. My grandmother could get around, but she was slow. Every time she was a hundred feet away from the car, the rain started. We spent the day walking around with umbrellas. We found a wheelchair for Granny, and two of my cousins pushed her so fast she nearly ended up in the reflecting pool. The adults took control of the chair after that. My dad stopped at one point and said he was never coming back to the gardens."

Kim struggled to keep from laughing. "Did he?"

"No."

They laughed together. "We had the same kind of outings," Kim said. "There's nothing like cowering under a shelter with a hundred other people while the storm rages on."

"I have something for you."

Kim opened the wrapped package to find a beautifully carved cross box. "I thought the cross might remind you of our first meeting. Then again, maybe it would be best if I didn't remind you of that."

"It's beautiful. And I'll always remember how you helped me with the play. Thank you so much."

"Open it."

Kim lifted the lid to find an exquisite cut-diamond ring tucked into the folds of velvet he'd placed inside the box.

Startled, she looked at him. "I don't understand."

"I love you, Kim."

"Wyatt?"

"Wait. Hear me out. I know I've blindsided you with this, but I wanted to state my intentions. I enjoy being with you. After Karen, I never believed I'd love again, but you changed that. I know we can have a good life."

"How can you be sure?" she asked. "When it comes to love, I've made more mistakes than I care to count. Truthfully I'm not sure I'm capable of making any relationship work. I wouldn't want to hurt you or Chase."

"You wouldn't," Wyatt said, shaking his head.

"There's so much I have to let go of before I could be a good wife. I have serious trust issues when it comes to men."

"You can trust me," Wyatt told her. "After we married, Karen was the only woman in my life. I didn't cheat on her or lie to her. I worked hard to provide for her and my son."

"But your life fell apart."

"Because we didn't have God. Don't get me wrong," he said when she started to object. "I know there's no promise life will be perfect with God in it, but I believe it's better because He's there for us. I have many regrets. My stupidity cost me a great deal, but I'm ready to move on. To have you as my wife, to give Chase a couple of siblings, and to make my house a home again."

"Oh, Wyatt, I can't say yes."

"That's okay, Kim. I didn't expect you to agree right away."

She felt confused. "Then why did you buy a ring?"

"To show I'm not giving up. I intend to persevere just as God has persevered all these years to make me His. I've prayed about this. I know we're right for each other, and I think that once you give your doubts over to God you'll agree."

She pushed the box back across the table toward him.

Wyatt rested his hand on top of hers. "Keep it. If you decide you can't marry me, you can return the ring, but the box is yours—a symbol of how God used you to touch my heart."

His words caused her to tear up. "I'm so sorry, Wyatt. Please don't think I don't love you and Chase. I just have to be sure. I can't risk having my heart broken again."

Wyatt looked almost sad. "You know, Kim, I think you should look at Chase as a prime example of how God works through us. My son has absolutely no reason to love me. I was a vague, shadowy figure in the background of his life, but when I came out of the darkness, he welcomed me with open arms. He prayed for my salvation and loves me with the innocence of a child. Who does that remind you of?"

"Jesus," she whispered.

Wyatt nodded. "I can't begin to promise to have Chase's ability to love so easily, but one thing is for sure—without God's grace I'd be more lost than I've ever been. Today and for the rest of my life I have a promise of light. I'd like for you to share that light with me."

When she didn't say anything, Wyatt only said, "Eat up. We have lots to see."

Chapter 18

W hat did you do yesterday?" Maggie asked at the fellowship following church the next morning. "I called the store to see if you wanted to go to dinner, but Ruby said you were off."

"I spent the day at Brookgreen Gardens with Wyatt," she admitted.

"I've never been there. I've heard the area is beautiful."

Kim was surprised Maggie didn't comment on her date with Wyatt. "I enjoyed myself. The statuary is outstanding, and they have so many other activities."

"I'm sure spending time with Wyatt made it even more fun."

"Oh, Maggie, I'm so confused," Kim told her. "I know Wyatt has given his life to God, but I can't get past the feeling that no one changes overnight."

"Do you feel God expects that of us?"

Kim shrugged. "I don't want to give away another chunk of my heart to a man who isn't interested in being there for me."

"And you think Wyatt would do that?"

"I'm too afraid of being hurt to take the risk."

"People in happy, loving relationships get hurt, too, Kim. But they communicate, forgive, forget, and move on with their lives. Have you put your life on pause forever because of the last guy you dated?"

Kim grimaced at the thought. "I guess I have."

"And you want to stay there, locked in the misery you feel?"

"No, I want a husband and children."

"Then shouldn't you be listening to God instead of yourself? How can God send you someone to love if you doubt every man He sends?"

Kim tossed the empty coffee cup into the trash. "How do I determine the ones He sends? Wyatt has a considerable past to deal with. I'm afraid his baggage and my own would be too much for us as a couple."

"Has he indicated it's more than a friendship?"

"He proposed."

Maggie gasped and grabbed Kim's hand, pulling her over to a private corner. "And you didn't call me?"

"I was in shock," Kim admitted. "Before the picnic, he handed me a hand-carved cross box. It's beautiful."

Maggie nodded. "Get to the part about the proposal. Did he give you a ring?"

"Yes, he put it in the box. The ring is beautiful. Expensive."

"What did you say?"

"That I wasn't ready yet. He's willing to wait."

"Did you have any idea?"

"He's made references to the future and needing me in his life. How can I be sure it's not seeing him so often with the kitchen renovation? Now that that's done, maybe I can get my jumbled life back in order—and be able to think more clearly."

"Good luck," Maggie said with more than a little sarcasm. "When you figure it out, let me know how. I haven't sorted out my thoughts since Mrs. Allene's death."

"I've seen Dillon here at Cornerstone a few times. Mrs. Allene would be pleased to know he's attending regularly—though I thought he'd be gone by now."

"He's decided to stay for the summer."

"Any word on the house?"

"He told me to call off my defenders. Said he got the message. What does that mean?" Maggie asked, her expression perplexed.

"You don't think someone confronted him about his behavior, do you?"

"Surely not," Maggie whispered. "I'd never want anyone to do that."

It occurred to Kim that Maggie and Dillon would make a nice couple. She must have love on the brain. "I think we have some powerful praying to do," Kim said. "I should tell Mari, Natalie, and Julie."

"Since you have the renovated kitchen to show off, why don't we plan a lunch at your place next week?"

Kim grinned. "Or we could go out and I could talk about my new kitchen."

"You don't have to cook. We can all bring something."

"I'll take care of everything," Kim promised. "And I'll be in prayer for you. You do the same for me."

~

It was the following Thursday night before the women could arrange their schedules to get together for dinner. Mari, Julie, and Maggie arrived together.

"Where's Natalie?" Kim asked.

"She has to drop off a birthday cake, and then she'll be here," Julie said. "She's bringing a special treat."

"Umm. Natalie's treats are always worthwhile."

"I think she's using us as taste testers," Julie told them. "She's experimenting with some new chocolate ideas and wants our opinion. She's getting ready to branch out into something new."

"I hope she doesn't overdo," Maggie said.

"I think she'll be sensible," Mari told them. "Look what she gave up when she realized it was too stressful for her. Hey, let's see this wonderful new kitchen."

The women oohed and aahed over the renovated kitchen. "Maybe one day

I'll get my own cabinetry by Alexander," Maggie said, running her hand along the smooth finish. "This is gorgeous."

"I wouldn't mind some new cabinets myself," Mari said. "Think the church would spring for a kitchen renovation?"

"I could donate—," Julie began.

"Don't even think about it," Mari interrupted.

"She's as bad as Joey," Julie grumbled. "They won't let me do anything."

Mari wrapped her arm around Julie's shoulders. "You help in more tangible ways. It's nice having an instant babysitter." She turned to Kim. "So what's for dinner?"

"Have a seat in the living room. I have appetizers."

Kim carried in a tray of veggies, fruits, and dips and poured water with lemon for everyone. "I kept it light."

"I'm delighted with any meal I don't have to prepare," Julie said.

"Did you and Noah find a place yet?" Kim asked after handing Julie a glass.

"Not yet. Noah thought Beth Erikson might want to sell her place, but she's planning to rent it week to week."

"I think she wants to keep it so she can vacation here."

"Cheaper than shelling out a couple of thousand for a week at the beach," Julie agreed.

The doorbell rang, and Kim excused herself.

"Sorry I'm late, but these will make up for it." Natalie slid the tray onto the new countertop, looking around. "You really did this place up right."

"Thanks," Kim said, checking out the chocolate-covered fruit and candies. "You didn't have to bring anything, but we're glad you did. What would you like to drink?"

"You have any soda? I've been craving it for weeks, but I don't dare keep any in the house."

"Caffeine-free okay?"

"Sounds wonderful."

The women visited for a few minutes longer before they moved to the table for the meal. Everyone enjoyed the lemon chicken and rice pilaf with green beans.

"That kitchen must have some powerful effects on your cooking abilities," Maggie teased. "I didn't know you had it in you."

"I can cook, I just hate cooking for one."

"I know what you mean," Natalie agreed. "Good thing I like salads."

"Kim, when are you going to tell them?" Maggie asked.

"Tell us what?" Julie asked eagerly.

"Wyatt proposed," Maggie volunteered.

"Do you mind?" Kim said with a look of dismay.

The other three women glanced from one to the other. "Okay, give," Julie demanded.

"Wyatt and I went out last Saturday, and he gave me this." She slid the box on the table.

"Oh, that's beautiful!" Mari cried, running her finger along the carving.

Kim nodded. "He said it's to remind me of our first meeting."

"So how did he propose?" Natalie asked.

"Lift the lid."

One by one the women studied the diamond inside.

"I was speechless."

"You told him no, didn't you?" Julie guessed.

Kim glanced down at the box that rested in her hands. "Actually, I told him I wasn't sure."

"Why?" Natalie asked.

"I have to be sure."

"You think he doesn't love you?" Julie asked.

"No. I'm sure about that. I just don't know if either of us can get beyond our pasts and move on."

"Don't let the past keep you from being happy. I nearly lost Noah for that very reason," Julie told her. "I judged him wrongly, and what we have today would never have happened if God hadn't directed our paths. I've never been happier, and I owe it all to God."

"I love Wyatt and Chase, but the fear of risking my heart again scares me to death."

"My very wise husband once reminded me God didn't give me the sense of fear," Julie said.

"What do you want most in the world, Kim?" Mari asked.

"To be loved and have a family."

"Then you know what you have to do, don't you?"

"Pray harder?" Kim asked with a playful grimace.

"We'll pray with you," Maggie said. "I like Wyatt. Of course, if you married him, you'd have to give up this wonderful kitchen."

"Who says?" Kim asked. "He could live here."

"But it would be more feasible for you to live at his house. His business is there."

"We have a ways to go before we reach that point."

"You think?" Julie teased. "I'd say you're closer to saying yes than you realize."

More than a little afraid Julie might be right, Kim changed the subject. "And what about Natalie? Aren't we concerned she's taking on too much?"

Natalie snorted. "You have to be talking about work. Everyone knows the only man I have chasing after me wants to run me out of town."

"No change between you and Avery?" Mari asked.

Natalie shook her head. "Now he's angry because I offered to help with the props. And because my photo cakes were noticed at the play reception. And maybe because it rained last Tuesday. Who knows?"

"Another reason we need to be in prayer for each other," Kim said.

"I already pray for each of you every day," Mari said.

They all nodded.

"Let's pray more specific prayers," Julie suggested. "That Kim can work out her relationship with Wyatt, Maggie and Dillon can come to an agreement over the estate, Maggie and Natalie will find the loves of their lives—and that I learn to keep my mouth shut."

"What about me?" Mari asked.

"We just thank God for you."

"Amen to that. Natalie, pull that tray of chocolates over here and tell us what you're planning," Kim said.

Dessert turned into the best part of the meal.

"I'm thinking of offering chocolate parties. I bought a chocolate fountain, and it got me to thinking it would be a good party-catering activity."

"Would you try to do it alone?"

"You don't have to worry about me. I know my limitations. I remember that attack, and I don't ever plan to have another one."

Mari held out her hand, and Julie grasped it in hers. They continued until they formed a circle around the table.

"Let's seek God's guidance."

Chapter 19

The power of prayer kept Kim going over the next few days. Now that Wyatt had finished the kitchen she didn't see him daily, but they talked on the phone every night just before bed. He'd promised not to rush her, and he hadn't.

They discussed their families and work, and Wyatt shared scriptures he'd read. She thought about how wonderful it would be to have him there with her. The first time he spoke of how different the church was from what he remembered, Kim whispered a prayer of thanks. She suspected God was working His changes in Wyatt.

He sat with her during church services, and she'd joined the Bible study. She helped him stain when he had a deadline, and he'd done a couple of favors for her at Eclectics. She'd even helped build Chase's bookcases, and desk, figuring out how to make the secret drawers for the desk.

She joined his family for Sunday lunch a couple of times. The experience gave Kim a glimpse into Wyatt's relationship with his father. The man had high expectations for his son and grandson and didn't mind voicing his opinion. Knowing Wyatt had made his peace with his father had done her heart a world of good.

Chase was playing soccer, and he invited her to his games. Kim enjoyed sitting in the bleachers with Wyatt and cheering for his son.

Everything was fine until she allowed fear to take control. Wyatt had become adept at figuring out the worst times for her, and those were the times when he backed off.

The past Saturday they'd gone out to breakfast, and while dining alfresco they shared the paper. She was taken aback by an old boyfriend's wedding announcement and voiced her thoughts. "What does she have that I didn't?"

"I'm thankful," Wyatt said when she tossed down the paper. "God intended you for me."

"Maybe He doesn't intend me for anyone."

"He does," Wyatt returned. "Having you in my life has made a major change in me. I am the happiest I have ever been."

Kim smiled at the thought. "I am happy, too, until I give in to these pity parties."

He squeezed her hand. "Then don't. Let yourself love and be loved."

"I'm trying." A tiny smile touched her mouth. "There's another major issue standing in the way of my decision."

"What's that?" he asked curiously.

"I could never give up my kitchen."

Wyatt laughed hard. "But wouldn't you prefer a house to the condo?"

"I suppose if I settled some of the details in my mind, I might not feel so overwhelmed. We should talk about what we both expect of marriage."

They drove to the beach and strolled along the sandy shore. Even at that early hour the beach was filled with families and sunbathers enjoying the beautiful spring weather. The roar of the waves provided a soothing background for their discussion.

"I could sell the house, and we could live in your condo," Wyatt offered.

"But your business. Ole Blue."

"I'd have to find another place to do my woodwork. And a home for the dog. But I'd do it for you."

"It wouldn't be fair to Chase. He's getting used to your place. You have to think about him, too."

"It's not as if he's not used to the condos."

"And you're willing to turn your life upside down to have me as your wife?"

"Not exactly," Wyatt said. "I'm willing to make sacrifices, but I'd expect equal consideration from you."

"We both know marriage is about give and take, Wyatt. But you'd be miserable in the condo, and you know it."

"We could sell both places and find something we all like."

Kim bent to pick up a seashell and examined the detail before dropping it onto the sand. "The condo isn't enough for a larger family."

"So you're agreeable to children?"

"Of course I am."

"That's one major issue out of the way. What about work? Do I need to find a job that pays better?"

"Would more money make you happier?"

"It's about supporting a wife and family, Kim."

"I have my income from Eclectics. I hadn't planned to stop working when I marry."

"So the only thing in question is where we'll live?"

"I think there's probably more to it than that."

Wyatt was silent for a few minutes longer before he stopped walking and reached for her hands. "Can I make a suggestion? I thought maybe we could talk to Pastor Joe about premarital counseling."

"But—"

Wyatt rested his finger against her lips. "It's a way to resolve more of your doubts."

"You don't have any doubts?"

"Not about making you my wife. My doubts have to do with my self-esteem. Mostly my handicap. And being a good husband and father."

"Do you think we might give people the wrong idea if we enrolled in pre-marital counseling?"

"What are you thinking, Kim? Is there any chance you'll marry me?"

"Wyatt. . .you know. . ."

"Sounds like we're both wasting our time," he said, releasing her hands. "I'll drop you at home and go pick up Chase."

Kim caught Wyatt's arm. "Talking to Pastor Joe is a good idea. Let's ask tomorrow after the service."

"Are you sure?"

"I care for you a great deal, and I'd never want to do anything to hurt you or Chase. If I didn't believe there was hope for us, I'd end this right now."

"Can you at least tell me what I'm fighting against? Are you expecting God to release you from your vow?"

"No. I'm more determined than ever to be sure I don't make another mistake."

"Does Chase frighten you?"

He raised a question she had considered. "What would I be to your son?"

"His mother, stepmother, guardian."

"But what do you expect of me?"

"To love and guide him in his life."

"And if we disagree? What if I see things differently from you?"

"I suspect you'd be softer on him than I'd be, Kim. I know what lies ahead for Chase. He's a good kid, and I pray he'll stay that way. But he's going to face some strong temptations. I don't want him to make the same mistakes I made. I know he may, but I pray he's willing to hear me out when the time comes. I have a lot to prove to both of you."

A lot to prove. His words echoed in her mind. She had promised to seek God's guidance, and yet she had allowed fear to keep her from accepting the love of a good man. The man she now believed God had placed in her life. Relief flowed through Kim as she laid her hand on his arm. "Wyatt?"

He looked at her expectantly.

"The answer is yes."

Joy filled his blue eyes, with a wondrous smile covering his face. "To my proposal?"

"To everything. I'll marry you. I'll be the mother of your children. I'll live in your home. And I'll love you for the rest of my life."

Wyatt pulled her into his arms. "Oh, Kim, what changed your mind?"

"God answered my prayers. You don't need to prove anything to anyone, Wyatt. God accepts you just as you are, and so do I."

Chapter 20

I t's a beautiful day for a wedding." Kim's mother placed the wreath of white baby roses on her daughter's head.

She watched her mother's reflection in the mirror as she stood behind her, pinning the shoulder-length veil into place. They had arrived two weeks before to help with the wedding and planned to stay until Kim and Wyatt returned from their honeymoon. "I was so happy to see the sun this morning," Kim said.

"Did Wyatt ever tell you where you're going on your honeymoon?"

"He finally told me last night that he's planned a long weekend in Charleston. Then we're coming home for Chase and taking a family vacation in Florida. We wanted to do something together before he goes back to school."

Kim turned to look at her mother. "You'll never guess what Wyatt gave me for a wedding present."

"Diamonds?"

"Better. He duplicated my kitchen at his place. You should have seen him and Chase. We went to the house after the rehearsal dinner. They were so excited they could hardly wait for me to open the door."

"That sounds more like a gift for the family than you."

"Oh, Mom, don't you see? The real gift is that he cares about what makes me happy."

"He's doing a good job."

"Wyatt tells me he loves me," Kim said with a big smile, "but he shows me in more ways than I can count."

After she'd said yes, they had decided to take their time and get to know each other better. Kim had enjoyed being Wyatt's fiancée. She'd never dreamed she'd find such a loving, caring man. Admittedly, at times, she expected to see the bad boy come through, but Wyatt worked hard at making sure that part of him was dead forever.

They had gone through premarital counseling, and only when they were both comfortable about getting married had they set the date. The last few months had been spent in a flurry of preparation.

Today, when she slipped into the white satin A-line dress with its sweetheart neckline, beaded bodice, and chapel train, Kim knew her every doubt had dissolved like snow in the summer heat.

She picked up a box from the countertop. "These are Wyatt's grandmother's diamond-and-pearl earrings."

"Something old and something borrowed," her mother said. "Here's your something new from your dad and me."

Kim opened the jewelry box and found inside a delicate gold necklace with a jeweled center. "Help me put it on."

"Do you have something blue?"

"My garter."

Her mother hugged her. "I'm happy for you, Kimmie."

"Ah, you're excited about becoming a grandmother," Kim said, giving her an extra squeeze.

"Not just me. You saw your dad and Chase fooling around last night during the rehearsal party. He's a great kid."

"We appreciate your helping Mrs. Alexander with Chase. Wyatt worries he's too much for his grandmother."

"It's been a few years since we did the parent-child thing, but I don't think we've forgotten how."

"How would you feel about a baby?" Kim asked. "Wyatt and I have talked about having a child right away."

Her mother's broad smile showed her approval. "Hold on to your condo. You give me a grandchild, and we're home to stay."

"Too late. I sold it to Noah and Julie Loughlin. Wyatt plans to put in connections for the RV at the house."

"You want us around for more than the occasional visit?" her mother asked with a teasing tone in her voice.

"You know I do," Kim told her, smiling. "There's always a place in my home for you and Daddy."

The door to the dressing area opened, and Mari, Maggie, Natalie, Beth, and Julie entered the room, wearing their tea-length, azalea-colored dresses.

"Okay, mother and daughter bonding time is over," Julie said. "You have an anxious groom and best boy out there."

Her dad tapped on the door. "Everyone ready? I have the photographer with me. He wants a shot of me with the bride."

Mari opened the door, and Kim's father came over to hug his daughter. "You're beautiful."

"Thanks, Daddy."

The photographer snapped several photos and left. There was a flurry of activity as Kim searched for her elbow-length white gloves. She pulled them on as her friends picked up their white rose bouquets, and Maggie passed Kim the red roses she'd chosen. Kim waited while her attendants moved slowly to the front of the church. When her turn came, her gaze fixed on Wyatt in his white tuxedo.

Kim had never been more thankful for waterproof mascara than when the joy of the moment overcame her. "Thank You, Lord," she whispered as they walked along the white runner that led her to Wyatt.

Her dad placed her hand in Wyatt's and stepped aside. Kim smiled at Wyatt, and he returned the smile. What a wonderful life she was going to have with him as her husband.

Time stood still from the moment Pastor Joe said, "Dearly beloved," until he pronounced them husband and wife and son.

"I love you," Wyatt said, and kissed her to the applause of their family and friends.

As she turned to walk back down the aisle, the Good Shepherd window caught her attention. And Kim thanked Jesus for the grace that had brought her love.

COMING HOME

Dedication

To those foster parents who find room in their hearts to provide homes to the children who need them.

And as always, special thanks to Mary and Tammy for taking the time to help me out.

Many thanks to the others who provided answers to my research questions.

Chapter 1

O kay, single ladies, we need you up front," Maggie Gregory announced to the reception party. "Kim's going to throw the bouquet."

Replacing the microphone in the stand, she scuttled off to the side with the furtiveness of a sand crab trying to avoid the incoming tide of women excited over the possibility of becoming the next bride.

"You, too, Maggie," Kim called when she spotted her friend's escape attempt. "There's no ring on that finger."

"Get over here," another girlfriend called from the center of the group.

Catching the throwaway version of the ribbon-bound bundle of red roses had never been a consideration for Maggie. Sure, she was a single attendant, but she was fifty years old. And she certainly didn't have a prince waiting to sweep her up into his arms and take her away from it all.

She moved around the outer fringes to the back of the group. When Kim turned for her toss, Maggie took a step back toward the crowd. Her high-heeled shoe slipped on the tile floor.

Feeling herself falling, Maggie struggled to regain her balance. A little scream left her lips when she failed.

Things moved in a blur of slow motion. She felt hands at her back as she tumbled backward, taking her would-be rescuer down with her into an ignominious heap on the fellowship hall floor.

"Are you okay?" a man's voice inquired.

She glanced up as the pastor's four-year-old's big eyes widened and he yelled, "Look, Mommy, Miss Maggie knocked Mr. Dillon down."

Maggie wanted to disappear as all eyes turned their way. "I'm fine. You?"

The bouquet chose that moment to bounce off the ceiling fan right into Maggie's arms, and the photographer recorded the scene for posterity.

"What a waste," Maggie Gregory muttered, grimacing at Kim when she walked over to where they sat on the floor.

"What happened?"

"I slipped on something. Everything's okay. Go toss your garter or something."

"You're next," Kim confirmed with a big smile.

"Cornerstone's going to have more than one old maid if they wait for me to get married," Maggie guaranteed, turning her head to look straight into Dillon Rogers's blue eyes.

Neither paid any attention when the single women moved aside for the men. Dillon extricated himself, and when he tried to stand, the sole of his leather dress shoe slipped on her satin dress. They both heard the ominous rip at the same time. "I'm sorry, Maggie."

Things couldn't get any worse. "Never mind."

The laughter started when the garter hit Dillon's chest. They both looked at Wyatt, who innocently held up his hands, and the camera flashed again.

Maggie felt her face flame with embarrassment. "I'm glad everyone finds this funny."

"Sometimes you just gotta laugh with them," Dillon said.

She wiggled her bare foot, checking to make sure she hadn't injured her ankle, and glanced around. "Do you see my shoe anywhere?"

Dillon scouted for the shoe, looking under the long cloths that draped the tables with no luck. Finally, he spotted it hanging out of a large handbag. "There it is," he said, indicating their predicament. "Do you know her?"

Maggie shrugged and shook her head, watching as Dillon tapped the guest on the shoulder. "Excuse me, ma'am, could I possibly trouble you for that shoe in your purse?"

The woman looked at him as if he'd lost his mind but pulled her bag out from under the table. Her surprise registered. She used two fingers to pass him the shoe before she grabbed a napkin and cleaned her hand. "You need to wipe the icing off the sole before it throws her down again."

He smiled. "We will. Thanks."

The humor of the moment struck, and Maggie covered her face with her hands as the laughter started.

"Maggie?" Dillon called in concern. "Are you okay?"

She looked at him, one hand shielding her face as the giggles refused to go away.

He realized she was laughing and offered his hand to help her stand. Maggie started to slide again when her other shoe found the same slippery substance on the floor.

"Here, sit down," he said, holding on to her as he slid a chair behind her. He used several paper napkins to wipe the cake icing from the soles of her shoes. When he knelt to slip them back onto her feet, the camera flashed again.

"Well, does the slipper fit?" Kim teased as she joined them.

"Perfectly," Dillon declared with a bow in the direction of the videographer.

"I got it all on tape," the man said happily.

Visions of ending up on a national TV wedding blooper program filled Maggie's head.

"Seriously, are you okay?" Kim asked them both.

"I'm fine. I can't speak for Dillon." Maggie surreptitiously fingered the seams of her gown, hunting for the tear. "Why didn't you just walk over and hand me the bouquet? It would have been much simpler."

Kim grinned. "But not nearly as much fun. That catch will go into the Cornerstone Hall of Fame."

"You mean shame, don't you?" Maggie countered.

"The real shame would have been not having a handsome man around to rescue you."

Maggie's gaze rested on Dillon Rogers. His white teeth flashed, and smile crinkles touched the corners of his eyes as he laughed with Wyatt.

Kim hugged Maggie and said, "We're leaving. Come toss birdseed at us. Just not too hard."

"I'll be right there," she promised. "Let me get the goody basket the ladies put together for you and Wyatt."

After Kim and Wyatt walked away, Maggie stood. "Dillon." She called his name softly and motioned him over.

"Look at my dress and tell me where it's torn."

She felt more than a little self-conscious as his gaze moved along the lines of the dress. "Pretty color," he commented.

"Same as Mrs. Allene's azaleas," Maggie said.

"I remember," Dillon said. "I look forward to seeing them again next spring."

Did he mean that? Maggie wondered. Spring was seven months away. He'd already stayed for four months when she'd been so sure he would return to his job overseas.

"Ah, here it is," Dillon said. "It's at the top of this slit up the back."

Maggie twisted in an attempt to see the damage.

"It's not noticeable," he assured.

"Thanks. I need to say my good-byes. We still have to put the church back together for services tomorrow."

"Anything I can do to help?"

Maggie paused. "Ask Joe. I'm sure he'd appreciate another strong back."

After waving the bride and groom off in their white limo, Maggie stopped by the bride's dressing room and exchanged her dress for the clothes she'd worn over earlier.

Back in the sanctuary, she collected bows and piled them on the front pew. After completing that task, she found a plastic bag and began picking up the rose petals that littered the aisle.

Dillon found her there when he came back inside.

"Feeling okay?" he asked as he bent to pick up the petals nearest to where he stood and dropped them into the bag.

With renewed humiliation, she said, "I'm fine. Thanks for trying to help. I hope I didn't hurt you with all that thrashing around."

"No harm done."

～

Dillon recalled the first time he'd laid eyes on Maggie Gregory. Back in the spring, when he'd come home from Saudi Arabia to care for his ailing mother, he'd been forced to revise his image of her. He hadn't expected someone closer to his own age, and in all the years his mom had talked about her friend, she'd never thought to share that information with him.

When his mother first mentioned Maggie, he hadn't recognized the name but figured more than a few things had changed in the more than twenty-five years he'd been away. Then he'd returned home, and when he'd felt those first stirrings of attraction toward his mother's friend, he'd been more than a little uncomfortable. Particularly since he'd had his doubts about the role she played in his mother's life.

"Dillon?" she called, bringing his attention to the bag she held open for the rose petals.

She'd changed into jeans and a T-shirt, her long blond hair still up in the jumble of curls from the wedding. Dillon decided he liked it best flowing about her face and shoulders. She stood nearly as tall as he, making it easy for those bright blue eyes of hers to look deep into his soul.

Why did he become a tongue-tied schoolboy around her? Their stilted conversation was indicative of their relationship. He'd gotten off on the wrong foot with Maggie from day one, and it seemed she didn't plan to let him forget it anytime soon.

"It was a beautiful wedding," Maggie said.

Dillon agreed. It had been interesting seeing yet another of his male friends surrender to marriage. Granted, he'd only known Wyatt for a few months, but Dillon knew Wyatt loved Kim a great deal and felt blessed to have her in his life. Dillon could understand that. Though he'd come to consider himself a committed bachelor over the years, there were times when he wished for someone to love.

Maggie disappeared and returned with the vacuum. "I'll finish up here if you'll find the remembrance table."

As he walked into the fellowship hall, Dillon allowed himself to consider what it would be like to have a wife. Unless he married a much younger woman or one with a ready-made family, there would be no children, but he could see himself happily married at this stage of his life.

"Hey, Dillon, you're a million miles away," Noah said as he and Joe walked past carrying a folded table.

"Maggie needs the remembrance table."

"It's in the hallway outside the office," Joe supplied. "The trays and Bible are on my desk."

"Thanks. Looks like you could use a hand with those."

"Always," Joe Dennis said with a broad grin, adding, " 'The harvest truly is plenteous, but the labourers are few.' "

Dillon admired the pastor's ability to quote appropriate scripture for any occasion. "Let me take care of this for her, and I'll be back to help."

Once they had readied the sanctuary for morning services, they moved to the fellowship hall. Maggie went off to help Mari Dennis while Dillon joined the men.

"You can break down tables or fold chairs. Noah and I will haul them to the storage room."

With the help of Kim's dad, they broke down two tables and walked along the hall, carrying one on each side.

"Hey, Joe," Noah called to his brother-in-law. "Dillon and Jimmy are carrying twice the workload."

"That means we'll finish in half the time. Then we can get home to eat. You, too, Dillon. You're more than welcome to join us."

"Can I bring anything?"

"No. There's enough food to feed a small army. Though if Mari had her way, we'd probably get chocolate and fruit. She's so disappointed that she missed out on the fountain today," Pastor Joe said. "My idea of comfort food is more substantial."

"Yeah, but you have to remember that their comfort with chocolate makes our lives comfortable, too," Noah pointed out. "I buy Julie a box of her favorite chocolates every couple of weeks or so."

The men laughed at his logic as they returned to clearing the room.

❧

"Are you coming back to the house for supper?" Mari asked as they collected the flower arrangements that would be distributed to the elderly congregation members the following morning.

"I'm looking forward to it." Maggie doubted Mari knew how much she appreciated the invitation. She certainly didn't want to go home and sit around by herself tonight.

"Sorry about Luke's commentary at the reception."

"Hey, the kid calls them like he sees them," Maggie said. "I've never been so embarrassed."

"But I saw you laughing."

"I couldn't help myself. During the free-for-all my shoe ended up in some stranger's big purse. You should have seen Dillon's face when he asked for it."

"You two were the highlight of the reception. You've forgiven him?"

Maggie wanted to. She really did. But his accusations had taken her back to a time and place in her life where she didn't want to go. The child who didn't belong anywhere had returned, and she blamed Dillon. Maggie had never imagined that Allene Rogers would leave her anything in her will. She'd tried to make Dillon understand that she had loved his mother a great deal, but he wouldn't listen. His belief that she would take advantage of Mrs. Allene had hurt so much. She had no idea how to explain her feelings to Mari and her other friends.

She doubted they would understand any more than she did.

"I'm trying. He's always around," Maggie declared. "He attends my church." She noted Mari's look and said, "Okay, God's church, but he's here. He lives in the house next door. He hangs out with my friends. The only place I don't see Dillon Rogers is at work."

"Let's hope for his sake that's the one place he can avoid."

"Definitely." Maggie wouldn't wish a hospital stay on anyone.

"Joe told me he invited Dillon to supper," Mari said, glancing at her friend as she spoke the words.

A surge of annoyance filled Maggie. Why did the man have to infiltrate her circle of friends? Couldn't he get his own? "That was nice of him."

Mari laughed. "Now that's a diplomatic response if I ever heard one."

Mari carried the box into the kitchen. Maggie followed with the last two vases. "You're pretty accepting of most people's failings. Why not Dillon's?" she asked.

"He sets me on edge. When Mrs. Allene was sick, I only wanted to help her. Then after she died and we learned about the will and house, he treated me like a con artist."

Allene Rogers had been a lifelong member of Cornerstone Community Church. When Maggie came to Myrtle Beach, she moved into Mrs. Allene's rental house. Her new landlord invited her to Cornerstone, and in time, Maggie had become a member. Over the years, the women had grown close. Maggie had cared for Mrs. Allene more as a loving daughter than a neighbor, and the woman had rewarded her by leaving Maggie the rental house in her will.

"He knows you didn't know about the house," Mari said.

After one last look around, they turned out the kitchen lights. They did one last walk-through of the sanctuary and stopped to pick up their dresses. Before plunging the narthex into darkness, Maggie pushed open the front door. The sweltering mid-August heat seemed even hotter after leaving the air-conditioned church.

"I know, but like I said, it's a feeling," Maggie defended.

"Maybe you feel guilty because Mrs. Allene left you the house."

Maybe so, Maggie agreed silently. "He commented on the color of the dresses, and when I said his mom's azaleas were that color, he said he looked forward to seeing them again. You don't think he's planning to stick around that long, do you?"

Mari turned to check the door lock and managed to step on her dress bag.

"Let me carry that before you trip yourself," Maggie offered, taking the long garment bag from her diminutive friend.

"Thanks. Joe said Dillon's enjoying his vacation and considering his plans for the future."

"He hasn't been home since I've known his mother. He flew her and his cousin over there a few times. Mrs. Allene was always so excited because she hadn't seen him in a while," Maggie said. "If my parents were alive, I couldn't imagine not seeing them for weeks, much less years, at a time."

"Men are different than women. A few calls reassure them. Women have to see for themselves."

Maggie shrugged. "But how can his employer afford to give him a year off?"

"I'm sure they have rules in place that address the situation. Will it bother you if he does stay longer?"

"Don't mind me," Maggie said. "I've been out of sorts lately. Let me drop this dress off at the house, and I'll come back to help."

"I'll walk with you," Mari said. Maggie's house was two doors down from the parsonage. "Other than Dillon and the house, what's troubling you?"

"Just having my own little pity party. All my friends have great lives."

"You're still down in the dumps?"

She nodded. Mari had recognized her grief and prayed with Maggie several times since Mrs. Allene's death. "I'm happy for Kim but sad because I know she's going to be busy with her new family."

"Perhaps you need to get out more," Mari suggested. "Find new activities to occupy your time. Joe says the Bible study is popular."

"Maybe I do. Okay, enough of this," Maggie declared. "I'm just feeling sorry for myself. It'll pass."

Mari slipped her arm around Maggie's and said, "Feel free to call when you need to talk. I can't say I remember what being alone is like, but I can listen. And when Kim and Wyatt come home, things will return to normal. You'll see."

Maggie had her doubts. "Thanks for caring, Mari."

"And you don't mind Dillon coming to supper?"

Now why did she have to go and bring that up again? "Why should I mind? It's your house. I don't have to entertain him. We'd better hurry, or there's going to be a house full of guests without a hostess."

Maggie prayed she could work through her discontent. It had been a long time since she'd felt so out of sorts about her life.

Chapter 2

I t's hot out tonight," Maggie commented, swiping the beads of sweat from her forehead. "I should have worn something cooler than these jeans."

"I hope we don't have a storm later," Mari said. "The twins don't sleep well during thunderstorms."

"That's August for you. Makes me long for fall."

"While the tourists long for endless summers. We took the kids down to the beach earlier in the week. We could hardly find a place to spread out our blanket. Can you believe summer is nearly over?"

"It's flown by. What did you decide about Matt and Mark and school?" Maggie asked. Her friends had been praying over whether they should enroll their two oldest sons in public school or homeschool them. Maggie knew their aunt Julie had offered to pay for a Christian school, but Joe and Mari had refused.

"We're leaning toward homeschooling. It'll be difficult for Matt and Mark to concentrate on their schoolwork with three younger ones running around the house. I'm not sure how we'll get past that."

"It's kindergarten. Give it a try, and if it doesn't work, you can put them in public school next year."

Mari sighed as she opened the screen door leading to her kitchen. "I can't believe how fast they're growing. Seems like yesterday they were keeping me awake half the night."

"Time truly flies," Maggie agreed.

"Any news on the foster parenting application?" Mari asked.

Maggie shook her head. "I don't really expect to hear anything for another month or two."

"Feel free to practice with my kids anytime you feel inclined," Mari offered with a laugh. "Then again, that might change your mind about taking on the responsibility."

"I love your kids," Maggie declared as she followed Mari into the house.

"There you are," Julie called as she juggled two large salad bowls. "We were getting ready to send out a search party."

"We took Maggie's things over to her house." Mari reached for her dress, and Maggie draped it over her outstretched arms. "I'll be right back."

"What do you need me to do?" Maggie asked.

"Grab those cups. There's ice in the cooler on the patio. Noah's taking the meat off the grill. There's a slab of ribs for you."

"Oh, I've been craving them forever," she declared. Maggie loved pork ribs. They were messy and not figure friendly, but they were delicious.

A couple of picnic tables covered in festive vinyl cloths sat on the patio area. Mari and Joe had strung fairy lights overhead, and citronella torches flickered about the outer perimeter of the yard, keeping mosquitoes at bay.

Maggie filled cups with ice and poured everyone's beverage of choice. After filling her plate, she opted to sit next to Natalie.

"This seat taken?" a male voice asked.

Maggie glanced up to find Dillon standing there. His neatly clipped, mixed gray hair hugged his head, and perfect white teeth flashed as he smiled at them. He had changed into a pair of khaki shorts and a pale blue golf shirt that complemented his tan.

How could he be totally oblivious to her discomfort around him? She'd have thought he would have kept his distance after their earlier escapade. Maggie swallowed quickly and wiped her hands and mouth with her napkin, casting a meaningful glance in Mari's direction before she said, "It's all yours."

He threw one leg over the seat, brushing up against her as he sat and maneuvered his other leg underneath the table. "Sorry. Never could figure out why the person who invented these things made them so hard to get into."

His comment generated general laughter and agreement around the table.

"I appreciate you inviting me over today," Dillon told Joe. "Nothing better than a meal cooked on the grill."

"I imagine you've had more than your fair share of different foods," Joe said.

"A few. Those look good," Dillon said, eying Maggie's barbecued ribs. He glanced back at the food table. "I didn't see any over there."

Maggie fought the urge to hide her plate. "That's because I'm the only rib fan in the bunch. Noah takes pity on me now and again."

Dillon's gaze drifted toward the plate again. "I haven't had ribs in years."

Since she'd lost her appetite the moment Dillon found his way to her table, Maggie picked up her knife and carved off half of the slab. "Here, take some of these. I can't eat them all."

She didn't add that she generally took home the leftover ribs to enjoy later. "Don't mind if I do."

He licked his finger and looked at Noah. "You'll have to give me the recipe for this sauce."

"No problem," Noah said with a broad grin. "They sell it in bottles at the grocery store."

Julie punched his arm. "You're supposed to say it's a family secret."

"It is some family's secret," Noah agreed. "Just not mine."

"So what were you talking about before I interrupted?" Dillon asked.

"Mostly we were stuffing our faces," Joe told him.

"I can see why. This food is excellent."

"There's something to be said for big receptions with sit-down dinners," Julie said.

Everyone nodded. Most of them had missed lunch and had only managed small plates of the hors d'oeuvres along with cake and punch.

"Did you hear what Wyatt and Chase gave Kim for a wedding gift?" Julie asked.

Wyatt had redone the kitchen in Kim's condo, and when she agreed to move into his house, he recreated the same kitchen as a wedding gift.

"I'm sure they've heard in some third-world countries by now," Noah told his wife. "I thought she was going to have Joe announce it from the pulpit before the wedding."

"Well, I think it's sweet," Julie told him. "That kitchen helped make them a couple."

"But the old rugged cross started it all," Joe said.

Everyone smiled and nodded. Kim had been so thrilled when Cornerstone allowed her to produce the Easter play she'd written. She'd approached Wyatt about building the cross, and they had maneuvered down a long, rocky road that culminated in marriage.

"Wyatt cleans up well," Natalie said.

"I almost didn't recognize him without the work shirts and boots," Maggie admitted.

"Yeah, we all razzed him about that white suit," Noah told the group.

"Isn't it wonderful what men will do for love?" Julie asked, flashing Noah a big smile.

The group chuckled when he leaned to kiss his bride of seven months.

"It was a beautiful wedding," Maggie said, glancing at Natalie. "You outdid yourself with that cake."

Dillon leaned forward and asked, "You made the cake? I thought she'd gotten it from a big-city cake designer."

"Thanks," Natalie said. "I lived in New York and worked for one of the best. She taught me a lot, and I taught her a few things in return."

"I can see how," Dillon agreed with a nod. "Hard to imagine, but it tasted better than it looked. Much better than the groom's cake."

"Don't let Avery hear you say that," Natalie warned.

"Avery?" Dillon asked, looking somewhat puzzled.

"Avery Baker. He made the groom's cake."

"Is he still around?" Dillon asked. "I hung out with his older brother when we were in school. Avery used to drive us crazy following us around and getting us into trouble with his parents."

"Obviously he hasn't changed much," Natalie said in a soft aside to Maggie.

"He owns his parents' bakery now," Mari told Dillon.

"I remember the Bakers. Still, his cake didn't compare to yours."

"Don't tell him that, or you'll elevate my status to archenemy number one."

"Over a cake?"

At Dillon's frown, Maggie considered he might have some redeeming qualities after all.

"It's a long story. Suffice it to say that Avery considers me the competition and never lets me forget it."

"You do make an extraordinary cake."

Natalie smiled. "Stop, or you'll make me blush."

He grinned at Natalie, and Maggie felt in the way. Then he winked at Maggie before focusing on his food again. The man used his charm on every woman in sight. She watched as he systematically piled items on his burger and smashed it down before lifting it from the plate. He took a big bite.

"I missed out on the chocolate fountain," Mari said. "I didn't dare risk getting it down the front of my dress."

"Well, break out the bibs," Natalie told her. "I had a cancellation for tomorrow and knew you wouldn't want all that fruit to go to waste."

"Did we tell you we love you?" Maggie asked happily.

"I think you love chocolate more," Natalie teased.

The conversation dropped off as everyone continued to eat. Maggie ate the wedge of watermelon she'd taken and toyed with the rind. Struck by the silence, she asked, "Where are the kids?"

Mari looked up from her food. "Diana thought taking Chase out would help him not miss Wyatt and Kim as much. She invited Matt, Mark, and Luke along. Robin took the twins over to her house for a while."

"Julie can tell you what a fun experience she's having," Maggie said, winking at her friend.

"I hope Luke doesn't decide to play hide-and-seek," Julie said. "Or sneak Puff along."

Her brother frowned. "No doubt Puff is around somewhere, lying in wait to pounce on some unsuspecting soul."

"Poor Joe," Mari said, rubbing a hand over her husband's shoulders. "He had to climb up and get him out of a tree yesterday. He nearly broke his neck."

"His or the cat's?" Maggie teased, wondering if he'd forgiven his sister for buying the pet without their permission. Mari loved the cat, but Joe often grumbled about the animal's mischievous antics.

Mari grinned at her husband. "His. He said he's calling the fire department next time."

Laughter rippled easily around the table at the thought of their pastor up a tree.

The women followed when Natalie went inside to set up the chocolate fountain. Soon they were stabbing fresh fruit with long skewers and dipping it in the sheets of chocolate that cascaded over the tiered edges of the tower.

The men came inside a few minutes later and laughed at the women as they enthusiastically encouraged each other to try the different items while dodging their efforts to share. They indulged in the cake and chocolate-dipped pretzels Natalie had brought.

Afterward, everyone helped clean up before settling on the patio to sit and talk. The summer evening was abuzz with the concert of frogs and grasshoppers and the scent of honeysuckle in the slight evening breeze.

The Elliotts returned and joined the group. The older boys chased fireflies around the yard, laughing with the abandon of the young. Robin brought the twins home, and they crawled into their parents' laps and fell asleep. All too soon, the wind picked up and the rumble of distant thunder forced them to call it a night.

Natalie stood and announced, "I'm out of here. Thanks for dinner. It was wonderful."

"Me, too," Maggie agreed. "I have to work tomorrow. I'll help with the fountain, Nat."

Dillon stood and said, "Let me help. Thanks for the invite. I'll have to return the favor soon."

After loading the fountain into her car, Natalie drove away and Dillon asked, "Um, Maggie, could I walk you home?"

Surprised by the request, she glanced at him and shrugged. "Sure. Let me get my things."

He followed her back inside and waited while she hugged her friends, said her good nights, and picked up the leftovers she planned to take for lunch the next day.

They walked through the side gate onto the sidewalk running in front of their homes.

"I suppose you're wondering why I asked to walk you home," Dillon said, breaking the noticeable silence.

"What's on your mind?" she asked.

"I think," he said hesitantly, then charged forward, "well, don't you think it's time we buried the hatchet and moved on?"

So long as he doesn't want to bury it in my head, Maggie thought wryly.

"It's what Mom would have expected of us. I said things I had no business saying. My mother's property was her business. Not mine."

"I didn't expect it, Dillon."

"I know you didn't. I don't think I ever truly believed any differently. Can we get past this?"

"I'll try if you will."

Even as she spoke the words, Maggie knew she had a ways to go before she could forgive Dillon Rogers. Until she could get past the pain, she didn't know how she could let go of the hurt he'd caused her.

Chapter 3

On Wednesday morning, Maggie woke early, eager to call Mari and share what had happened the previous day. She fixed breakfast and read the paper while giving her friend time to get the kids settled before making her call.

"I've never been so shocked in my life." Maggie filled her glass from the refrigerator door ice maker and poured freshly made lemonade. She took a long, refreshing drink.

"You mean he just walked in and gave you flowers and candy? No, Luke. Let Puff eat. Sorry."

"You sound a bit frazzled," Maggie said.

"They're all in high gear today."

Maggie didn't know how Mari managed with five children under the age of six. "I told him I'd make sure all the nursing staff knew they were from him."

"And that's when he said they were for you?" Mari prompted.

"Exactly," Maggie declared, leaning against the French door and looking into her backyard. The grass needed mowing, and weeds had taken over her flower beds. Maybe this afternoon. Already the heat from the August day radiated against the insulated glass. "You could have knocked me over with a feather."

Mari giggled.

"It's not funny. He said they'd grown very fond of me during his wife's hospitalization."

"They?"

Maggie detected subdued laughter in Mari's tone. "William Smith and his six sons, ages thirteen to eighteen."

"You think he's looking for a working woman to help put them through college?"

Maggie grinned at Mari's comment. "Probably. His wife died two months ago. I refuse to believe he's over her death. I saw the way he took care of her at the hospital. He loved her."

"I'm sure he isn't, but men get on with their lives pretty quickly. Particularly men with six growing boys. So you're truly not interested?"

"He's a nice man but not for me. I thanked him for the flowers and candy, reiterated that I would make sure the entire nursing staff knew they were from him, and said I needed to get back to work."

"How did he take it?"

"He seemed disappointed." Maggie sighed and asked hopefully, "Do you think he got the message?"

"You tell me."

"He'll probably contact me again." William Smith's determined effort to assure she knew the flowers were for her told Maggie he didn't intend to give up easily. "I'm not interested in becoming involved with someone grieving the love of his life. They were married for more than twenty-five years. And I really liked his wife."

"I'm sure it will work out," Mari offered. Maggie could tell she was washing dishes. "You never said why Dillon asked to walk you home the other night."

"Could be he's old-fashioned and didn't want me walking alone at night," Maggie offered evasively.

"Try again."

Maggie sighed and told the truth. "He asked if we could be friends."

Mari burst into laughter. "Oh, this is better than daytime television."

"Hey," Maggie called with mock affront, "this is my life you're laughing at."

"And you don't think it's funny? Just days ago you were down because everyone else had great lives. Now you have two men in pursuit. How do you feel about becoming Dillon's friend?"

"I don't know."

"He's a handsome man. It wouldn't hurt to get to know him better."

"And have my heart broken when he goes back overseas?"

"You said yourself he's not in such a great hurry. Maybe you could change his mind."

"And what if I don't want to change his mind?" Maggie challenged.

"Then you don't. You know we're praying for you to find the right man."

A few months back, their group of friends had agreed to pray for each other to find happiness with the men God intended for them.

"We want you to be happy," Mari said. "The right man will bring you joy you've never known before."

"Pray for Natalie. She's younger and deserves to find her Mr. Right."

"You deserve yours, too."

"You and Julie already meddled once," she reminded.

Maggie hadn't had a clue what Dillon meant when he'd confronted her back in April, saying he'd gotten the message and for her to call off her defenders. She'd been horrified when Mari and Julie admitted they'd talked to Dillon about his behavior.

"We do these things out of love for each other," Mari told her. "What are you doing for lunch? Care to join us for cold ham and potato salad?"

"Sounds. . ." Her words trailed off with the deafening *crash*. "What on earth?"

"Maggie? What's going on? I hear a horn."

She ran into the living room and paused. Half of the hood of a large old Caddy sat right where her picture window had been. Shattered glass and debris from the front of her house covered the car's hood and littered the floor. Stunned, she noted the car had rammed the sofa where she'd sat reading the paper only minutes before. Where she'd still be if she hadn't gone into the kitchen to call Mari.

The strong odor of gasoline mobilized Maggie into action. She tossed the cordless phone onto the chair and moved cautiously toward the vehicle. Though she couldn't be sure from the way he was slumped against the steering wheel, Maggie suspected the driver to be Max Carter. She knew him from church.

"Maggie? Where are you?" Dillon Rogers's horrified cry gave her pause. He yelled again, sounding frantic.

She panicked when Dillon began ripping away boards. She had no idea whether the car would continue to move once the barricades were removed.

"Stop!" Maggie screamed.

Doubtful he could hear her over the car's engine and blaring horn, Maggie considered her options.

Praying all the while that the car wouldn't lurch forward and kill her, Maggie grabbed the chenille throw from the recliner. Bits of glass fell to the floor as she gave it a quick shake then used it to brush the remaining glass from the car hood. She barely felt the warm metal as she crawled through the opening to reach the passenger side door. Tears of joy sprang to her eyes when it opened easily. She entered the vehicle, turned the key, and sighed in relief when the revving engine sputtered once, then twice, and died.

Maggie turned her attention to Max, checking his vitals and determining he was no longer with them. Tears trailed down her cheeks as she sent up a prayer for his family.

"Are you trying to get yourself killed?"

Taking Dillon's anguished question in stride, she gently shifted Max's body to lean his head back against the seat. The horn ceased blaring. She closed his eyes before backing out the passenger door. "I had to do something before you ripped those boards away."

Dillon pulled her into his arms. "You took ten years off my life."

"Couldn't you hear the engine?" she asked, not minding that he held her.

"I thought he'd hit you. I saw you sitting on the sofa when I went out to the mailbox earlier."

"I was in the kitchen."

"Thank God." His heartfelt declaration shook her to the bottoms of her feet.

Despite the August heat, Maggie trembled from shock.

"It's okay," he comforted, hugging her again.

She remained within the confines of his arms until Mari's and Joe's cries reached her ears.

"Over here," Dillon called. "I need to call an ambulance."

"What happened?" Mari called.

"Max drove into the house. He's dead."

Mari gasped.

"He just left the church," Joe said. "He wasn't feeling well."

"They're sending an officer and an ambulance," Dillon said after he used his cell phone to speak with the 911 dispatcher. Dillon wrapped his arm around Maggie's waist and guided her around the vehicle and out into the yard, relinquishing his hold to Mari. "She's in shock," he said softly before walking over to talk with Joe.

"Oh, Mari, Max is dead," she said and burst into tears.

"Shh, it's okay," her friend comforted. "Thank God you're safe."

Maggie swiped her eyes and said, "What's wrong with me? I never cry."

"I think having a car driven into your house is reason enough. Thank God you were in the kitchen."

"Linda will be devastated," Maggie declared sadly. She knew Max's wife from the church nursery, and they had talked many times about her husband's refusal to see a doctor.

"When I came into the living room, the car hood was half in the house with the engine running and the horn blaring. Dillon was yelling my name." Maggie's voice broke as she gulped in a deep breath and shook harder at the memory. "I suppose he's thinking it serves me right," she murmured, feeling guilty the moment the words passed her lips. He'd obviously been very concerned when he came to her rescue. "I'm sorry. He doesn't deserve that."

"No, he doesn't," Mari admonished. "Why would you even think that? This unforgiving woman isn't the Maggie I know."

Her comment hit Maggie like a dousing of ice water on a hot summer day. It had never been her intention to behave so poorly toward another of God's children.

Joe and Dillon walked up, and Dillon said, "Why don't you come over to the house and sit on the porch?"

"I need to stay here."

"It was the most awful noise," Mari told them, describing what she'd heard over the phone.

Their gazes turned to the police car as it pulled into the driveway, siren blaring and blue lights flashing. A fire truck followed.

Mari greeted the officer, another member of Cornerstone.

"Mrs. Dennis. Pastor Dennis. What happened, Miss Gregory?"

Before Maggie could tell him, the ambulance arrived. She turned away when the attendants removed Max's body from the car and took him away to be officially pronounced. As a nurse, she'd witnessed death before. Maggie had no idea why it bothered her so much this time. Burt pulled out his notepad and began asking questions.

Minutes later, a wrecker arrived and slowly pulled the car from the home. The large car cleared the house, taking out one of the porch supports, and the A-frame of the roof slapped against the front with a *thud*.

"We should have shored up the roof," Dillon told Joe.

The car retreated across what had once been a well-landscaped lawn, leaving the fountain and statuary in shambles. Maggie considered how long she'd searched for those pieces and how thrilled she'd been when Kimberly called to say she'd found exactly what Maggie wanted.

Now their loss was nothing compared to the tragic loss of Max's life. Fresh tears welled in Maggie's eyes, and Mari wrapped her arms around her friend. Maggie groaned when the television van pulled up behind the officer's car just as the fire truck and ambulance pulled away.

"I'll handle this, Miss Gregory," Burt said, walking over to greet the reporter. They shot footage and then left the scene after getting a statement from the officer.

"Max's fifteen minutes of fame," Maggie whispered.

"It *is* more than we're used to on Maple Street," Joe said.

The officer returned. "Sorry about that. They heard it on the scanner."

"Thanks for keeping me off camera," Maggie told him.

"I didn't want them releasing anything until we notify Max's wife."

"Can I come along when you do that?" Joe asked.

"I'd appreciate it, Pastor Joe. That's one of my least favorite job-related tasks."

"Mine, too."

"I think that does it, Miss Gregory." He ripped off a piece of the form and handed it to her. "You'll need this for your insurance. Have a nice day," he said, tipping his head politely before he walked over to the cruiser.

Just how does he suppose I do that? Maggie wondered. Struggling to regain her composure, she asked, "Where are the kids?"

"With Noah."

Joe came over and said, "I'm going with Burt to notify Linda Carter. Maggie, I'll come back later to help secure your house."

"I'd better get back to the kids. Will you be okay?" Mari asked Maggie.

"I'm fine."

Dillon stepped up beside her. "I'll stay."

Mari nodded and asked Maggie, "Will you come to the house for lunch?"

"I have to secure everything first."

"We'll take care of it for you," Dillon promised with a caring smile.

Maggie's heart thumped.

Mari moved to the sidewalk and looked back once more, waving good-bye. Maggie waved listlessly in return.

"Why don't you go with her and call your insurance agent?" Dillon suggested.

"I need to take care of my home."

"You need to know what your agent wants you to do," Dillon said. "I'll stay here and keep watch. Do you have any tarps? We need them for the roof."

Maggie shook her head.

"We'll find some. I have plywood. And we need to make sure the house is safe to enter."

"Thanks, Dillon." The adrenaline that had pumped through her minutes earlier had evaporated, leaving nothing but feelings of sadness behind.

He looked at her for what seemed a long time. "It'll be okay, Maggie. We'll have it sorted out in no time. A couple of boards over the opening and you'll be safe and secure."

Maggie didn't know how secure she'd feel with a bit of lumber keeping intruders at bay. She rubbed her hands over her face, images of Max Carter and the car coming clearly to mind.

"Once the insurance adjustor gets the claim processed, we can get contractors in and have the place looking better than ever," Dillon continued.

It would be so nice to drop all this on him, but Maggie didn't feel that was fair. "You're busy with your place."

He'd spent the last couple of months updating the house that had been around since the thirties.

"It will be okay, Maggie. I promise."

She smiled at him. "I'm sorry, Dillon. Truly I am."

"For what?"

"The way I've treated you. You don't deserve my anger. You had every right to feel I'd stolen your inheritance."

Dillon looked shocked. "Don't say that. This house belonged to my grandparents. They gave Mom and Dad the house next door when they married, so it's not as if they worked themselves to death for their land. And I don't think I did anything to deserve my inheritance, either. Nothing beyond having the good fortune to be my parents' son."

A pained look spread across her face.

"What is it, Maggie? What did I say?"

"I was my parents' daughter. And then they were gone, and I was nobody's child. I lived in foster homes from the time I was eleven years old. The Floyds and your mom were the only adults besides my parents who ever made me feel truly at home. I didn't help Mrs. Allene because I wanted something from her. I loved her."

Dillon enveloped her in his arms and whispered, "Shh. I know. I'm sorry, too, Maggie. I hurt you with my accusations. I know you loved Mom. The house doesn't matter to me. It was fear that I'd allowed someone to take advantage of my elderly parent. Guilt because I hadn't been bothered to care for her myself."

"Why didn't you come home earlier?"

"I wish I had."

Maggie wished he had, too. She regretted that he'd missed his mother's last years. "I'll never be too busy to help you, Maggie. Go make your call," he said when she looked at the house again.

Dillon settled into the swing hanging beneath the shade of the old gnarled tree. If only the car had veered a couple of feet to the left, it would have struck the tree rather than the house. "I'll wait here."

"I'll be right back."

"Take a few minutes," he advised gently. "You're still in shock."

Maggie supposed she was. She trembled and felt chilled despite the sun. "I don't want to impose."

"It's not imposing. It's called being neighborly."

"Can I at least offer you a glass of lemonade?" He raised his brows as if asking how she planned to accomplish that. "The back door is unlocked. I can go around the house."

"I'm fine. Go make your call so we'll know how to proceed."

She took a couple of steps and then turned back, dropping onto the seat beside him. "It just occurred to me that I don't have insurance on the house. The estate isn't settled. I have content insurance."

Dillon thought for a minute or two. "Homeowners probably won't cover it anyway. Max Carter's vehicle insurance should."

"Then I should call his company?" Maggie fished the insurance information Burt had given her from her pocket and named the national company listed there.

"Let's call Mom's agent and have him advise us."

"I have the same agent," Maggie volunteered. "Mrs. Allene told me about him when I rented the house."

"Do you have the number?"

"In my purse. Inside the house."

"Tell you what," Dillon said. "You stay here and take it easy. I'll grab the phone book."

❧

As Dillon ran across to his house, he understood Maggie's confusion more and more. Seeing that old Caddy in her house had been the ultimate shock for him.

He forced himself to breathe more slowly when fear swamped him again. She could have been killed. And he would have cared.

Dillon admitted the truth to himself. He'd grown fond of Maggie Gregory. She might be as prickly as a cactus, but she had a good heart. He knew he had to help her get past the hurt he'd caused. He'd do it, too. No doubt, she'd give him fits, but he knew the end result would make it worthwhile.

❧

After Dillon disappeared inside his house, Maggie dropped a foot to the ground and gave the swing a push. So many things filled her head—Max's death, Mari's words of admonishment, Dillon's caring. Why did she doubt his intentions? He'd done nothing to make her believe he wanted anything more than to help her through a trying situation.

"Maggie."

She smiled at Julie and Noah Loughlin. Julie hugged her. "Are you okay? I know I'd be freaked out if a car drove into the front of our place."

The idea made Maggie giggle. They lived in a second-floor beach condominium. "Let's hope no car ever gets that high."

Julie and Noah smiled.

"What will you do?" Noah asked.

"Dillon's getting the phone. It's such a mess. The house is tied up with the estate, and we don't know whether to call the homeowner or vehicle agent."

"I'd say the vehicle," Julie volunteered.

Noah nodded agreement. "You may have to get the homeowner's agent involved before it's over, but Max's insurance is definitely liable."

"How's Linda?" Maggie asked.

"Joe's with her now."

"I feel so bad for her," Maggie said in an almost whisper. "She wanted him to see a doctor, but he refused. Said it was indigestion."

"Men can be so stubborn," Julie agreed, glancing at her husband.

"Hey, we don't have a monopoly on stubborn. You're pretty stubborn, too, Mrs. Loughlin."

Julie grimaced at him, and Maggie watched the couple's loving playfulness and wondered what life would be like with someone who loved her that much.

"Noah's going to come over later and help board up the house. Are you sure it's safe to be inside?"

"I don't know," Maggie said.

"Dillon, hi," Julie called when she saw him walking toward them. "A bit too much excitement in the neighborhood, I hear."

"You're not kidding." He passed Maggie the phone book. "Give me the agent's name, and I'll call him for you."

"I can talk to him."

"Like you said, the estate isn't settled, so he'll probably have to talk to me anyway."

Maggie didn't feel like arguing, so she flipped to the yellow pages and calmly recited the agent's office number.

Dillon dialed and a few minutes later told her they could do what they needed to secure the house until the adjustor could get there. "He said he'd be over shortly to take pictures. Turns out he has Max Carter's car insurance, too."

He glanced at Noah and said, "We need tarps to cover the roof. If we pile the worst of the debris out of the way, we should be able to secure the front with plywood."

"That doesn't sound very safe," Julie offered.

"Mom always said locks only keep honest people out," Noah pointed out.

"But still. . . ," Julie began, cutting off at her husband's warning look. "You can stay with us."

"Thanks, but I'd just as soon stay here," Maggie said. "Perhaps thieves will be less inclined to break in if I'm here. I can take some personal days."

"Noah and I will help in every way possible," Julie said.

"Me, too," Dillon promised.

As she sat and studied the devastation to her home, her thoughts centered even more on the Carter family. Her loss seemed minute compared to theirs. They'd lost their beloved husband and father.

"Dear Lord," she whispered, "please be with Linda and her family as they deal with the loss of their loved one. Help them to find great joy in knowing Max was Your child and has gone home to be with You.

"And please help me let go of the pain and anger that keep me from being the witness You would have me be. Amen."

Chapter 4

The insurance adjustor finally showed up on Friday and determined the majority of the damage was limited to the house front. Dillon's structural engineer friend had basically said the same thing on Thursday.

Dillon made a long list of things for her to ask but came over when the man arrived and recounted every item. If the adjustor found Dillon's actions puzzling, he didn't say anything. He just jotted on his forms and did the math. When the totals were completed, Maggie was shocked to learn there was more than twenty thousand dollars' damage to her house and gardens.

Everything was included—the structure, furniture replacement, landscaping, and labor. The list seemed endless. Maggie's head was spinning by the time the adjustor told her he'd get a check in the mail.

"What about damage that might not be found until the work gets under way?" Dillon asked.

"Here's my card," the man said, handing it to Maggie. "Give me a call if anything comes up."

"Unbelievable," Maggie said after he'd driven off. "For a few minutes there, I thought he was going to declare the place totaled."

Dillon smiled. "I'm sure he deals with far more vehicle collisions than house-and-car. So where do you want to start?"

"I don't know."

"We need a contractor. Anyone from church you do business with?"

Maggie shook her head. "I'll ask around and see if I can get a recommendation."

"Want me to handle this for you? I can call the contractors. See what they say."

"You don't have time."

"Sure I do. Now that we know the place isn't going to fall down on your head, we can take our time and do it right."

"Not too long, I hope," Maggie offered quickly. Somehow the very thought of repairing the housefront as quickly as possible made her hope she could forget the incident that plagued her still.

The living room might be usable, but she found the darkness depressing. Plywood obstructed sunlight that had flooded the room. She couldn't even welcome visitors at her front door. They had to come around the house and enter through the back.

She'd spent Wednesday night on the sofa in Mari and Pastor Joe's study. Despite Julie's invitation, she hadn't felt right about intruding on the newly-weds. Thursday night, she'd spent a restless, nightmare-filled night in her own bed. She prayed her anxiety would stop soon.

"Depends on how busy they are," Dillon said. "We want recommendations from past jobs. I think we can get the work under way soon enough. That is, if you'll trust me to do this for you."

She looked at him, seeing the question in his expression. "I do trust you, Dillon, and I appreciate everything you've done for me. But I don't feel right about dumping my responsibility on your shoulders."

"When do you work again?"

"Tomorrow. I'm on the night shift this week."

"Why don't I make a couple of calls and see if we can get someone out today? I doubt anyone's available, but it can't hurt to try."

After Dillon left, Maggie went inside and sorted laundry. He returned just as she was taking her uniforms from the washer. "What did you find out?"

"Pretty much what we thought. One guy can come by tomorrow."

Maggie sighed and reminded, "Max's funeral is in the morning."

"Let me help," Dillon requested again. "Give me a key. We'll look at the house and lock up after we finish."

"It's too much to ask," Maggie declared with a shake of her head. "You can't finish your place if you're working on mine."

"My house is at a stopping point. And I won't be doing the work myself," he insisted. "Just supervising. Carrying out your decisions."

Maggie didn't understand why Dillon made it sound almost critical that he do this. "But you're on vacation. You don't want to spend your time off work-ing. What about your job?" she asked. "If you get called back before the house is finished, I won't have a clue what to do."

"I'll keep you informed every step of the way," Dillon said. "And I won't be called back."

"You've been here for months, Dillon. Surely your employer doesn't plan for you to remain on leave indefinitely."

"Actually, I retired. I notified them a couple of months after I came home."

Surprise filled her. "I thought you liked your work."

"I did, but I don't want to go back. I don't have to work."

"Then you're a very fortunate man." Early retirement wasn't in her future. She hoped to increase her retirement plan contributions now that she didn't have to pay rent, but that had to wait until after she'd sorted out tax and insur-ance costs. "I'm sure you worked hard to get to that point," she added.

"So you'll let me help?"

She shook out another uniform top, slipped it on a hanger, and hung it on the rod over the utility sink. "You'll let me know if it gets to be too much?" she questioned.

"We'll get everything knocked out in a week or two, and you'll be back to normal before you know what happened."

"I'll be in your debt."

"No charge," he said softly.

She looked up, and their gazes caught and held. The idea that something of great import had just happened grabbed hold and refused to let go. He smiled, and she smiled back.

"Now, how about we go out to lunch. I have a taste for seafood."

She glanced at the washer. "I need to do a couple more loads."

"It's just lunch," he offered. "Unless you want to run by the hardware store and look at windows and doors."

She was hungry. And she could do laundry this afternoon as easily as now. "Give me time to brush my hair."

He glanced at his watch. "I'll meet you out front in fifteen minutes."

"Better give me thirty. I have to finish here."

"Go comb your hair," he said, reaching for a wet shirt. "I'll do this."

"No!" Maggie cried, horrified by the idea of leaving Dillon to handle her laundry.

"Okay," he declared, stepping away. "Thirty minutes."

He must think I'm crazy, Maggie thought as she pinned pants onto a hanger. But there was something too personal about allowing the man to handle her garments.

Dillon was getting very personal. Maggie considered the way he'd pursued helping her with the house. And now offering to hang up her laundry. . . She definitely felt confused by his behavior.

In her bedroom, she glanced down at the clothes she wore and decided to change. She didn't know where he planned to lunch but decided a pair of capri pants and sleeveless top in a rose color would probably be fine.

After changing, she brushed her hair and slid on a pair of sandals, all the while keeping an eye on the clock. Ready with a couple of minutes to spare, she secured the back door and walked over to where Dillon waited by his mother's car.

"You look nice," he said, holding the car door open for her.

"Thank you," she returned, both for the compliment and gentlemanly gesture.

He walked around and slid behind the wheel. Mrs. Allene's car was a fully loaded, newer model, far more advanced than Maggie's economy car. She'd always found it very comfortable. Dillon had cooled the interior while waiting for her.

Thinking he'd name one of a multitude of local restaurants, Maggie asked, "So where did you have in mind for lunch?"

"I'm thinking Calabash. That okay with you?"

She knew the little town just off the North Carolina border well. They had a reputation for being crazy about seafood, and Maggie had eaten more than her share of "Calabash-style" seafood.

So much for an hour for lunch. The drive there would take almost that long. "Sure," Maggie agreed. "I just need to get back in time for Max's visitation tonight."

At least she had clothes to wear tomorrow. She'd planned to grocery shop, but she could pick up something from the cafeteria.

"Mom loved Calabash."

"Yes, she did. How does it feel to be eating American again?"

"My waist is bearing the brunt of it," he said with a laugh. "If I keep eating like this, I'll have to buy new clothes."

Maggie considered his trim appearance. She felt certain he was one of those people who could eat anything and never gain weight. She should be so fortunate. "What was the food like there?"

"Different but good. Lamb and grilled chicken were staples. I'll have to prepare some of my favorites and let you be the judge."

"Sounds like fun," Maggie agreed. "Where did you live?"

"In Riyadh, the capital. The company has a private compound with a pool, small store, book and video libraries, even a barbershop."

Maggie found Dillon to be quite an accomplished storyteller as he spoke of his years in Saudi Arabia.

Upon their arrival, he parked and then escorted her inside the restaurant. After they were seated, Maggie picked up their conversation where it had left off. "What made you choose to live there?"

He paused for a moment then said, "A woman."

Her head went crazy with thoughts of unrequited love that might have driven a man like Dillon Rogers to such a place to overcome his pain.

"We met in our third year at NC State and dated for years. I thought one day we'd marry and come back to live next door to my parents.

"Needless to say, she didn't feel the same way. When she accused me of not having an adventurous bone in my body, I took the job in Saudi to prove her wrong. I fell out of love with her and in love with the challenges of my new life and didn't look back. Last I heard, she's living in some little one-horse town with her third or fourth husband."

"Did she ever contact you again?"

"I think Mom forwarded a letter sometime between husbands two and three."

"Is she the reason you never married?"

Dillon rested his arm over the back of the chair next to him. "I don't think so. Every now and again, the idea of a wife and family appealed, but I didn't want to give up my job and move back to the States."

"Weren't there families over there?"

"Yeah," he said with a nod. "Some of the guys were married. Even had children. I didn't want that life for my family."

"Do you have regrets?"

He shrugged. "A few. Mostly when I hear people talking about their kids and grandkids. I know it probably disappointed my parents that I didn't produce an heir to carry on the Rogers family name. But there are male cousins with boys, so the name continues."

No doubt, Mrs. Allene would have adored a couple of grandchildren for reasons other than preserving the family name. She'd loved kids, particularly Pastor Joe and Mari's bunch.

"What about you? You never married, either. Why?"

Turnabout was fair play. He'd answered her question and now awaited her answer. Did she really want to tell him fear had kept her from falling in love?

"My mom died when I was very young, and then my dad died when I was eleven. There was no family left, so I ended up in the foster care system. I lived in a few homes, but when I turned fourteen, they placed me with the Floyds. They were a loving couple, and I was the only foster child they ever had."

"They never adopted you?"

"No, but I'm thankful for all they did for me. The money from the state stopped when I turned eighteen. They had no obligation, but they wanted me to get my education. I chose to become a registered nurse because of my foster mother."

"Do you stay in touch with them?"

"We talk on the phone. They live in a retirement village just outside DC."

"So why didn't you marry?" he asked again.

"I wanted a family, to be loved, but I was too afraid to make it happen."

"What made you afraid?" Dillon asked.

"I could never get it just right." Maggie could tell her comment baffled him. "Like the three bears, I was either too this or too that in every relationship."

"So the men moved on?"

Maggie nodded. "To women who were less complicated. Then I moved here, and your mom invited me to Cornerstone. I found contentment in my Lord and Savior that I'd never known before. I didn't feel as alone anymore. I had my new family at Cornerstone, and everything was wonderful."

"Until I showed up?"

"Everything fell apart when Mrs. Allene got sick," Maggie admitted. "Like God and Cornerstone, your mother had become a stabilizing influence in my life. When I felt depressed, Mrs. Allene prayed for me and helped me accept that things wouldn't always be so bad. When I needed to talk, she listened. And when I needed good advice, she gave it."

Dillon nodded slowly. "Sounds like Mom. She refused to allow me to feel sorry for myself. I remember the times she told me to get a backbone."

"Ouch."

He grinned. "She could be tough when she needed to be. And I suspect having me as a son made that need surface rather often. She never sent me to talk to Dad. She had her own discussions, making what she would and would not tolerate very clear.

"We butted heads on lots of issues, but I knew she loved me. I never realized how much until I took the Saudi job and she didn't try to change my mind. Told me I needed to finish growing up." A poignant smile touched his face. "It's tough when you're nearly thirty years old and your mom says you need to grow up. But I knew she was right."

"Did you feel abandoned?"

"No. Mom sent care packages, and we talked regularly. She helped direct my path, just as she'd always done, except she did it from thousands of miles away.

"When Dad died and I came home for the funeral, I considered coming back for good, but she told me not to do it for her. Said she didn't need me giving up the life I loved to come home and make us both miserable," Dillon said with a distant smile.

"That explains her resistance to calling you when she got sick."

He looked surprised. "She didn't want to call?"

Maggie shook her head slowly. "Told me to mind my own business when I said it wasn't fair to you."

"She'd do that," he agreed, sadness touching his expression. "I wish she'd told me sooner."

"I should have known things weren't right with her," Maggie said. "Should have seen how sick she was. Maybe she'd still be alive if I had."

"Sounds like she protected you, too."

The waitress arrived with platters of hot seafood, French fries, coleslaw, and hush puppies. Dillon said grace and they started to eat.

Maggie considered what he'd said. How long had Mrs. Allene known she had a terminal illness? "Kim's mom said Mrs. Allene needed time to strengthen herself."

"Maybe it's a mom thing," Dillon said. "She didn't want me to grieve her loss before I had to."

"We're all creatures of habit. We hide our emotions behind brick walls and don't let our loved ones see how much we're hurting when life could be so much easier if we shared the load."

"Do you think mankind will ever catch on?"

Maggie shook her head. "No. We'll keep on bumbling our way through. That's human nature. I'm sorry I didn't call earlier."

Dillon laid his fork on the plate and wiped his mouth. "I need to admit something. After you called, I had problems believing things were as bad as you indicated. I felt Mom would have told me if that were the case. Still I couldn't get what you said off my mind and called my cousin Leslie. Once she told me how sick Mom was, I caught the next plane home.

"I'm sorry, Maggie. I suppose I should have kept that to myself, but since the subject of communication came up, I think it's important that you know. I don't want to risk it coming up later and hurting even more."

"I don't blame you," she said, her voice raspy with emotion. "I was a stranger."

Dillon covered her hand with his and squeezed. "You were Mom's friend. You were there. I should have listened."

"I wondered why you were being so bullheaded," Maggie told him. "I was positive you'd realize your mother was trying to protect you."

He shook his head. "When Mom said she was okay, I believed her."

Maggie understood his distress. She'd felt the exact same way when Mrs. Allene told them to stay out of her business. "Don't beat yourself up, Dillon. You were there in time. That's all that matters."

"I could have been a better son."

"You can't change the past. Mrs. Allene got what she wanted. You didn't sit around watching her die. She couldn't bear the thought of that."

"But she allowed you to be there," he pointed out.

"I didn't ask permission," Maggie told him. "I kept showing up, and she was too weak to throw me out."

"Thanks, Maggie. For everything."

She nodded and watched Dillon for a few moments as he returned to his meal. Dillon Rogers had grown into a fine man. Mrs. Allene would be proud of her son.

Chapter 5

Maggie had many things on her mind when she returned to work the following day—the Carter family's grief, Dillon's lunch revelations, and her home repairs. Finding yet another flower arrangement from her admirer only added to the mix. "When did they arrive?"

"Around lunchtime. Who sent them?" her coworker asked.

Praying she was wrong, Maggie reached for the card. Just as she'd suspected. "Would you believe William Smith?"

"You mean the man who lost his wife a couple of months ago? Are you dating?"

"No," Maggie denied hotly. "I don't date." Although yesterday with Dillon had been like a date. The first one she'd been on in years. "Mr. Smith sent flowers and candy last week. I left them for the staff."

"So he's interested in you?"

"How can he be interested in anyone? You saw how much he loved his wife."

"Maybe he doesn't like being alone," Belinda said with a shrug. "He wouldn't be the first."

"I'm not interested. I tried to tell him, but I don't think he got the message."

"He has nice taste in flowers."

Belinda fingered the large sunflowers in the massive arrangement that held so many colorful summer flowers.

"Take them home with you," Maggie offered.

Belinda asked, "You sure?" At Maggie's nod, she said, "Okay, I will. How were your days off?"

"You wouldn't believe me if I told you," Maggie said with a grim smile.

"What happened?"

"A car drove into my house. Right into my living room."

"That was you? I saw it on the news. Poor Maggie. You're blessed that you weren't killed."

She shuddered. "When I consider I was sitting on the sofa not fifteen minutes before. . . If I hadn't gone into the kitchen to make a call. . ."

Maggie drew a deep breath. "I feel so bad for the man's family. His wife works in the church nursery with me occasionally. The funeral was today."

"That's right. The driver died."

Maggie nodded. "He had a heart attack."

Belinda shook her head in disbelief. "What are you doing about the repairs to your house?"

"My neighbor is handling things."

"The one whose mother owned the place?"

Maggie nodded. "He's agreed to help me find a contractor and get things straightened out."

"That's nice of him."

Very, Maggie agreed silently. She just wished she didn't feel so suspicious of Dillon's motives.

"I know that's a gigantic weight off your shoulders." Belinda yawned. "We'd better get through this before I fall asleep. Madison has been feverish and cranky for a couple of days now."

"Did it occur to you to call in sick?"

"Bobby took care of her last night and said she's better today. Hopefully we'll have her back in day care on Monday."

Belinda launched into a summary of the day's activities. After she left, Maggie reviewed charts and started her routine of checking in with the patients and carrying out the doctors' orders. One patient went off for a test, three more were admitted, and before she realized it, suppertime had arrived.

As she ate her sandwich, Maggie wondered about the outcome of the contractor's visit but restrained herself from calling Dillon. She'd promised to trust him and felt certain he'd let her know.

By morning, she was glad to see her replacement arrive. Just as she was finishing for the day, a nurse from emergency called up to say a woman was asking for her.

Wondering who it could be, Maggie grabbed her purse, called good-bye, and headed for the elevator. In the ER, she stopped by the desk, and the attendant pointed to the seats along the side of the room. She recognized Mrs. Pearson and a screaming Chloe Turner from church. She hurried over to where they sat.

"Maggie, thank God you're here!" the woman cried.

Chloe's wails had everyone in the waiting area looking at them with raised brows. She lifted the little girl from Mrs. Pearson's arms and whispered a few soothing words as she patted the baby's back. Soon Chloe's sobs became hiccups. "What's going on? Why are you here with Chloe? Where's Peg?"

Maggie knew Peg Turner rented Mrs. Pearson's garage apartment. Peg's husband had left her for another woman a few months before.

"I hadn't seen her in a couple of days, and I thought I'd better check on them," Mrs. Pearson explained as she patted the child's shoulder. "Peg was so sick. I called an ambulance. Chloe and I followed in my car."

Maggie rocked gently, soothing the little girl. "Did you bring her bottle or a diaper bag?"

"I didn't think about that. Everything happened so fast."

Maggie glanced down, relieved to find the little girl had drifted off to sleep. "Take her and let me check on Peg. I'll be right back."

Peg was indeed very sick. She had a ruptured appendix and would be staying in the hospital for a few days.

"Maggie, where's Chloe? Why is she crying?" asked Peg.

"Mrs. Pearson has her in the lobby. She's fine. Don't worry. We'll take care of her during your hospital stay."

"I can't stay," Peg protested weakly, trying to rise from the bed. "I have to take care of Chloe."

Maggie rested a hand against her shoulder, holding her still. "Peg, you have to get better to do that. I'll be happy to take Chloe home with me if that's okay with you. She knows me from the church nursery. And I'll let Pastor Dennis know what's going on with you. I'm sure he'll stop by."

"You won't let them take her away?"

The fear in Peg's softly spoken question tugged at Maggie's heart. She had no doubt the single mother worried about what would happen to her child if she weren't around to care for her.

"Your church family will take good care of Chloe," Maggie promised. "You'll be back at home with her before you know it."

The woman sagged weakly against the bed. "Thanks, Maggie. I was so afraid. Mrs. Pearson has a key to the apartment. She can let you in to get what you need for Chloe. She's a good baby."

Maggie listened as Peg weakly outlined a few basics for caring for her child before insisting, "You rest now. I'll check on you tonight."

Sometime later, Maggie carried the baby into her house. She had scarcely gotten inside when Dillon knocked on the door.

"Where have you been? I thought you'd be home. . ." His voice trailed off as his gaze rested on the sleeping baby in her arms.

"Something came up," Maggie told him. "Here, hold her while I get some bedding."

"Uh, Maggie," Dillon muttered uncomfortably when she placed the child in his stiff arms and adjusted them into a cradle.

"Oh come on, Dillon. She's asleep. Just hold on to her. Here, sit down. You'll feel more comfortable."

"Whose baby is this?" he asked when she started to walk away.

"I'll fill you in once I get her settled."

"Maggie!" Dillon called in alarm when she started to leave the room.

"Shush," Maggie warned. "You'll wake her."

Dillon glanced down and back at Maggie with total uncertainty in his expression.

"You're doing fine," she said. "I'll be right back."

Maggie folded and tucked bedding until she'd made a small pallet on the floor. She lifted the child from Dillon's hold, shushing Chloe when she woke briefly.

"Whew." She blew out a deep breath and dropped back on the chair arm. She noted Dillon watching her, allowing his gaze to drop to the sleeping baby before coming back to her.

Weary, she rubbed her face and explained how she'd been called to the ER after work to find Chloe crying so loud she had everyone in the waiting room cringing. "She stopped when I took her."

"So where's her mom?"

"In the hospital. Peg's very sick. I promised to take care of Chloe until she's released."

"How can you do that and work, too?" Dillon asked.

"I have a plan. Don't look at me like that," she said defensively. "It was the right thing to do."

"And you need one more thing to take up your time, I suppose?" Dillon asked.

"She's not a thing. She's a baby."

"I know, but with your job and now the house situation, wouldn't it be better if someone else cared for her? Maybe Mari Dennis."

"Mari doesn't need another child, Dillon. She has five of her own. Chloe is comfortable with me, and I promised Peg."

"She'll probably keep you awake all day."

"It wouldn't be the first time I've lost a bit of sleep," Maggie assured.

"Where's her father?"

"Peg said he spends his time barhopping and getting himself into trouble. He doesn't even pay child support. You think I should entrust Chloe to him?"

"He's her father. Maybe taking responsibility for his child would force him to rethink his life."

Maggie refused to consider contacting the man. "Peg's already lost her husband and her home. I won't let anything happen to Chloe. She stays right here with me until her mother can take over."

He looked thoroughly chastised. "Okay, I'm sorry. You're right. I just thought maybe we could go to dinner later and talk about the contractor."

"Losing your mom is a big deal when you're grown, but you'll have to admit it's even bigger when you're Chloe's age," Maggie said. "If you really want to go out, I can handle a baby at a restaurant. But you're welcome to eat with us. I have spaghetti sauce defrosting in the fridge and thought I'd make garlic bread."

"She won't be a happy camper when she wakes up and finds her mom missing."

Maggie found it interesting that Dillon had already determined what Chloe would be like when she woke. "She'll be fine. Did the contractor show up yesterday?"

He looked disgusted. "Yeah, he came. Two hours after he said he'd be here. Didn't offer any explanation for being late. No apology. Poked around for another hour and said he can't start work until late September."

Maggie's brows lifted at that. "Why so long? I'd hoped that with his quick response, he'd be available right away."

"After talking to him, I don't think he could handle the job anyway."

"Really? Why?"

"He couldn't give me references, and there was something about his attitude. He got too excited when I mentioned you wanted the job completed as quickly as possible.

"I think he's saying late September so we'd feel we should pay him more when he moves you up on the schedule. He kept asking about overtime. And his quote was on the high side. I went over to see Wyatt."

"Was Kim there?"

"At the store. Chase was hanging out at the shop with his dad. All he could talk about was Florida."

Maggie laughed. "He's excited about the trip."

"Wyatt's going to give me the name of a couple of contractors he knows. And he'll do what he can to help get things sorted out when he gets back."

"That's sweet of him."

Dillon studied her for a moment. "You didn't say it was sweet of me."

Maggie smiled. "How do you know? Maybe I've told everyone that you're wonderful for doing this."

He shrugged. "Maybe you have. You should get some rest. What can I do to help?"

"Could you pick up the playpen from Mari's after church? She said Joe would bring it later, but there's no telling when he'll have time."

"How about Chinese?"

"It won't take long to fix the spaghetti."

He nodded toward the sleeping child. "She might need you. It would be difficult to care for her and cook."

Maggie nearly laughed at his logic. Women had juggled babies and housework for years. She'd feel insulted if she didn't know he had good intentions. "I don't mind not cooking. Chicken and broccoli would hit the spot. Let me get some money."

"I've got it."

Maggie protested, "I don't expect you to feed me, Dillon."

"You can return the favor next time."

After he'd gone, Maggie considered the implications of there being a next time. Apparently, Dillon Rogers planned to make himself at home in her life.

Right at home. How did he do that? Dillon believed he belonged everywhere he went. She'd craved that elusive feeling since her father died.

Was it her? What kept her from accepting her right to belong? Despite the fact that her friends welcomed her into the community with open arms, there were still times when she felt like an outsider.

Maggie doubted Dillon had any idea how she felt. Nor did she feel an overwhelming need to share her lack of self-esteem.

Little Mary Margaret Gregory had once had self-esteem, before foster homes had left her drifting in the wind, as homeless as tumbleweed blowing through the desert. She hadn't fit in there, either, because she was the outsider—the child the family allowed to live in their home. Even adopted children knew they had a special place in their parents' hearts, but foster children were more like nomads.

In her foster care years, Maggie had become acquainted with more than one child placed in the system because their parents couldn't be bothered to accept their responsibility. Then there were the kids like her whose lives had taken a turn for the worst and left them homeless wards of the state.

Maggie understood Peg's concern about her daughter. Where would Chloe go if something happened to her mother? Back to the father who couldn't put aside his own selfish needs to care about his wife and small child? She didn't even want to consider that possibility.

Maggie pushed herself off the recliner and ran out to the car to get the bags she'd brought from Peg's home. In the kitchen, she sorted the items. No doubt, Chloe would be hungry when she woke. Maggie smiled at the worn stuffed teddy Peg reminded her Chloe couldn't be without. She remembered seeing it in the little girl's arms when she came to the nursery. Obviously, Mrs. Pearson hadn't known that when she grabbed Chloe and headed for the hospital.

They napped until well after lunch. When she woke, Maggie called Natalie to ask if she could stay with Chloe that night. She agreed and said she'd come over to get acquainted with the child before Maggie left for work.

Dillon returned midafternoon and brought their meal inside before going back to his car for the playpen and high chair. "Mari showed me how to set them up. I'll show you when she wakes up."

"Chloe," Maggie said. He looked at her strangely. "Her name is Chloe. Her mother's name is Peg."

His bewildered expression told her he didn't understand. "I'm sure Peg and Chloe appreciate your efforts on their behalf. I wanted you to know their names."

Dillon shifted uncomfortably. "Well. . . Um. . . It's the least I can do."

She found his discomfort surprising. "I appreciate your help, too. It's sweet of you."

He grinned widely. "Let's eat before our food gets cold."

Maggie checked on Chloe and returned to the kitchen. She sat down at the table and served her plate from the various containers. "I really should wake her up. She won't sleep tonight."

"Give her a few more minutes—just until you finish eating."

Maggie chose a seat where she could keep Chloe in sight. "What's the next step with the house?" she asked as she removed her egg roll from the wrapper. "If this contractor can't start until September, that's probably going to be the case with all of them."

"Let's see what Wyatt has to offer. I wouldn't have hired this man. I didn't feel good about him."

They finished, and Dillon helped Maggie set up the playpen in her bedroom and the high chair in the kitchen. Chloe woke hungry, and he entertained the baby while Maggie prepared her meal.

Afterward Chloe played on the floor at their feet as she and Dillon watched television. When Chloe started to fuss, Maggie joined the baby on the quilts and made her laugh.

"You're good with her," Dillon commented.

"It's good experience for when I become a foster parent." He grew quiet. "Is something wrong, Dillon?"

"No. No," he denied quickly.

"You seem troubled."

"Just thinking. You want me to keep an eye on her while you get dressed for work?"

"Natalie should be here shortly. She's spending the night."

He stood up. "Call me tomorrow if you need someone to care for her so you can rest."

"Thanks, Dillon. We'll be fine. She goes to day care."

He took Maggie's hand in his and squeezed gently. "Have a good night. I'll be in touch about the house."

⁓

After letting himself out Maggie's back door, Dillon headed for the gate that separated their yards. *That was close,* he realized, thinking how easily she'd picked up on his mood. She was too perceptive. He did feel troubled. Maggie's maternal behavior seemed out of place with the woman in his head.

The child's needs would preempt his opportunity to spend time with Maggie. Working on the house gave him a good excuse to visit often, but now he'd have to share Maggie with a little girl.

And what was that about becoming a foster parent? She'd never mentioned that before.

Oh, don't be so selfish, he told himself as he secured the gate and walked across his freshly mowed lawn. What had Mom always said? When something's meant to be, God works it out.

⁓

After he left, Maggie concentrated on getting Chloe bathed. She felt worn out from entertaining the little girl.

The phone rang around four thirty, and she left Chloe playing on the quilt while she grabbed the cordless phone from the kitchen.

"Maggie, I hear someone tried to take a shortcut through your living room!" Kim exclaimed.

"Welcome home," Maggie said, happy to hear from her friend. She walked back into the living room. "How was Charleston?"

"Okay, I guess. I only had eyes for Wyatt."

"Says a woman in love," Maggie teased. "He should have saved his money and kept you at home."

"No way."

"From what Dillon said, I take it Chase is eager to see Florida."

"That child is wearing me out," Kim said. "I know I'll never want to see some of these rides he's talking about again."

"They are easier on the body when you're Chase's age."

Chloe screamed, and Kim said, "I didn't realize you had company."

Maggie handed the baby her toy as she explained the situation.

"Is Peg okay?"

"She will be. I'm watching Chloe until she's back on her feet. I think I'll bring Peg here after she gets out of the hospital. Her place is too small for me to stay there, and I have the guest room and can help with Chloe until she's able to take over."

"Let me know if I can help," Kim said. "Wyatt said Dillon is looking for contractors for you."

"He's been a great help," Maggie said, unsure she wanted to explain the matter further.

"So you two are getting along?"

"I think we'll be able to get past the history. He went over to Mari's for the playpen and high chair, and he picked up lunch today. He acted like a woman my age never dealt with children or something. He'd freak if he saw me with all those kids in the nursery."

"Probably. Wyatt just called him with a list of contractors. Hopefully, he'll find someone soon."

"I hope so. I miss my windows. And my door." At least the space was usable. The men had boarded the opening with plywood inside and out and cleaned up the debris. It might look a little rough, but she felt secure in her home.

"I know, but consider the possibilities," Kim told her. "Now you can do some of that exterior remodeling you've always thought would suit the house."

"My fountain's broken."

"Oh," Kim moaned. "Don't worry. We'll find one that's even better."

"I'll hold you to that. When do your parents leave?"

"Next weekend. We'll be back on Friday so we can spend time with them, and then the next Monday is the first day of school."

"You're going to have a busy week. Have fun with your new family."

"I will," Kim said with a laugh.

"Let's get together soon."

"I'll call you."

"Say a prayer for Chloe tonight. She misses her mommy. I hope she doesn't give Natalie a hard time."

"Already done. Take care."

Chapter 6

Early Monday morning, Natalie reported that she and Chloe had a good night and took the little girl off to day care so Maggie could sleep. Maggie picked Chloe up that afternoon, and Natalie returned to stay the night just before Maggie went to work.

On Tuesday, Maggie insisted Dillon stay for supper. He'd stopped by to discuss an estimate from the contractor he had met with Monday evening after Maggie had left for work and offered to care for Chloe while she finished their meal. Maggie laughed when Dillon showed his horror at the way Chloe smeared food from head to toe and across the high chair in her efforts to feed herself.

"Hey, we don't do that," he protested when she banged her bowl on the high chair and then tossed it on the floor. Dillon ripped off several paper towels to clean up the mess.

"You might not do it now, but you did when you were her age," Maggie told him.

"I can't imagine Mom allowing me to be that messy."

"It's learning to be independent, Dillon. How else will she learn to feed and dress herself?"

He deposited the towels in the trash. "So I should be telling her 'good job'?"

Maggie grinned and nodded. "While encouraging her to get more in her mouth than on her body, of course."

She set a bowl of rice on the table and added the beef stew she'd cooked with onions, potatoes, and carrots in the slow cooker. "Eat your dinner. I'll take over with Chloe."

He served his plate and took a bite. "This is delicious."

"Thanks. So tell me about the contractor."

He changed gears quickly, wiping his mouth as he said, "He's the one we should use. I'm impressed with his knowledge level, and he can start right away."

"Right away?" she questioned. He'd told her most of the others he'd called were backlogged for months.

Dillon reached for his iced tea and took a long drink before he nodded. "My advice is to give them the job. Unless you want to wait for more estimates."

Maggie wasn't sure. "You're comfortable with this guy?"

"Keith Harris gave me references, and they all checked out. Three satisfied customers said both he and his brother do excellent work."

"Then why is he available so soon?" Maggie asked.

"It's the craziest story. He and his twin brother, Erik, are married to sisters. Both wives were expecting, and the babies were born on the same day. They cleared their calendars to help at home. Now they're ready to start booking again and willing to make yours their first project. Answer to a prayer, wouldn't you say?"

Maggie remembered reading about the couples in the paper. "Oh yes," she agreed without further hesitation. "I'm so tired of that cave I call my living room. I need light."

"I'll call Keith right now."

"He might be busy," she said.

"He's expecting my call." Dillon unclipped his cell phone and dialed her new contractor. "He'll be here tomorrow," he told her after disconnecting.

"You were sure I'd say yes, weren't you?" Maggie asked, mildly put out by his actions.

"We need to act fast, before they get more projects in the works. Keith gave me a materials list. I placed the order this morning and picked these up while I was at the hardware store." He indicated the door and window brochures he'd laid on the tabletop earlier.

"What happened to carrying out my decisions?" she demanded.

His pleading blue gaze begged her forgiveness. "I'm sorry. When he told me they could start tomorrow, I knew they needed supplies."

"And you couldn't pick up the phone to call and ask?"

He frowned and said, "You were sleeping. Do you want me to cancel the order?"

It annoyed her more that he tried to use charm to coax her into a better mood. "No, Dillon. Did you pay for the stuff?"

He reached for his wallet. "I have the receipt right here. You can reimburse me when you get your check from the insurance company."

Maggie didn't like being in his debt. She had planned to use her credit card. She'd known this would happen. "Fine."

"What about the door and windows? Do you have any idea what you want?"

"A few, but I'll look at the brochures tonight after I get Chloe into bed."

"We should visit a couple of stores so you can see the doors and windows before you decide."

"I'm off the rest of the week. I bring Peg home from the hospital on Friday."

Dillon finished his meal and indicated she should eat. He used paper towels to wipe Chloe's face and hands and wiped the high chair down with a sponge. "You're bringing her here?"

"She's still recovering, Dillon. She can't take care of Chloe on her own."

He grimaced when Chloe let out a loud wail of protest because he didn't take her from the high chair. "I still don't understand why you're making this your problem."

"It's not a problem. While she recovers from her surgery, Peg's not allowed to lift more than ten pounds. If she goes home alone with Chloe, she won't have a choice, and then she'll be back in the hospital. I've discussed it with Natalie and Mari, and they're willing to help."

"You don't leave anything to chance, do you?"

Maggie laid her fork on the plate and went to get Chloe a cookie. "Rarely. It's never been an option for me. Not if I want my life to run smoothly."

"Your life would glide if you didn't take on so much."

"What would you do, Dillon?" Maggie demanded. When he said nothing, she said, "Let me answer that for you. When it's something you can handle, like finding my contractor, you're on it without hesitation. But this situation with Peg and Chloe isn't something you can handle, is it?"

He looked sheepish. "I suppose not."

"There are too many people in the world who never ask anything of their fellow man until they're knocked off their feet and forced to seek help. Do you think Peg likes giving up her independence? Not in the least. And she'll spend weeks trying to figure out some way to repay me. But that's not my reason for helping. I'm doing this for Chloe." Maggie ran her hand over the child's red curls. "You need me, don't you, sweetie?"

The baby laughed.

"So if it were just Peg, you wouldn't be doing this?"

She forced herself to settle down. "I'd still help, but she wouldn't need more than a few groceries, maybe a ride home from the hospital or to the doctor's office, and perhaps a bit of medical advice," she explained. "I'm a nurse. Taking care of people is what I do best."

"Another good reason not to take it on in your private life."

"We're not going to agree. Until Peg's able to care for Chloe without endangering herself, I'm helping out."

"Do you think Natalie or Mari would keep an eye on her when we go shopping?"

Maggie studied the messy baby. "We could take Chloe with us."

"To the hardware store? There are a million things she could get into."

Chloe took that moment to toss her spoon on the floor. It clattered against the tile. "That's why they put child seats on shopping carts."

Dillon looked doubtful. "Fine. What about tomorrow?"

"I think I need to be here to make sure the Harris brothers understand what I want. What about Friday afternoon? It'll probably be close to noon before I get Peg home and settled."

"What about day care?" Dillon asked. "You are planning to take Chloe, aren't you?"

Maggie had no plans to change the baby's schedule. Besides, it would be hard for her to rest with demolition and construction going on. And as for Friday, she knew Peg was eager to see her daughter, but things would be easier all around if she left Chloe at day care until later that afternoon. "I'll run it by Peg."

"Coming home is going to take a lot out of her. She can rest and then spend quality time with her child Friday night."

Dillon was right. Peg was exhausted from the exertion of the trip home and agreed she needed time to get herself together before seeing Chloe. Maggie brought Peg home, fixed her lunch, and helped her into bed for a long nap. She apologized for the construction noise, but Peg assured her she didn't mind. After making sure Peg had everything she needed nearby, Maggie called Dillon.

He took her to a discount hardware store, and they looked through the various windows and doors on display. A beautiful oak door with a leaded glass panel and matching sidelights struck her fancy, and even though Maggie told herself it was more than she had planned to spend, she kept trying to work it out in her head.

"You should get it," Dillon said when she went back to examine the door for the third time.

"It costs three times as much as the others," she argued. "And if I get a cheaper door, I can have those bigger windows."

"I could look around for something similar that costs less," he offered. "Only thing is the Harrises will need them soon."

"I'm sure I can find one here," Maggie said.

"What about carpet for the living room?"

"Just a new area rug," Maggie said. Thankfully, her old rug had protected the floor from the gas, oil, and radiator fluids that had poured from the car. "I love the hardwoods. I worked hard to restore them."

He looked surprised. "You did the floors?"

She nodded. "Mrs. Allene said I could. I ripped up the old carpet and rented a sander. Once I got used to the machine, it wasn't bad." Maggie grinned and admitted, "A time or two, I thought I'd gone too deep, but thankfully I hadn't."

"What else did you do to the house?"

"Painted, replaced the bathroom vanity and kitchen counters, and tiled the kitchen floor."

"Mom let you pay for all that?"

Maggie shrugged. "Why should she pay? I rented a perfectly good house. I wanted the changes."

"But you improved her property."

The reality of the matter was that she'd improved her own property, but

Maggie had no way of knowing that would be the case. She wondered if her work had been the reason Mrs. Allene left her the house.

"Did you landscape the yard, too?"

"I love to garden. That reminds me. Did the adjustor cover that in the estimate?"

"He did, but I don't think he paid what the statuary was worth."

"They were all secondhand pieces. I have the receipts. Kim found the fountain for me."

"I looked it over and think we might be able to salvage it with epoxy and concrete paint."

"Won't it leak?" Maggie asked.

"If it doesn't work, all we've lost is the cost of the supplies. If it does, you'll have your fountain back."

Maggie walked back to the oak door. "I'm going to buy this one. If I don't, I'll kick myself later when I start wishing I had. Besides, I won't need bigger windows with the glass in the door and panels."

"Good point. Today's your lucky day. Wyatt has an account with this store, and he gets a discount. He said to charge whatever we need, and we'll settle up later."

Pleased with how things were falling into place, Maggie laughed joyously. "I need to shop with you more often."

After picking out her windows and shingles for the new roof, they headed for home.

"Thanks for your help, Dillon. I didn't look forward to handling this alone."

"No problem. I'll pick up the fountain later and take it over to my workshop."

"I doubt it can be repaired, but you're welcome to give it a try."

"I like making things work when people think it's impossible."

Maggie had seen that facet of his personality in action numerous times. Maybe it was something to do with being an engineer. "Are you coming over for dinner?"

"No. I'm sure your houseguest will want to get to bed early."

"Well, thanks again," she said as she opened the car door. "I'm going to pick up Chloe. Peg's waited long enough to see her child."

Later that night, when Peg and Chloe were sleeping, Maggie found herself missing Dillon. Sure, there were times when she considered him controlling, but the good outweighed the bad.

She thought about the door they'd found that day. It was perfect. Something else she'd never considered she'd have—a home of her own with a beautiful leaded glass and oak front door to welcome her friends.

Chapter 7

On Sunday, Maggie dressed Chloe for church and then took her in to say good-bye to her mother.

"Wish I were going," Peg said as she righted Chloe's hair bow. The baby's hand immediately went to her head.

Maggie knew how Peg felt. She didn't have her strength back, but she was tired of being a convalescent. They had become better acquainted since Peg had moved in. Last night, after Chloe was in bed, they sat and chatted until time for bed.

"Is Peg short for Peggy?" Maggie asked.

"No. Mary Margaret."

Maggie smiled. "I'm Mary Margaret, too."

"Your mom's best friend?" Peg asked.

"Grandmothers," Maggie offered. "Both died before I had an opportunity to know them."

"It's old-fashioned," Peg said. "I wanted Chloe to have something unique. Of course, now that I think about it, there will be hundreds of Chloes and only a few Mary Margarets."

Peg thanked Maggie for stepping in to care for her daughter. Maggie understood Peg's concerns and felt thankful for the opportunity to be of service to someone in need.

"No, Chloe," Peg said, bringing Maggie's thoughts back to the present.

Maggie tried to clip the hair bow back in place and gave up when Chloe wouldn't leave it alone. "We'd better go."

She told Chloe to tell Mommy good-bye and smiled when the child worked her fingers in response. Grabbing the stroller from the laundry room, they went outside and saw Dillon coming out his back door.

It was a gorgeous day, the sun shining brightly and not a cloud in the sky. No doubt the beach was already filled with sun worshippers. Maggie sent up a quick prayer for them as she struggled to keep her hold on Chloe while opening the stroller.

"Good morning, ladies," Dillon said, coming over to complete the task for her. "It's a beautiful day for service to the Lord."

"I'm putting Chloe in the nursery and attending worship service today."

"Want to sit with me?"

"I'll meet you in the sanctuary after Sunday school."

As Maggie went off toward the nursery, Dillon headed to the room where his Sunday school group met. He enjoyed being in fellowship with men his own age. His worship in Saudi Arabia had been much different.

One of the things Dillon appreciated most was the freedom to worship. It might have been something he took for granted in the past, but having lived in a Muslim country for so many years, he found himself very appreciative of Cornerstone.

After greeting the others, he took a seat and allowed his thoughts to drift back to Maggie in her caregiver mode. She seemed so comfortable with Chloe.

Maybe it was because she was a nurse, but no matter how he tried, Dillon couldn't help but feel Maggie allowed people to take advantage of her. Awareness washed over him like waves washing up on shore. No wonder he'd hurt her with his insinuations. Now that he knew her better, he realized she wasn't capable of what he had implied.

The class began, and soon it was time to meet Maggie. They sat in the pew his parents used to sit in. Having her by his side was nice. When they sang, he enjoyed her alto voice. When Joe Dennis invited them to read along in their Bibles, she shared.

"No doubt some of you in here today are carrying a load of guilt over past sins," Pastor Joe began. "Something you can't let go of even though your heavenly Father has removed this sin to the depths of the ocean.

"And we all know that ocean is pretty deep. You can't dive to the bottom without oxygen, and even then you can only stay down a brief time. Forgiven sin isn't like that. It doesn't bob to the surface when we least expect it. Once you've repented and been forgiven, that sin no longer exists in God's eyes.

"Oh, we hold on to it," Joe Dennis pronounced gravely. "Maybe as penance for our wicked ways. Self-punishment to keep us from forgetting. Or maybe we hold on to remind ourselves we're not worthy of Jesus Christ dying for our sins. But friends, we are worthy indeed. Christ made us worthy.

"Now listen carefully. I'm not saying we should ever take the gift for granted. We should embrace His love with open arms and freely offer it to anyone with ears to listen."

As the sermon continued, Dillon's discomfort increased. He glanced at Maggie to find her listening to the pastor's words, nodding in agreement.

"If there's a burden on your heart today because you need to seek forgiveness from someone, then you should pray and take action to resolve the situation immediately. Only then can you walk with God as He would have you walk."

Each word stabbed Dillon in the heart. He was a Christian. He had given his heart to Jesus as a child of seven, but he still had to fight the ways of the world. And he definitely needed to seek forgiveness of someone he'd hurt by his actions.

When Maggie decided not to stay for fellowship and collected Chloe from the nursery, Dillon joined her for the walk home.

"Can we talk for a few minutes?"

She seemed eager to escape. "I'm sure Peg is ready for lunch."

"Just a few minutes, Maggie. Please," Dillon pleaded. "Chloe is happy right now, and I'm sure Peg can wait that long."

"Not today. Not now."

"Why?" he asked. "I'm trying to say I'm sorry. Is it too much for you to accept my apology?"

"Yes," Maggie said. "There's nothing to forgive."

"You know there is," Dillon insisted with a stubbornness reminiscent of his mother.

"What I know is that Mrs. Allene was your mother, not mine. You should have doubts about me," Maggie said, stooping to pick up the toy Chloe tossed from the stroller.

Dillon bent at the same time, and they butted heads. "Why are you saying this, Maggie?" he asked as he straightened up, rubbing his skull.

"Because I heard that sermon today, too, Dillon. I haven't been able to see my role in our problems because of the beam in my own eye."

Dillon shook his head and insisted, "I was wrong. Now that I know you better, I know you'd never willingly take advantage of another living soul. I misjudged you, and I'm sorry."

"You don't understand."

Confusion drove him to ask, "Understand what?"

"It's stupid, but I felt I no longer belonged."

"Belonged where?"

"Here," Maggie explained. "In your mother's life. In my hometown."

"But how could you feel that way? You're a member of the community. A member of Cornerstone. People love you."

"But I took something that wasn't mine to take."

"How do you figure that?"

"You'd have to understand my past," she said, looking everywhere but at Dillon.

He lifted her chin and gazed into her eyes. "Tell me."

"You remember I was a foster child?" Dillon nodded, and she continued. "I became a loner. Being a foster child does that to you. You wander in and out of people's lives, like going through a revolving door.

"My problem was I tried too hard. Whenever the parents said, 'Why can't you be more like Maggie?' I saw the writing on the wall. A good foster kid learns to fly under the radar, but I wanted to be loved. I thought being good would help. But I was wrong."

"But surely the parents knew it wasn't your fault if their children were jealous."

"It didn't matter," Maggie declared. "The foster parents weren't going to make their lives miserable. Oh, some of them showed regret. After all, I was an easy foster child. I did more than my fair share of chores and made good grades in school."

"What about your last foster parents? Did they make you feel that way?"

"The Floyds are good people," Maggie said. "But my insecurities were well established by that time. I'd been in the system for years, and I didn't dare get too comfortable for fear I'd get sent away again."

"But it didn't happen."

"No, but I lived daily with the knowledge that it could. You grew up and made the decision to leave home, Dillon. I had no home to leave. You can't begin to imagine what it's like to be forced to depend on the kindness and mercy of strangers."

"Like Peg?" he asked with a dawning understanding.

Maggie nodded. "My needs have always been pretty basic. I have to feel people love and want me in their lives."

"And I made you feel you don't belong?" he repeated.

"No, not you. Me," Maggie stated, resting her hands against her chest to emphasize her point. "When you questioned my intentions, I went on the defensive because I felt this sense of entitlement about Mrs. Allene. I became that little girl who wanted to be someone's daughter. Your mother's daughter."

"There's nothing wrong with that," Dillon said. "My mother loved you and rightfully so, because truth be told, you were a better daughter than I was a son. I knew she wasn't going to live forever. I just didn't know how little time I had."

"None of us do, Dillon. That's why it's important to tell people you love them at every opportunity. I felt envy when she talked about you. I sound like a candidate for a psychologist's couch."

"Not really. Sometimes when we can't have what we want in life, we reach out and take. You wanted a mother, and I had one I took for granted."

"She was a wonderful woman."

"I'm glad we can share our memories of her," Dillon said.

"So where do we stand?"

"I consider you a good friend, Maggie, but I feel the need to explore another depth to our relationship. I care for you."

What is she thinking? Dillon wondered, watching her expression as she considered what he'd just shared with her.

Chloe started to fuss, and Maggie glanced down at the child. "I'd better get her home."

"Maggie?" Dillon said as she pushed the stroller forward a couple of steps. "You won't let what I just told you scare you off, will you?"

She glanced back at him. "No, Dillon. If God has something more in store for us, I'll be around to learn what it is."

He smiled broadly.

"I'm glad we talked. I'll have to thank Pastor Joe for his sermon."

"There's so much we don't know about each other," Maggie warned.

"There's time."

They shared another smile. Maggie invited him to lunch, and Dillon quickly accepted, eager to spend more time with her now that she'd given him a glimpse of the real Maggie Gregory.

Chapter 8

Her return to day shift and the ongoing work on the house presented Maggie with a new dilemma. She knew Peg couldn't rest comfortably with all the noise and activity. Peg suggested she could go home, but Maggie knew she couldn't care for Chloe alone yet.

Natalie solved the problem by offering to take Chloe to day care and Peg back to her apartment for the day. Mari would pick up Chloe from day care before they closed, and then Maggie would pick up Peg and Chloe after work and bring them back to her house for the night.

Maggie let Natalie in the next morning and left Chloe in her care while she showered and dressed for work. She found them in the kitchen.

"You don't have to be here so early. I don't think they plan to start work until around seven."

"I wasn't sure," Natalie said as she fed Chloe fruit. The baby smiled shyly. "She's such a sweetie."

Maggie noted Chloe's hair had been brushed up into little pigtails on each side of her head. "How did you manage that? She won't leave her bows alone."

"I sidetracked her with food. I'm sure she'll catch on shortly."

Chloe offered her own baby-speak greeting when Maggie spoke to her before pouring coffee into her travel mug. "How's Peg this morning?"

"Good. She said the pain isn't as bad. Didn't want any pills when I took her breakfast a few minutes ago."

Maggie yawned widely. "Thanks, Nat. See you tonight."

<hr/>

Maggie took Peg for her post-op appointment on Friday. The doctor released her to return to work but cautioned her about overdoing.

"Are you sure you can care for Chloe?" Maggie asked when Peg announced her plans to return home.

They stopped by the church day care, and Peg watched as Maggie secured Chloe in the car seat. "You've done enough. It's time we gave you your house back."

"I haven't minded having you there."

"I know, but I'm feeling stronger every day. You gave me time to recuperate, and I thank you for that. If it hadn't been for you and Natalie, I would have had no choice but to care for Chloe myself."

"When do you want to go?"

"Today. I have everything packed."

Maggie felt tears well in her eyes. "I'm gonna miss you both so much."

"We'll miss you, too. I hope we can stay in touch," Peg offered uncertainly.

"You're not getting rid of me that easily," Maggie said with a grin. "I consider you a friend. Besides, your daughter has taken control of a chunk of my heart."

"Oh, Maggie, I can never thank you enough for all you've done."

"Seeing you well and happy is all the thanks I need," Maggie said.

Back at the house, Maggie insisted Peg rest while she loaded the car. "What about food?"

"I need a few things."

"I'll take you to your place. You can make a list, and I'll do the shopping." When Peg started to protest, Maggie held up her hand and said, "Last time, I promise."

"Okay, but you have to let us do something for you."

"Just get better."

Three hours later, Peg and Chloe had settled in at home. Maggie had restocked the kitchen, and Mrs. Pearson promised to check in on them regularly.

Overwhelming sadness filled Maggie as she walked outside and climbed into her car. She'd known she'd miss Peg and Chloe but not how much.

A public service announcement about foster parenting played on the radio, reminding Maggie to follow up on the application she'd submitted back in the spring. The four- to six-month review period had passed, but the accident had put things on hold. She hoped she would soon have the house repaired and get a placement.

She still couldn't believe the idea had never occurred to her until recently. And now she anticipated the prospect of sharing her home again.

Maggie parked and walked over to talk with Keith Harris for a few minutes before going inside to load the dishes into the dishwasher. Maggie smiled when she found Chloe's dish. It would give her a reason to visit sooner. She turned off the faucet after rinsing the last plate and grabbed a towel to dry her hands before answering the knock at the back door. "Dillon? What's wrong?"

She touched his arm and noted the pale dampness of his skin.

"Pain in my side. Nausea after I eat."

She took his arm and guided him toward a chair. "Why didn't you say something before?"

"Men don't whine."

Maggie grinned at that. "Suffering in silence doesn't make sense. How is the pain on a scale of one to ten?"

"A thirteen," he said, grimacing as he spoke.

"Let me grab my purse. I'll take you to the ER." She knew he was sick when he didn't argue.

An hour later, she sat by his bed in the small cubicle. The diagnosis was pancreatitis caused by gallstones.

"For now, we'll admit you in the hospital and restrict all food and water until we get this under control," the doctor said. "I'm ordering a GI cocktail. That should help some. We'll give you medication for the pain, and I'd like to do a CAT scan. Then we can look at options to eliminate the problem."

"Whatever you need to do," Dillon told them, all the while struggling to keep a stiff upper lip.

Maggie patted his hand. "You'll feel better soon."

"All that big talk about others taking advantage, and now I'm doing the same thing," he mumbled.

"It's not taking advantage if I do something willingly," Maggie said.

"I'm so thirsty," Dillon moaned.

"I'll bring you a few ice chips. Be careful though. We don't want to make things worse."

Dillon lay back against the bed. "I don't ever recall being this sick."

Maggie smoothed her hand over his forehead, and upon realizing what she'd done, jerked her hand away. That certainly wasn't very professional. "Rest for a bit."

He reached for her hand and kissed it, whispering his thanks just before he dozed off.

Maggie hated seeing Dillon like this. She prayed for him throughout her shift and had the church members doing the same. Joe and Noah came to visit, as well as Wyatt and Kim Alexander. The members of Cornerstone filled his room with flowers, cards, and balloons. By Saturday, he seemed to be doing better when she stopped in to check on him.

"I'm sorry, Maggie. I let you down."

"Don't be ridiculous, Dillon. You couldn't know you'd get sick. Besides, the Harris brothers are doing an excellent job. They got the porch roof back on and promised me a working door and new windows by next week."

"They work fast."

"They've had plenty of men checking up on them. Wyatt, Joe, and Noah drop by every day."

"All of them?"

"Well, I suspect Joe and Noah started out by witnessing, but now that they've learned the Harrises attend church, they're inspecting their work."

He managed a weak smile.

⁓

On Sunday, Dillon woke feeling much better. The surgeon did his rounds early that morning.

"We can proceed with surgery or wait until a later date."

"I don't want to risk a recurrence of what just happened. Let's get this over with."

295

"I'll check on an operating room. Maybe this afternoon but probably tomorrow."

Dillon went to surgery, and by Monday night, Maggie was encouraging him to walk. She told him the sooner he became mobile, the sooner he'd get to go home. He managed to make it around the floor a couple of times.

"Hey, Maggie," one of the aides called, "I see you got more flowers."

She looked up just as he walked by. Dillon noted the large bouquet in the nurses' station.

Who could be sending Maggie flowers? Dillon wondered as he continued his shuffle down the hall. He'd never seen any other man at her home. But no doubt she had her share of men who appreciated her beauty and personality, including him. Of course, his feelings went beyond appreciation.

In all the times he'd been in Maggie's home, he'd never seen flowers. Most women would take such a large, extravagant bouquet home to enjoy, wouldn't they?

Whatever the case, maybe it was time he sent some flowers of his own. Just to let her know he'd been serious when he'd talked about advancing their relationship.

When the doctor released him the next day, Dillon was glad to leave the confines of the hospital. When Wyatt offered to pick him up, Dillon accepted. He might be sore and stiff, but he was sick of the hospital. Well, most of it. Having Maggie as his caregiver had been a plus.

Of course, being a convalescent at home when you couldn't do anything wasn't much fun either. When the nurse reviewed his release orders with him and warned him not to lift more than ten pounds, he thought about Peg and Chloe. Funny how being in the same predicament put the situation in a completely different light.

Restless, Dillon read the paper and his e-mail and finally decided to walk over and look at Maggie's house. The Harris brothers were well on their way to completion of the job.

Keith Harris came outside and spotted Dillon. "How are you feeling?"

"Much better. It was rough going there for a while."

"I can imagine. Maggie asked us to keep you in our prayers."

"Believe me, I appreciated every prayer sent up on my behalf." He pointed at the house. "Looks good. I'm sure Maggie will be glad to have her door and windows in."

The contractor chuckled. "She's mentioned it a time or two. She'll probably do a victory dance when she opens the door the first time."

Dillon could see her doing exactly that. "Be sure to put me on your reference list."

"Business is starting to pick up again now that word is getting around, but we appreciate the referrals. The pastor stuck our card on the bulletin board over at the church."

"I appreciate the great job you've done for Maggie." The twinges of discomfort warned Dillon he'd done too much. "I'd better head on home. This surgery makes me feel like an old man."

Maggie had been called in to work extra shifts but checked on Dillon when she got home on Wednesday and Thursday. On Thursday afternoon, he remembered his plan and placed a floral order. He suspected she would have preferred going to the nursery for rosebushes but decided this would work for now.

The next morning, he watched through the window and smiled at the sight of her carrying the roses into the house. At least she hadn't given them away.

A few minutes later, he saw Maggie crossing the yard. She tapped on the door, and he invited her in.

She smiled at him. "Good morning. How are you feeling?"

"Better."

"Did you eat?"

"Toast and coffee."

"Well, go easy on the food for a few days. You might find yourself unable to eat things you used to eat."

Dillon nodded. "How was work?"

"Good. Thanks for the flowers. They're gorgeous, but you shouldn't have."

"They were the least I could do after all you've done for me and my mom."

"I told you, Dillon, I did what I did for Mrs. Allene out of love."

"And me?"

Maggie blushed as she said, "There's a certain degree of affection involved."

"The flowers are my way of saying thank you to the beautiful woman I care for a great deal."

"Thanks. You want to come over for a late celebratory lunch after I wake this afternoon? Keith left the bill on the kitchen counter. Everything is officially back where it belongs."

Maggie's pleasure radiated out through her smile. "I should send you flowers. I owe you a great deal of thanks. You helped make a major inconvenience much easier."

"The Harris brothers did the hard work," Dillon said. "I just wandered around making comments and asking questions."

"I know you did more than that," Maggie told him.

"You want me to take care of lunch? I could order pizza or something."

"No pizza for you. I picked up a roasted chicken at the grocery store yesterday. Or I have sandwich fixings if you prefer."

"Call me when you wake up."

❧

As Maggie got into bed, her gaze drifted to the arrangement on the nightstand.

She smiled as she recalled Dillon's "beautiful woman he cared for" compliment.

Sleep didn't come easily as she considered the changes in her life. She didn't feel as sad as she had after Mrs. Allene's death. Maybe because she had Dillon to occupy her time?

All she knew was that he was his mother's son. He had inherited many of the traits she'd admired in her friend. "You'd be proud, Mrs. Allene," she whispered, wishing the woman was around so she could tell her what a wonderful son she had.

After a while, exhaustion won out, and her eyes drifted shut. It was after two o'clock p.m. when she woke, and Maggie took a quick shower and washed her hair before she called Dillon. After she spoke to him, she reheated leftover green beans to go along with the chicken and potato salad. She poured glasses of lemonade just as he made an appearance.

"You want to eat in the kitchen or on the patio?"

"Let's sit outside," Dillon said. "It's a nice day. I never imagined I'd spend Labor Day in the hospital. What did you do?"

"Kim and Wyatt invited everyone to their place for an afternoon cookout."

"I can hardly believe the summer is over."

"The town was full of tourists for the holiday weekend."

"One final hurrah?"

"Some will come as long as there are sunny days," Maggie said, "but Labor Day generally marks the end of the season."

After appeasing their hunger, the conversation drifted from subject to subject.

"You lived in DC?" Dillon asked as she talked about the Floyds.

"Just outside in Virginia. Mr. Floyd worked at the Pentagon. Tell me about Saudi Arabia. What did you do in your free time?"

"Camped, scuba dived in the Red Sea, and followed softball tournaments. They were very popular. I went to the souk often."

"The what?"

"Souk. The market. You should see the gold souks. Walls covered in gold. They keep thievery to a minimum by chopping off the right hand."

"Sounds cruel," Maggie said.

"It's a different culture," Dillon told her. "Women don't have freedoms like here in the States. But they are a very family-focused country."

"Tell me more about the souks."

"They had some great handwoven baskets. And Persian rugs."

"Like your mom's?"

Dillon nodded. "I shipped them home to her. I have more at my place. I want to show you the ornate camel saddle I have. I really need to check into having my things sent home."

"Mrs. Allene often mentioned your letters. She loved those packages you sent."

Maggie shared a story about his mother, and Dillon seemed eager to hear more.

"I shouldn't have let time get away from me like I did."

His regret-filled words struck a chord in Maggie. She remembered her own judgmental comments but accepted that life had gotten in the way. He'd lived thousands of miles away and used the telephone as his contact.

"She would want you to look ahead, Dillon. Not back. I'm sure she told you that many times."

"Too many," he agreed. "Thanks for taking care of her."

"We took care of each other. She was a good friend."

He didn't say anything, only nodded, and Maggie saw the sheen in his eyes. Dillon still grieved his mother as she did her friend. She reached over and touched his hand gently.

"We were both very blessed to have her in our lives, and we will see her again one day."

"Another blessing," Dillon agreed. "So what are your plans now that the house is finished?"

"I'm going to put my home back together and notify foster care."

"About what?" he asked.

"I told you about my plans to become a foster parent."

"How are you going to manage that? Won't working alternating shifts every week make it impossible?"

"A number of mothers work alternating shifts at the hospital, Dillon."

"Yes, but they have husbands to help take care of the children."

"Not all of them. There are more single moms than you realize," Maggie said, adding, "but they do have family to help. I have it worked out. Once I get a placement, I'll request a day-shift schedule. Mari's agreed to help out when I have to work."

"A child is a big responsibility."

"I know that," Maggie said, finding herself a bit put out by his comment. "Believe me, I prayed over this when the idea presented itself. It's the right thing to do. There are kids who need love in their lives, and whether I provide that love for days or months, it's something I need to do."

"You need to think about what you're taking on," he argued.

"Why would you assume I haven't?"

"I didn't say that."

"You implied I hadn't. You did the same thing when I brought Chloe and Peg home."

"I offered my opinion as your friend. I'm sorry if that bothers you."

His huffy response troubled Maggie. "As my friend, you should know I do consider how my decisions affect my life."

"I'm sorry. I shouldn't have said anything."

"I'm sorry, too. It was a major decision, but it's time I gave back."

Resigned, Dillon asked, "How can I help?"

"Pray for me."

Maggie continued to make certain that Dillon didn't overdo. On her next day off, she made a dish of his mother's macaroni and cheese casserole recipe and took it over to him.

She found him sorting through old pictures at the kitchen table. After placing the casserole in the oven, Maggie walked over and picked up a photo of what appeared to be him at around age five.

"Thinking of taking up scrapbooking?" she teased.

"Strolling down memory lane. I ran across these boxes and thought I'd see if I recognized anyone."

"Have you?"

Dillon nodded. "These appear to be the family photos. Mom and Dad, me. Grandparents, aunts, uncles, cousins."

Maggie pulled out a chair and sat down. "I love old family photos. I suppose ours got dumped in the trash with the rest of our things after Daddy died."

"I'm sorry, Maggie. I wish I could give them back."

She smiled. "I'll be happy to share yours." Maggie felt herself grow warm at the implication of her words. "I mean. . . Well, I love old photos."

Dillon chuckled and pushed the box over. "Help yourself. There's at least five or six generations of old here."

She playfully tapped him on the arm and reached for a photo of a young couple, the man dressed in uniform. "Your parents?"

He nodded. "Mom always said Dad was the most handsome man she knew."

Maggie disagreed. She considered Dillon better looking.

They sorted through photos for half an hour before the timer went off and Dillon said, "Mac and cheese time."

Maggie filled plates, and Dillon poured tea. They abandoned the photo-strewn table in favor of the island.

"Your mom has lots of pictures."

"Mom had too much junk. I've donated bins of clothes and whatnots to charity."

Maggie hated to consider what he'd given away. "Some of those whatnots were probably valuable."

Crinkles of confusion formed about his eyes as Dillon asked, "Like what?"

"Since I don't know what you donated, I can't be sure, but she collected Fenton glass and was always saying she needed more display space."

He grimaced. "I guess someone will find a real bargain at the resale shop."

His cavalier response astonished Maggie. "You don't feel any attachment? These things belonged to your mother."

"I'm not the sentimental type," Dillon declared. "I don't care for clutter.

You wouldn't believe some of the stuff I've run across. This morning I found bundles of letters Dad sent Mom when they dated. And the cards I sent for birthdays and Mother's Day."

Maggie gasped. "Please tell me you didn't throw them away."

He shrugged. "Not yet. But why not?"

"It's your family history, Dillon. Your parents' love story. Don't you want to read the letters?"

"Not particularly. They're private correspondence."

"They're a treasure. A written testimony of your parents' love for one another," Maggie argued. "I don't have any of that from my parents."

"While I have an overabundance I could care less about?"

This isn't my concern, Maggie thought. But words of advice tumbled from her lips. "You don't have to keep everything, but be careful not to dispose of things you can't replace."

"I have Dad's tools. And I kept their books. I'm going to build shelving around the fireplace in the family room to hold them all."

"Some of your mom's knickknacks would look good on those shelves," Maggie suggested. "And if you're so determined to get rid of stuff, at least talk with Kim. She'll give you a fair deal."

Dillon eyed her for a moment. "You think I'm heartless, don't you?"

Maggie knew it was unfair to judge others based on her own situation. Maybe if she had several lifetimes of possessions to choose from, she'd feel the need to give up things, as well.

"No," Maggie said. "I just hope you kept a list for tax purposes."

"It wasn't worth the trouble."

Maggie had never known anyone who didn't need tax write-offs.

"How do I know what to keep?" Dillon asked, sounding somewhat dismayed by the idea.

"Surely you have favorites."

"A few. What do I do with the rest?"

"No one in the family wants anything?"

"My cousin wanted a quilt our grandmother made for Mom."

Maggie recalled the beautiful quilt that his mother had treasured. She felt sad that he hadn't held on to it for his mother's sake. "She loved that quilt."

"Leslie wants to give it to her daughter," Dillon said. "At least that way something gets passed on to another generation."

"That's a true negative of being single," Maggie admitted. "Of course, most kids today don't want their parents' junk, either." She covered her mouth. "I'm sorry. I didn't mean that as a criticism."

"I know. I doubt Mom was so attached to her things that she'd want me holding on to stuff I don't want. I promise not to dispose of anything else without asking first."

"You don't need to ask me," Maggie said hastily.

"But you know what was important to Mom."

"It needs to have special meaning for you, Dillon."

"You can tell me about the truly special pieces. I've been meaning to ask if you wanted any of her jewelry."

Maggie thought about the valuable pieces Mrs. Allene had worn over the years. Particularly the string of pearls Maggie adored. "Keep the jewelry, Dillon. You might want it for your wife one day."

"And supposing there's no future Mrs. Rogers?"

"At least hang on to it for a couple of years before you decide," Maggie suggested. "You could share some of her costume pieces with the elderly ladies at church. Just sort out the expensive stuff first."

"I think most of that might be in the wall safe," Dillon said. "Though I've yet to find the combination."

Maggie recalled the time Mrs. Allene had the safe lock drilled. She'd asked Maggie to help her remember the combination. "Seems like she told me she'd used her anniversary and your birthday. I don't know the order or anything. She said the hint would jog her memory if she forgot again."

Dillon grabbed a pad and scribbled the information. "I'll give it a try. The attic is bursting at the seams, too," Dillon told her. "Some stuff has to go. I promise to be more selective in my disposal, but they're only things. Nothing here brings back the good memories of my parents. They're right here," he added, tapping his temple lightly.

Maggie considered her lack of good memories. There were a few with her dad, but they seemed so distant now.

"That's because you've always known exactly where home was. It seems like I've searched my entire life for the place that made me feel that way. South Carolina is as close as I've come."

"Until I came back and made you feel as if you'd done something wrong?"

Maggie avoided his gaze. "I never had an ulterior motive except maybe to experience some of that magnanimous love Mrs. Allene heaped on everyone."

He smiled regretfully. "I'm sorry. I never meant to hurt you. You know all your friends don't hesitate to rush to your defense. I felt like a jerk when Julie told me I should be ashamed for thinking negative thoughts about you. Mari backed her up."

"They told me," Maggie admitted. "I never asked them to talk to you."

He grinned at her. "We may be getting to know each other, but that's one thing I already know about you. You fight your own battles."

"I have been known to run away from a few," she countered.

Dillon tipped her chin and kissed her gently. "That's okay, too, just as long as you don't run away from us."

Chapter 9

As September moved forward, Maggie appreciated their growing friendship even more. She and Dillon spent a lot of time together—at church, dining out, even taking long walks along the beach. It seemed only natural that he would be on the list of people she called to share her news.

"I'm getting a foster child today. A short-term placement. Her name is Marsha Kemp, and she's ten."

"When does she arrive?"

"After school. I have to run. There's so much to do before she gets here. I need to buy groceries and get her a welcome present."

"Slow down, or you'll burn yourself out before she gets there."

Maggie laughed and said, "Talk to you later."

After three that afternoon, Maggie heard a car door slam, and it was all she could do not to meet the caseworker in the driveway. She opened the door, smiling widely as she viewed the child who had come to stay with her. Preteen and rail thin with long, dark hair and a doubt-filled expression summarized her best.

The caseworker introduced them. "Marsha Kemp, this is Maggie Gregory."

Maggie held out her hand, and the child offered hers in return. "Welcome, Marsha. Let me show you where you'll be staying."

She led the way down the hall to her converted guest room. Maggie had packed away her things and splurged on a few items she thought Marsha might enjoy. When Maggie talked about painting the room in colors that would appeal to children, Dillon had helped. The room sported aqua and purple walls that matched the new striped bedspread and drapes. "Come into the living room after you unpack, and we'll get to know each other."

The girl nodded, appearing quiet and withdrawn.

"God, help me deal with this," Maggie prayed softly as she followed Mrs. Prince back into the living room.

"This is Marsha's first time away from home," the caseworker said. "Her mother got involved with the wrong man and has been incarcerated for thirty days."

"I'll do everything possible to help her."

"I know you will. Don't hesitate to call with any question." The woman handed her a business card. "We appreciate your willingness to help."

After Mrs. Prince left, Maggie waited in the living room, glancing repeatedly at the clock. What was taking so long? The phone rang, and she reached for the handset she'd left on the arm of the sofa earlier.

"Hi. How's it going with your foster child?" Dillon asked.

"She's unpacking."

"I thought maybe we could order pizza later."

"It's better if it's just me and her tonight. It's tough on her, Dillon."

"Yeah, I can imagine. How about you ladies let me take you out this weekend?"

"I'll see what Marsha thinks and let you know."

"You will let me spend time with you, won't you?"

She heard Marsha coming down the hallway. "Gotta go. Talk to you later."

Maggie smiled at the child, noting her red-rimmed eyes. "How's your room?" Marsha shrugged. "Anything you need?"

Marsha's head barely moved in response.

"What's your favorite food?"

Marsha shrugged, her gaze fixed on the floor.

"Come on," Maggie urged. "There's something you really like. How about pizza? I like everything on mine."

"Cheese."

Maggie felt as though she'd received a gift in the one word. "How about a half and half for dinner tonight?"

Marsha nodded.

"Are you hungry? Or would you like to visit for a while?" Even as she asked, Maggie could see the child was hungry but afraid to say so. "Let's order now. I have soda, and I think we have chips. We can have a few while we wait. Let me show you the kitchen."

Maggie held the phone between her head and shoulder as she placed the order and poured soda for Marsha and iced tea for herself. She dumped a few chips into a small bowl and carried it over to the table. "Pizza will be here in twenty minutes. So you want to tell me about you, or should I go first?"

Marsha pushed a chip into her mouth and pointed at Maggie.

"I'm Mary Margaret Gregory. Everyone calls me Maggie. I'm single, and I don't have any children. I'm a nurse and work at the hospital. I go to church at Cornerstone Community Church and have some really great friends. Do you go to church?"

Maggie's heart wrenched when the child's head moved from side to side.

"My pastor and his wife have five kids. They're younger than you, but I'd like you to meet them. My friend Kim and her husband, Wyatt, have a son named Chase. He's twelve. There's also Julie and Noah. He's the associate pastor at the church. And my friend Natalie. Dillon, he's my neighbor and a good friend, He'd like to meet you, too," she said, the words rushing out in a nervous gush. "You're ten?" The child nodded. "When's your birthday?"

"October twenty-fifth."

Maggie made a note of the date. Marsha would still be with her. Maybe the idea of planning something special would help the child settle in. "I'm scared, too, Marsha. You're my first foster child. I know you miss your mom, but I'd like to be your friend."

The doorbell rang. "There's our pizza."

Back in the kitchen, Maggie took paper plates and napkins from the cabinet and refilled their glasses. She set the pizza box on the table.

"Let's say grace," Maggie said, holding out her hand. After a few moments' pause, Marsha laid her hand in hers. Maggie thanked Jesus for their food and for Marsha. When she pushed the open box in the child's direction, she took one slice.

Maggie slid two onto her plate and encouraged Marsha to eat. The room grew quiet. "Since neither of us knows what to expect, how about we set some ground rules. I know I'm a stranger, but I want to be a good parent. That means I do the things your real mom does. I have to be sure you eat and get your rest and do your homework."

"Why did they make her go away?" the child asked, tears trailing down her cheeks.

"Sometimes adults make bad choices," Maggie explained as she drew the girl into her arms and rocked back and forth. "Your mom didn't want to leave you, but she had to for a while. I'll take good care of you, Marsha. I promise. Will you let me?"

The child nodded.

"Let's finish our dinner. Did you decide what you're wearing to school tomorrow?"

Marsha shook her head.

"How about I help you choose something after dinner?"

"Okay."

Maggie felt as if she'd hurtled over a high jump. And tonight was just the beginning.

Later, after Marsha had gone to sleep, Maggie reached for the phone and called Mari.

"How did it go?"

"She doesn't understand why they took her mom away."

"Poor kid. Life is such a struggle without being removed from your loved ones."

"Tell me about it."

"Do you think your experience as a foster child will help?"

"I never really understood why my parents had to die, but I survived. Marsha will, too. At least her mom is coming back for her."

"Hopefully a wiser woman," Mari said. "I'd hate to see Marsha end up in the system when she could be with her mom."

"But I'd rather she stayed there than have this happen over and over again," Maggie said.

"We'll pray for her and her mother," Mari promised.

"Her birthday is in October. She's turning eleven. I thought maybe I could plan something for her."

"That's a good idea. Planning a party will take her mind off things."

"I need to figure out what girls her age like."

"Are you allowed to give her gifts?"

"Yes. We're encouraged to celebrate events. I told her about my friends. And about church. She doesn't attend."

"Maybe another reason God placed her in your life."

Maggie considered Mari's words. When she'd prayed about becoming a foster parent, it had been to help a child who needed a parent. She hadn't considered the possibility that the child would need her heavenly Father.

"Could be. I'd better get to bed. I have to take her to school in the morning."

"Did you get your shift change?"

"They're working on it. I arranged for the church day care to pick her up from school."

"And I'll pick her up from the church on the days you work and bring her here."

Maggie had approached Mari with the plan back when she first started to think about foster parenting. "I talked with my supervisor today, and she's going to arrange for me to get off early this week. If it's okay, I thought I'd bring her by tomorrow night."

"Come for dinner."

"Okay. Night, Mari."

Maggie looked in on Marsha and found her asleep, hugging a worn Raggedy Ann doll. She adjusted the covers and turned on a night-light in the bathroom before going to her own room.

She woke early the next morning, her thoughts filled with getting Marsha to school on time. In the kitchen, Maggie considered the possibilities for breakfast.

After everything was prepared, she knocked on Marsha's door. The child was nearly dressed. "I fixed grits and eggs for breakfast. That okay?"

Marsha nodded.

Back in the kitchen, Maggie placed a package in the chair. Marsha looked at it in surprise.

Maggie had chosen the book bag and accessories after making sure Marsha didn't already have one. "It's for you."

They developed a routine. The first day, Maggie took Marsha to and from school. That night, she introduced her to the Dennis family. Marsha immediately bonded with the children. The first time she laughed at Luke and their cat, Maggie knew everything would be okay.

On her first Sunday, Maggie took Marsha to church. She knew it would be yet another new experience, but she showed the child her Sunday school classroom and depended on Julie to make Marsha comfortable. Afterward, Julie mentioned how well Chase and Marsha had gotten along.

That afternoon they went to visit Peg and Chloe. Marsha's fascination with Chloe was obvious. They played together as Peg and Maggie talked.

"She'll make a good babysitter," Peg said as she observed Marsha's gentle ways with her daughter. The child responded softly to the baby as they rolled a musical ball back and forth.

Maggie was glad to hear Peg had no problems since her return to her florist job. "Is there anything you need? I mean. . . Well, being out of work is difficult."

"We're fine. Besides, I should be asking that question," Peg said. "I can't tell you how much I appreciate all you've done. You're a wonderful friend."

"I didn't do a thing you wouldn't have done if the roles had been reversed."

"I just hope you remember that when my time comes."

"It doesn't have to be for me. Just pass it on. Help someone who needs help." Maggie glanced at her watch. "We need to be going soon. Dillon's taking us to dinner."

"How is he?"

"Much better. He understands how you felt."

"Most men can't stand being sick."

Maggie knew Peg was thinking of her husband, and her heart went out to the woman. It must hurt her badly to have her husband walk away like that.

❧

Dillon took Maggie and Marsha to a popular cafeteria. They chose foods and placed them on their trays, carrying them into the large dining room. They chose a table and emptied their trays. "I have to go to Columbia. Would you and Marsha like to ride with me?"

"I can't take her out of school."

"I have a teacher workday on the ninth," Marsha volunteered.

"That's a good day. How about you, Maggie? What's your calendar like?"

"I'll check. I could probably arrange a vacation day if I'm working. And I need to get permission from the caseworker."

"I thought we could visit the zoo. What do you think, Marsha?"

She shrugged.

"You'll like this place," Dillon said.

"Could we invite Mari and the Dennis children?" Maggie requested softly.

Dillon looked disappointed. "I'd hoped to get to know her better."

"Just her?"

Dillon grinned at Maggie. "I've missed you."

"You could have visited."

"I thought Marsha needed you more."

"Okay. We'll do this your way. Just the three of us. What time do you plan to leave?"

"It's a little more than a two-hour drive. I have to go by the courthouse to sign papers, and then we can head for the zoo. How about six thirty or so?"

They made their plans, and early on the morning of their trip, Maggie and Marsha crossed the backyard to Dillon's house for breakfast.

"Thanks for doing this," Maggie said as she took the plate he handed her. "I overslept."

He smiled and winked. "I didn't mind. I got up with the chickens anyway."

"You have chickens?" Marsha asked.

Dillon laughed. "No, honey. That's just something my mama used to say about getting up early. Roosters were their alarm clocks. They'd be up doing chores when that old bird cock-a-doodle-dooed."

"I've never seen a rooster."

"They strut about the yard like they're king of the roost," Maggie said.

"That they do," Dillon agreed, sliding his plate onto the table. "Let's eat so we can get on the road. I'm eager to see the zoo. How about you, Marsha?"

Her head hardly moved in response as she attacked her food. The child ate every meal with such gusto that Maggie wondered how well her mother fed her.

No, she warned herself. The idea that Marsha deserved a better parent teased her, and Maggie already knew she would have problems letting go when the time came. She'd become very attached to the girl in a short time.

Dillon's gaze rested on her, and she picked up her fork and started eating. "This is good," she said, and Marsha nodded.

"Eat up. I made plenty." Dillon rose from the stool and topped off their juice glasses.

As soon as breakfast was over and the dishes were in the dishwasher, Dillon said, "Why don't you ladies finish whatever you need to do and meet me at the car?"

"Come on, Marsha. Let's brush our teeth and comb our hair."

"Don't be long, or I'll leave without you," Dillon joked.

The child looked nervous. Maggie rested her hand on Marsha's shoulder. "He's teasing, honey. He really wants us to go with him. We'll be right back, Dillon."

"I'll wait," he promised solemnly.

Within minutes, they were on the road. Dillon had poured coffee into travel mugs and placed juice boxes in a cooler for Marsha.

Maggie noted how Dillon's gaze frequently went to the rearview mirror and the child reflected there. "Bet you're glad to have a day off from school. I loved teacher workdays. Of course, it's been a long time since I had one. How do you like school?"

When she shrugged, Maggie said, "You need to answer Mr. Rogers. He can't look at you while he's driving."

"Okay," Marsha mumbled.

"A woman of few words," he said softly to Maggie. She nodded.

They arrived in Columbia a little after nine o'clock. Dillon found the courthouse and parked. "Did you want to come in or wait here?"

"We could visit the ladies' room," Maggie said.

"I'm not sure how long this will take." He handed her his car keys.

Dillon concluded his business quickly, and they drove over to Riverbanks Zoo and Garden. He paid their admittance fee and accepted the brochures.

As they strolled through the area, Dillon reached into his pocket. "I have something for you, Marsha."

He handed her a small digital camera. "The printer is at my house. Take all the pictures you want. We'll print them off when we get home. I can take some of you to send to your mom in your next letter."

Why didn't I think of that? Maggie wondered. Maybe because she didn't want to encourage interaction with the mother while she was in jail. That wasn't fair. If it were her parents, she would want to see them. Perhaps she should ask the caseworker about visitation.

"I plan to give her the camera and printer for her birthday," Dillon told Maggie.

"I don't know if her mother can afford the supplies," Maggie said.

"I hadn't considered that."

Maggie watched Marsha as she worked the digital camera the way Dillon had showed her, checking each picture in the viewfinder before taking the photo. "It's a great idea for today. She can take her photos, and you can help her print them. I doubt Marsha has had much quality time with a good father figure, so that will be nice, too."

The child insisted that Dillon and Maggie pose at the monkey cage. Marsha giggled when Dillon waved his arms and scratched his head.

"Hey, I want a copy of that one," Dillon enthused when Marsha ran over to share the image on the camera. "That fellow likes Maggie's golden hair."

Marsha nodded and giggled again.

The next hours were some of the best Maggie could ever recall. When Marsha had filled the camera with photos, Dillon pulled another memory card from his pocket and sent her off to take more pictures.

"The ink to print all those is going to break you."

Dillon shrugged. "It's worth it if it makes her happy. Let's take a breather.

All this walking is wearing me out."

"Are you feeling okay?" Maggie asked, afraid the activity had been too much for him. "Everything healed up nicely?"

"My doctor says so. Those staples were the worst."

"But you grimaced and took it like a man?"

"Sure I did. After the initial 'Hey, that hurts,' I became an iron man."

Maggie laughed. "I'm so glad you're feeling better. I worried about you. And thanks for this idea. You've really made Marsha happy."

"Every child should feel that way every day," Dillon said.

"I doubt she's had much opportunity to feel special in her life. Not with a mother who has problems."

"You don't know that to be a fact," he quickly pointed out. "Her mother could be the most loving woman in the world who messed up one time."

"That's all it takes to ruin someone's life."

"Don't hold a lapse in good judgment against the woman," Dillon warned.

Maggie had prayed over her feelings regarding Marsha's mother. For the life of her, she couldn't understand how any mother could allow a man to separate her and her daughter. No mother should do that to her child. As far as Maggie was concerned, a parent should put her child first.

Marsha ran back to where they sat on benches. She paused in front of Dillon, her expression happy when she asked, "Will you come to my party?"

He nodded. "Sure. If you want me to. I'm kind of old, though."

The child leaned against his leg. "You're my friend. Maggie said I could invite my friends."

A knot formed in Maggie's throat as she watched them together.

"I'd be honored. What should I bring you? Tell me your favorite things."

Dillon paid a great deal of attention to the child as she told him about her life. "It's just me and my mom. We take care of each other. I'd like to give her something special, too."

"What did you have in mind?" he asked, and Marsha shrugged. "Why don't we think about it and decide later," he suggested.

As the child's hand slipped into Dillon's, Maggie couldn't help but wonder what made the child bond so quickly with him. What was it about him that charmed the female species?

She'd grown to care for Dillon Rogers in a way she'd never cared for another man. A way that had her thinking about their future. But how could it work? They were worlds apart.

"Maggie?"

"Yes?" she responded, jumping guiltily as she shifted from daydreams to reality.

"Marsha and I were discussing lunch. Would you like a hot dog?"

"Sounds good."

All too soon, their day was over. Hearing Marsha chatter about what she'd seen and the pictures she'd taken made Maggie even happier. Their silent girl had opened up.

When Marsha grew quiet, Maggie glanced back to find she'd fallen asleep. Marsha's head rested against the seat, the long arms of the monkey Dillon had given her wrapped about her neck just as he'd placed the stuffed animal she'd chosen.

"I've never heard her talk so much," she whispered to Dillon. "You made her day."

"How about you? How was your day?"

"I enjoyed myself. I love the zoo. I plan to go back and visit the gardens."

"We could have done that today."

Maggie shook her head. "Marsha wouldn't have enjoyed them as much. I'd come back to the zoo, too."

"And bring the Dennis children?"

"It would make a great educational outing. I could see them there."

"Terrorizing the animals?"

"They're good kids," Maggie objected. "What scares you most? Luke and his questions?"

"The numbers," Dillon said. "I prefer one-on-one like today. And yes, Luke petrifies me. I'm afraid he'll find out I don't know anything."

"Oh, I doubt that. Luke tells everyone you're smart. He always searches you out."

"He likes hearing about my camel rides."

"So do I. You know there are going to be more kids one of these days. Julie and Kimberly are both planning to start families."

Dillon glanced at her. "Does that bother you?"

"Not really. It just changes our relationships. It's hard to get together when children are involved."

"But these children have willing fathers who I'm sure will take over so their wives can have time with their friends."

"I hope so. I enjoy spending time with them."

"You'll still have Natalie. And me. I'm single."

"And not likely to become a mother anytime soon," Maggie countered with a big grin.

Dillon laughed loudly, and Marsha jumped in the backseat. "Sorry, honey. Maggie made me laugh."

She rubbed her eyes. "Are we there yet?"

"Almost. Why don't you get us a juice box out of the cooler?"

Marsha dug juice boxes from the melting ice and busied herself putting in straws and passing them around.

Dillon took a sip. "Ah, that's good. What plans do you ladies have for the weekend?"

"We have chores in the morning, and then I thought we'd go shopping for party items. We need to pick a theme."

"That sounds like fun. Are you interested in burgers and hot dogs for the guests? I could fire up my new grill."

"What do you think, Marsha?"

"Yes. And cake and ice cream and candy."

Maggie glanced at her. "Whoa. That's a serious sugar rush. How about some veggies?" Marsha grimaced. "Maybe lettuce and tomato for the burgers?"

"Okay."

Maggie would let the other parents worry about getting veggies into their kids. "I think we should have a menu. What's your favorite cake?"

"Chocolate."

"Mine, too."

"Is Natalie making the cake?" Dillon asked.

"What do you think?"

"Well, there's always Avery."

Maggie shook her head. "Marsha will have a cake to remember this birthday. Natalie's already planning."

"Then I can only imagine what she will come up with."

"Whatever Marsha wants. Once we pick the theme and decorations, Natalie will design the cake."

"Gives me something to look forward to."

"When's your birthday?" Maggie asked.

"December eighth."

She nodded. "I'll have to share that with Natalie and see what happens. Your favorite cake?"

"Orange."

Long after she'd tucked Marsha in for the night, Maggie found herself still awake. She turned on the lamp and picked up her Bible, reading scriptures and thanking God for the wonderful day He'd given them. Marsha could hardly wait to see the other kids so she could tell them about the zoo. Maybe once Dillon got the photos printed, she could show them.

Memories of the experience with Dillon that day made her smile. He had been so thoughtful and focused on them having fun. She hoped he enjoyed himself, as well. God was so good. She'd been so alone, and now she had a child living in her house and another good friend. She felt very blessed.

Chapter 10

The theme was flower power.

And Natalie had not only baked a larger cake for the birthday girl; she'd given the kids their own smaller cupcake versions as well. There were even iced flower cookies. More than one kid would be on a sugar high before the afternoon ended.

After taking Marsha's gift to the church fellowship hall, Dillon went to Maggie's to retrieve the plate of burgers and hot dogs. "Everything looks nice."

"Marsha's so excited. She barely slept last night. She's never had a party. It won't be long before she's gone," Maggie said glumly.

"You heard from her caseworker?"

She nodded, feeling the growing knot in her throat. Dillon folded Maggie into a hug. They stood silently for several seconds before Marsha bounded into the room wearing the tie-dyed T-shirt that she and Maggie had made along with bell-bottomed jeans that sported big flower patches on the legs. A peace symbol dangled on a long string around her neck, and she wore big plastic flower rings on her fingers.

"Hello, birthday girl," Dillon said. The child beamed at him. He lifted the plate from the counter and said, "I'll take these over to the fellowship hall."

"Thanks, Dillon."

Later, he stood by Maggie's side as they watched a mob of kids run around. "You didn't go crazy by much, did you?"

"It's been fun. The caseworker is taking her to visit her mom tomorrow."

"Are you okay with that?"

"I have to be. When Marsha looks back at her time with me, I think she'll remember this party. And the zoo trip."

"I found a special gift for her to share with her mom."

Excited, Maggie turned to him and asked, "Really? What?"

"Two necklaces with one heart charm. Each of them gets half."

"That's perfect!" Maggie exclaimed. She threw her arms around his neck and kissed his cheek.

"Whoa," Dillon said, his arm slipping about Maggie's waist before allowing his lips to touch hers gently. Remembering where they were, they parted and took a step back.

Maggie turned pink. "Sorry, I didn't mean to attack you."

"Are you truly sorry?" he asked softly.

She wiped the lipstick smudge from his cheek. "No."

"I love you, Maggie."

Her eyes widened. She loved him, too. It had come slowly, creeping up on them, and she knew as surely as she drew her next breath that he held her heart. "Let's talk about this later. After the party."

"Definitely," Dillon promised with a tender smile.

He loved her. Maggie felt as if she were walking on air. What exactly did that mean? They were both a bit old to go steady, weren't they? Oh well, maybe not.

It thrilled her that he'd taken the little girl's wish for something special to share with her mother and made it happen. Maggie considered her own wishes. She'd wished for a home ever since her dad had died. Could Dillon give her that?

"Those kids are going to mutiny if we don't get the games under way," Dillon told her.

She and Marsha had found the perfect party games and then had fun at the dollar store finding prizes for the winners. Marsha would be able to plan her own parties in the future if her mom fell short. Particularly her sweet sixteen. Maggie paused as she considered that leap into adulthood. Marsha was only eleven. Thirteen would be the next milestone.

Why couldn't she have met Dillon Rogers years ago when she could have had children of her own to guide through these milestones?

Because it wasn't meant to be. She refused to live her life crying over spilled milk. *Look for the positives.* Tonight when she wrote in her gratitude journal, she'd be thankful that she'd given one little girl a happy day, but she'd be joyous over the good friends in her life and now the love of one special man. What could be better than that?

"Whew," Dillon exclaimed later as he stuffed the last trash bag in the Dumpster. "What a day. Where's Marsha?"

"She wanted to watch her new DVD with the Dennis kids. I told Mari I'd pick her up when I finished here."

"So have you thought any more about what I told you earlier?"

She looked at him. "A time or two."

"And what are you going to do about it?" he challenged.

"What do you suggest?"

"You could return the sentiment."

"And if I did?"

"Who knows what would happen?"

Reality washed over her. "I do care for you, Dillon. A great deal."

He lifted one brow and asked, "But you aren't using the *L* word just yet."

" 'I love you' has never been easy for me to say," Maggie admitted.

"What do you want, Maggie?"

"To feel I've come home."

"Tell me what that means."

"A place where I belong, where I feel loved and protected. The place we come to and know we're important to everyone there."

"How do you know when you're there?"

"You just do."

"That's an ambiguous response."

Sadness encompassed Maggie as her description fell short of making him understand. "If I knew how to explain it better, I would."

"Let me give it a shot. I think you mean like when I was in first grade and a bully picked on me and I knew my mom would take my side."

"Exactly. A dragon slayer."

"I'll slay your dragons, Maggie. Just share them with me."

She rested her hand against his cheek. "You've done a wonderful job, Dillon. That damage to the house was a dragon. You took care of that. This party was a dragon. You've helped so much today."

"And do you feel like coming home?"

"I'm closer than I've ever been. I'd better get Marsha home. I'm sure she's exhausted."

"Can I walk with you?"

Maggie slipped her arm through his. "I wouldn't expect anything less from my dragon slayer."

He laughed and worked his fingers through hers.

"Natalie did a fantastic job with that cake. I'm thinking about placing a weekly order so I can have it for dessert every day."

She stared at him and then burst out laughing. "I'm sure Marsha will share her cake if you come to lunch tomorrow."

"I thought the caseworker was taking her to see her mom."

Maggie sighed. "I forgot. Oh well, come over anyway, and we'll drown our sorrows in leftover birthday cake."

Chapter 11

Marsha's gone."

Maggie's heartbroken expression and the tears on her lashes tore at Dillon. "I didn't want you hurt. I liked Marsha."

"I'm sorry." She sniffed and grabbed another tissue. She'd used a box since saying good-bye to the child that morning. "You should go home. I'm not fit company."

"Let's do something to take your mind off what's happened. How about getting together with friends and going out to dinner?"

"I wouldn't be good company."

"Didn't you divert Marsha's attention to keep her from missing her mother?"

"That was different. She's a child."

"And you have to be miserable because you're an adult?"

"Don't be silly."

"I'm only trying to help, Maggie. If you continue to act as a foster parent, you'll have to love them enough to let them go. Pray for her. Pray that her mom will turn their lives around in a good way. You took her to church. Now Marsha knows about God's love. She's never been exposed to that before."

"I want to be happy for Marsha," she whispered. "I really do."

Dillon hugged her. "So about those friends and dinner. . ."

Maggie shook her head.

"Do you want me to go?" Dillon asked gently.

Maggie grasped his hand and shook her head.

"Come on. We need to get out of here. How about a show at one of the musical theaters? We could play putt-putt or go fishing. Tell me something you've always wanted to do."

"Ripley's." Other than she'd always thought she'd go one day, Maggie had no idea why it had popped into her head now.

"You're on. I'll get the car."

"Give me a few minutes to get myself together."

An hour later, Maggie pointed at the pamphlet and laughed. "Look, Dillon, they call it an Odditorium."

He grabbed her hand, pulling her through the turnstile and to the first display. They had the place to themselves as they moved up stairs that glowed in the dark and through a labyrinth of semidark passages, reading the placards describing each exhibit Robert L. Ripley had gathered in his world travels.

"Check him out," Dillon said, indicating the tallest man either of them had ever seen.

They continued, studying the facts, viewing the illusions, examining Cleopatra's barge made entirely out of sugar, as well as a matchstick roller coaster, oddities of nature, and artwork made of everything from jelly beans to butterfly wings.

"Look at this," Maggie said, indicating a picture of Jesus with the book of John written in the background.

Dillon leaned closer and said, "You can actually read the words."

Maggie shuddered at the old torture devices on display.

When they approached a bridge that warned them to enter if they dared, Maggie looked askance at the walls that seemed to turn about them.

"Come on," Dillon said. They stepped onto the bridge, and she found that it moved from side to side.

They entered a room and sat on the benches and watched videos of outstanding feats.

"Marsha would like this place." She grew silent as the sadness returned. "Do you think she's okay?"

"Yeah, I do. Marsha's a tough kid."

"She's just a little girl."

"Who had to grow up faster than most. Like you, Maggie."

"I wish it could be different for her."

"It is. She has a mother to love and care for her."

Her anger peaked, shattering the last shreds of her control. "Much better than a foster parent."

"I didn't say that," Dillon said quickly. "God blessed Marsha with you at the time when she needed you most. She knew you cared and took that knowledge and those memories home with her. You planted the seed of Jesus in her heart, and we both know what God can do."

Shamed by her angry outburst, Maggie said, "I hope so. I want her to be happy."

He took her hand in his and asked, "Are you sure foster parenting is right for you? I don't like the thought of seeing you heartbroken every time you lose a child."

They sat in silence for a couple of minutes, idly watching the television screen. "I suppose in time I'll learn to protect my heart, to accept that I'm making a difference by just being there and loving my fellow man as God directs."

"How about you love as freely as you like and let me help protect your heart?"

Confused, she looked at him. "How. . ." she began, trailing off when Dillon slipped off the bench onto one knee.

"I love you, Maggie. I want to marry you." He held her hand in his, and the firm grip made her feel protected. "I thank God for blessing me with you in my life."

"You really mean that?" Maggie asked. "You're thankful for me?"

"Very much so."

"Why do you want to marry me?"

"I want to be your husband," he said simply. "To love you. To share your generous heart. To be the one you come home to."

"I love you, Dillon. I didn't want to, but I couldn't help myself. It came as naturally as breathing. Well, actually you sneaked up on me and knocked me breathless with your love."

"I hope to keep you breathless," Dillon said with a broad smile. He reached into his pocket and removed a jeweler's box. Opening the lid, he held it out to her. The large diamond gleamed in the overhead light.

Maggie hesitated. "Dillon, that's. . ."

He nodded. "Mom's ring. I considered buying a new one but decided this one would mean more. You did tell me to save her jewelry for my wife," he reminded. "I had it cleaned. We can update the setting, or I'll buy you a new ring if that's what you want."

"No, you can't change the ring. It's perfect." Mrs. Allene had worn it with pride for a great number of years. Maggie wanted to do the same.

"Maggie?" he prompted, pushing the box in her direction.

She hesitated. "I'm scared, Dillon. I don't know how to be a good wife."

"I don't know how to be a good husband, either. We can learn together."

Maggie felt so helpless.

"Did you doubt you could be a good foster parent?"

"I had my moments," she admitted.

"But you were willing to try."

"And if I'd failed, they would not have allowed me to have other children. They have a word for failed marriages, too, Dillon."

"I wouldn't have proposed if I wasn't certain about us."

"I don't have doubts about you, Dillon. It's me."

"You don't want to marry me?" he asked, trouble lines appearing in his forehead.

"I do."

"Then say yes," he prompted.

"You realize I'm a fifty-year-old old maid?"

"So I'm the fifty-five-plus male equivalent. I never thought I'd meet the right woman, and now that I have, I don't want to let you go. Remember the vows, Maggie. For better or worse, richer or poorer, in sickness and in health. I'm committed to you. Forever."

She touched his cheek, feeling the bristle of his five o'clock shadow beneath her hand. Tears welled in her eyes as she absorbed the promise he'd just made to her. "Yes, Dillon. I'd love to be your wife."

He rose to his feet and pulled her into his arms. "Thank God. My knee was about to give out."

Maggie flashed him a playful frown. "Now that's not very romantic."

"I'll make it up to you. I didn't intend to propose like this. I wanted it to be someplace special. Done up right."

"This feels pretty right to me," Maggie said.

"You're a cheap date," Dillon said as he reached for her hand and slid the ring in place. It fit perfectly.

"You think so? This looks expensive."

He leaned forward and kissed her. "Romantic?"

"I thought Kim's was big," Maggie said.

"And that's good?"

She tapped him on the chest. "No, silly. It's not the size of the diamond. It's the love that puts it there."

"Well, if we're measuring in love, I couldn't afford the carats to match my feelings for you. Dad gave that to Mom on their twenty-fifth anniversary. He never gave her an engagement ring and looked a long time for the perfect ring."

"That makes it even more special." Maggie twisted her hand back and forth, appreciating the shine of the diamond as it reflected in the light. "Oh, Dillon, I'm like doubting Thomas when it comes to love. I don't want to be insecure in my love for you, but I am."

"Then let me prove my intentions are honorable. I won't let you down, Maggie."

"I know you won't. I don't doubt that for a moment. I'm afraid I'll let you down. Can we tell Mari and Joe?"

Dillon smiled and said, "I thought you didn't feel like seeing anyone."

Maggie remembered Marsha and felt guilty.

"I think we should," Dillon said quickly. "When do you want to get married?"

"Probably early next year."

"So long?" Dillon countered with a frown.

"Well, I want to be married at Cornerstone, and Joe requires marital counseling. That takes some time."

"How about Valentine's Day?" Dillon suggested.

Maggie nodded. "We can say our vows after church the Sunday before Valentine's Day."

"You sure you don't want all the trimmings?"

Maggie paused for a moment as thoughts of her childhood dream wedding filled her head. "I'm too old for all that."

"No, honey, you're never too old for anything you want to do," Dillon countered.

"I would look silly," she objected. "We'll be just as married with a simple wedding as an expensive one."

"Whatever you want," Dillon said amicably.

What do I want? Maggie wondered. Definitely to marry Dillon. She loved him a great deal.

"We can live in Mom's house and rent yours."

That caught her attention.

"It's not like that," he protested immediately upon seeing her expression. "The house is yours. I don't have anything to do with the property."

"But what about two becoming one?" Maggie asked. How could she marry him if she doubted his actions? "I don't have lots of worldly possessions, but what I do have will belong to us both. Including the house."

He lifted her hand to his lips. "I don't want anything to stand in the way of our happiness. My possessions will belong to you, too. I plan to change my will."

"Let's do it together," Maggie suggested.

Dillon took her hand, and they continued their tour. As they exited onto the stairs leading to the game room, he asked, "Feel better?"

Maggie smiled at him and nodded. "Much."

Chapter 12

Maggie Gregory was getting married.

That was the buzz around the community, her church, and her job. She'd flashed her beautiful diamond more than she could imagine and never tired of the comments.

It seemed like a dream. Maggie Gregory had caught a man. Incredible. A wealthy, handsome one at that. Who would have thought it could happen? Certainly not her.

Mari and Joe had been delighted for them both. When Joe insisted on putting them on the calendar for counseling after the first of the year, neither she nor Dillon protested. They might be older and wiser in some respects, but neither of them knew what to expect when it came to marriage. Maggie planned on forever and knew this was a step in the right direction.

She was talking with Mari when Julie, Natalie, Kimberly, and Peg found them after the service on Sunday morning.

"I'm so happy for you," Julie cried, hugging Maggie. "When did he propose? Details. We need details."

"The day Marsha went home to her mother. I was so blue, and he took me to Ripley's and got down on one knee and proposed right there."

"Believe it or not?" Kimberly teased.

"Oh, believe me, I'm still pinching myself. It doesn't seem real."

"Well, that ring is. It's beautiful," Julie said.

"It was Mrs. Allene's," Maggie said, twisting her hand side to side.

"Dillon obviously loves you. It doesn't get better than that. So what do you plan for the wedding?" Julie asked.

"Very simple. We're standing up after Sunday morning services to say our vows."

"What?" they all chorused.

"It's what we want."

"Is it?" Julie demanded. "There are no memories in that kind of ceremony. You might as well go to the wedding chapel in Dillon, South Carolina."

"It's best for us both. And I will have memories. We'll be married in our church home by our pastor," Maggie told her.

"And you'll make more memories," Mari consoled upon realizing that Julie's argument troubled their friend.

"That's right. Dillon's planning our honeymoon, and there's no telling where we'll end up."

"I wouldn't take anything for my wedding memories," Kim said.

"Me, either," Julie agreed. "We may have put the wedding together in a week, but it was beautiful."

"Maybe I'm just too practical to be romantic," Maggie said. "Big weddings are for young girls. Not old women like me."

Dillon waved at her from across the room. "I have to go. Dillon's taking me to lunch with his family. See you tonight."

❧

After Maggie left with her new fiancé, Julie cried, "We can't let her do this."

"It's not our decision," Mari reminded.

"We'll see," Julie countered.

The women looked at each other and groaned. What was Julie thinking? They were all more than a little familiar with her escapades.

"Ready, honey?" Noah asked.

"Oh, I'm more than ready," she said, grinning at the others before she took his arm and walked out of the church.

"I don't like this," Mari said, obviously worried that her sister-in-law would do something foolish. "You know how Julie is."

Kim shrugged. "She's right. Maggie deserves more than this little nothing wedding she's planning."

"We can pray over it," Mari said. "But we need to respect Maggie and Dillon's decision."

"We need to talk some sense into her," Natalie said. "Why would they choose to get married at the time when everyone is eager to get home to their lunch? Even something simple in the afternoon for a group of their close friends would be better."

"It's Maggie and Dillon's wedding," Mari reminded yet again.

"But do you honestly think it's the best choice for a wedding ceremony?" Kim asked her.

"I'd prefer that they do something more special," Mari admitted.

"Then we need to convince Maggie to change her mind," Kim said. "I'm going to talk to Julie this week and see what she's thinking."

Chapter 13

W hen do you have days off again?" Dillon asked.

"The first of the week. I work next weekend. Why do you ask?"

"I wanted to visit Charleston. How about Monday? We could leave early and make a day of it."

"What's in Charleston?" Maggie asked curiously.

"Lots of history," he enthused. "Fort Sumter. Horse-and-buggy tours. Boat and bus tours, too. What do you think?"

There were a million things she needed to do, but Maggie decided she'd rather spend the day with Dillon. "Sounds wonderful as long as we don't spend all day at that fort place."

"We can stop at Mount Pleasant and visit Boone Hall Plantation if you'd like."

"I've never been to Charleston. My foster parents took me all around DC when I lived with them, but I've never had much opportunity to do the tourist thing here."

"You don't take vacations?"

"Now and then. Usually I stayed home and worked on whatever project I had going at the time. You'll find I'm more of a homebody than world traveler."

"There's never been anywhere you wanted to go?"

"Not that I could afford. I did the cruise thing once. And I've been to Disney with a couple of church groups."

"So if you could go anywhere you wanted, where would you go?"

Maggie considered the question. "I don't know. Australia maybe."

"What about Europe? China?"

"You've seen those places?"

Dillon nodded. Another difference between them, Maggie considered glumly. How could he be content with someone like her?

"I've done more than my share of exploring," Dillon said. "I'd like to show you my favorite places, but I'm ready to keep my feet planted on solid ground if that's what you want. We'll take it slow. You'll have fun. I promise."

And Dillon kept that promise. On Monday they headed for Charleston. Their first stop was Boone Hall Plantation in Mount Pleasant. As they drove along the world's longest oak-lined avenue to the house, Maggie said, "I feel like I'm heading for Tara. Or was it Twelve Oaks? Come to think of it, I don't think Tara had trees like these."

"I wouldn't know."

Maggie looked at him. "You never saw *Gone with the Wind*?"

"Never."

"Well, that's a part of your education I can remedy. I have the movie on tape. It's four hours long."

Dillon looked surprised. "You're kidding."

"It has an intermission."

For the next hour, they toured America's most photographed plantation, learning the history of the Low-Country estate and still-working plantation.

"So what do you think? Would you like a house like this?" Dillon whispered as they followed the guide.

Maggie shook her head. "Give me cozy and quaint anytime."

"Me, too."

They drove the six miles into Charleston.

Dillon marveled over the incredible bridge. "I read that it's the longest cable-stayed bridge in the nation."

Their next stop was the visitor's center. After studying what was available, Maggie said, "We can visit the fort first. I know you're eager to do that."

"This says the tour is two and a half hours long. Let's pick a Charleston tour, too, so we can see the city."

His willingness to please her did all sorts of things to Maggie's heart.

Later, after they visited Fort Sumter, Maggie commented on his obvious interest in history. "Tell me what else you like," she said. Puzzlement touched his face. "I know you like to travel."

He took her hand in his. "I like spending time with you."

"Good thing," Maggie teased. "I'll soon be around twenty-four hours a day. You'll get a break on the days I work."

He brought her hand up to his lips. "I'll miss you on those days."

She smiled at his romantic gesture. "I'll miss you, too. So what else do you like?"

Dillon held on to her hand as they walked around. "Staying busy, mostly. I thought that once I get the house finished, I might offer to head up a small home repair group at the church. For seniors and single moms. What do you think?"

"It's a good mission. And will probably keep you busier than you realize."

"I thought maybe some of the other guys might be interested. Wyatt's helping Kim with her Christmas program plans, but he's not interested in the choir. He'd like to help others in some way, as well."

It thrilled Maggie that her future husband was a godly man who cared about others.

After lunch they caught the next bus tour. Maggie noted that all their tour guides today were well versed in their ability to share Charleston's history. Their driver showed them various aspects of South Carolina's second-most-populous city. They toured historic houses and a theater before they were delivered back to the visitor's center. It was getting late by the time they left Charleston.

"What are you looking for?" Dillon asked as she rummaged through her purse.

"My cell phone. I must have left it charging at home. I wanted to check my voice mail."

He unclipped his from his belt and handed it to her.

There was one message, and Maggie immediately recognized Mrs. Prince's voice. "They want to place two small children with me," she said after listening to the caseworker's message.

"When do you have time to care for two children, work, and plan a wedding?"

"What plans are there beyond buying a dress and you getting a new suit?"

"What about our counseling sessions?"

"What's going on, Dillon? You obviously don't want me to take these children."

"You have a lot going on right now," he said smoothly, with no expression on his face.

"So are you being protective or selfish?"

He looked sheepish. "A little of both. I want to spend time with you. It's difficult when you're caring for children."

"But I enjoyed my time with Marsha. And Chloe."

Dillon glanced at her and said, "And got your heart broken."

"All of them don't leave so soon," Maggie objected. "What's the real problem? Are you saying you don't want me to be a foster parent?"

He glanced at her and asked, "What if I said yes? Would you choose being a foster parent over being my wife?"

Maggie frowned and shook her head. "No. I like providing a secure, loving home to the children who need them, but to continue after we're married, you'll have to be part of the experience. I realize that's probably something you haven't had time to consider."

"I don't know what to say, Maggie. I'm an old guy who has never been exposed to children. I'm not a father or an uncle. Very few of my friends had children, so when you talk about parenting, it's really something I don't know if I want or not."

He spoke freely about his feelings, and Maggie did the same. "My experience is limited to my friends' children and the church nursery, but it proved worthwhile."

"And no doubt I'd find it just as worthwhile, but right now there are things I want more."

"Like what?"

"Time with you. Maybe I am selfish, but I want more than a few days between placements. Most newlyweds take time before they start families. I know we're not so young anymore, but I'd still like my couple time."

"I understand, Dillon. Truly I do. It's just that I feel I'd be letting the program down."

He sighed. "Maybe it's because I haven't had time to adapt to the idea. I'm sure you were 100 percent behind the plan from day one, but I'm trying to decide how I feel."

"Is it because they're foster kids?"

"Good grief, Maggie, don't you think I have enough sense to know how blessed I was to have good parents?" he demanded. "And to realize that not everyone is that fortunate?"

"That's why I want to do this," she explained. "To help those kids."

Dillon pulled into the opposite lane to pass a slow-moving vehicle. "Can we at least adapt to married life before you add another person to the mix?"

His reluctance troubled her. "It took months to get approved for foster care. I just started."

A few moments of silence elapsed before Dillon spoke. "It sounds sappy, but I just found you. I don't particularly care to share you all the time."

And romantic, Maggie thought as she suggested, "I don't want you feeling overwhelmed, either. How about for now, I take only short-term placements—for children who need a place until the wedding—and then we can look at it again later next year?"

He glanced at her and smiled. "After the long honeymoon I plan to take you on. Anywhere you want to go."

"The place doesn't matter, Dillon. Just so long as we're together."

He reached for her hand. "Hearing you say that makes me even more determined to do something truly outrageous. Maybe even a trip around the world."

"I do have a job, you know."

"Yes," he acknowledged glumly. "That's something I'd love to change."

"What if I found a job at a doctor's office?" Maggie asked.

"Part-time?"

"Maybe if I rented the house and got enough income to offset my expenses. I wouldn't be able to contribute much to our budget, though."

"I can support you."

"Do you have any idea what you're suggesting?"

"It would give us more time together."

"Yes. Maybe too much time. We need to think about this. Pray over it."

"So we put that on the list with foster care for later discussion?"

"I think so. Not that I'm totally opposed to the idea of not working," she admitted with a little laugh.

Soon they turned onto their street. Dillon parked in his driveway and escorted her home. Her words swirled in his head as he unlocked his back door. When he'd realized he was in love with Maggie Gregory, he decided to make her part of his life. He hadn't calculated children into the mix.

How did he really feel about being a foster parent? Dillon knew Maggie would expect an answer to her question sooner rather than later. And he truly didn't have one.

In the kitchen, he took a glass from the cabinet and filled it with ice and water from the new stainless steel refrigerator he'd recently bought. His house was certainly up to code with all the renovations he'd done.

Admittedly, getting to know Marsha had been nice. She was a sweet child, but it was more than the kids. He wanted time with Maggie, not the world. Already she had a multitude of friends that filled much of her off time.

That was something else in the way—her job. He didn't care for sitting around, waiting for her to get off work and then hoping she wasn't too tired to spend time with him. If she didn't have to work, they could travel and see the places she'd never seen. Being foster parents wouldn't allow that. They'd be stuck in Myrtle Beach.

Would Maggie understand his selfish desire to have her to himself? Maybe after a year or so, they could foster kids again, but first he wanted time alone with the woman he loved. That wasn't too much to ask, was it?

❧

Maggie glanced at the clock and headed for the shower. She'd enjoyed their trip. Dillon was a lot of fun. Things had gone well until she'd called home to check her messages.

She'd assumed Dillon would be willing to continue foster parenting after they married. Of course, she hadn't considered the intrusion on his privacy with the check-in visits by the caseworkers and having children around all the time. He had gotten along well with Marsha, but then he hadn't been around her that much. Was it reasonable to ask this of him? She could tell Dillon that if he loved her, he would agree, but that wasn't fair to him.

And just as she'd adapted to Marsha, Maggie knew it would take time for them to adapt to living together. She hated to let the foster care program down, but she needed to be fair to Dillon. He said he'd think about foster parenting, but she wouldn't pressure him.

If Dillon wanted to do this, they would proceed. Otherwise, she'd do what she could to help before the wedding. Content with her decision, Maggie turned on the hair dryer.

❧

A few days later, Mari asked, "You and Dillon are coming for Thanksgiving dinner, aren't you?"

Mari had issued an invitation days before, but Maggie hesitated. "You have family coming."

"It's just us. Julie and Noah are visiting his parents that weekend. Julie wants to spend Christmas with her Cornerstone family. Last year's Christmas celebration at the church was such a success that we're planning to do the same thing again." The year before when Luke had destroyed Mari's list, Julie planned Christmas dinner for everyone at Cornerstone who didn't have special plans.

"Has she already started on Joe about the kids' gifts?" Maggie asked.

"You know she has," Mari said, her voice filled with loving exasperation. "She wants to buy them one of those huge blow-up slides and a ball pit for the backyard. So when Joe says we don't have storage, she offers to buy a building. Honestly, I don't know how Joe refuses. She offers the most convincing arguments."

"You think they'll spoil their own kids?"

"You know they will. Noah tries to curb her generosity, but there are times even he can't refuse her."

Julie's talent for software design and her investment in her employer's company had provided her with more than enough money to share. "Particularly when she's doing so much good for others?"

Mari nodded. "I know the kids would love the slide, but it's not practical."

"But you know she'll come up with something equally as good, don't you?"

Mari grinned and nodded. "Did I tell you Joe's taking the singing Santa over to their place while they're away?"

The Santa had been yet another of Julie's inspirations for the kids. The motion detector activated the thing every time someone came near.

Maggie laughed. "She'll be surprised it's still around. She was sure you'd sell it at a yard sale."

"I'm afraid it's going to set them both off with the practical jokes. So will you come?" Mari asked.

"You have your hands full with Joe and the kids."

"You could always relieve some of the burden. Another set of hands would be appreciated."

"Okay. I'll ask Dillon. But only if you let me contribute to the meal."

"We'll plan a menu with all our traditions."

"Sounds good, but I don't have any traditions. Perhaps you can share a few of yours."

"I imagine you and Dillon will come up with a few of your own. But you can start with Mrs. Allene's mac and cheese casserole. It would be a perfect addition to Thanksgiving dinner."

"Ah, so that's the real reason you want me to come," she teased.

"The real reason is because you're my friend and the kids will love you forever."

"You got it. What else should I bring?"

⟨⟨⟨

Thanksgiving with the Dennis family had proved enjoyable. Maggie wasn't sure, but she felt Dillon had become more comfortable around the kids. They certainly seemed to enjoy his company.

When she'd talked with her caseworker the day after their trip, Maggie learned they placed the children with another family when she wasn't available. She explained her situation, and Mrs. Prince said she'd keep Maggie in mind, but there hadn't been another placement.

She zipped her jacket and pulled on a pair of gloves. "I can't believe Christmas is in two weeks." Colder than usual weather had certainly put a zip in the day they had chosen to visit Simpson's Tree Farm. "Are you sure you don't want a tree?"

"Just a wreath for the door," Dillon replied. "I might put out one of those ceramic trees Mom had. That's enough."

"Not for me," Maggie declared. "I love to decorate for the holidays. I got a later start than usual this year."

"And you plan on catching up this weekend?"

She pulled a list from her pocket and read, "Tree, garlands, wreath. That's a beginning. The other stuff comes out when I unpack my coat closet, which never sees a coat."

"Let's go. I'll drive."

Upon their arrival at the farm, Dillon reached for her hand and said, "Let's go find your tree."

A couple of hours later they found the perfect one. "This is it," Maggie pronounced.

"You're sure?"

Maggie had already picked and discarded numerous trees. "Positive. I'll stand right here while you get Mr. Simpson. I don't want to risk not being able to find it again."

Minutes later, Dillon grinned at her childlike exuberance when she grabbed the tip of the netted tree and walked toward the car. She sang Christmas carols and stepped aside while the men fitted the tree into the trunk. They walked over to a display of evergreen wreaths, and she chose the largest one on the rack along with six garlands.

Dillon chose a smaller wreath and reached for his wallet. "What's the total?"

"I'll pay for mine," Maggie said.

"I plan to enjoy your tree, so it's only fair that I pay," Dillon offered.

She shrugged, and the two men came to an agreement.

"Julie came by yesterday with Mari and the boys," Mr. Simpson told them.

"Does this year's tree rival last year's?" Maggie asked with a big grin.

Mr. Simpson laughed. "The boys tried, but she didn't fall for it this time."

On the ride home, Maggie told Dillon the story of the monstrous tree the Dennis boys had talked their aunt Julie into buying the previous year.

"It was the biggest, ugliest tree on the farm. Then Luke let the cat out of the bathroom and ended up turning the monstrous tree over on Julie. Noah can hardly tell the story without laughing. He said the look on Julie's face was priceless. They'll never celebrate another Christmas without that story being told."

At Maggie's, they worked at getting the tree into a stand. Following Maggie's instructions, Dillon rearranged the furniture and centered the tree in front of her new windows.

"Perfect."

"Where are the lights?" When Maggie pointed to a plastic bin that contained several strands, he asked, "All of those?"

"A tree needs lights," she defended. "I wrap every branch."

Dillon pulled the first reel of lights from the box. "You really don't mess around, do you?"

"I pack them away in good working order." She took the reel and laid it to the side. "Those are twinklers. They go on last."

"Okay, you wrap. I'll keep them untangled and follow."

Much later, when Maggie declared the completed tree the most beautiful ever, Dillon agreed with her. "You almost make me want one of my own."

"You should. Your mother has some beautiful ornaments. I used to help with her tree, too."

"What do you think about adding some of them to this tree?"

"And making it our first tree?"

"Sounds good to me," Dillon agreed.

"Me, too," Maggie said with a happy sigh. "I love Christmas. I have all sorts of plans for the holidays. You are coming to the Christmas Day dinner at church, aren't you?"

He nodded. "Leslie invited us, but I told her we had plans."

Dillon had taken her to Leslie's home for lunch right after they announced their engagement. She'd enjoyed spending time with his cousin and her family. "Are you sure you wouldn't rather be with your relatives?"

"I'd rather be with you."

Lost in his beautiful blue eyes, Maggie knew he meant every word. "We could go to Leslie's."

"I told her we'd stop by on Christmas Eve. Is that okay?"

Maggie slipped her arms about his waist and hugged him. "It's fine."

"How about a break to admire our handiwork over hot chocolate?"

"Sounds good. You make the chocolate. I'll unpack my figurines," Maggie said.

They sat on the sofa, drinking big mugs of chocolate and discussing the remaining decorations.

"The outside stuff is in the building," Maggie said. "I'll work on that tomorrow."

Early the next morning, Dillon found Maggie hard at work. Several boxes sat in the yard as she systematically organized her outside decorations. Three wire trees stood nearby. "I've already put the net lights on the shrubs."

"Am I going to be able to sleep at night?" Dillon teased after he kissed her.

"Probably not. I will be putting the megalights on your side of the house."

"Then don't be surprised if they mysteriously get unplugged."

Maggie grinned at him. As they worked their way into the front yard, Maggie paused to examine the sago palm she'd added last year. "It's not going to survive."

"We'll have to get a replacement. I fixed the fountain."

Maggie whirled around. "It's working?"

Dillon nodded. "You'll have to decide whether it meets your standards."

"I loved that fountain."

"We'll walk over after we finish and see what you think."

⟷

Life was good, Maggie thought as she wrapped her last gift. She'd found some things for Dillon today that she felt certain he would like. She studied the ribbon spools on the table and chose one to match the paper. After tying a big bow and adding Dillon's name to the tag, she placed it beneath the tree.

Because they were going to the church on Christmas Day, Dillon and Maggie had decided to open their gifts to each other on Christmas Eve after they returned from dinner with his family. Dillon had warmed up to the idea of celebrating Christmas. They'd attended the programs at church and the annual parade, and he'd taken her to a holiday show at the theater. They had even visited a couple of neighborhoods to check out their light displays. When Wyatt and Kim mentioned the Nights of a Thousand Candles at Brookgreen Gardens, he'd asked if she wanted to go. He'd even suggested the Festival of Trees at Ripley's Aquarium. Maggie told them there wasn't enough time for everything. He admitted his previous lack of cheer had stemmed from many years of very little celebration in Saudi.

Maggie considered her relationship with Dillon. Feeling loved was so wonderful. She never wanted it to end. But fear was her constant companion. No matter how much she prayed about the situation, she hadn't found total peace. She wanted to be Dillon's wife but feared her insecurities would stand in the way of their happiness.

Chapter 14

Hey, Dillon, this is Julie. Can you come over to Mari's today for lunch?"

"Maggie's at work."

Julie laughed. "We know. We're inviting you."

He couldn't help but feel suspicious. "What's up?"

"We'll tell you when you get here. Come around noon. See you then."

Dillon wondered what her friends had in mind as he hung up the phone. It didn't make sense they'd invite him without Maggie. Oh well, he had to eat. And he'd been meaning to discuss his mission idea with Joe. Maybe he'd be around.

Over soup and sandwiches, the women outlined their plan.

The more they talked, the more concerned he became. "I don't know, Julie. I don't feel right about deceiving her."

"It's not deceit," she insisted. "It's surprise. You don't honestly think Maggie wants her wedding to be some little stand-up affair after church, do you?"

"She said she did."

"Only because she believes she doesn't deserve better."

Her statement confused Dillon. "Why would she think that?"

"She thinks people would consider a big wedding for an old maid foolish. We don't agree. Maggie didn't think she'd ever find her Mr. Right. We prayed for her, and God gave her you."

"I want her to be happy. I'll do whatever it takes."

"Then help us make this happen for her," Julie encouraged. "I promise to take the heat if she gets upset. But I don't think she will. She'll be delighted with the end result."

"She's never going to agree. She said simple."

"That's the beauty of our plan. You and Maggie make the simple plans. We rev them up. And you're not deceiving her. You're helping us surprise her."

"So far the wedding is just us in dress clothes after church. We haven't taken it any further."

"Trust us, Dillon," Mari said. "I felt the same as you at first. But after serious consideration, much prayer, and some conversations with Maggie, I changed my mind. We're her friends. We'd never do anything to hurt her."

"But what if she truly doesn't want a big wedding?"

"She didn't think she wanted a husband, either," Kim pointed out.

"Exactly," Julie agreed. "She didn't believe her prince would ever come."

Dillon looked skeptical. "You wouldn't ask me to dress in tights and ride a white horse, would you?"

They all giggled like little girls at the thought. "Ah, come on, Dillon," Julie teased. "Couldn't you just see Maggie's face?"

He thought about his practical Maggie and all the things she'd missed in life. Her friends were right. She deserved a memorable wedding. "Okay, I'm in. But no tights."

"And we've got it under control," Julie said. "Mari and I are going dress shopping with her next week. What woman can resist trying on wedding gowns? Once she picks her favorite of the real dresses, I'll make sure it's in the dressing room on her wedding day."

"Julie, that's ingenious," Kim declared. "Can I come, too?"

"Me, too," Natalie chimed in.

Mari and Julie glanced at each other and smiled. "The more the merrier. We need one promise from you, Dillon. Every time she acts suspicious, you kiss her and say, 'I can't wait to have you as my wife.'"

"I can handle that."

"Whatever you do, don't give us away," Julie instructed. "Miss Maggie Gregory is about to get the surprise of her life, and she's going to love you for it."

"It may be the stupidest thing I've ever done," Dillon told them.

"Actually, I'd rate it up there with the best," Julie said. "Just wait until you see her on your wedding day. You'll put every doubt behind you."

"We're planning a shower," Mari said.

"We already have more than we need in the two houses, not including what I have in Saudi," Dillon offered.

"A new bride needs pretties," Kim pointed out.

His face turned red.

"We're calling the wedding Project Love Day," Mari said. "We're decorating the church and planning a formal sit-down dinner for the reception. Several women have signed up to provide food. Of course, Maggie will know nothing until it's time to write the thank-you notes."

"And I'm doing your cake as a gift," Natalie said.

"You were doing this with or without my help, weren't you?" Dillon asked, his gaze shifting from woman to woman.

Julie nodded. "If we had to. Maggie's very important to us."

"And to me. I love her a great deal."

He noted the way the women smiled at each other.

"Where are you taking her on your honeymoon?" Natalie asked.

Dillon shrugged. "I don't know. I've suggested a few places, but she doesn't seem interested."

"Why not Saudi? She'd love to see where you lived, meet your friends, help sort through your stuff."

"That's not a honeymoon," he objected.

"You'll find Maggie's idea of a honeymoon is being with you wherever you are," Mari said.

"There's always the Alaskan cruise she's talked about," Kim said.

"Or Australia. Remember she has the pen pal friend over there," Mari pointed out.

"Why can't Maggie tell me this?"

"Maggie isn't a *me* kind of person, but every once in a while she shares a tidbit about herself. You have to pay close attention or you'll miss it."

Dillon believed that. She'd surprised him more than once. Hopefully he could keep his mouth shut and not spoil this for Maggie or her friends.

~

"So what's the plan for your day off?" Dillon asked Sunday night before leaving for the evening.

"The girls are taking me dress shopping."

"Want to come over for breakfast? I could make one of those omelets you love so much. Or I could make pancakes."

"Definitely pancakes," Maggie agreed, adding, "I will need my strength. They plan to take me to a bridal shop."

He leaned forward and kissed her. "I can't wait to have you as my wife."

She considered him thoughtfully. "You've been saying that a lot."

"Not too much, I hope."

Maggie slid her arms around his neck. "That would be impossible. I can't wait to have you as my husband. Is something wrong? You've been acting strange for a few days now."

"I'm a strange man," Dillon explained with a mischievous leer, hoping his guilt wasn't obvious. Why did he feel that surprising Maggie was a negative when the others didn't?

"Yes, you are," she agreed with a huge grin. "But you're being stranger than usual."

"Now, should my future bride talk that way about her beloved?"

"Sweetheart, only your future bride can talk that way about her man."

"You gonna go mama bear on anyone who talks bad about me?" Dillon teased.

"And how would you feel about that?"

He shrugged. "It's okay. As long as I get to do the same. Maggie, how do you feel about surprises?"

"I'm all for them. What did you have in mind?"

"It would hardly be a surprise if I told you."

"True. At least give me a clue. What's it for?"

"Our wedding," Dillon responded truthfully.

"Something outrageous and shocking, I hope."

"Do you mean that?" he asked somewhat doubtfully.

She laughed. "I doubt either of us could come up with outrageous or shocking. We're too practical for our own good."

Your friends can, Dillon thought. *Prepare for the surprise of your life, Miss Maggie.*

⤙⤚

"Dillon's acting strange," Maggie told Mari when she called later that evening.

"How so?"

"I can't put my finger on it exactly. You don't think he's getting cold feet, do you?"

"No way. That man's so eager to marry you. I'm surprised he's waited this long."

"He seems withdrawn. Almost as though he's keeping secrets. I suppose he could be. He did ask if I liked surprises."

"And you told him you do, I hope?"

"I did."

"What do you think is on his mind?" Mari prompted.

"For one thing, he doesn't want to be a foster parent."

"Did he say that?"

"Not in so many words, but he keeps saying he wants couple time."

"Makes sense. The more people in the mix, the more confusing it becomes," Mari pointed out.

"I feel like I'm letting the program down."

"You didn't plan on falling in love, Maggie. Does that mean you should give up your own happiness for the sake of the foster children?"

"No. . .but you know what I mean."

"They'll understand once you explain you're getting married and your future husband wants you to himself for a while."

"They did," Maggie said. "I've already told the caseworker. She said she'd keep me in mind until the wedding, but I haven't heard from them. I enjoyed Marsha and looked forward to working with other children. I don't know why it didn't occur to me sooner."

"It wasn't God's plan."

"True. How are the kids? It's been awhile since I've seen them."

"They miss you. Luke asked to go see Miss Maggie earlier. Right after I told him to pick up his toys."

Maggie laughed. "That's one wise kid you have there."

"Too wise for his own good. It's all I can do to stay two steps ahead of him. Thankfully the others are nothing like Luke."

"Give them time. With a brother like him, I'm sure they'll soon learn."

"Gee, Maggie, thanks for brightening my day."

"You know you love it."

"I do. My children are as precious to me as we are to God."

"I love being a child of God," Maggie agreed.

"Me, too. I'd better go. Matt's yelling at the twins. Don't forget, we're going to the bridal shop tomorrow."

"It's a waste of time."

"Come on, Maggie, be a sport. Joe's taking care of the kids so I can have the day off. You wouldn't deprive me of that, would you?"

"Never."

❧

"You're looking particularly beautiful this morning," Dillon said after Maggie kissed him.

The heavenly smell of the pancakes made Maggie's mouth water. "You know this is going straight to my hips, don't you?"

"A few pancakes never hurt anyone."

"I don't have your metabolism."

He handed her a plate. "We could take long walks on the beach every morning."

Maggie settled at the table, shaking out her napkin. "That's difficult with my shifts. You'd think all that walking the floors would help, but it doesn't."

After they said grace, she cut off a bite of pancake and forked it into her mouth.

"You could always quit your job," Dillon said.

She took a sharp, deep breath. "You don't quit, do you?"

He stared wordlessly.

"You're changing everything," Maggie declared stubbornly. She could see from his shocked expression that she'd come at him out of left field with this one. "Slowly easing me from my life. Your place for mine. . ."

"We can live in your house," Dillon interrupted. "I just thought Mom's place would give us more space."

"There you go with the logic. Who wouldn't want a bigger house? To retire at fifty? To travel the world? You're changing my life."

"Mine, too," Dillon defended as he turned away and scraped a burned pancake off the griddle.

"Because you chose to change," Maggie pointed out.

"Okay, if you don't want these things, tell me," Dillon all but shouted, flinging the spatula at the sink. It clattered against the stainless steel interior.

She regretted making him angry. "That's the problem. I do," she admitted in a tiny voice.

Dillon sat down next to her. "What's going on, Maggie?"

"I'm scared."

He reached for her hand. "Why?"

"Of what happens when things get too good. I dreamed of early retirement, but that's all it was—a dream. There's no way I could afford not to work. And now you've proposed that I'll not only retire early but travel, as well. This is a fairy tale, Dillon. Not real life."

"You know I'd never hurt you."

"Maybe not intentionally, but we can't promise it'll never happen. Couples argue."

"Is that what we're doing? Arguing?"

"I'm trying to tell you how I feel," she declared, irritation changing her tone. "You've veered so far from that man who thought I was out to cheat your mom."

"I said I was sorry."

"I don't want apologies, Dillon. I need you to understand that sometimes I don't know how to accept the good. There's too much pessimism in me to believe nothing bad will happen."

"If I'd known asking you to quit work would set you off like this, I would have kept my mouth shut."

She rested her hands on his arms. "Oh, Dillon, I should have told you how bad I can get."

"You're not bad, Maggie. And maybe it's past time some good came into your life. I'm not saying you have to quit work, but if you felt inclined, I'd love to have you at home with me."

"I'm so overwhelmed."

His worried expression made her feel even worse. She'd allowed her insecurities to burden them both. "I do want to marry you," she shared quickly. "But remember, I've steered my own course for years."

"And it's going to be difficult to allow someone else to chart changes in the map?"

"Exactly."

"I don't plan to sink your ship, honey. Maybe help steer you around a few obstacles."

"I've provided for myself since I was eighteen years old. The Floyds paid for my education, but I worked to pay for my incidentals. I can't imagine not working. What would I do all day?"

"Whatever you want. Watch the sunrise. Sleep in. Enjoy the sand between your toes. Spend hours listening to the ocean roar. You could help with my handyman project. Wouldn't it be nice to do whatever we want and not have to rush back home so you can go to work?"

"Well yes," Maggie admitted, feeling calmer than before. "I'm not arguing that point."

"So it's fear of change?"

Maggie nodded slowly. "You must think I'm crazy."

"You scared me."

"I don't usually act this way. Maybe it's this outing with the girls that has me acting batty."

"You don't want to go?"

"I do. I don't know what to expect."

"They can't force you to do anything you don't want to do."

Maggie laughed. "Maybe I want to do it all, but I'm afraid to take the leap."

Dillon wrapped his arms around her. "Jump, darling. I promise to catch you. Think of it in terms of being a Christian. We try to offer God advice, but things always go His way, in His time, particularly when we place our faith in Him."

It was the perfect analogy for her. She'd struggled with God's plans for her, too.

"Don't stress so much. As long as we're flexible and communicate, we'll be okay."

Maggie gazed into his eyes. "You promise to love me even when I'm crazy?"

"What choice do I have?" he asked, leaning forward to kiss her.

A horn blew. "Gotta go." Maggie hugged him one last time, forked another bite of pancakes into her mouth, and ran out the door.

"Call me when you get home," Dillon called. "I want to hear about this dress."

"Not until our wedding day," she called back to him.

Dillon dropped into the chair and thought about what had just transpired. Maggie Gregory kept him on an emotional roller coaster. Her reaction to his suggestion had been startling. Was he doing the right thing by keeping her friends' secrets? He wished he knew. Maybe Joe could offer some insight into the situation.

He phoned the church and learned Joe was at home. He called his minister and friend and asked if he had a few minutes to talk. Joe told him to come over.

"Hi, Dillon, come in," Joe invited, closing the front door behind them. "What can I do for you?"

"I wanted to discuss the ladies' plans. I'm not comfortable with the surprise element."

The patter of children's feet sounded down the hall. "Ready, Daddy," Luke announced. When he saw their guest, he shouted, "Hey, Mr. Dillon!" Then he turned around and bellowed, "Mr. Dillon is here."

"Hey, Luke," he said, returning the child's hug when he wrapped his arms about his lower body. Turning to Joe, he said, "I can come back. You're busy."

"We're going outside to play. Come on. We'll talk."

The children ran for the swings and sandboxes, and Joe took a seat on the patio, inviting Dillon to do the same. "Haven't you ever surprised Maggie with something?"

"Her ring when I proposed." And his suggestion she quit work. Dillon didn't mention that. Her reaction had surprised them both. He still didn't understand why it had blown up in his face.

"And you didn't consider it wrong to surprise her with the proposal?"

He shrugged, shaking his head. "No."

"Consider this. God gifted Maggie with a good man and good friends who want to gift her with the perfect wedding."

"There's something else," Dillon offered almost tentatively. "Maggie's foster parenting. She assumes it's a given we will continue to foster children. Our marriage necessitates another review process. I don't have anything to hide, but I have mixed feelings. I never imagined I'd find the love of my life, and I'm not thrilled about sharing her with kids."

"Have you told her?"

He shrugged and nodded. "I shared my doubts. I want to spend time with her. Am I being selfish?"

"I can't answer that, Dillon. Is there another reason you're hesitant? Maggie's only had one foster child, and it went well."

"She was devastated when Marsha went home," Dillon told Joe. "I'm afraid that would happen with every child she brings into her life."

"Maggie would learn to protect her heart with time. Letting go becomes easier with practice. Is that the only reason, Dillon? You don't like seeing Maggie hurt?"

He nodded. "I wish like crazy that we'd met when we were younger and she could have a family of her own. Maggie needs to feel grounded. I'm afraid that denying her foster parenting will take away that outlet for the love she needs to share. I said we could look at it again in a year or so, but neither of us is getting any younger."

"Pray over it."

"I have. Believe me. I'm waiting on God's answer."

"And He will provide. Just let Him guide you both."

Chapter 15

And why is it you want to go to the bridal shop?" Maggie asked her friends when they immediately suggested the store. "You know I plan to wear a suit."

"They sell suits," Julie said. "Just dressier than the department stores. You can't have a plain-Jane wedding. There has to be more bling than that ring on your finger."

"So I'll get silver shoes," Maggie countered. "Or maybe white with sparkles."

"You have to try on dresses," Kim insisted. "We plan to live vicariously through you today."

"I'm buying a suit."

Her determined response made Mari ask, "Why are you afraid to try on wedding dresses?" Maggie didn't answer.

"You think you'll want a big wedding if you do," Kim guessed.

"It's not what Dillon wants," Maggie told them. "We agreed to keep it simple."

"It doesn't hurt to look," Julie said. "Wait until you see all those beautiful gowns. You need to try on at least a dozen just because you're the bride-to-be and you can."

Maggie frowned. She hated trying on clothes. "I learned a long time ago not to want what I can't have."

"I don't get it, Maggie. Why can't you have a wedding dress?" Julie asked.

"I'd look silly."

"Because you're fifty?"

"I'm plain old me. Not a movie star or blushing young bride."

"Surely you don't believe any member of Cornerstone would feel you don't deserve a beautiful gown or a fancy wedding because you're an older woman?" Julie asked.

"No, but Dillon and I agreed on simple."

"Simple can be many things," Julie pointed out. "My wedding was simple but beautiful. Dillon doesn't care about the wedding. He cares about you being happy."

"Humor us for a couple of hours," Mari suggested, taking her arm and leading her inside. "Then we'll take you to lunch."

Maggie sighed and relented, "Oh, okay, lead on. Let's find the most expensive gowns in the place."

Julie grinned and said, "Now that's the right attitude." Inside, they waited in the upscale showroom, and everyone laughed when Maggie mentioned the television sitcom where two friends dressed in borrowed gowns and pretended to be brides, tossing bouquets back and forth.

"I don't think we'd better try that here," Mari whispered. A well-dressed woman came over and introduced herself as the owner. "Which of you lovely ladies is our bride?"

Maggie felt her skin grow warm when her friends pointed in her direction.

"Congratulations. When's the wedding?"

"The Sunday before Valentine's Day."

The woman nodded. "What did you have in mind?"

"A simple white suit."

"But she wants to try on gowns first," Julie said. "Right, Maggie?"

"My friends insist I have to try on wedding gowns though they know my plans are very simple."

"There are gowns that would be glorious on you," the woman offered, switching into salesperson mode. "Let me show you."

When Maggie stepped up on to the dais wearing the first gown, she had to admit the owner knew what suited her. She felt like a fairy princess wearing a satin halter dress with a tulle skirt and beaded Alençon lace.

The next dress was a satin ball gown adorned with back buttons and a long train detailed with lace appliqué cutouts.

She tried on dress after dress as each of her friends chose their favorite. Then Maggie tried on the dress she'd picked, and they all sighed in delight.

The satin floor-length halter gown with the side drape and flower detail was a perfect fit. The woman produced a long tulle veil that trailed along behind Maggie.

"So what do you think?" Maggie asked as she pirouetted before the mirror and looked over her shoulder at the back of the gown. They all agreed she should choose this one.

She took one more look and remembered her intent. No matter how she felt in the dress, it wasn't part of her plans. "I don't know why I let them talk me into this," she told the owner. "Do you have white suits?"

"Of course. I'll bring a couple into the dressing room."

"Maggie, wait!" Julie cried, stepping up on the dais next to her. "Don't you think she should choose this one?" she asked the owner.

"It suits her, but if she doesn't want the gown, then we'll find her what she wants."

"But it's perfect. It doesn't even need alterations. Even the length is exactly right."

"Julie, please," Maggie requested softly. "Don't make me want this more than I already do."

"Okay," her friend agreed with a heavy sigh. "Pick out your suit, but I'm paying."

They all knew better than to argue with Julie when she got into this mood. Maggie stepped into the dressing room and removed the dress with Mari's help.

"Julie's disappointed."

Mari looked up from undoing the buttons and nodded at Maggie in the mirror. "She only wants you to have a beautiful dress. We all do."

Her friend came into the dressing room. "Here, try this one," Julie said, handing her a very feminine white lace suit with satin lapels.

The owner brought a knee-length raw silk suit in white and one with a long skirt, but Maggie chose the one Julie had picked. After the decision was made, the owner called in her seamstress to take Maggie's measurements.

On their way out, a display caught Maggie's eye. She paused to finger the gorgeous lilac dress and sighed in delight. The dress featured the same halter-top style as the wedding dress she'd loved. "If I were having attendants, this is the dress I'd choose."

"We could wear the dresses and serve as honorary attendants," Natalie suggested.

"And you'd know we wanted to be up front with you," Julie agreed.

"It's not practical," Maggie said with a shake of her head. "We'd freeze with our shoulders out in February."

"Ready for lunch?" Natalie asked. "I'm starving."

Maggie agreed. The couple of bites she'd managed that morning had long since left her.

"Thanks again for your help," she told the owner.

"My pleasure. You'll make a beautiful bride."

They were in the car when Julie cried, "I forgot to pay for your dress. Noah says I'd forget my head," she muttered. "Everyone stay put. I'll be right back."

"You really should let me pay for it," Maggie insisted one final time.

"You'll hurt my feelings if you don't let me give you this gift."

Maggie couldn't help but wonder why Julie was so adamant. She hadn't insisted on giving Kim her dress. But then Kim's parents had paid for her wedding. And Julie had worn her mother's gown for her wedding. Maybe it was because Maggie didn't have a family.

Julie was gone for several minutes and grinned like a Cheshire cat when she crawled into the backseat with Natalie and Kim and said, "Mission accomplished."

At their favorite restaurant, Mari took Maggie's arm and led her inside while the others removed packages from the trunk.

"What are they doing?" she asked, glancing back over her shoulder.

"You'll see." They followed the hostess to a small private room in the rear of the restaurant. The others arrived, stacking their packages on a nearby table.

"Okay, give," Maggie demanded, her gaze shifting from face to face.

"Welcome to your shower," Kim said.

"That's right, practical one," Julie said, "even if you act like Scrooge over the wedding, we're giving you a shower. We decided not to embarrass you by having this particular event at church, but there are a few necessities every new bride must have."

Maggie groaned. "You'll be the death of me yet, Julie Loughlin."

Everyone chuckled and reached for their menus. After choosing their entrées, they enjoyed their iced tea and the blooming onion appetizer Natalie ordered.

"So what did you think about the gowns?" Mari asked.

"They were all beautiful. That one would have been perfect if we were having a formal wedding. But the suit serves the purpose, and I can wear it again."

"What would your dream wedding be like?" Kim asked.

"Marrying Dillon is a dream for me. I never expected to fall in love with him."

"Not after the way he treated you when you first met," Kim said.

Kim had been her faithful defender when it came to Dillon's treatment of her. "Dillon feels guilty that he allowed strangers to care for Mrs. Allene. He knows I loved her like a mother."

"And wishes she could be here for the wedding?" Mari asked.

"Yes. And my parents, of course. They've been dead for years, but I miss them still."

"You always will," Mari said, her eyes tearing up. She, too, had lost her mother. Julie reached over to squeeze her sister-in-law's hand.

"I'm sorry," Maggie whispered. "I didn't mean to upset you."

"You didn't," Mari said with a gentle smile. "I was blessed to have my mother sitting in the front pew when I married Joe. You, Joe, and Julie weren't as fortunate."

"I need to call Mom tonight," Kim said with a sheepish look.

"Let me tell you what Dillon said this morning," Maggie said, steering the conversation to a happier subject.

"That he loves you?" Julie asked.

Surprised, Maggie said, "Yes. He says that all the time lately."

Julie shrugged. "All men in love should say it often. So what did he say?"

"He suggested I retire."

Everyone looked startled.

"And what did you say?" Julie demanded.

Maggie looked embarrassed. "I accused him of trying to change everything about my life. He thinks I'm crazy."

"I doubt that," Mari comforted. "Is early retirement something you'd consider?"

"He says he doesn't want to sit around for long days waiting for me to get off work and that he can afford to support us both."

"You'd be crazy to say no," Julie said.

"He keeps knocking my feet out from under me with these surprises," Maggie explained. "Helping with the house, the proposal, this ring, and now this."

"Sounds as if he's smitten," Julie declared.

Maggie nodded, and everyone laughed.

"You deserve to be loved, and now that we know Dillon better, we know he's the man for you," Mari said.

"I hope I'm the woman for him."

"Don't ever doubt it, Maggie Gregory," Julie said sternly. "Dillon Rogers is the lucky one. Not every man has you in his life, and don't ever let him forget it."

"That's right," Kim agreed. "Our husbands are blessed to have us as their wives, and now that you're about to get married, we're going to find Natalie her Mr. Right."

"Oh, Lord, deliver me," Natalie said, raising her gaze heavenward in supplication.

After their meal, they ordered dessert and lingered over the bridal shower.

"This is for your wedding night," Mari said, passing Maggie a beautifully wrapped package.

Maggie opened the box to find a virginal white satin nightgown and matching robe—the nightwear a mother often gave her daughter. Tears welled in her eyes as she considered Mari's thoughtfulness. "Thank you."

"And these go with that," Julie said with a teasing grin, passing her what appeared to be a shoe box.

Inside, Maggie found a pair of white satin and marabou slippers with three-inch heels. "I'll break my neck."

"But just think, when you fall, Dillon will be there to catch you."

The laughter started and didn't stop as Maggie opened box after box.

"It's only a matter of time before you're wearing one of Dillon's old T-shirts and sleeping in drawstring pajama pants again," Kim said, handing Maggie another box. "You won't be able to help yourself. They're just too comfortable. But if there's a time when you need to remind Dillon you're all woman, this should do the trick."

Almost afraid to open the box, Maggie found a short red satin nightie inside.

"Wow," Julie said.

Maggie adored the romantic garments she would have never bought for herself. "This is too much," she declared tearfully.

"It's never too much for our friend," they said.

Julie lifted her tea glass into the air. "To Maggie."

"To Maggie," they repeated in unison.

~

"Are you having second thoughts?" Maggie asked Dillon later that night after she told him about the trip to the bridal shop and the surprise shower. Was it her imagination, or did he seem to withdraw with the question?

"Why would you ask that?"

"Well, after my attack this morning, I wouldn't be surprised if you were reconsidering. And I can't put my finger on it, but you're different somehow."

Dillon slipped his arm around her and pulled her against his chest. "I'm thinking about counseling and being a good husband, but I'm not about to change my mind. February can't get here fast enough."

She smiled at him. "I started sorting through some stuff that I'll probably give away."

"You don't have to do that. We'll find a place for everything."

"We should talk about what we want to keep for our place."

"Your sofa is more comfortable than Mom's," Dillon said, settling further into the deep sofa.

"We could flip-flop pieces and rent the house furnished."

"Or donate them to charity. We're bound to have more than we need."

"Mari could use a new couch. The kids are hard on their furniture."

"I still haven't gone through the attic," Dillon told her. "Let's see if there's anything up there they can use."

"That sounds like a plan."

Chapter 16

Shopping for her dress and being surprised by her shower had made the approaching nuptials even more real for Maggie. Then Joe Dennis called to set an actual start-up date for their premarital counseling. On the first night, Maggie couldn't quiet the butterflies in her stomach as she and Dillon sat with Pastor Joe in his home study.

He closed the door and settled in an old recliner while they sat on the sofa. "It's not often I get to give these sessions one-on-one," Joe told them. "I'm really glad to have this opportunity to counsel you both. Loving each other is important, but you'll find areas that require negotiation if you want a happy, long-lasting marriage.

"I'll outline the plans for the meetings in a few minutes, but first I want to ask what your biggest concerns are. Maggie, ladies first; what's your major concern about marriage?"

She laughed nervously. "You want me to pick just one?" When Joe nodded, she said, "Fear."

He shrugged. "Define 'fear.' "

She wrung her hands. "That I won't be the wife Dillon deserves."

"We've discussed that," Dillon objected. "I have no expectations."

"And you feel that's realistic?" Joe asked.

Perplexed, Dillon glanced at Maggie and back at Joe. "I feel we can work things out as we go. That's the way we've handled things so far."

"Have you considered that continuing to do it that way will put unnecessary stress on your marriage?"

Dillon's brows drew together. "How so?"

"What side of the bed do you prefer?"

"The left."

"You, Maggie?"

"The left."

"Only one left side of the bed." They looked at each other. "So someone has to take the right side. How do you decide? Does one of you opt to be the bigger person and make the sacrifice? Do you flip a coin? Does the one who gets there first get the left side? Or will you discuss it and come to an agreement that works best for you both?"

"I suppose we'll discuss it," Dillon said.

"I know it seems simple, but it's just the beginning. You'll agree to accept things about each other, little things that drive you crazy and can cause major problems if you're not prepared to handle them. What about you, Dillon? What's your biggest issue?"

He looked at her. "I'm not sure Maggie trusts me to do what's best for her."

"Trust is important," Joe agreed. "Do you trust Dillon, Maggie?"

She nodded. "I wouldn't have said yes to your proposal if I didn't believe you love me."

"But do you trust him?" Joe repeated. "Do you feel you can put your life in his hands and know he'll take care of you?"

"I hadn't considered that marriage was turning yourself over to another person and depending on them to take care of you. I think of it as a partnership—both of us looking out for each other."

"What about Dillon being the Christian head of your household? Him making decisions that you might not wholeheartedly agree with?"

"I've made my own decisions for years, and I'm not likely to stop once we're married."

"I don't plan to take over her life."

"But you will," Joe said. "You say you don't have expectations, but you do. You expect Maggie to trust you to do the right thing. How can you know what the right thing is if you don't discuss it?"

"I don't think we need to talk every little thing to death," Dillon objected.

Joe rested his chin on steepled fingers and said, "I can see you're already uncomfortable, but these sessions are intended to help you grow as a couple. We may move out of your comfort zones, but please don't shut down on me."

They nodded, and Joe asked, "Do you need to communicate?"

"Sure," Dillon agreed. "I can't understand what she wants if she doesn't tell me when I ask."

"Does she have to wait until you ask?"

He frowned. "No. Maggie's not a game player, and I like that."

"I know you had issues with her when you first met and that you've resolved them. Do you feel guilty for the way you treated her?"

"I've apologized, and she's accepted my apologies. But yes, I do feel guilty."

"What about forgive and forget? Maybe Maggie doesn't want you to bring that up anymore. She wants to forget it ever happened."

"Is that true?" Dillon asked. "Did you tell him that?"

"No," she defended, looking at Pastor Joe with surprise. "I can't really tell anyone how I feel."

"Not even me?" he asked, sounding disappointed.

"Not even me," she countered. "I have issues from the past, Dillon. Things that will affect our marriage more than I'd like."

"Maggie hasn't shared anything with me, Dillon, but look at how easily you made an assumption that she had."

"I'm sorry."

"You allowed a communication you heard to affect your thought processes. Rather than thinking it over, you reacted, and that knee-jerk reaction can sometimes haunt your marriage forever. Once words leave your lips, you can't pull them back. And regardless of how the old saying goes, words can hurt."

Once more, both Maggie and Dillon nodded.

"Here's how I'd like to proceed. We have six weeks until the wedding. In the past, I've done four-, six-, and even eight-week sessions, depending on the couple."

"And one week," Maggie said, reminding him of Julie and Noah.

"If I hadn't already known my sister and Noah so well, I'd never have allowed that," Joe said. "Anyway, I believe we can do this in four weeks. Tonight, I want you to complete a test. You need to answer the questions without discussing them with each other. We'll discuss the answers as we go into our sessions."

The room grew quiet as Joe gave them each a clipboard and suggested Dillon move to his chair.

"There are no right or wrong answers. Just questions that will provoke you to consider a number of pertinent points that relate to marriage. If you have any questions, ask. I'll be glad to help. Mari baked cookies today. You get started, and I'll get our refreshments."

Occasionally, Maggie glanced up to find Dillon looking thoughtful. She wondered where he was on the questionnaire. And while she knew the answers were supposed to be her own, she couldn't help but wonder how he had responded.

Later the mood was contemplative as they walked toward home.

"That test was something else," Dillon said.

It had been rather eye-opening, Maggie thought. "Amazing how many things we never really considered."

"Like preferring the same side of the bed?" When Maggie nodded, he assured her, "That's not really a problem."

"Something else you'll give up for me?"

He reached for her hand. "You'd do the same for me. I can see where counseling will be beneficial. And just because we're not always in full agreement over everything doesn't mean things can't work out. That's where compromise comes into play. I think we're pretty good at that."

Are we? Maggie wondered. How many times had she gone along with Dillon's decisions? What other differences would the test answers reveal?

"Come look at the ceiling. I finished it today. I'll make you a berry smoothie."

Maggie loved the fruity taste of the smoothies Dillon blended for her. He'd started keeping ingredients on hand and sometimes brought supplies to her house, as well.

"I want to know how you answered those questions on bank accounts," she said as he let them into the house.

Maggie admired the ceiling and sat at the kitchen island while Dillon whirled ingredients in the blender. "Did you take the shirt back yet?" she asked. She'd given him the shirt for Christmas and had guessed at his size. She didn't think he liked the shirt but knew he'd keep it for fear of hurting her feelings by taking it back.

"No. It's okay."

"It's too big," Maggie argued. "Give it to me. I'll exchange it for a smaller size."

"I'll handle it," he promised. "You already have enough to do."

"Exchange it for something you like. I don't mind," she said.

"I used my new woodworking tools yesterday. I can't believe how long I looked and waited to buy them. Now I have several projects in mind."

It pleased her that she'd found something he liked.

"How's the new purse working out?"

Dillon had given her a very expensive handbag, and while Maggie wasn't thrilled with the various compartments, she carried it daily. Soon she'd fill him in on how personal the preference for handbags really was. "Good. The girls at work love it."

He slid a glass on the island before her and shuffled through the drawer.

"What are you looking for?"

"I found something for you at the grocery store. I'm positive I stuck them in here," he muttered. "Ah, here they are."

Maggie laughed when he handed her a straw with a spoon on the end.

"How's this for when your smoothie is too thick to drink?"

Maggie trailed her fingers along his jaw. "You're a keeper, Dillon Rogers."

He sat on the stool next to her, his hands cradling her face as he kissed her. "No matter what the test results say?"

"It's not a test," Maggie said. "More of a 'getting to know you' tool."

"Like those icebreaker things at meetings?"

"Exactly. And I look forward to learning everything about my future husband."

"And changing the parts you don't like?" he asked.

Maggie shook her head. "No. We accept those things and celebrate our differences."

"I can't tell you how much I appreciate hearing that from you."

"They're not just words, Dillon. I'll respect your role as head of our home, but I expect you to communicate with me."

"I do."

"Yeah, like that plant list Keith Harris sent me. I thought you promised to let me make the decisions about my house."

"I did. But if you look, you'll find everything is the same as what you had in your yard before."

"I saw a couple of hundred dollars in flowers."

He quickly swallowed the sip of smoothie and said, "Those were for here."

"My future home, you mean?"

"I know you love flowers, and I thought I'd have him bring a few things over."

"I'd rather go to the nursery and pick them out myself. I go every spring to choose what I put in my planters and add to my landscaping. Your beds are full of bulbs. Haven't you noticed the crocuses and daffodils pushing through?"

"You'll have to show me."

"Don't you garden?" It was high on Maggie's retirement list. She looked forward to spending more time in her yard.

He shrugged. "Until this summer, I hadn't used a lawn mower since I was a teenager."

"Your life has been so different."

They finished their smoothies, and Maggie took the glasses over to the sink. She rinsed them and the blender before putting everything in the dishwasher. "So how did you answer those banking questions?"

"I'm flexible. Mom and Dad had a joint account, but if you'd rather keep them separate, that's okay. We could have a household account."

If she took advantage of Dillon's plan for her to retire early, what would she put into the account? Rent money from the house maybe. Possibly a little money from her retirement, but it wouldn't amount to much.

"Did I tell you Natalie might be interested in renting my place?"

"No. That's a great idea."

"We're going to talk about it next week. She'd like a bigger kitchen."

"Hope it works out. It would be nice to have that resolved before our wedding. Definitely before the honeymoon."

"Where are we going?" she asked.

"It's a surprise."

Maggie pushed her hair behind her ears and said, "It'll be an even bigger surprise when you end up going by yourself because I didn't get enough time off from work."

Dillon frowned. "Why won't you just give up your job?"

"Because I have personal expenses that I can't expect you to cover."

"My money will be yours, Maggie."

She didn't want to argue about this again. "Should I ask for a week of vacation? I need to get my request on the books."

"Can you swing two? I have something special in mind."

She sprayed the countertop with a disinfectant spray and used a paper towel to wipe it away. "I'll ask."

Chapter 17

January slipped away, and the groundhog predicted another six weeks of cold weather. Though cold outside, Maggie felt warmly cocooned in Dillon's love. At least during those times she allowed herself to be happy.

Dillon's determination to make everything special for her showed through in the attention he showered on her. Maggie had never known what being spoiled could be like, but his behavior certainly mirrored what she'd imagined. He took care of her in so many ways. She couldn't begin to count the number of times she'd come home to prepared meals or they had dined out when she was tired after work. He'd even offered to run errands when she so much as mentioned a need.

The counseling sessions were going better than she'd thought. Joe had expertly talked them through the few things they disagreed on, including foster care. Maggie hadn't been surprised to learn Dillon's main objection had to do with her being hurt when the children went away. And she'd made the decision to give him the couple time he needed.

They discussed Dillon's love of travel and Maggie's admitted preference for home. When Joe asked why, she could only admit how much she had always considered home the place where she belonged.

Both Dillon and Joe had impressed upon her that home wasn't always a building.

"What if Dillon had to go back to Saudi?" Joe asked. "Would you let him go rather than give up your home and friends here?"

Maggie shrugged. "I wouldn't want to. But I can't say what I'd do, and truthfully I'm thankful I don't have to make the decision."

"But it's always a possibility. When Mari and I married, I'm sure she thought we'd remain in Colorado. Our lives changed, but she was willing to follow me." He picked up his Bible and flipped through the tissuelike pages.

"In Ruth 1:16, we read, 'Intreat me not to leave thee, or to return from following after thee: for whither thou goest, I will go; and where thou lodgest, I will lodge: thy people shall be my people, and thy God my God.' When you marry, this becomes your promise to each other," Joe said.

"And I will promise that," Maggie said, glancing at Dillon as she spoke. "I just know I need roots. And I need Dillon to understand why home is so important to me." To her dismay, her voice broke slightly.

Dillon reached for her hand. "And I'm trying, Maggie. But you have to move forward with me. I want nothing for you but happiness."

"I suspect Maggie's nomadic existence in her childhood has a great deal to do with her need for a home," Joe offered. "You did say you lived in a number of foster homes after your father's death."

Maggie nodded.

"You stayed with the Floyds the longest. Why not remain in Virginia?"

"A college friend grew up in Myrtle Beach. She brought me here for a visit once, and I fell in love with the area. After Mr. Floyd retired and they began to travel, I decided to make the move. Sometimes I think God orchestrated it so I'd come here and find Him."

"And me," Dillon offered. "I've been studying my Bible, too, praying for scripture that would bring you comfort," he told her. "I ran across Psalm 90:1 last night. 'Lord, thou hast been our dwelling place in all generations.' "

"Very good, Dillon," Joe agreed. "There's no more perfect dwelling place than in the Lord."

"I understand what you're saying," Maggie told them. "And I want to feel that way. Truly I do."

"We'll pray over this," Joe promised. "Your happiness is in God and the love He's given you. Not in a place."

❧

On Tuesday night, Dillon had a church meeting, and Natalie called to invite Maggie out to dinner at their favorite restaurant.

"So what have you been up to lately?" Maggie asked.

"Avery and I are working together on a special cake."

That surprised Maggie. "What kind of cake?"

"For Love Day."

"What's that? A Valentine celebration?" she asked curiously, surprised no one had mentioned the event to her. Natalie nodded and concentrated on adding dressing to her salad. "Why didn't anyone tell me? I would have helped."

"You've been busy with your counseling sessions."

"Not too busy to help out at church," Maggie protested.

"It's no big deal, Maggie. You do a lot for Cornerstone. Give others an opportunity to do their part."

"I suppose the bigger deal is that you and Avery are actually working together. How did you manage that?"

Natalie shrugged. "Same committee assignment. I think Avery agreed so he could get my cake batter recipe."

Maggie laughed. "That sounds paranoid."

"I gave it to him."

Maggie's head shot up, and she stared at her friend. "You did?"

"Sure. The biggest thing about my cakes is originality. I know what combinations taste good together and what makes them pretty. Believe me, it's not just the cake alone."

"Whatever it is, it's delicious. What do you think about making a cake to serve at the after-church fellowship on our wedding day?"

"I could do that."

"On second thought, I'm not so sure it's a great idea," Maggie said. "We're already holding people up from their Sunday lunch. How do you think they'd feel about a sugar high on top of that?"

"They're going to stay and wish you well anyway. And you've seen how they gobble up the cookies and coffee. What did you have in mind?"

"My favorite is chocolate, and Dillon likes orange. Surprise us."

Natalie nodded. "How is counseling going?"

Maggie sipped her tea. "Good. I didn't realize it would be so involved, but we worked through some things, and I think our marriage will be stronger because of that."

"You said 'think.' Are you still having doubts?"

Maggie sighed and nodded. "Never about Dillon."

"Don't let the past stand in the way of your future," Natalie advised. "Remember a few weeks back when Pastor Joe spoke on God forgiving our sins? Doubting yourself doesn't make you a good Christian, nor will it make you a good wife."

"I love Dillon. I thank God for him all the time. Still, I can't go along with every suggestion he makes and feel comfortable."

"Like what?"

"Giving up my job. I have expenses. I don't feel right about letting him pay them. And it doesn't seem fair for him to support our home solely with his income."

"That comes from being a sole provider for so long. You're used to doing for yourself, but you have to accept that Dillon needs to take care of you, too."

"But how do I take care of him?"

Natalie grinned at Maggie. "My mom sat me down years ago and told me how to keep a man. Plain and simple, you love him. That's all he wants from you.

"Mom said men see themselves as providers. That's how it works, and divorce happens when two people can't communicate their needs to each other."

"It's good advice," Maggie agreed. "I've been praying that God would help me."

"I think we need to get together and pray for you like we did for Kim."

"I wouldn't mind. It's been awhile."

"Let's do it then. Is Dillon having a bachelor party?"

"I don't think so."

"Maybe Wyatt and Joe can plan something for him, and we can have a bachelorette party. I'll call everyone."

"It doesn't have to be about my wedding," Maggie protested.

"We love you, Maggie. But God loves you more. He sent you Dillon. He will equip you to become the wife you need to be."

~

"We got our marriage license today," Maggie announced as they settled in Kim's living room. "This wedding is really going to happen."

"Did you doubt it?" Mari asked.

Maggie glanced at Natalie then back at Mari. "Natalie told me God will strengthen me, and I believe that. I'm praying hard."

"We're praying, too," Julie assured. "We haven't stopped since we asked God to send you a husband."

"Maggie, you've come a long way in life, and you deserve to be happy," Kim said.

"I know how she feels," Julie said. "I married Noah knowing I wasn't cut out to be a minister's wife, but God makes it work. I love Noah more today than when I married him."

"I feel the same about Wyatt," Kim said. "Every day gets better and better."

"Hey, you're depressing me," Natalie offered with a little laugh. "I wouldn't mind having what you all have."

"Don't worry. It's in God's hands," Mari reassured.

"I've got news to share before I bust," Kim said.

"You're pregnant," Maggie guessed immediately.

Kim radiated her delight. "Wyatt is very happy."

"And so is your mom," Maggie added. "When are they moving back?" Everyone laughed at Maggie's teasing.

"Not to steal Kim's thunder, but I have an announcement myself," Julie said with a wide grin.

"You, too?" Maggie asked. When Julie nodded, Maggie glanced at Mari. "Did you know?"

"I knew Julie thought she might be."

Maggie hugged her friends. "I'm so happy for you both. I can't wait to see your babies. I know they'll be as beautiful as their mothers."

"Thanks, Maggie," Julie said. "You're a good friend. You deserve all the happiness God has in store for you."

Chapter 18

S houldn't you be getting dressed for a wedding?"

Maggie glanced at Julie and smiled. "It won't take me long to change."

"You're not nervous?"

Maggie shrugged. "I have a few jitters."

"Then you're blessed. I'm sure my shakes registered on the Richter scale."

As she laughed at Julie's comment, the nursery room door opened and Joe stepped inside. "Maggie, they had to rush Chester Simpson to the hospital this morning, and I need to go over and be with Geneva. Noah is going to preach the second service. If it's okay, I thought we might do the ceremony at six this evening. Dillon says it's up to you."

A postponement by the pastor. *What next?* Maggie wondered. "We can wait, I suppose."

"Thanks, Maggie. I don't want Geneva to be alone."

"Me, either," Maggie agreed, flashing him a big smile. "Besides, it's not as if you're throwing off a major production."

"Thanks for understanding. Noah could perform the service if you'd rather not wait."

"No." She glanced across the room to where Julie knelt between two toddlers and looked back at Joe. "No offense to Noah, but I consider you my pastor."

Joe squeezed her hand. "I'm glad. I want to hear you say your vows."

"We'll see you at six then. Tell the Simpsons I'm praying for them."

"Will do," Joe said, waving at his sister as he hurried from the room.

"What's going on?" Julie asked.

Maggie settled a toddler at the table and gave him a toy. "Chester Simpson had to go to the hospital. Joe asked if we could delay the ceremony until this evening."

Julie looked startled. "And you're okay with that?"

"It's fine. Dillon will be my husband, and that's all that matters."

"Um, Maggie, I need to take care of something. I'll be back in a few minutes."

"Take your time. We've got plenty of help this morning."

After church, Mari, Kim, Julie, Natalie, and Peg gathered around Maggie. She explained what had happened.

"We're picking you up at four thirty so you can dress here at the church," Kim told her.

"I can put my suit on at home."

"I thought I'd put your hair up," she offered.

"I don't have a veil, so that might be better than wearing it down around my shoulders."

"And I want to do your makeup," Julie said.

"Dillon's not going to recognize me."

"Oh, he's going to know his beautiful bride," Mari declared. "Go home, rest a bit, and take a bubble bath. We'll be there before you know it."

The afternoon sped by. After gathering what she needed for the wedding, Maggie finished packing for their honeymoon. They had decided to leave the next day though Dillon still insisted on keeping his plans a surprise.

As promised, her friends arrived en masse. She got her dress from the bedroom, along with the bag containing her other necessities. "We can walk to the church," Maggie said as she slipped her new shoes on and took a couple of steps. "On second thought, let's drive. I don't know why I let you talk me into these things."

"You'd wear those white nursing clogs if we'd let you," Kim said.

"Flip-flops would have been better if it weren't so cold."

At the church, they ushered her into the room where all Cornerstone brides dressed for their wedding.

"I need to make sure everything is okay in the sanctuary," Maggie said.

"I'll do it," Mari said, guiding her toward Kim.

Kim pushed a chair up behind Maggie. "Let's do your hair first. What if we pull it up in curls?"

"I'd like that."

Mari returned and pronounced the sanctuary to be in perfect order.

Several minutes later, Kim held up a mirror. "What do you think?"

Maggie touched the mass of curls. "Thanks, Kim. This is so much better than wearing it down."

Julie stepped forward. "Now for the makeup."

"I don't wear much."

"More won't hurt tonight. You're paler than usual."

"In shock from all this attention," Maggie teased.

"It's only just begun," Natalie said.

Maggie looked at her. "What else are you planning?"

"To marry you off to Dillon," Natalie said.

Maggie relaxed and allowed Julie to work on her face. When Julie held up the mirror again, Maggie could hardly believe her eyes. "You're a miracle worker."

"Brides are the best makeover candidates. They glow."

Maggie laughed. "This skin hasn't glowed in years."

"Well, it does now," Kim declared. "Let's get you into your dress, and then we can change."

Confusion filled Maggie when Julie unzipped a second garment bag. "That's not my suit." She stared at the material that flowed from the bag when Julie shifted it out. She immediately recognized her dream dress from the bridal store.

"Oh, honey, please don't cry," Mari said, jerking tissues from a nearby box.

"It is your dress," Julie said. "You looked so beautiful in it. Please don't be upset that I bought it for you."

Maggie looked into their expectant faces and knew there was no way she could be angry. "You're right. I deserve to be a princess on my wedding day."

"That's the spirit," Julie declared. "Sit down, and let Kim pin the veil in your hair."

Kim put the tulle veil into place and secured it with hairpins.

Maggie looked around at Julie. "What would you have done if I'd said no?"

"Begged and pleaded," Julie said. "And the suit won't be a waste. You can wear it for another formal event."

"I love you all."

"We love you, too," Mari said, hugging her close.

"There's more than the dress, isn't there?" Maggie asked.

The women looked at each other.

"Yes," Mari answered truthfully.

"What have you planned?"

"Every minute detail," Julie said.

"Including Mr. Simpson's hospital visit this morning?"

"No. That's was God's intervention," Julie assured. "We struggled to find a way to change the time, and it just happened. And praise God, Mr. Simpson only had indigestion and not a heart attack."

Maggie shook her head in disbelief. How could she not love these women? "So what do we do?"

"Just let the ceremony unfold as planned. We did all the stressful worrying for you."

"Does Dillon know?"

"Not everything. Please don't be upset with him, either. We dragged him into our scheme to surprise you. We told him to say he couldn't wait to have you as his wife anytime you acted like you suspected something."

Maggie grinned. "That explains his strange behavior."

"He had his reservations, but he couldn't find anything wrong with doing this for you."

Truthfully, Maggie couldn't either. Knowing her friends loved her enough to make her day extra special meant a lot.

The group of them soon had her in the gown. As they smoothed and tucked, she found it difficult to take her eyes off the bride reflected in the cheval mirror. She had fought this so hard, but Maggie knew this was what she wanted for her wedding. Over the last few days, she'd struggled, reassuring herself the lace suit would be fine, but now she understood what they had tried to tell her.

When they unzipped their garment bags to reveal duplicates of the lilac tea-length gown she'd admired at the bridal shop, Maggie shook her head.

"You did say this was the dress you would have picked," Kim pointed out.

"But I didn't mean you had to buy it. You could have worn something you already had."

"Oh please!" Julie cried. "I didn't want my picture taken on your wedding day wearing some old dress I'd worn a million times."

"I suppose all the guys are wearing tuxedos?"

"You've never seen a more handsome bunch," Kim told her.

There was a tap on the door.

"Can we come in and say hello to the bride?"

Maggie gasped at the sight of the Floyds. Though they had stayed in contact by phone, she hadn't seen them in years. She moved to hug them.

"You look stunning," Sharon Floyd declared, taking Maggie's hands in hers.

"I can't believe you're here. I would have invited you, but Dillon and I planned to say our vows after church and didn't think it was practical to ask you to come so far for a fifteen-minute ceremony."

"We're glad your lovely friends planned this beautiful wedding. You deserve it, Maggie."

Mari introduced herself to the Floyds and then looked at Maggie and whispered, "We thought perhaps Mr. and Mrs. Floyd could walk you down the aisle and give you away."

A lump formed in her throat. "I'd love that."

Mari wrapped an arm around Maggie's waist for support. "Wyatt is Dillon's best man. Noah and Avery are groomsmen."

"Avery?"

"Yes," Natalie said. "I'll tell you the story of how we became friends while working together on your cake design."

"Love Day?" Maggie asked.

Natalie nodded. "That's the code name for your wedding."

"I can't wait to hear that story. It sounds as miraculous as mine and Dillon's."

Mari took Maggie's hand in hers. "Just enjoy and accept this gift from the people who love you. You deserve this, Maggie. Now don't cry," she whispered when tears welled in Maggie's eyes. "We can do a lot, but we can't work miracles with red eyes."

Maggie giggled and blinked away the tears. These women were her true sisters.

"Ready?" Julie asked.

"Wait!" Peg cried. "The flowers." She handed each of the women a single purple rose. "These are my contribution. To repay you for your kindness to Chloe and me."

Maggie hugged her.

Natalie pinned corsages on the Floyds. Peg removed the bridal bouquet from its box. "Dillon sent this. There are fifty miniature white rosebuds. Here's the card. He put it in the envelope. No one else read it."

Maggie felt the tears surge again as she read, *"Please be happy about this. Your friends had me the moment they said you deserved the best. I agree. I love you. Dillon."*

Kim smacked her forehead. "Dillon sent your something old." She shuffled through the items in her bag and pulled out a jewelry box.

Inside, Maggie found Mrs. Allene's pearls and gasped. When she'd suggested he save his mother's jewelry for his wife, she'd never imagined she would fill that role.

"Everyone's waiting," Julie declared as she secured the pearls around Maggie's throat.

Her mouth fell open when the sanctuary doors opened to show the church fully decorated for her Valentine wedding. Candles, greenery, and two tall vases of red roses rested on the pulpit. More candles gleamed in the dark windows. Kim's white ribbons decorated the pews.

Maggie's gaze focused on the Good Shepherd window. Jesus held out His hand, encouraging her to take that first step. She had never felt the presence of the Lord more fully in her life than at this particular moment.

Her attendants started down the aisle.

"When did you have time?" she asked as Mari adjusted the veil.

"It started the day you told us what you planned, and it just snowballed. We had a meeting at church, and your wedding became Project Love Day. I think every member of the church has been here at one time or another this afternoon. You have a ton of thank-you cards to write."

Too choked up to speak, Maggie nodded.

"Maggie, look at me!" Marsha cried, twirling in the beautifully embroidered white and lavender junior bridesmaid's dress.

"You're beautiful, honey." Tears welled in Maggie's eyes. If she made it through this wedding without looking like a raccoon, it would be a miracle.

Luke stood nearby holding her ring pillow with pride.

"Thank you," she whispered to Mari.

"No more tears," Mari ordered. "This is a joyous day."

Very much so. Maggie had not known such joy since before her parents' death. This was exactly the type of wedding she would have chosen if they'd been alive.

"Ready?" Mr. Floyd asked, patting her hand when it trembled against his arm.

When her gaze shifted to Dillon, the love in his expression stole her breath away. He looked very handsome in his black tails.

Love more encompassing than she'd ever known came over her. The love of Jesus—Maggie was sure of that. All those years she'd felt so alone, God had cared. Before she'd ever known Him as her Savior, He'd known and loved her.

He had given her parents to replace those she'd lost, friends to enrich her life, and the man she loved with all her heart. And He'd given her another family—that of God. Nothing could make this day better.

Mari kissed her cheek. "See you down front." She whispered directions to the children before she walked in carefully measured steps toward the front.

This is so surreal, Maggie thought as she waited. And then it was her turn. The music changed and everyone stood as she took her first step. She felt like a princess as she heard the soft gasps of several women in the audience.

Maggie nearly cried again when Joe asked who gave this woman to be married and Mr. Floyd pronounced, "We do, in her parents' honor." Her focus never left Dillon as they spoke their vows.

"I present to you Mr. and Mrs. Aaron Dillon Rogers. You may kiss your bride."

Applause filled the church as Dillon kissed her for the first time as her husband.

"Ready?" he asked, taking her arm and heading toward the exit.

In the background, Maggie heard Joe announce, "The reception will be held in the church fellowship hall."

"Pictures first," Julie declared when they exited the sanctuary doors. They returned to the front of the church and went through the formal poses.

Maggie held Dillon's hand. "I can't believe this is real."

"Quite a leap from that simple service we planned."

"Do you mind?"

Dillon raised her hand to his lips. The camera flashed. "All I wanted was you as my wife. I didn't care how we got there. I had reservations when they started talking about surprising you. You're not upset, are you?"

"Actually I think they know me better than I know myself. This has been wonderful. I'd highly recommend surprise weddings."

Dillon's laughter drew everyone's attention to them. "She recommends surprise weddings," he explained.

The laughter echoed throughout the group.

The reception was just as stunning. Snowy white cloths draped tables filled with white china and silver. The food was tremendous, and each setting had its own miniature version of the beautiful wedding cake.

"You must have spent hours doing all these cakes," Maggie declared as she and Dillon sliced into the cake for the photographer. The bride and groom atop the cake looked like a caricature of the two of them.

"You're worth it," Natalie said, turning to speak to a woman who asked about a cake.

Avery walked over.

"You did a fantastic job," Maggie told him.

"Glad you like it. I know I've been wrong for the way I've treated Natalie. I apologized to her."

"Sometimes we can't see beyond ourselves," Maggie told him. "The important thing is to be friends in Christ. In the end, that's all that matters."

"Did Avery tell you we're planning to enter a version of your cake in a contest?" Natalie asked after she finished her conversation and turned back to them.

"Wow. You two really have come a long way."

"All thanks to you and Dillon," Natalie pointed out. "If not for this surprise wedding, we'd probably still be at odds with each other."

"God works in mysterious ways," Dillon said.

"That He does," Maggie agreed, slipping her arm around Dillon's waist. "I love you, Mr. Rogers."

"And I love you, my incredible Maggie Rogers. You've made coming home the best thing I ever did." He kissed her, and Natalie and Avery playfully cleared their throats.

Joe came over to offer his congratulations.

"I hope you didn't mind rescheduling," he said.

"We didn't mind at all," Dillon said. "I'm sorry Chester Simpson ended up at the hospital though."

"He didn't stay," Maggie said. "He gave me a thumbs-up when I walked down the aisle."

"And you're not upset over all the secrecy?" Joe asked.

"Not at all."

Joe clapped Dillon on the shoulder. "I think he lost sleep over keeping it from you."

"But I'm glad he did," Maggie announced. "The memories of this special day will stay with us forever. Having so much love focused on us helped me realize that in Jesus we will never be foster children. We're the real thing, and we always have a home with our heavenly Father."

All three sets of eyes grew misty with her revelation.

"Welcome home, darling," Dillon declared as he wrapped his arms around her.

"Amen," Joe Dennis declared.

Epilogue

Two years later

S till tired?" Dillon asked as they walked toward the church.

Maggie nodded. They had arrived home from a month-long Australian tour just two days before. Though tired, she knew she'd never forget the experience. "It'll take time to get over the jet lag."

"By next week I hope," Dillon said. "We're getting a foster child placement on Monday."

Maggie smiled. Over the past two years, Maggie Rogers had seen more of the world than she'd ever imagined. She'd given up her job and concentrated on being a good wife. They'd honeymooned in Paris and then gone to Saudi Arabia so Dillon could introduce her to his friends. They'd taken an Alaskan cruise and frequently traveled in the United States. She'd even accompanied him on a couple of mission trips.

"Oh, I almost forgot," she said, drawing the strand of pearls from her coat pocket.

Dillon leaned to kiss her after he secured the necklace in place. "I love you, Maggie. Not a day goes by that I don't thank God for bringing us together."

She turned in his arms. "I love you more every day, too, Dillon. Having you as my husband has made me so happy." The sounds of slamming car doors and people's laughter intruded on their moment. "We'd better hurry, or we'll be late." Inside the church, Maggie touched his cheek and said, "See you down front."

He paused a second longer and winked at her.

She smiled and opened the door to the bride's room.

"There you are," the women called in unison.

Maggie's gaze moved from friend to friend. Each one so precious—her sisters in Christ—the family she'd longed for.

She was proud to call Mari Dennis her friend and Joe Dennis her pastor. The Dennis children were growing up so fast; and Luke had become even more attached to Mr. Dillon. Maggie knew Dillon felt the same about him.

Julie, Noah, and little Joshua had arrived the day before. Noah had been called to a church in Tennessee, and they all missed Julie a great deal. They remained in touch and were delighted that she'd grown to love being a pastor's wife.

Maggie walked over and hugged her. "Where's Josh?"

"With Diana. She's keeping him and Sarah today."

Kim's mother was truly in her element with the little girl who had stolen all their hearts.

"She said to tell you she's sorry she can't be here, Natalie," Kim said as she pinned the veil in place. "Though I'm pretty sure you'd prefer not to have them carrying on during your ceremony. Mom has Sarah spoiled rotten."

Maggie walked over and hugged Kim. "I don't think your mom is the only culprit."

Kim grinned and said, "Welcome home."

"Thanks. How are you feeling today?" Maggie asked, noting Kim's expanded waistline and thinking it wouldn't be long before little Sarah had a brother or sister.

"Okay. Mom's taken a lot of the load off by helping with Sarah and the store."

"Are we still on for tonight?" Julie asked. "I told Noah we're having girls' night. Sure you don't want to stick around, Nat?"

Natalie shook her head and said, "Not this time."

Peg called hello, and Maggie decided she looked much happier. Peg's estranged husband had been killed in a bar fight the year before. Six months later, Maggie and Peg had gone out to lunch and encountered William Smith. Maggie introduced them, and he had asked Peg out. All the Smith men adored Peg and Chloe, and Maggie saw a wedding in her friend's future.

Maggie walked over to help Peg sort the flowers. "Where's Chloe?"

"Will and the boys are keeping an eye on her."

Maggie smiled and said, "Hey, Nat, you need to aim that bouquet in Peg's direction today."

"That's my plan," their friend declared.

Kim grinned at Maggie and said, "You should give her some advice on the best way to catch one."

Maggie laughed at her teasing. "Just jump right out in front and accept the inevitable. It makes things easier all around."

"Well, what do you think?" Natalie asked as she twirled about in her wedding dress.

"You look like you belong on top of a cake," Maggie teased, hugging her friend.

Maggie and Dillon's wedding had brought Natalie and Avery together in Christian fellowship, and they had become quite a team. Recently, she and Dillon had watched when they won the grand prize at a wedding cake competition on television.

"You make a beautiful bride."

"Who would have thought it?" Natalie asked.

"Jesus," Maggie supplied. "The very Cornerstone of our existence."

The music started and Natalie said, "Can we pray?"

They all bowed their heads, each thanking God for this precious family He'd given them.

A Letter to Our Readers

Dear Readers:

In order that we might better contribute to your reading enjoyment, we would appreciate your taking a few minutes to respond to the following questions. When completed, please return to the following: Fiction Editor, Barbour Publishing, Inc., P.O. Box 719, Uhrichsville, OH 44683.

1. Did you enjoy reading *Palmetto Dreams* by Terry Fowler?
   ❏ Very much—I would like to see more books like this.
   ❏ Moderately—I would have enjoyed it more if _____
   _____
   _____

2. What influenced your decision to purchase this book?
   (Check those that apply.)
   ❏ Cover   ❏ Back cover copy   ❏ Title   ❏ Price
   ❏ Friends   ❏ Publicity   ❏ Other

3. Which story was your favorite?
   ❏ *Christmas Mommy*   ❏ *Coming Home*
   ❏ *Except for Grace*

4. Please check your age range:
   ❏ Under 18   ❏ 18–24   ❏ 25–34
   ❏ 35–45   ❏ 46–55   ❏ Over 55

5. How many hours per week do you read? _____

Name _____

Occupation _____

Address _____

City _____ State _____ Zip _____

E-mail _____

If you enjoyed

PALMETTO DREAMS

then read

MAYHEM IN MARYLAND

THREE ROMANCE MYSTERIES

by Candice Speare

Murder in the Milk Case
Band Room Bash
Kitty Litter Killer